PRAISE FOR *Javier Marías*

"Marías is one of the best contemporary writers."   —J. M. Coetzee

"By far Spain's best writer today."   —Roberto Bolaño

"A great writer."   —Salman Rushdie

"It is a rare gift, to be offered a writer who lives in our own time but speaks with the intensity of the past, who comes with the extra richness lent by a foreign history and nonetheless knows our own culture inside out. Yet, strangely, Javier Marías—who is famous in Spain and garlanded with prizes from the rest of Europe—remains almost unknown in America. What are we waiting for?"
—*The New York Times Book Review*

"Javier Marías is one of the greatest living authors. I cannot think of one single contemporary writer that reaches his level of quality. If I had to name one, it would be García Márquez."
—Marcel Reich-Ranicki, *Das Literarische Quartett*

"The most subtle and gifted writer in contemporary Spanish literature."   —*The Boston Sunday Globe*

"Marías is simply astonishing."
—*The Times Literary Supplement* (London)

"Javier Marías is such an elegant, witty, and persuasive writer that it is tempting simply to quote him at length."   —*The Scotsman*

"Marías uses language like an anatomist uses the scalpel to cut away the layers of the flesh in order to lay bare the innermost secrets of that strangest of species, the human being."   —W. G. Sebald

"His prose possesses an exquisite, almost uncanny observation, re-creating moments and moods in hypnotic depth."
—*The Telegraph* (London)

Javier Marías

TOMORROW
IN THE
BATTLE THINK ON ME

Javier Marías was born in Madrid in 1951. He has published thirteen novels, two collections of short stories, and several volumes of essays. His work has been translated into forty-two languages, in fifty-two countries, and won a dazzling array of international literary awards, including the prestigious Dublin IMPAC award for *A Heart So White*. He is also a highly practiced translator into Spanish of English authors, including Joseph Conrad, Robert Louis Stevenson, Sir Thomas Browne, and Laurence Sterne. He has held academic posts in Spain, the United States, and in Britain, as Lecturer in Spanish Literature at Oxford University.

INTERNATIONAL

ALSO BY JAVIER MARÍAS

(in order of US publication)

TOMORROW
IN THE
BATTLE THINK ON ME

A NOVEL

Javier Marías

Translated from the Spanish
by Margaret Jull Costa

VINTAGE INTERNATIONAL
VINTAGE BOOKS
A DIVISION OF RANDOM HOUSE, INC.
NEW YORK

*The translator would like to thank Javier Marías,
Annella McDermott, Antonio Martin, and Ben Sherrif
for all their help and advice.*

M.J.C.

A VINTAGE INTERNATIONAL EDITION, MARCH 2013

Translation copyright © 1996 by Margaret Jull Costa

Vintage ISBN: 978-0-307-95075-8

www.vintagebooks.com

TOMORROW
IN THE
BATTLE THINK ON ME

NO ONE EVER EXPECTS that they might some day find themselves with a dead woman in their arms, a woman whose face they will never see again, but whose name they will remember. No one ever expects anybody to die at the least opportune of moments, even though this happens all the time, nor does it ever occur to us that someone entirely unforeseen might die beside us. The facts or the circumstances of a death are often concealed: it is common for both the living and the dying – assuming that they have time to realize they are dying – to feel embarrassed by the form and appearance of that death, embarrassed too by its cause. Seafood poisoning, a cigarette lit as the person is drifting off to sleep and that sets fire to the sheets or, worse, to a woollen blanket; a slip in the shower – the back of the head – the bathroom door locked; a lightning bolt that splits in two a tree planted in a broad avenue, a tree which, as it falls, crushes or slices off the head of a passer-by, possibly a foreigner; dying in your socks, or at the barber's, still wearing a voluminous smock, or in a whorehouse or at the dentist's; or eating fish and getting a bone stuck in your throat, choking to death like a child whose mother isn't there to save him by sticking a finger down his throat; or dying in the middle of shaving, with one cheek still covered in foam, half-shaven for all eternity, unless someone notices and finishes the job off out of aesthetic pity; not to mention life's most ignoble, hidden moments that people seldom mention once they are out of adolescence, simply because they no longer have an excuse to do so, although, of course, there are always those who insist on making jokes about them, never very funny jokes. What a terrible way to die, people say about certain deaths; what a ridiculous way to die, people say, amidst loud laughter. The laughter surfaces because we are talking about an enemy at last deceased or about some remote figure, someone who once insulted us or who has long since inhabited the past, a Roman emperor, a great-grandfather, or even some powerful person in whose grotesque death one sees only the still-vital, still-human justice which, deep down, we hope will be dealt out to everyone, including ourselves. How that death gladdens me, saddens me, pleases me. Sometimes the trigger for hilarity is merely the fact that it is a stranger's death, about whose inevitably risible misfortune we read in the newspapers, poor thing, people say, laughing, death as a performance or a show to be reviewed, all the stories that we read or hear or are told as if they were mere theatre, there is always a degree of unreality about the things other people tell us, it's as if nothing ever really happened, not even the things that happen to us, things we cannot forget. No, not even what we cannot forget.

There is a degree of unreality about what has happened to me and which is still not over, or perhaps I should use a different tense – the classic storytelling tense – and say, instead, what *happened* to me, even though it is still not over. Maybe now, when I tell it, I'll find myself laughing. I have my doubts though; it is not yet remote enough and my dead person has not long inhabited the past, she was neither powerful nor an enemy, and I cannot really say that she was a stranger either, although I knew very little about her when she died in my arms – now, on the other hand, I know more. Fortunately, she was not naked, at least not entirely, we were in the process of undressing, of undressing each other as one tends to do the first time it happens, that is, on those first nights that have all the appearance of being unforeseen, or which you pretend to yourself were unpremeditated in order to save your modesty, so that later on, you can experience a feeling of inevitability and thus shrug off any possible guilt, people believe in predestination and the intervention of fate, when it suits them. It is as if, when it comes to the point, everyone wanted to say: "I never sought it, I never wanted it," when things turn out badly or depress you, or when you regret something, or end up hurting someone. I neither sought nor wanted it, I should say now that I know she is dead, and that, even though she hardly knew me, she died in my arms inopportunely – undeservedly too, for I was not the one who should have been at her side. No one would believe me if I said it, not that that matters much, since I am the person doing the telling and people can either choose to listen to me or not. Now, however, whilst I can say that I never sought it, never wanted it, she cannot say that or anything else, she cannot contradict me, the last thing she said was: "Oh God, the child." The first thing she had said was: "I don't feel well, I don't know what's wrong with me." I mean that was the first thing she said once the process of undressing had been interrupted, we were already in her bedroom, half-lying down, half-dressed and half-undressed. She suddenly withdrew from me and covered my lips with her hand as if not wanting to make the transition from kissing my lips to not kissing them until she had replaced this with some other affectionate gesture or touch, she pushed me gently with the back of her hand and then turned over and lay on her side, facing away from me, and when I asked her: "What's up?", that is what she replied: "I don't feel well, I don't know what's wrong with me." That was when I first saw the back of her neck, which I had never seen before, with her hair slightly lifted (as it is in certain nineteenth-century portraits of women) and somewhat tangled and sweaty, and yet it wasn't hot in the room, an old-fashioned neck traversed by striations or threads of black, sticky hair, like half-dried blood, or perhaps mud, like the neck of someone who slipped in the shower, but still had time to turn off the tap. It all happened very fast and there was no time to do anything. There wasn't time to call a doctor (and what doctor could you call at three o'clock in the morning? doctors don't even do house calls at lunchtimes these days) or to call a neighbour (and which neighbour, I didn't know them, I wasn't in my own house and had never before been in that house which I had entered as a guest and where I was now an intruder, I had never even been in that street before, hardly ever been in that part of town, and then only a long time ago) or call her husband (and how could I, of all people, phone her husband, besides, he was away and I didn't even know his full name), or wake up the child (and what would be the point of waking the child, when it had taken so long to get him to sleep), or even to try and help her myself, her illness came on very suddenly, at first, I thought or we thought that the meal, with all its interruptions, had disagreed with her, or I thought that perhaps she was already becoming depressed by or beginning to regret what had happened, or had felt suddenly afraid, those three things often take the form of malaise and illness, fear and depression and regret, especially if the latter coincides with the acts that provoke it, all at once, a yes and a no and a perhaps and, meanwhile, everything has moved on or is gone, the misery of not knowing what to do and of having to act regardless, because one has to fill up the insistent time that continues to pass without waiting for us, we move more slowly: having to decide without knowing, having to act without knowing and yet foreseeing, and that is the greatest and most common of misfortunes, foreseeing what will come afterwards, it is a misfortune generally perceived as quite a minor one, yet experienced by everyone every day. It is something you get used to, we take little notice of it. She felt ill, I hardly dare write her name – Marta, that was her name, and her surname was Téllez – she said that she felt sick and I asked her: "But what do you mean, in your stomach or in your head?" "I don't know, I feel absolutely deathly, I just feel horribly queasy all over, all over my body." That body that was now in my hands, the hands that touch everything, the hands that squeeze or caress or explore or even strike (I didn't mean to, it was an accident, don't hold it against me), the sometimes mechanical gestures of hands feeling their way over a body about which they are still undecided as to whether or not it pleases them, and then suddenly that body feels sick, that most diffuse of malaises, all over her body, as she put it, and she had also said, "I feel absolutely deathly," she had not meant it literally, but as a figure of speech. She did not think she was dying, nor did I, besides, she had said: "I don't know what's wrong with me." I kept asking questions because that is a way of avoiding having to do anything, and not only asking questions, for talking and telling all avoid the kisses and the blows and having to take steps, putting an end to the waiting, and what could I do, especially at first, when according to the rules of what should and shouldn't happen – rules that are, at times, broken – it should have been only a passing phase. "Do you actually feel like being sick?" She didn't reply in words, she shook her head, the back of her neck with its threads of hair like half-dried blood or mud, as if it were too much of an effort to speak. I got off the bed and walked round it and knelt down by her side so that I could see her face, I put a hand on her forearm (touch consoles, the hand of the doctor). She had her eyes tight shut at that moment – long lashes – as if the light from the table lamp hurt her eyes, the lamp we had not as yet switched off (although I was thinking of doing so shortly, before she became ill I had wondered whether to switch it off now or later: I wanted to see, I had still not seen that new body that was sure to please me, so I had not switched it off). I left the lamp on, now it might be useful to us in view of her sudden indisposition, her sudden illness or depression or fear or regret. "Do you want me to call a doctor?" and I thought of those unlikely accident and emergency numbers, the phantasmagoria of the telephone book. She shook her head again. "Where does it hurt you?" I asked and she feebly indicated a vague area comprising her chest and her stomach and below, in fact her whole body apart from her head and her extremities. Her stomach was uncovered now, her chest less so, she was still wearing (although the hook was undone) her strapless bra, a vestige of summer, like the top half of a bikini, it was slightly too small for her, perhaps she had put on an older, smaller bra precisely because she was expecting me that night and because, despite appearances and despite the carefully engineered coincidences that had led us to that double bed, it had all in fact been premeditated (I know that some women wear their bra a size too small on purpose, to give them more uplift). I was the one who had undone her bra, but it had not come off, Marta was gripping it now with her arms or armpits, perhaps unintentionally. "Is it passing off a bit?" "No, I don't know, I don't think so," she said, in a voice that was now not merely diminished, but distorted by pain or, rather, by anxiety, because I don't actually know that she was in any pain. "Wait a bit, I can hardly speak," she added – being ill makes you lazy – but nevertheless she did say something else, she wasn't so ill that she had forgotten about me, she was considerate regardless of the circumstances and even though she was dying, in my brief acquaintance with her she had struck me as being a considerate person (but then we didn't know that she was dying): "Poor thing," she said, "you weren't expecting this. What an awful evening." I hadn't been expecting anything, or perhaps I had, the same thing that she had been expecting. The evening hadn't been awful up until then, perhaps a touch boring, and I don't know if she sensed what was about to happen to her or if she was referring to the excessively long wait we had had, because the child had not wanted to go to sleep. I got up, walked back around the bed and lay down on the side I had occupied before, on the left side, thinking (again I saw the nape of her motionless, striated neck, hunched as if she were cold): "Perhaps I should just wait and not ask her anything for a while, just leave her to be quiet and see if it passes off, not force her to answer questions or try and assess every few seconds if she's a little better or a little worse, thinking about an illness only intensifies it, so does watching it too closely."

I looked at the walls of the bedroom which I had not even glanced at when I first entered it, because I had been looking at the woman who, before, had been by turns vivacious or shy and who was now in a bad way, the woman who had led me there by the hand. There was a full-length mirror opposite the bed like in a hotel room (they were a couple who liked to look at themselves before going out into the street, before going to bed). The rest of the room, on the other hand, was a domestic bedroom, for two people, there were telltale signs left by a husband on the table on my side of the bed (she had immediately gravitated towards the half she occupied each night and each morning – something beyond dispute, mechanical): a calculator, a letter opener, a sleep mask given out by some airline to shut out the glare of the ocean, a few coins, a dirty ashtray and a radio alarm, in the lower compartment there was a carton of cigarettes of which only one pack remained, a bottle of extremely virile Loewe cologne that someone must have given him as a present, possibly Marta herself on the occasion of a recent birthday, two novels, also presents (or perhaps not, but I couldn't imagine myself ever buying them), a tube of Redoxon, an empty glass he hadn't had time to put away before leaving on his trip, a magazine supplement listing the television programmes, programmes he would not see, for he was away that night. The television was at the foot of the bed, beside the mirror, they were people who liked their comforts, for a moment it occurred to me to use the remote control to switch it on, but the remote control was on the other bedside table, on Marta's side, and I would have to walk around the bed again or bother her by stretching my arm above her head, what would she be thinking about now, if it was just depression or fear that had gripped her. I stretched out my arm and picked up the remote control, she didn't notice even though the rolled-up sleeve of my shirt brushed her hair. On the left-hand wall, there was a reproduction of a rather kitsch painting by Bartolomeo da Venezia that I happen to know well, it's in Frankfurt, it depicts a woman with rather straggly ringlets and wearing a laurel wreath, a circlet and a diadem on her forehead, she is holding a bunch of small flowers in her raised hand and has one (rather flat) breast exposed; to the right, there were fitted wardrobes painted white like the walls. Inside would be the clothes that her husband hadn't taken with him on his trip, most of them, it was a short trip according to what his wife Marta had told me during supper, to London. There were also two chairs with clothes draped over them, the clothes were perhaps dirty or newly washed and still unironed, Marta's bedside lamp did not cast enough light on them for me to see. On one of the chairs I saw some men's clothing, a jacket slung over the chairback as if the chair were a clothes hanger, a pair of trousers with a large-buckled belt (the zip was open, as it always is on trousers that have not been put away), a couple of pale, unbuttoned shirts, the husband had only recently been in that room, that morning he would have got up from that very place, from the pillow I was now leaning against, and he would have decided to change his trousers, he was in a hurry, maybe Marta had refused to iron them for him. Those clothes were still breathing. On the other chair there were women's clothes, I saw a pair of dark stockings and two of Marta's skirts, they weren't like the skirt she was still wearing, they were smarter, perhaps she'd been trying them on, unable to decide, until a minute before I had knocked at the door, one never knows what to wear for romantic assignations (I had had no such problems, I wasn't even sure if it was a romantic assignation and my wardrobe tends to be rather monotonous anyway). In the posture she had adopted, the chosen skirt was now horribly creased, Marta was doubled up, I could see that she was squeezing her thumbs with her fingers and had drawn up her legs as if trying to use that pressure to calm her stomach and her chest, as if trying to contain them, that posture revealed her knickers and, in turn, part of her buttocks, they were very small knickers. Out of a sudden sense of modesty and to avoid her skirt becoming still more creased, I thought perhaps I should smooth it and pull it down, but I couldn't help liking what I saw and it was doubtful that I would go on seeing it – seeing any more of it – if she did not get any better, and, besides, Marta had possibly expected those creases, they had begun to appear already, as usually happens on those first nights, which are no respecters of the clothes you take off or of those you leave on, although there is a certain respect for the new, unknown body: perhaps that was why she hadn't ironed any of the clothes draped over the chairs, because she knew that the next day she would have to iron the skirt she put on tonight, which one, which is the most flattering, the night on which she would receive me, in such cases everything becomes creased or stained or crumpled and momentarily unusable.

Before switching on the television, I turned the sound down with the remote control, and, just as I had intended, a voiceless image appeared and Marta did not notice, even though the room immediately grew brighter. A subtitled Fred MacMurray appeared on the screen, it was an old movie on late at night. I flicked through the channels and returned to MacMurray in black and white, to his rather unintelligent face. And at that point, I could no longer keep myself from thinking, although no one ever thinks very much or in the order in which those thoughts are later retold or written down: "What am I doing here?" I thought. "I'm in an unfamiliar house, in the bedroom of a man I've never seen, a man I only know by his first name, which his wife has mentioned – naturally and irritatingly – several times throughout the evening. It's also her bedroom which is why I'm here, watching over her illness after having removed some of her clothes and having touched her, I do know her, although not very well, I've only known her for two weeks, this is the third time I've seen her in my whole life. Her husband phoned a couple of hours ago when I was already having supper in his house, he called to say that he'd arrived safely in London, that he'd dined extremely well at the

Bombay Brasserie and that he was in his hotel room getting ready to go to bed, he had work to do the following morning, he's away on a short business trip." And his wife Marta didn't tell him that I was there, here, having supper. That made me almost certain that this was a romantic supper, although at the time her little boy was still awake. Her husband had doubtless asked after the boy, and she had told him that he was about to go to bed; her husband had probably said: "Put him on so that I can say good-night to him," because Marta had said: "No, I'd better not, he's still wide awake and if he talks to you, he'll get even more excited and there'll be no getting him to sleep at all." In my view, that whole discussion was absurd, because the boy, nearly two years old according to his mother, spoke in a rudimentary, barely intelligible manner and Marta had to interpret and translate for him, mothers are the world's first interpreters and translators, who interpret and then articulate what is not even language, they interpret the child's expressions, their frantic gesturing and their different ways of crying, when the crying is still inarticulate and cannot be put into words, or excludes or impedes them. Perhaps his father could understand him too, which would explain why he asked to be allowed to speak to him on the phone; to make matters worse, the boy always spoke with a dummy in his mouth. I said to him once, while Marta was in the kitchen for a moment and he and I were left alone in the living-cum-dining room, me sitting at the table with my napkin on my lap, he on the sofa clasping a small toy rabbit, the two of us watching television, he directly and I obliquely: "I can't understand you with the dummy in your mouth." And the boy had obediently removed the dummy and, holding it for a moment in his hand, in an almost eloquent gesture (in the other he held the rabbit), he had repeated whatever it was he had said before, although equally unsuccessfully with his mouth unencumbered. The fact that Marta did not allow the boy to speak on the phone made me even more certain that this was a romantic supper, because the boy, in his garbled half-language, might, despite everything, have communicated to his father that a man was there having supper. I soon realized that the boy tended only to pronounce the last part of words with two or more syllables, though not always the whole syllable (instead of "moustache" he said "tache", instead of "ice cream" he said "scream": I don't have a moustache, but a moustachioed mayor had just appeared on the screen; Marta had given me ice cream for supper); even knowing that, it was difficult to decipher, but possibly his father was used to it, his interpretative senses also attuned to that primitive language spoken by only one speaker who, moreover, would soon cease to speak it. The boy still used very few verbs and so barely spoke in sentences, he got by using nouns and the occasional adjective, and he said everything in the same exclamatory tone. He had refused to go to bed while we were having supper or not having supper but waiting for Marta to come back to the table after her comings and goings to the kitchen and her patient solicitude towards the child. His mother had put on a video of a cartoon on the TV in the living room – at the time I didn't know there was another television in the house – to see if the flickering screen would send him to sleep. But the child remained alert, he had refused to go to bed, for all his ignorance or his precarious knowledge of the world he knew more than I did, and he was watching over his mother and watching over that guest whom he had never before seen in the apartment, he was guarding his father's place. There were several points in the evening when I would happily have left, I already felt more of an intruder than a guest, and more and more of an intruder the more certain I became that this was a romantic assignation and that the child knew this intuitively – the way cats do – and was trying to impede it with his presence, dead tired and battling against sleep, sitting quietly on the sofa watching a cartoon he didn't understand, although he did recognize the characters, because sometimes he would point at the screen and, despite the dummy, I was able to understand what he was saying because I could see what he was seeing: "Titin!" he would say, "Cap'n!" and his mother would stop talking to me for a second and turn her attention to him and translate or reinforce what he had said, so that not one of his incipient, admirable words would remain uncelebrated, unechoed: "Yes, sweetheart, it's Tintin and the Captain." When I was little, I used to read Tintin in large-format books, nowadays, children watch him moving and hear him speaking in a ridiculous voice, so I couldn't help but be distracted from the fragmentary conversation and from that much-interrupted supper, I not only recognized the characters, but their adventures too, the Black Island, and I could not help but follow them out of the corner of my eye from my place at the table.

It was the child's refusal to go to bed that finally convinced me of what awaited me (if he did finally go to sleep and if that was what I wanted). It was his vigilance and his instinctive distrust that betrayed the mother, more so even than her silence when she spoke on the phone to London (her silence regarding my presence there) or the fact that she was too smartly dressed, too made up and too flushed for someone merely having supper at home at the end of the day (or perhaps she was just very hyped up). The revelation of one's fear gives ideas to the person causing that fear or to the person who could cause it, the preventative measures taken against what has not yet happened cause it to happen, suspicions decide what was as yet unresolved and set it in motion, apprehension and expectation force the ever-deepening cavities that they create to be filled, something has to happen if we want to dissipate that fear and the best thing to do is to let it run its course. The child was accusing his mother by his irritating reluctance to go to sleep and the mother was accusing herself by her tolerance of him (it's best to try and have supper in peace, she would be thinking, would have been thinking since the evening began; if the boy has a tantrum, we're sunk), and both those things completely undermined the pretence that is always necessary on first nights, the pretence that allows us to say or believe later on that no one sought or wanted anything: I never sought it, I never wanted it. I too felt accused, not only by the child's efforts to avoid giving in to sleep, but also by his attitude and the way he looked at me: he had mostly kept his distance, he regarded me with a mixture of incredulity and a need or a desire for trust, the latter was particularly noticeable when he spoke to me in his blunt, solitary syllables, almost always enigmatic, in a voice that was unexpectedly loud in someone of his size. He had not shown me many things and he wouldn't let me hold his rabbit. "The child is right, he's right to do that," I thought, "because as soon as he goes to sleep, I will occupy the place usually occupied by his father, albeit only for a while. He senses that and wants to protect that place which is also a guarantee of his place, but because he is ignorant of the world and does not know that he knows anything, he has smoothed my path with his transparent fear, he has given me all the signs I might not otherwise have seen: he, despite everything and despite knowing nothing, knows his mother better than I do, she is the world he knows best and for him she holds no mysteries. Thanks to him I will not hesitate to act, if I choose to act." Gradually, overwhelmed by sleep, he had slumped further down in his seat and had ended up lying on the sofa, too tiny for that large piece of furniture – like an ant in an empty matchbox, except that an ant moves – and he had continued watching his video with his cheek resting on the cushions, his dummy in his mouth like a reminder or a superfluous emblem of his extreme youth, his legs drawn up as if he were going to sleep or about to go to sleep, his eyes still wide open though, he wouldn't let himself close them not even for a moment, from where she was sitting, his mother peered across every now and then to see if her son had finally succumbed as she hoped he would, the poor woman wanted to be rid of him even though he was her whole life, the poor woman wanted to be alone with me for a while, not for long, just for a while (but I say "poor woman" now, I didn't think it then, perhaps I should have). I asked no questions and I made no comment because I did not want to appear impatient or lacking in feeling and, besides, she herself informed me quite naturally every time she leaned back again: "Oh dear, his eyes are still like soup plates, I'm afraid." Although he had been quiet, the child's presence had dominated the whole evening. He was a tranquil, apparently good-humoured child and he really was very little trouble, but there was no way he was going to leave us on our own, there was no way he was going to disappear and go alone to his room, there was no way he was going to lose sight of his mother, who was now lying in the same position as her son had on the vast sofa while he battled against tiredness, except that she was battling against illness or fear or depression or regret and she did not look tiny lying there on her own double bed nor was she alone, for I was by her side, holding the remote control in my hand, not knowing quite what to do. "Do you want me to go?" I asked. "No, wait a moment, I'm sure it'll pass, don't leave me," replied Marta Téllez and when she did so, she turned her face towards me, at least that was her intention, she couldn't have seen me because she didn't turn her head quite enough, what she did see was the television screen and Fred MacMurray's foolish face which I was beginning to associate with that of the absent husband while I thought about him and about what had happened, or what, until then, had not happened but had been planned. Why did he not phone now, sleepless in London, it would be a relief if the phone rang and she picked it up and explained to her husband in her enfeebled voice that she was feeling really ill and didn't know what was wrong with her. He would take charge then, even though he was far away, and I would be free of all responsibility (the responsibility of one who merely chances to be there, nothing more), I would cease to be a witness, he could call a doctor or a neighbour (he would know them, they were his neighbours not mine), or a sister or a sister-in-law, so that they could be startled from their sleep and in the middle of the night go to his house to help his sick wife. And meanwhile I would leave, I would come back another night if the opportunity arose, when there would be no need for preliminaries or pre-ambles, I could visit her tomorrow at the same time, late at night, when the child would be certain to have gone to bed. I couldn't go waking people up, but her husband could.

"Do you want to phone your husband?" I asked Marta. "It might make you feel better to talk to him and to let him know that you're not well." We can't bear those close to us not to know about our troubles, we can't bear them to continue to believe that we are more or less happy when, suddenly, we are not, there are four or five people in everybody's life who must be informed immediately of whatever is happening to us, we can't bear them to go on believing what is no longer true, not for a minute, for them to believe that we are married when we have just been widowed or that we still have parents when we have suddenly become orphans, that we have company when that company has just left, or are in good health when we have suddenly fallen ill. That they should think us still alive when we are dead. But that was a strange night, especially for Marta Téllez, doubtless the strangest night of her whole existence. Marta turned her face more now, I saw it full on, as she would have seen mine, for some time now I had seen only the back of her neck, growing ever damper with sweat, ever more rigid, the crisscrossing threads of hair growing ever more matted, as if becoming impregnated with mud; and her smooth, bare back. When she turned round, I saw that her eyes were screwed so tight shut that it was unlikely she could see anything, her eyes almost supplanted by her long lashes, I don't know if the strangeness of the look which I could only guess at was due to her having momentarily forgotten about me and to her failure to recognize me or my question or my remark, or perhaps to the fact that she had never felt what she was feeling then. I suppose she was dying without my realizing it, dying is a new experience for everyone. "You're mad," she said, "how can I possibly phone him, he'd kill me." When she turned, her bra, which she had been holding in place – intentionally or not – with her arms or armpits, dropped on to the mattress. Her breasts remained uncovered but she did nothing to cover them: I suppose she was dying and I didn't realize it. And she added, proving that she hadn't forgotten about me and that she knew what I was talking about: "You've switched the television on, poor thing, you must be bored, turn the sound up if you like, what are you watching?" While she was saying this (though she said it as if she were talking to herself) she placed one hand on my leg, the suggestion of a caress she could not complete; then she removed it to return to her previous position, with her back to me, curled up like a little girl, or like her little boy who was sleeping in his room at last with no thought for me and for her, probably in a cot, I don't know if two-year-olds still run the risk of rolling out of bed in the night on to the floor if they sleep in a bed like grown-ups, or if they sleep in cots where they're safe. "It's an old Fred MacMurray film," I replied (she was younger than me, I wondered if she would know who Fred MacMurray was), "but I'm not really watching it." In London, her husband would also be asleep, oblivious to her and ignorant of my existence, why did he not wake up, anxious, why did he not guess what was happening, why did he not call her in Madrid, seeking consolation, only to be greeted here by a voice filled by an even greater anxiety, one that would make him forget his own, why did he not save us? In the middle of the night, though, everything was in order for all the other possible people or characters behind with the news: for the child, close at hand, unaware of the world beneath his own roof, and for the father far off on that island where usually one sleeps so soundly; for the sisters-in-law or sisters who would be dreaming of the abstract future in this city that is never still and where it is always hard to sleep – more a giving in, never a habit; for some overworked, exhausted doctor who might perhaps have saved a life if someone had dragged him from his nightmares that night; for the neighbours in that same building who would be growing increasingly desperate, thinking in their sleep of the next morning coming ever closer, with less and less time before they had to wake up and look at themselves in the mirror and clean their teeth and turn on the radio, another day, how dreadful, another day, how fortunate. Only for me and for Marta were things not in order, I was not oblivious or immersed in sleep and it was already very late, before, I said that it all happened very fast and I know that it did, but remembering it is as slow as witnessing it was, I had the feeling that time was passing and yet only very slowly according to the clocks (the clock on Marta's bedside table, the watch on my wrist), I wanted to let it pass unhurriedly before each new remark I uttered or each new movement I made, but I couldn't manage it, barely a minute passed between my remarks and my movements or between movement and remark, when I thought ten minutes had passed or at least five. In other parts of the city something, though not much, would be happening, in orderly and disorderly fashion: I could hear the cars some distance away, there was not much traffic in that street, it was called Conde de la Cimera, and what I did know was that there was a hospital very near, called the Hospital de la Luz, where night nurses would be dozing, head resting on one hand, a superficial sleep born to be broken, legs crossed, wearing whitish stockings with lumpy seams, perched on uncomfortable chairs, whilst, beyond, some bespectacled student would be reading pages of law or physics or pharmacy for some pointless exam in the morning, forgetting everything he had learned the moment he emerged from the exam room; and beyond that, further off, in another part of town, at the bottom of the hill in Hermanos Bécquer, a solitary whore would take a few expectant, incredulous steps towards the kerb every time a car slowed down or stopped for the traffic lights: dressed in her best clothes on a cold Tuesday night, in order to be seen from either much too close to or else only from a distance, or perhaps she was a man, a young man dragging the heels of his stilettos because he is still not quite used to them or is ill or tired, his footsteps and his infrequent encounters with men in cars all destined to leave no mark on anyone, or to become superimposed one on the other in his confused, fatalistic, fragile memory. A few lovers would perhaps be saying goodbye to each other, they can't wait to go back home alone to their own bed, the one rumpled, the other intact, but they still hang back, exchanging kisses at the open front door – he is the one leaving, or she is – while he or she waits for the lift that has remained motionless for a whole hour without anyone calling for it, not since the most noctambular of the other tenants returned home from a discotheque: the kisses of the one who is leaving, standing at the front door of the one who is staying, become confused with those of the day before yesterday and those of the day after tomorrow, there was only ever one memorable first night and it was immediately lost, swallowed up by the weeks and the repetitive months that succeeded it; and somewhere a fight will have broken out, a bottle flies or someone slams it down on the table of the person bothering him – grasping the bottle by the neck as if it were the handle of a dagger – and the bottle doesn't break but the glass table does, although the foam from the beer gushes out like urine; or someone somewhere is committing a murder, or, rather, homicide, since it is unpremeditated, it just happens, an argument and a blow, a cry and the sound of something tearing, a revelation or the sudden realization that one has been deceived, finding out, listening, knowing or seeing, death is sometimes brought on by affirmation and activity, driven away or perhaps postponed by ignorance and tedium and by what is always the best response: "I don't know, I'm not sure, we'll have to see." You have to wait and see and no one knows anything for sure, not even what they do or decide or see or suffer, each moment sooner or later dissolves, its degree of unreality constantly on the increase, everything travelling towards its own dissolution with the passing of the days and even the seconds that appear to sustain things but, in fact, suppress them: the nurse's dream will vanish along with the student's vain wakefulness, the tentatively inviting footsteps of the whore, who is possibly a sick young man in disguise, will be scorned or go unnoticed, the lovers' kisses will be renounced after a few more months or weeks that will bring with them, unannounced, the final night, the bitter, relieved farewell; the glass table top will be replaced, the fight will disperse like the smoke that harboured it that night, even though the person who started it may continue to make trouble; and, as if it was just another insignificant, superfluous tie or link, the murder or homicide is simply lumped in with all the crimes – there are so many others – that have been forgotten and of which no record remains and with those currently being planned and of which there will be a record, even though that too will eventually disappear. And things will happen in London and all over the world about which neither I nor Marta will have any knowledge, in that respect we will be alike, it's an hour earlier there, perhaps her husband isn't sleeping on the island either, but spending a sleepless night staring out of his wintry hotel window – a sash window, in the Wilbraham Hotel – at the buildings opposite, or at other rooms in the same hotel which forms a right angle with its two rear wings that are invisible from the street, Wilbraham Place, most are in darkness, staring at that room where, in the afternoon, he saw a black maid remaking the beds of those who have left, in preparation for those who have not yet arrived, or perhaps he can see her now in her own attic room – those rooms are on the top floor, the narrowest rooms with the lowest ceilings, and are reserved for the employees who have no home of their own – getting undressed after her day's work, removing her cap and her shoes and her stockings and her apron and her uniform, then standing at the sink and washing her face and under her arms, he too can see a half-dressed, half-naked woman, but, unlike me, he hasn't touched her or embraced her, he has nothing to do with that woman who, before going to bed, has a perfunctory wash, British-fashion, at the wretched sink of one of those English rooms whose tenants have to go out into the corridor to use a bathroom shared with other people on the same floor. I don't know, I'm not sure, we'll have to see, or, rather, we'll never know, the dead Marta will never know what happened to her husband in

London that night while she lay dying beside me, when he comes home she won't be here to listen to him, to listen to the story, possibly fictitious, that he has decided to tell her. Everything is travelling towards its own dissolution and is lost and few things leave any trace, especially if they are never repeated, if they happen only once and never recur, the same happens with those things that install themselves too comfortably and recur day after day, again and again, they leave no trace either.

At the time, though, I still did not know to which category of event my first visit that night to Conde de la Cimera – an unfamiliar street – belonged, I considered leaving and not coming back, it really was bad luck on my part, but then again it was possible that I might come back the next day, today according to the clocks, and whether I did or did not come back, from the moment I left there and as the day advanced, there would soon begin to be no trace of this first or, rather, this unique night. "My presence here will be erased tomorrow," I thought, "when Marta is well again and recovered: she'll wash the dirty dishes from our supper and iron her skirts and air the sheets, even those I didn't use, and she'll prefer not to remember her folly or her failure. She'll think of her husband in London and feel comforted and long for his return, she'll look out of the window for a moment while she tidies up and re-establishes order in the world – in yesterday's hand one unemptied ashtray – although there is still perhaps a slightly dreamy look in her eyes, growing weaker every moment, a look that belongs to me and to my few kisses, the memory and the temptation and the effect all cancelled out now by malaise or fear or regret. My presence here, so apparent now, will be denied tomorrow with a shake of the head and a turning on of a tap and, for her, it will be as if I had never been here and I won't have been, because even the time that refuses to pass in the end does pass and is washed away down the drain, and I need only imagine the coming of morning to see myself leaving this house, I might leave it even sooner, when it's still night, crossing Reina Victoria and walking for a while along General Rodrigo in order to clear my head before hailing a taxi. Perhaps all it needs is for Marta to go to sleep and then I'll have a reason and an excuse to leave." Suddenly the bedroom door opened, it had been left ajar so that Marta could hear the child if he woke up and cried. "He never does wake up, whatever happens," she had said, "but, that way, I feel more relaxed." I saw the child in his pyjamas leaning in the doorway with his inevitable rabbit and his dummy, he had woken up without crying, possibly sensing the imminent death of his world. He was looking at his mother and looking at me out of the simplicity of the dreams he had not quite abandoned, uttering none of his few, truncated words. Marta didn't realize he was there – her eyes tight shut, her long lashes – although I made a rapid, alarmed move to do up my shirt which I had not yet taken off, but which she had unbuttoned for me (too many buttons then and now too many to do them all up). Marta Téllez must be very ill indeed not to notice the presence of her son in her bedroom in the middle of the night, or not to sense it, since she wasn't looking in his direction, nor anywhere else. For a few seconds, I was afraid that, at any moment, the child might enter the room screaming and clamber on to the bed next to his sick mother or burst into tears to attract her attention – her attention was focused entirely on herself and on her disobedient body. He looked at the television and saw Fred MacMurray who, in this scene, as he had been in other scenes for some time now, was accompanied by Barbara Stanwyck, a woman with a cruel, rather disagreeable face. He must have felt disappointed that it was in black and white and that there were no voices, or that it was Fred MacMurray and Barbara Stanwyck instead of Tintin and Haddock or one of the other important characters from his cartoon, because his eyes did not remain fixed there, as children's eyes normally do when they alight on a television screen, instead he looked away at once, back at Marta. I blushed to think that it was my fault he was seeing his mother half-naked – almost half-naked, her bra had slipped off and she had made no attempt to cover herself – although perhaps he was used to it, he was too small for this to be a matter of importance to his parents and, besides, some parents consider it proof of a healthy lack of inhibition to share their own nakedness with the inevitable nakedness of their children, so frequent when they are very young. I still blushed despite this modern thought, however, and very awkwardly scooped up the bra from where it had fallen – it lay on the bed like a cast-off – in order, in a feeble, half-hearted manner, to cover up its owner's breasts. I did not, in fact, do so, because I realized that any movement, the touch of the fabric on her skin, would wake Marta up if she had gone to sleep or that she would, at any rate, open her eyes, and I thought it better for her not to know that the child had seen us, as long as the child allowed, I mean, as long as he did not cry or climb on to the bed or say anything. He obviously didn't sleep in a cot or, rather, if he did, the bars must be quite low, just high enough so that he wouldn't roll out in his sleep, but not high enough to prevent him from getting up if he wanted to. So I remained for a few seconds with that undersized bra in my hand, like a pale, paltry trophy, as if highlighting a conquest I had been unable to make, and which, in fact, was nothing of the sort: at that moment, I saw it as proof of my folly and my failure, and of hers. The child was obviously awake because he was there, standing in the doorway with his eyes wide open, but, in fact, he was still almost asleep, or at least that's what I told myself. He looked at the bra, attracted by my gesture, and I immediately hid it, screwing it up in the hand I had dropped down to the covers, hiding it behind my back. He probably didn't quite recognize me, he doubtless remembered my face rather as he remembered those of the childish characters in his videos or the faces of the dogs he dreamed about, except that he hadn't yet put a name to me, or perhaps he had, my name had been spoken several times by Marta during supper, perhaps he knew it but, in his struggle against sleep, could not quite say it. No words came into his mouth, there was no expression in his eyes, I mean, no recognizable expression, nothing that fitted any of the normal adult terms – perplexity, hope, fear, indifference, confusion, anger; the slight frown was due to his fragile wakefulness, nothing more, at least that's what I told myself. I got up carefully and went slowly over to him, smiling slightly and saying to him in a very low voice, a whisper: "You must go back to sleep now, Eugenio, it's very late. Come on, you must go back to bed." From my great height, I placed a hand on his shoulder – I still had the bra in my other hand, as if it were a used napkin. He allowed me to touch him, and placed his hand on my forearm. Then, he turned obediently and I watched him disappear down the corridor taking short, hurried steps, on his way back to his room. Before going in, he stopped and turned towards me, as if expecting me to accompany him, perhaps he needed a witness to watch him get into bed, to be sure that someone knew where he was when he was asleep. Noiselessly – on tiptoe, I still had my shoes on, I thought that now I would probably not be taking them off – I followed him and stood by the door of the room in which he slept and which was still in darkness, the boy hadn't switched on the light, perhaps he didn't know how to, although the blind was raised and the glow of the yellowish, reddish night outside came in through the window – it was not a sash window. When he saw that I was following him, he climbed, still clutching his rabbit, into his bed again, a wooden cot, not a metal one, with the bars lowered as I had imagined. I think I stayed there for some minutes, although I didn't look at the clock when I left Marta's bedroom nor afterwards when I went back. I stayed until I was certain that the child had gone back to sleep again and I knew this from his breathing and because I moved closer for a moment to see his face. When I did so, my head bumped against something, though nothing that hurt me, and only then, in the half-light, did I notice that, hanging from the ceiling, out of his reach, were a few toy aeroplanes suspended on long threads. I took a step back and then returned to the door where I stood leaning against the doorframe – as he had done before, not daring to enter his mother's bedroom – so that I could see them more clearly against the diffuse light. I saw that they were made out of cardboard or metal or were, perhaps, painted models, there were a lot of them and they were all old-fashioned propeller planes that doubtless had their origin in the far-off childhood of the father who was now in London, who would have waited until he had a son in order to get them out and restore them to their proper place, a little boy's bedroom. I thought I could make out a Spitfire, a Messerschmitt 109, a Nieuport biplane and a Camel, as well as a Mig Rat, as this Russian plane was known during the Spanish Civil War; and there was a Japanese Zero and a Lancaster too, and possibly a P-51H Mustang with the smiling jaws of a shark painted on the lower part of its snout; and there was a triplane too, it might have been a Fokker, which, if it was red, would be Baron von Richthofen's: fighters and bombers from the First and Second World Wars all mixed up together, along with some from the Spanish Civil War and others from the Korean War, I had some when I was a child – though not as many, I quite envied him – which was why I recognized them silhouetted against the mottled, yellowish sky in the window, just as I would have recognized them in flight during my childhood had I seen them. With my hand, I had steadied the plane that my head had bumped against: I considered opening the window, it was closed and so there was no breeze, the planes did not move or sway, apart from a very slight toing and froing – a kind of inert, or perhaps impassive, oscillation – inevitable in any light object suspended by a thread: as if above the head and body of the child they were all languidly preparing for some weary night-time foray, tiny, ghostly and impossible, which would, nonetheless, have taken place several times in the past, or perhaps it still anachronistically took place each night, when the child and the husband and Marta were all at last asleep, each one dreaming the weight of the other two. "Tomorrow in the battle think on me," I thought or, rather, remembered.

BUT TONIGHT THEY did not sleep, possibly none of them did, at least not well, not straight through, not as they would hope to, the mother, ill and half-naked, lying on the bed watched over by a man whom she knew only superficially, the child with the covers half off (he had got into bed on his own and I didn't dare rearrange the miniature sheets and blankets and tuck him in properly), and the father, who knows, he would have had supper with someone or other; after hanging up and looking thoughtful – lightly scratching one temple with her forefinger – and a touch envious (she may have had company, but she was still stuck in Conde de la Cimera as she was every night), all Marta had said was: "He told me he'd just had a fantastic meal at an Indian restaurant, the Bombay Brasserie. Do you know it?" Yes, I did know it, I liked it a lot, I had dined in its vast colonial-style rooms on a couple of occasions, a pianist in a dinner jacket sits in the foyer, and there are respectful waiters and maîtres d'hotel, and huge ceiling fans winter and summer, it's a very theatrical place, rather expensive by English standards, but not prohibitively so, a place for friends to meet and celebrate or for business meetings, rather than for intimate, romantic suppers, unless you want to impress an inexperienced young woman or a girl from the working classes, someone likely to feel slightly overwhelmed by the setting and to get absurdly drunk on Indian beer, someone you won't have to take to any intermediate place before hailing a taxi with tip-up seats and going back to your hotel or your flat, someone with whom there will be no need to speak after the hot, spicy supper, you can merely take her face in your hands and kiss her, undress her, touch her, framing that bought, fragile head in your hands in that gesture so reminiscent of both coronation and stran-gulation. Marta's illness was making me think morbid thoughts and although I was breathing easily and felt better standing in the doorway of the boy's bedroom, watching the aeroplanes in the shadows and vaguely remembering my own remote past, I thought that I really should go back in to the other bedroom, to see how she was and to try and help her, perhaps take off her clothes, this time in order to put her to bed and cover her up and evoke the sleep which, with luck, might have overtaken her during my brief absence, and then I would leave.

That wasn't how it was. When I went back into the room again, she looked up at me with her dull, clenched eyes, she was still hunched and unmoving, the only change being that now she was hiding her nakedness with her arms as if she were ashamed or cold. "Do you want to get under the covers? You'll get cold like that," I said. "No, please don't move me, don't move me an inch," she said, adding at once: "Where were you?" "I went to the bathroom. You're not getting any better, you know, we ought to do something, I'm going to call an ambulance." But she still insisted that she did not want to be moved or bothered or distracted ("No, don't do anything yet, don't do anything, just wait"), nor did she want voices or movement around her, as if she were so full of foreboding that she preferred everything about her to be in a state of utter paralysis and preferred to remain in the situation and posture that at least allowed her to go on living rather than risk any variation, however minimal, that might upset the temporary and precarious stability – her already frightening stillness – that was filling her with panic. That is the effect panic has, which is why it is so often the downfall of those who experience it, for it makes them believe that they are somehow safe inside the evil or the danger. The soldier who stays in his trench barely breathing, scarcely moving, even though he knows that the trench will soon come under attack; the pedestrian who feels unable to run away when he hears footsteps behind him at dead of night along a dark, deserted street; the prostitute who doesn't call for help after getting into a car whose doors lock automatically, and realizes that she should never have got in beside that man with the large hands (perhaps she doesn't ask for help because she doesn't believe she has a right to it); the foreigner who sees the tree split in two by lightning and falling towards him, but doesn't move out of the way, he merely observes its slow fall on to the broad avenue; the man who watches another man walk over to his table with a knife in his hand and doesn't move or defend himself because he believes deep down that this cannot really be happening to him and that the knife will not plunge into his belly, the knife cannot be destined for his skin and his guts; or the pilot who watched as the enemy fighter managed to tuck in behind him, but made no last attempt to escape from the enemy's sights by some feat of acrobatics, certain that, although everything was in the other man's favour, he would, nonetheless, miss the target because this time he was the target. "Tomorrow in the battle think on me, and fall thy edgeless sword." Marta must be conscious of every second, mentally counting each one as it passed, aware of the continuity which gives us not only life, but the sense of being alive, the thing that makes us think and say to ourselves: "I'm still thinking or I'm still speaking or I'm still reading or I'm still watching a film and therefore I must be alive; I turn the page of a newspaper or take another sip of my beer or do another clue in the crossword, I'm still looking at things, noticing details – a Japanese man, an air hostess – and that means that the plane in which I'm travelling has not yet fallen from the skies, I'm smoking a cigarette and it's the same one I was smoking a few seconds ago and I know that I will manage to finish it and light the next one, thus everything continues and I can do nothing about it, since I'm not in a mood to kill myself nor do I want to, nor am I going to; this man with the large hands is stroking my throat, he's not pressing that hard yet: even though he's stroking me more roughly now, hurting me a bit, I can still feel his hard, clumsy fingers on my cheekbones and on my temples, my poor temples – his fingers are like piano keys; and I can still hear the steps of that person in the shadows waiting to mug me, but perhaps I'm wrong and they're the footsteps of some inoffensive person who simply can't walk any faster and therefore overtake me, perhaps I should give him the chance to do so and take out my glasses and pause and look in a shop window, but then I might stop hearing them, and what saves me is the fact that I can still hear those footsteps; and I'm still here in my trench with my bayonet fixed, the bayonet I will soon have to use if I don't want to be run through by that of my enemy: but not yet, not yet, and as long as it is not yet, the trench hides and protects me, even though we're in open country and I can feel the cold air on my ears not quite covered by my helmet; and that knife that approaches me in someone else's hand has still not reached its destination and I'm still sitting at my table and nothing has yet been torn or pierced, and, contrary to appearances, I will still take another sip of beer, and another and another; since that tree has not yet fallen and won't fall even though it's been snapped in two and is falling, it won't fall on me, its branches won't slice off my head, it's not possible, I'm just a visitor to this city, I simply happened to be walking along this avenue, I might so easily not have done so; and I can still see the world from on high, from my Supermarine Spitfire, and I still have no sense of descent and weight and vertigo, of falling and gravity and mass which I will have when the Messerschmitt at my back, who has me in his sights, opens fire on me and hits home: but not yet, not yet, and as long as it is not yet, I can go on thinking about the battle and looking at the landscape and making plans for the future; and I, poor Marta, can still see the glare from the television that continues to broadcast and the warmth of this man who has lain down beside me again and keeps me company. As long as he is by my side, I won't die: let him stay here and do nothing, I don't want him to talk or to phone anyone, I don't want anything to change, just let him warm me a little and hold me, I need to be still in order not to die, if each second is identical to the previous second, it makes no sense that I should be the one to change, that the lights should still be lit here and in the street and that the television should still be broadcasting – an old Fred MacMurray film – while I lie dying. I can't cease to exist while everything and everyone remains here and alive and while, on the screen, another story follows its course. It doesn't make sense that my skirts should remain alive on that chair if I'm not going to put them on again, or that my books should continue to breathe on the shelves if I'm not going to look at them any more, my earrings and neck-laces and rings waiting in their box for their turn which will never come; the new toothbrush that I bought just this afternoon will have to be thrown away because I've already used it now, and all the little objects that one collects throughout one's life will be

thrown away one by one or perhaps shared out, and there are so
many of them, it's unbelievable how many things each of us owns,
how much stuff we accumulate in our homes, that's why no one
ever makes an inventory of their possessions, not unless they're
going to make a will, that is, not unless they're already contemplating those objects' imminent neglect and redundancy. I haven't
made a will, I haven't got much to leave and I've never given
much thought to death, which it seems does come and it comes in
a single moment that upends and touches everything, what was
useful and formed part of someone's history becomes, in that one
moment, useless and devoid of history, from now on, nobody will
know why or how or when that picture or that dress was bought
or who gave me that brooch, where and from whom that bag or
that scarf came, what journey or what absence brought it, if it was
a reward for waiting or a message from some new conquest or
intended to ease a guilty conscience; everything that had meaning
and history loses it in a single moment and my belongings lie there
inert, suddenly incapable of revealing their past and their origins;
and someone will make a pile of them and, before bundling them
up or perhaps putting them in plastic bags, my sisters or my
women friends might decide to keep something as a souvenir or
a spoil, or to hang on to a particular brooch so that my son can
give it to some woman when he's grown up, a woman who has
probably not even been born yet. And there'll be other things
that no one will want because they are only of use to me: my
tweezers, or my opened bottle of cologne, my underwear and
my dressing gown and my sponge, my shoes and the wicker chairs
that Eduardo hates, my lotions and medicines, my sunglasses, my
notebooks and index cards and my cuttings and all the books that
only I read, my collection of shells and my old records, the doll
I've kept since I was a child, my toy lion, they might even have
to pay someone to take them away, there are no longer eager,
obliging rag-and-bone men as there were in my childhood, they
wouldn't turn their nose up at anything and would drive through
the streets holding up the traffic, car drivers then were still prepared to slow down for their mule-drawn carts, it seems incredible
that I should have seen that, not so very long ago, I'm still young
and it wasn't that long ago, the carts that grew to impossible

heights as they picked things up and loaded them on until the carts were as tall as one of those open-topped double deckers you see in London, except that here the buses were blue and drove on the right; and as the pile of things grew higher, the swaying of the cart drawn by a single, weary mule became more pronounced – a rocking motion – and it seemed that all that plundered detritus – defunct fridges and cardboard boxes and crates, a rolled-up bedside rug and a sagging, broken-down chair – was constantly on the point of toppling over, unseating the gypsy girl who invariably crowned the pile, acting like a counterbalance, or as if she were an emblem or Our Lady of rag-and-bone men, a rather grubby girl, often blonde, sitting with her back to the load, with her legs dangling over the edge of the cart, and from her perch or peak, she would look back at the world and at us in our school uniforms as we overtook her, and we, in turn, clutching our files and chewing our gum, watched her from the top deck of the buses that took us to school in the morning and back home in the afternoon. We regarded each other with mutual envy, the adventurous life and the life of timetables, the outdoor life and the easy life, and I always wondered how she managed to avoid the branches of the trees that stuck out over the pavements and knocked against the high windows as if in protest at our speed, as if wanting to reach through the windows and scratch us: she had no protection and was alone, perched up high, suspended in the air, but I imagine that her cart moved slowly enough to give her time to see them and to duck down, or to grasp them and hold them back with one grimy hand that protruded from the long sleeve of a torn, woollen, zip-up cardigan. It isn't just the minuscule history of objects that will disappear in that single moment, it's also everything I know and have learned, all my memories and everything I've ever seen – the double-decker bus and the rag-and-bone men's carts and the gypsy girl and the thousand and one things that passed before my eyes and are of no importance to anyone else – my memories which, like so many of my belongings, are only of use to me and become useless if I die, what disappears is not only who I am but who I have been, not only me, poor Marta, but my whole memory, a ragged, discontinuous, never-completed, ever-changing scrap of fabric, but, at the same time, woven with such patience and such extreme care, undulating and variable as my shot-silk skirts, fragile as my silk blouses that tear so easily, I haven't worn those skirts for ages, I got tired of them, and it's odd that this should all happen in a moment, why this moment and not another, why not the previous moment or the next one, why today, this month, this week, a Tuesday in January or a Sunday in September, unpleasant months and days about which one has no choice, what decides that what was in motion should just stop, without the intervention of one's will, or perhaps one's will does intervene by simply stepping aside, perhaps it suddenly grows tired and, by its withdrawal, brings our death, not wanting to want any more, not wanting anything, not even to get better, not even to leave behind the illness and the pain in which it finds shelter, for want of all the other things that illness and pain have driven out or perhaps usurped, because as long as they are there, you can still say not yet, not yet, and you can still go on thinking and you can still go on saying goodbye. Goodbye laughter and goodbye scorn. I will never see you again, nor will you see me. And goodbye ardour, goodbye memories."

I obeyed, I waited, I did nothing and I phoned no one, I just returned to my place on the bed, which was not really my place, though it was mine that night, I lay down by her side again and then, without turning round and without looking at me, she said: "Hold me, hold me, please, hold me," meaning that she wanted me to put my arms around her, so I did, I put my arms around her from behind, my shirt was still unbuttoned and my chest came into contact with her hot, smooth skin, my arms went around her arms, covering them, four hands and four arms now in a double embrace, and that was clearly still not enough, while the film on TV proceeded soundlessly, in silence, oblivious to us, I thought that one day I would have to see it properly, in black and white. She had said "please", our vocabulary is so deeply embedded in us that we never forget our manners, we never, for a moment, relinquish our language and our way of speaking, not even in time of desperation or in moments of anger, whatever happens, even when we are dying. I remained like that for a while, lying on her bed with my arms around her as I had not planned to and yet, at the same time, as I had known I would, it was what I had been waiting for from the moment I entered the apartment and from before then, ever since we arranged to meet and she asked or suggested that we should meet at her place. This was something else, though, a different, unexpected kind of embrace, and now I was certain of what until then I had not even allowed myself to think, or to know that I was thinking: I knew that this was not something that would pass and I thought that it might well be final, I knew that it was not due to regret or depression or fear and that it was imminent: I thought – she's dying in my arms; I thought that and, suddenly, I had no hopes of ever leaving her, as if she had infected me with her desire for immobility and stillness, or perhaps with her desire for death, not yet, not yet, but then again, I can't take any more, I can't take it. And it may well be that she couldn't take it any more, that she couldn't stand it, because a few minutes later – one, two, three or four – I heard her say something else, she said: "Oh God, the child" and she made a sudden, slight movement, almost certainly imperceptible to anyone watching us, but I noticed it because I was so close to her, it was like an impulse from her brain that her body only registered as the faintest flicker, a cold, fleeting reflex, as if it were the tremor, not entirely physical, that you experience in dreams when you think you're falling, falling over a precipice or plummeting earthwards, your leg kicks out as it misses its footing and tries to halt the feeling of descent and weight and vertigo – a lift hurtling downwards – of falling and gravity and mass – a plane crashing, a body leaping from a bridge into the river – as if, just at that moment, Marta had felt an impulse to get up and go and find the boy, but had only managed it in her thoughts, in that tremor. And after another minute – and five; or six – I noticed that she was lying very still, even though she was already still, that is, she lay even stiller and I noticed the change in her temperature and I no longer felt the tension in her body, pressed against me, as if she were pushing back hard, as if she wanted to find refuge inside my body, to flee from what her own body was suffering: an inhuman transformation, an unknown state of mind (the mystery): she was pressing her back against my chest and her bottom against my belly and the back of her thighs against the front of mine, the bloody, muddy back of her neck against my throat and her left cheek against my right cheek, jaw against jaw, and my temples, her temples, my poor temples and her poor temples, her arms beneath mine as if one embrace were not enough, and even the soles of her bare feet against my shoes, resting on them, she laddered her stockings on my shoelaces – her dark stockings that came to mid-thigh and which I had not removed because I liked that old-fashioned image – all her energies thrown back and against me, invading me, we were glued together like Siamese twins who had been born joined the whole length of our bodies, so that we would never see each other except out of the corner of one eye, she with her back to me, pushing, pushing, almost crushing me, until all that stopped and she lay still or stiller, there was no pressure of any kind, not even that of leaning against me, and instead I felt the sweat on my back, as if a pair of supernatural hands had embraced me from in front while I was embracing her, and had rested on my shirt leaving yellowish, watery marks on it, leaving the cloth stuck to my skin. I knew at once that she had died, but I spoke to her and I said: "Marta," and I said her name again, adding: "Can you hear me?" and then I said to myself: "She's dead," I said, "this woman has died and I'm here and I saw it and I could do nothing to stop it, and now it's too late to phone anyone, too late for anyone to share what I saw." And although I said that to myself and I knew it to be true, I felt in no hurry to move away or to withdraw the embrace that she had requested, because I found it or, rather, the contact with her recumbent, averted, half-naked body pleasant and the mere fact that she had died did not instantly change that: she was still there, her dead body identical to her living body, only more peaceful, quieter and perhaps softer, no longer tormented, but in repose, and I could see again out of the corner of my eye her long lashes and her half-open mouth that were still the same, identical, her tangled eyelashes and her infinite mouth that had chatted and eaten and drunk, and smiled and laughed and smoked, that had kissed me and was still kissable. For how long? "We are both still here, in the same position and occupying the same space, I can still feel her; nothing has changed and yet everything has changed, I know that and I cannot grasp it. I don't know why I am alive and she is dead, I don't know what either of those words means any more. I no longer have any clear understanding of those two terms." And only after some seconds – or possibly minutes, one, two, or three – I carefully removed myself from her, as if I did not want to wake her or as if I might hurt her by moving away, and had I spoken to someone – someone who would have been a witness there with me – I would have done so in a low voice or in a conspiratorial whisper, born of the respect that the mystery always imposes on us if, that is, there is no grief or tears, because if there is, there is no silence, or else it comes only later. "Tomorrow in the battle think on me, and fall thy edgeless sword: despair and die."

I still did not dare to turn up the sound on the television, because of that silence, but also because of an absurd thought: it suddenly occurred to me that I should avoid touching the remote control or anything else, in order not to leave my fingerprints anywhere, when I had already left them everywhere and, besides, no one would be looking for them. The fact of someone dying while you remain alive makes you feel, for a moment, like a criminal, but it wasn't just that: it was that suddenly, with Marta dead, my presence in that place was no longer explicable or only barely so, I couldn't even invent a story that would explain it, I was more or less a stranger and now it really didn't make sense to be spending the early hours of the morning in a bedroom that was perhaps no longer hers, since she no longer existed, but her husband's, in a house to which she could only have invited me in his absence; but who could now affirm that she had invited me, since there was no one there to witness it? I leapt off the bed and then I felt panicked, mentally rather than physically, it wasn't so much that I had to do things as to think about them, to set in motion everything that had until then been muffled by the wine, the expectation and the kisses, by our flushed faces and our fantasies, by perplexity and alarm, although I don't know if in that order; and by the present grief. "No one knows that I'm here, that I was here," I thought, immediately correcting the tense of the verb because I could already imagine myself outside that room, that apartment, that building, and even in a different street, I saw myself hailing a taxi after crossing Reina Victoria or in the avenue itself, there are always taxis passing, however late, it forms the final stretch of an old boulevard that ends up lined by houses and the first of the university campus trees. "Nobody knows that I've been here and there's no reason why anyone should," I said to myself, "therefore, I'm not the one who should warn anyone or run in a panic to the Hospital de la Luz and wake up the nurse sitting in her chair asleep, with her legs crossed or, grown forgetful, slightly apart, I won't be the one to drag her from her ephemeral, avaricious sleep, nor will I be the one suddenly and prematurely to drive out everything that the anxious, bespectacled student has managed to learn, nor will I be the one to interrupt the farewells of the satiated lovers lingering at the door of the one staying behind and, at the same time, longing to part, perhaps on this very floor; because no one must know nor will yet know that Marta Téllez has died, I won't make an anonymous phonecall to the police either or ring at the door of the neighbours opposite, I won't go out and buy a death certificate at the local late-night chemist's, for all those who know her she will remain alive tonight while they dream or lie sleepless here or in London or anywhere else, no one will know of the change, the inhuman transformation that has taken place, I will do nothing and speak to no one, I should not be the one to break the news. Were she still alive, no one would know today or tomorrow or perhaps ever that I was here, she would have concealed it and that's how it should be, even more so now that she's dead. And the child, oh God, the child." But I decided that I would think about that afterwards, after a few moments, because another thought interposed itself, in fact, two thoughts, one after the other: "Perhaps there's someone, a friend or a sister, whom she would have talked to about me tomorrow, possibly blushing and smiling. Perhaps she already has talked to someone about me, someone to whom she announced my visit – news travels fast by telephone – and confessed her hesitant desire or her certain hope, perhaps she was talking about me and only hung up when she heard me ring the doorbell, he's here already, you never know what was happening in a house the second before you rang the bell and interrupted it." I buttoned up the shirt that Marta's now stiff fingers had undone when they were still agile and cheerful, I unzipped my trousers and tucked my shirt in, my jacket was in the living room, draped over the chairback as if the chair were a clothes hanger, but where were my overcoat, my scarf and my gloves, where were they, she had taken them from me when I came in and I hadn't noticed where she had put them. That too could wait, I didn't want to go into the living room just yet because my shoes would make a noise and the child hadn't long since got back to sleep, and anyway, the idea of going past his room and making the aeroplanes tremble with my footsteps made me feel awkward, his whole life had changed, the world had changed, and he didn't yet know it, more than that: his present world had ended, because, after a short while, he wouldn't even remember it, it would be as if it had never existed – brittle, erasable time – the memories of a two-year-old do not last, at least I remember nothing from my own life when I was two years old. I looked down at Marta, from the viewpoint of a man standing up and looking down at someone lying on a bed, I saw her firm, round buttocks beneath her scanty knickers, noticed how her skirt had ridden up, observed the hunched position that allowed me to see all that, though not her breasts which were still covered by her arms, she was a remnant, a cast-off, something not to be kept, but discarded – to be burned, to be buried – just as so many of the things that had belonged to her would suddenly become redundant, like the things that get thrown out with the rubbish because they continue unstoppably to change and to rot – the skin of a pear or some fish that's gone off, the outer leaves of an artichoke, chicken giblets, the fat from the Irish sirloin steak that she herself had scraped off our plates into the bin only a short time before, before we went into the bedroom – a lifeless woman, not even covered up, not even under the sheets. She was mere detritus and yet for me she was the same woman as before: she hadn't changed, I still recognized her. I should put her clothes back on so that they wouldn't find her like this, I immediately rejected the idea, it was too difficult, too dangerous, I might break one of her bones putting her arm in the sleeve of whatever I put on her, where was her blouse anyway, perhaps it would be easier just to pull back the sheets and cover her over, you could do anything with her now, poor Marta, manipulate her, move her, at the very least, cover her up.

I stood for a few moments paralysed, immobilized by my own mental haste, doing nothing, haste makes us think very contradictory things, it occurred to me that, had she foreseen this or known about it, it would have distressed her that those close to her should be left in ignorance, that they should believe her still alive when she wasn't, and for how long, that they would not be informed immediately, that everything would not be thrown into instant disarray by her sudden death, that those imprudent telephones would not at once start to ring, talking about her, and that everyone who had known her would not be exclaiming over her, thinking about her; and, later, those who had known her would find unbearable their ignorance of the fact of her death, an ignorance of which they were about to be or already were the victims, for the husband remembering, later on, that he was peacefully asleep on an island – for how long, and that he got up and had breakfast and went to a business meeting in Sloane Square or in Long Acre, and perhaps even went for a walk – while his wife was dying and was dead with no one at her side, no one to tend to her, first the one and then the other, because he would never know for sure that there had been no one else with her, although he might suspect it, it would be difficult for me to cover up every trace of the hours I had spent there, should I decide to do so. He must have left his London telephone number and address somewhere, next to the phone, I saw that there was no paper next to the phone on Marta's bedside table, a phone and answering machine combined, perhaps by the phone in the living room, where she had spoken to her husband before, with me there in the room. It would be a good idea for me to have that address and that telephone number anyway, in case several days passed, not that they would, that was impossible, too long a silence, suddenly the idea terrified me: someone would come, and soon, Marta went to work and would have to leave the child with someone, she couldn't possibly take him with her to the university, she would have arranged for the child to be looked after by a child minder or a friend or a sister or her mother, unless, another terrifying thought occurred to me, unless she left the child at a nursery and took him there herself before going to her classes. And then what would happen, tomorrow no one would take him, or perhaps tomorrow Marta didn't even have any classes or only in the afternoon and no one would come to the house until then, she hadn't seemed worried about having to get up early in the morning, and had remarked that she had some classes in the mornings and others in the afternoon, and not every day of the week, which days though, or were they just tutorial times when she had to be there in the morning or the afternoon, I couldn't remember, when someone has died and can no longer repeat anything, you wish you had listened more carefully to each and every word, other people's timetables, no one ever pays much attention to them, mere preliminaries. I decided to go into the living room, I took off my shoes and went on tiptoe, I wondered if I should close the door of the child's bedroom as I passed by, but the door might creak and wake him up, so I continued on, barefoot and on tiptoe, my shoes hooked over the middle and index fingers of one hand, like the villain in a cartoon or a silent movie, still making the floorboards creak despite all my efforts not to. Once in the living room, I closed the door and put my shoes back on – I didn't tie the shoelaces, already thinking about the return journey, because I would have to go back – there were the bottle and the wine glasses, the only things that Marta hadn't tidied away, she was particular about such things, and the wine had been left not by accident, but because we were still drinking a little of it as we sat on the sofa that had been occupied and finally vacated by the boy, after eating our Häagen-Dazs vanilla ice cream and before we kissed and moved into the bedroom. That hadn't happened so very long ago, now that it was all over: everything seems as nothing to us, everything becomes compressed and seems as nothing to us once it is over, then we always feel that we were not given enough time. Next to the telephone in the living room there were a few yellow post-its stuck to the table – three or four had notes scribbled on them – along with the little rectangular block from which they came; on one of them was what I was looking for, it said: "Eduardo" and underneath that: "Wilbraham Hotel", and underneath that: "Wilbraham Place" and underneath that: "4471/730 8296". I tore off another post-it from the block and I started copying it all out with the pen I took from my jacket as I was putting it on (the time for me to leave was drawing closer), it was where I had left it, on the back of the chair that had served as a clothes hanger. I didn't, in fact, copy out the information, when you first get hold of a telephone number, you always feel tempted to dial it at once, I had the London number of that Eduardo whose surname I still didn't know, but in his own house it shouldn't be a problem to find out what his surname was, I looked around, on the coffee table I saw a few letters which I had had no reason to notice before and so hadn't, it was probably the day's mail that had arrived after his departure and would have been allowed to accumulate there until his return, except that now he would have to return very soon and nothing would accumulate. "Eduardo Deán", said two of the three envelopes and the other said even more, an envelope from a bank with his two surnames on it, and if I called London there would be no problem with the surname that counted, the first, rather unusual one, there would be no need to spell it because I would ask for Mr Dean which is how the hotel would know him or recognize him, in spite of the accent on the "a", which the English would ignore. If I phoned, what would I say, I wouldn't give my name just the news, I would force him to take charge of the situation now, since he hadn't saved us before, and then I could wash my hands of the affair, I could simply leave and start to forget, a piece of bad luck, I could start to hone the memory and reduce it to just that, a piece of bad luck, perhaps an anecdote or, more dignified, a story, one I could tell to close friends, not now, but one day, when it had acquired the necessary degree of unreality that would make it all more benevolent and bearable, that particular businessman had spent far too long not worrying about his family (you have to worry ceaselessly about those closest to you), no, that wasn't true, he had phoned after his supper at the Indian restaurant, but Marta Téllez was not my wife but his, and the boy, Eugenio Deán by name, was not my son, Deán, the father and the husband, would have to take responsibility sooner or later, why not now, why not from London. I looked at the clock for the first time in ages, it was nearly three, but on the island it would be an hour earlier, almost two o'clock, not particularly late for a native of Madrid even if he had things to do the following day, and besides, in England, people don't get up particularly early. While I was dialling, I thought (one's dialling finger bypasses one's will, bypasses any decision one has taken, acting without knowing, deciding without knowing): "It doesn't matter what time it is, if I'm going to give him such news anonymously, it's irrelevant what time it is or if I wake him up, he'll wake up quickly enough once he's heard it, he'll think it must be a joke in the worst possible taste or the product of some enemy's incomprehensible grudge, he'll call back at once and no one will pick up the phone; then he'll call someone else, a sister-in-law, a sister, a friend, and ask them to come over and find out what's going on, but by the time they arrive, I will have gone."

The English voice took a while to answer, five rings, the porter had probably dropped off to sleep, it was a Tuesday night in winter, and before returning to consciousness, he would have imagined that he was dreaming he could hear a phone ringing, his head perhaps resting on the counter like a future decapitee, his ankles wrapped around the legs of the chair, one arm hanging limply down.

"Wilbraham Hotel, good morning," that voice said in English, rather indistinctly, but in keeping with the clock.

"May I speak to Mr Dean, please?" I said.

"What room number, sir?" replied the voice, which had recovered its harsh, neutral, professional tone, the voice of a factotum.

"I don't know his room number, his name's Eduardo Dean."

"One moment, please." I waited a few seconds during which I heard the porter whistling quietly, rather odd in an English person who has just been woken up in what, for him, would be the middle of the night, the small hours. The next thing I would hear, when the whistling stopped, would be the hoarse voice of Marta's husband startled awake. I prepared myself, prepared myself mentally rather than the precise, gabbled words I would have to say before hanging up, without a goodbye. But that isn't what happened, instead the English voice came on again and said: "Hello, I'm afraid there's no Mr Dean in the hotel, sir. Is it spelled D-E-A-N, sir?"

"D-E-A-N, that's right," I repeated. In the end, I had had to spell it out. "Are you sure?"

"Yes, sir, there's no Mr Dean in the hotel tonight, sir. When is he supposed to have arrived?"

"Today. He should have arrived today."

"You mean yesterday, Tuesday, isn't that right, sir? Just a moment," said the porter, for whom the day and the night that for me seemed endless were already distant entities, and again I heard him whistling, he was obviously a jovial man, a man of spirit, possibly a young man despite the dignified, professional tone he adopted; or perhaps he had been sleeping soundly until shortly before and was feeling refreshed, the night shift. Appropriately and ironically enough, he was whistling "Strangers in the Night", now I had time to recognize it, which meant that he couldn't be that young, young men don't whistle Sinatra songs. After a few more seconds he said: "There was no reservation in that name for yesterday, sir. He might have cancelled, of course, but there was definitely no reservation in that name yesterday."

I was on the point of insisting and asking him if perhaps there was a reservation for today, Wednesday. I didn't, though, I merely thanked him, he said: "Goodbye, sir" and I hung up, and only after hanging up did a possible explanation occur to me: in England, as in Portugal and in America, if someone has three names, what counts is the last name, Arthur Conan Doyle, for example, is usually listed under Doyle. When they saw Deán's identity card or passport, they would probably have registered him under his second surname, Ballesteros, which, for a Spaniard, barely counts at all. I could have tried asking for Mr Ballesteros and then I realized that I shouldn't and that I shouldn't even have asked for Mr Dean and that I had had a narrow escape. If I had managed to leave him my tragic message, Deán might have called not only a sister-in-law, a sister or a friend, but a neighbour or even the porter, who would have been up to the apartment in no time at all and would have discovered me going down in the lift or down the stairs or right there: by the time they had arrived, it was more than likely that I would not even have left. I had to leave soon though, I shouldn't waste time, even though, as yet, no one knew anything and no one was likely to turn up at that time of night. But there were still things I needed to sort out: I took my shoes off again and went back to the bedroom. When I passed the boy's room, I clearly thought what had been in my mind all the time, throbbing, postponed, Marta's last words, "Oh God, the child." I walked on and, now, having made contact with the outside world, even if it was only with a foreign porter about whom I knew nothing and never would know anything, I saw the situation differently when I went back into the bedroom, for the first time I felt ashamed at the sight of Marta's half-naked body, ashamed of the part I had played in that nakedness. I went over and pulled back the cover and the sheets on the unoccupied side of the bed, the side occupied by me that night and by her husband on other nights, I pulled the sheets right back, from the pillow down to the foot of the bed, then I walked around the bed and, from the other side, I managed to push her, with due consideration for what had passed between us, then rather harder when I noticed the resistance put up by the slight mound formed by the puckered sheets down the middle of the bed and this time I did feel a certain repugnance towards her dead flesh (one hand on her shoulder, my other hand on her thigh, pushing), that contact no longer felt pleasant, I think I averted my gaze as much as possible as I was moving her. I had to roll her over, there was no other way of getting her across the ruck of woollen cover and sheets, and when she was on the side of the bed where she never slept (she rolled over twice and remained as she had been before, lying on her side, looking to her right), I pulled up the sheets and the bed cover that I had previously drawn back and I managed to lay them over her. I covered her up, I tucked her in, I drew the sheets right up to her neck, to the nape of her neck, which now no longer looked as if she had just emerged from the shower, and I even wondered if I should perhaps cover her face too, as I have seen people do countless times in films and on the news. That, however, would be evidence that someone had been with her, when, at present, there would be only a suspicion, which, however strong (and suspicion was inevitable), was still not a certainty. I looked at her face, still so like the face it had been, still instantly recognizable to herself had she been able to see her reflection, much as it would have been day after day when she looked at herself in the mirror on every countable morning of her life – when things come to an end they have a number, and nothing forewarns us of this and nothing changes from day to day – still recognizable to me too when I compared it to the face in the photo on the dressing table, the photo of her wedding that would have remained there for reasons of implacable, enforced inertia ever since it was first placed there and which neither of the bedroom's inhabitants would have looked at in ages: five years ago, she had said, a little younger and with her hair up, the back of her neck, old-fashioned somehow, would have been on view throughout the whole ceremony, and on her face is a look of mingled joy and surprise – the laughter of alarm – she's wearing a short dress, but she's wearing white (though it might be cream, it's only a black-and-white photo), her arm linked conventionally through that of her serious and rather inexpressive husband, like all husbands in wedding photos, the two of them seemingly isolated in the picture when, in fact, they would have been surrounded by people, Marta is holding a bouquet in her hands and is looking neither at him nor straight ahead, but at the people who must have been standing to her left – sisters, sisters-in-law and girlfriends, the amused and excited girlfriends who remember her from when she was a little girl, from when they were all little girls, they're the ones who can't believe that she's getting married, the ones who still see everything as a game whenever they get together and are thus a source of relief, they are her confidantes, her best friends because they are like sisters, and her sisters are like friends, all of them both envious and supportive. And I look at her husband, Deán, he isn't just serious, with his long, strange face, he looks rather uncomfortable, as if he had landed up at a party held by the neighbours of some acquaintances or at a celebration that has nothing to do with him because it is a purely female occasion (weddings are the province of women, not just of the bride, but of all the women present), a necessary intruder but, ultimately, mere decoration, someone who can be dispensed with at any moment, apart from at the altar – just the back of a neck – throughout the whole of that celebration which might last all night, much to his despair and his jealousy and his loneliness and regret, knowing, as he does, that he will only become necessary again – an obligatory figure – when all the guests have gone or when he and the bride leave and she does so unwillingly, looking back, still wearing in her eyes the dusky night. Eduardo Deán has a moustache, he's looking directly at the camera and biting his lip, he's very tall and thin and, although his face struck me as memorable, I didn't remember it once I had left the apartment and left Conde de la Cimera and that part of town. I could no longer see him.

As yet, though, I was still there, and, again, I was delaying leaving, as if my presence could remedy something that was entirely irremediable; as if I had qualms about abandoning Marta and leaving her alone on our wedding night – for how long? but I never sought it, I never wanted it; as if as long as I was there things still had some meaning, a thread of continuity, the silken thread, she's dead, but the scene begun when she was alive continues, I am still in her bedroom and that makes her death seem less definitive because I was also there when she was alive, I know how it all happened and I myself have become the thread: her shoes, forever empty now, and her creased skirts, which will never now be ironed, can still be explained, they still have a story, a meaning, because I was a witness to the fact that she wore them, that she had them on – her high-heeled shoes, rather too high for wearing at home, even for the benefit of a guest, a near stranger – and I saw how she pushed them off with her own feet when she got to the bedroom and how she suddenly diminished in height, which made her seem somehow more carnal, more placid, I can tell the story and I can therefore explain the transition from life to death, which is a way of both prolonging that life and of accepting that death: if someone has been present at both things, or perhaps I should say states, if the person dying does not die alone and if whoever is with the person can give witness to the fact that the dead person was not always dead, but was once alive. Fred MacMurray and Barbara Stanwyck were still speaking in subtitles as if nothing had happened, and then the phone rang and I panicked. The panic was not instantaneous, it happened in two stages, because, for a second, I wanted to believe that the first ring had issued from the screen, but phones had a different ring then and, besides, there wasn't a phone in that particular scene and so neither MacMurray nor Stanwyck turned round to look at it or to pick it up, the way I immediately turned towards Marta's bedside table, the phone in Marta's bedroom was ringing at three o'clock in the morning. "It's not possible," I thought, "I haven't spoken to her husband, I called him but I didn't speak to him and nobody knows what has happened, I didn't say anything to the porter, not a thing." And more thoughts thronged in as they do in moments of stress: "Perhaps he dreamed about it in his bed in London, intuited or guessed what had happened, and woke up filled with despair and jealousy and loneliness and regret and preferred to call in order to allay his night sweats and to calm himself, even at the risk of waking her up and possibly the child too." It didn't occur to me to close the bedroom door in order to avoid the latter happening, and at the third ring, out of sheer panic and to stop the strident ringing, I picked up the phone, but I didn't say hello or anything and only then, with the receiver in my hand but not to my ear – as if that contact might betray me – I realized that the answering machine was on – I saw a red light vibrate and flicker – and that it would have answered for me and for her. And when I realized that, I immediately hung up, in response to my growing panic when I heard a man's voice say: "Marta?" and again: "Marta?" That was when I hung up and stood absolutely still, holding my breath, as if someone had seen me, I took three steps towards the door and then I did carefully close it, out of panic and so as not to wake the child, and I prepared myself for the renewed ringing that would not be long in coming, and indeed was not, one, two, three, four, and then the answering machine cut in, I couldn't hear the recorded voice, I didn't know if it was her voice recorded when she was still alive or that of her husband who was far away. Then the beep sounded, I checked with my finger that the volume was up high and I heard the man's voice again, I heard everything he said: "Marta?" he began again. "Marta, are you there?" And this question was impatient or, more than that, irritated. "Did we get cut off before? Are you listening?" There was a pause and some annoyed tutting. "Are you there? What are you playing at? Are you out? When I phoned you just now, you hung up on me! Oh, for Christ's sake, pick up the bloody phone!" There was another second's wait, Deán seemed rather foul-mouthed to me, he began to bluster. "Oh, I don't know, anyway, you must have the volume turned down or perhaps you've gone out, I don't understand it, you must have got your sister to look after the boy. Anyway, I've just got home and so I only just got your message, honestly, fancy forgetting that Eduardo was going away today, you can't be very keen to see me, the one night when we could have seen each other at our leisure, without having to resort to a hotel or the car. Shit, if I'd known about it, you could have come over here or I could've come over to you for a bit, instead of wasting the whole bloody night as I just have. Marta? Marta? Are you stupid or something, why don't you pick up the phone?" There was another pause, a slight groan of exasperation, I thought: "It isn't Deán, but he's a bully, and rude with it." The voice went on talking, quickly, irritably, but firmly, it was like the sound of an electric shaver, steady and hurried and monotonous: "Oh well, I don't know, I don't think you have gone out, and then there's the boy, oh well, if you have gone out and you come back soonish, say, before half past three or a quarter to four, call me if you like, I'm not going to bed just yet and, if you want, I could still come over for a while, I've had the most ridiculous night, disastrous, I can't wait to tell you all about the mess I've got myself into, it makes no difference if I go to bed a bit later still, I'll be wrecked tomorrow anyway. Marta? Are you there?" There was a final, infinitesimal pause, the time it took for him to click his sharp tongue disapprovingly again. "Right then, I don't know, perhaps you're asleep, if not, we'll talk tomorrow. But Inés isn't on duty tomorrow, so there's no chance of seeing each other. You might have remembered before, honestly, you're bloody useless you are."

He didn't say goodbye. His voice was hectoring, battering, condescending, he took liberties or was used to being allowed to do so, he was speaking to a dead woman and he didn't know it. He was speaking angrily, reproachfully, urgently, to a dead woman, in a voice accustomed to tormenting others. Marta would never know, and he would never be able to tell her what had happened to him that night, he wasn't the only one to whom something both ridiculous and disastrous had happened, it had happened to me as well, and more especially to her. And there would certainly be no chance of their seeing each other, he had no idea how remote that chance was, they would never see each other again either hastily or at their leisure, at a hotel or in the car or anywhere, and that fact momentarily and strangely gladdened me, I felt a glimmer of retrospective or imagined jealousy, as brief and discreet as the red light on the answering machine that flickered when the man hung up, then became a steadfast "I". "So, I was just playing second fiddle," I thought and I thought it using exactly those words, that expression. And I felt a flash of disappointment when I thought immediately afterwards: "She really had forgotten that her husband was going away on a business trip, it wasn't a pretext to invite me in his absence, in which case, perhaps she too didn't seek it or want it; perhaps nothing was planned, or perhaps she just waited to see what would happen." We had arranged to have supper together that night in a restaurant, then, in the afternoon, she had called me to ask if I would mind having supper at her place instead: she was so distracted lately what with problems and overwork, she said, that she had forgotten that her husband was going to London that day, she had been counting on him being able to look after the boy; then she hadn't been able to find a babysitter, and she would have to cancel our date altogether unless I was able to have supper there, here, where we did, in fact, have supper, our glasses of wine were still in the living room. The invitation made me feel a bit awkward, I suggested leaving it for another day, I didn't want to complicate things for her; she insisted that I wasn't complicating anything, she had some freshly bought Irish sirloin steak in the freezer, she said, and she asked if I liked meat. I had arrogantly taken that as an initial indication of her romantic interest in me. Now I learned that she had first tried to locate the man with the electric voice who hadn't got Marta's message until three o'clock this morning, a message left when, it must have been after Inés, whoever she was, presumably the man's wife, had gone on duty – on duty as what? – she wasn't on duty tomorrow, but today she was, she can't have gone out very early, possibly a nurse, a pharmacist, a policewoman, a magistrate. "If Marta had been able to get in touch with him, she would certainly have called me back to cancel our supper and my first visit to Conde de la Cimera, she would not have welcomed me but him, he would have been the one here now, which would have made much more sense, with him it would not have taken so long to get started; perhaps on another occasion my place in the bed had also been his, perhaps it wasn't always Deán's place, but occasionally his and tonight mine, there's no point in regretting one's bad luck, it's all the same, even though we choose

47

to forget that and refuse to think about it so that we can continue to be active and to act without knowing, to decide without knowing and to take those poisonous steps; it's all the same, walking down a particular street or getting into a car at the invitation of the driver who, from his seat at the wheel, pushes open the passenger door for us, taking a plane or picking up the phone, going out to supper or staying in our hotel staring distractedly out of the sash window, celebrating a birthday and growing up and going on having birthdays and getting called up, initiating a kiss that leads to other kisses that will force us to linger and for which we will be called to account, asking for or accepting a job, watching the growing storm without bothering to seek shelter, drinking a beer and looking at the women sitting on their stools at the bar, it's all the same, and every one of those things can bring in its train knives and broken glass, illness and malaise and fear, bayonets and depression and regret, the tree struck by lightning and the fishbone in the throat; as well as the fighter plane at one's back and the barber's blunder; the broken high heels and the large hands pressing on your temples, my poor temples, the lit cigarette and the back of the neck averted and damp with sweat, the creased skirts and the undersized bra and then the naked breast, a woman tucked up in bed apparently sleeping and a child who dreams in blissful ignorance beneath his inherited scene of aerial combat. "Tomorrow in the battle think on me, when I was mortal; and let fall thy lance." I again stood looking at her and thought, addressing my thoughts to her: "How many other phone calls did you make today or, rather, yesterday, when you realized that your husband was going away and leaving you free? How many other men would you have preferred to me, how many others did you call to come and keep you company and celebrate your night of singledom or widowhood? You were too late for all of them. Perhaps the only person left was the person you hardly knew, the one you already had a date with, a date made days before, unthinkingly, not realizing that you couldn't waste on him that particular night on which you had forgotten you would be free; perhaps you had to make do with me, once you had gone through your address book and had dialled number after number from this same telephone that still rings for you by this bed, the people who don't yet know that you have died in this bed and that you died in my arms still keep calling and will go on calling until someone tells them that they can cross out your number, there's no point phoning Marta Téllez, because she won't answer, the now useless number that must be forgotten by all those who once made an effort to remember it, including myself, by those who dialled it without even thinking, like that man whose electric-shaver voice has been recorded so that anyone in this room can listen to it, anyone except the person it was intended for; or perhaps I'm being unfair and I was only the second on the list, poor Marta, the one who might have displaced that insistent first choice if the night had truly been a first night, the first of many others that would have led us to linger at my door in order to exchange the insatiable kisses of lovers saying goodbye, the first of many others that no longer wait in the future, but will sleep now for ever in my unsleeping consciousness, the consciousness that gives due consideration to what happens and doesn't happen, to the facts and to the failures, to what cannot be undone and to broken promises, to the chosen and to the rejected, to what recurs and to what is lost, as if it were all the same: error, effort, scruples, the dark back of time. "How many other calls like that would you have made during your now completed lifetime, of which I only came to know the end but not the whole story? I'll never know. Although I will try to remember, on the reverse side of time along which you are already travelling."

I put aside such thoughts. I had avoided looking in the full-length mirror until then, but then I saw myself, my eyes seemed sleepy and apathetic, they felt sore and so I rubbed them with my hands, what they revealed was indifference. I could still recognize myself, my appearance had not changed as Marta's had; I even had my jacket on, it wasn't hard for me to remember the man who had arrived at that house as a supper guest some hours before, a few hours, too many hours. I had to leave there without further delay, I suddenly had the feeling of being caught in a spider's web, in a state of stupefaction, in a state of doubt that had gone unrecognized by my tireless consciousness. I was in my stocking feet and, like that, I could neither act nor decide anything, I put my shoes on and tied the laces, resting the soles on the edge of the bed,

I was no longer careful. I glanced around me without looking properly at anything, I did only two things before leaving the room: I opened the lid of the answering machine, removed the tiny tape and put it in my jacket pocket, I believe that when I did so, I thought two things (or perhaps I only thought those things later on and, at the time, I acted purely mechanically): Deán probably didn't know anything with any certainty, because there would be no ignoring that and certainty is not something that should be forced on anyone, there should always be room or space for doubt; and if Deán did already know, then it was best that the possibility should remain open that the person who had had supper with Marta that night was that other man and not me; and if Deán found and listened to that tape, the other man would be out of the running. (The first thought was considerate or perhaps kind and a little false; the second was prudent, not that anyone would know anything about me, not a thing, I thought again.) The second thing I did was still more mechanical, entirely stripped of solemnity, intention, meaning, in fact, it didn't make any sense at all: I deposited the briefest of kisses on Marta's forehead, I barely brushed it with my lips and then withdrew. I left the bedroom without turning off the television, leaving MacMurray and Stanwyck there for a while, for as long as they lasted – like solitary, momentary witnesses, silent but subtitled, of the two states of Marta Téllez, of her life and of her death, and of the change from one to the other. I didn't turn the light out either, I could no longer think about what would be best or most convenient for me or for her or for Deán or for the boy, I was exhausted, I left everything as it was. Then I walked down the corridor with my shoes on, not worrying whether I made any noise or not, I was sure that nothing would wake the boy. I went into the living room, picked up the bottle and the two wine glasses and took them into the kitchen, I saw the apron that Marta had put on to fry the meat. I washed the glasses with my own hands, placing them upside down on the draining board to dry, I emptied what remained in the bottle down the sink – very little: we drank in order to seek and to want; Château Malartic, though I know nothing about wine – and I threw the bottle in the bin, where I saw the ice-cream carton, potato peelings, torn-up bits of paper, a slightly bloodstained piece of cotton wool, the fat from that Irish meat that I had enjoyed, the leftovers that had been placed there by the dead woman when she was still alive, such a short time ago, the fat from the meat and the hands were the same now, dead, discarded meat, both undergoing a subtle transformation. "My overcoat, my scarf and my gloves," I thought, where had Marta put them after she had opened the door to me? Next to the front door there was a built-in wardrobe, I went over there, opened it and, when I did so, a light went on, the way the light goes on when you open a fridge. There they were, carefully placed on a hanger, the blue scarf folded over the left shoulder of my darker blue overcoat, the collar still turned up the way I always wear it, my black gloves protruding a little from the left pocket, just enough to see that they were there and wouldn't be forgotten, but not so much that they might inadvertently fall to the floor. She was a careful woman, she knew how to look after other people's things. I took them out of the cupboard and put them on, the scarf first, then the overcoat, although not the leather gloves, I might still need my hands free. For a moment, I studied the other clothes, in three different sizes, Deán had an expensive pale blue raincoat, he was obviously very tall, how odd that he hadn't taken it with him to London; Marta had several coats, zipped inside a plastic cover was a fur coat, whether real or fake I don't know; a diminutive anorak and a diminutive navy blue overcoat with gold buttons dangled high above the floor of the cupboard and so they would remain until they grew a few sizes; on the upper shelf there were hats, almost no one wears hats these days, amongst them I noticed a pith helmet and I couldn't help picking it up, it seemed quite old, with its leather chin strap and its worn green lining bearing a very old, cracked label on which the maker's name was still legible: "Teobaldo Disegni" and underneath: "Avenue de France 4" and underneath that: "Tunis". Where had it come from, it must belong to Deán's father or to Marta's, they must have inherited it, as the boy had inherited the hanging fleet of aircraft from his father's childhood. I put the pith helmet on and went in search of a mirror in which I could look at myself, I found one in the bathroom and I had to smile when I saw myself, a colonial in winter wearing scarf and overcoat, my smile didn't last long though, the boy, in all that time I hadn't wanted to think about him, I mean, concentrate my thoughts on him, but I knew, I knew it intuitively right from the start, I knew the three possibilities available to me and I knew which one I would choose. I took off the pith helmet, returned it to its place and closed the cupboard (the light went out). I could stay there and take care of the child until someone turned up, that made no sense, I might as well keep phoning Deán until I got through, or call the porter or a neighbour, and thus betray myself and Marta too. I could take him with me, I could keep him with me until his mother's body was found, and then return him later, I could always do so anonymously, deposit him the next day, or the following day, a few yards from the front door and then just go, I could even leave him at the porter's lodge and then run off, and meanwhile what, twenty-four or even forty-eight hours spent in the company of a miniature fury, he might not even want to come with me or to leave the house, I would have to wake him up and get him dressed in the middle of the night and prevent him going in to see his mother, he would probably cry and kick and hurl himself to the floor, I would feel like a kidnapper, it was absurd. Lastly, I could just leave him: I had to leave him, there was no real alternative. The child would go on sleeping until he woke, then he would call out for his mother or perhaps get up on his own and go and look for her; he would climb on to her bed, he would start shaking the body, motionless under the covers, doubtless not much different from any morning; he would protest at her indifference, he would shout, he would have a tantrum, he wouldn't understand, a child that age doesn't know what death is, he wouldn't even be able to think: "She's dead, Mama is dead," neither the concept nor the word would enter his head, nor would the word "life", neither thing exists for him, what a blessing. After a while, he would grow tired and watch the television (perhaps I should leave the one in the living room switched on too, in case he wanted to watch it and so that he wouldn't have to stay in the bedroom next to the body) or he would get up and go about his business – toys, food, he would be hungry – or he would cry endlessly and very loudly, children have superhuman lungs, they can cry for hours, so much so that one of the neighbours would hear him and ring the doorbell, although neighbours don't much care what goes on as long as it doesn't bother them. Someone was bound to turn up in the morning anyway, a child minder, a cleaning lady, her sister, or Deán would phone again between business deals and no one would answer, not even the answering machine, the tape was in my jacket pocket; and then he would get worried and would make enquiries, he would set things in motion. One thought remained after thinking all this: the child would be hungry. I went to the fridge and I decided to prepare him something to eat as if I were putting out food for a pet I was leaving behind while I went away for a couple of days on a trip: there was ham, chocolate, fruit, I peeled two mandarins to make it easier for him to eat, salami, I took off the skin, I didn't want him to choke, his mother wouldn't be there to put her finger down his throat to save him; I cut up some cheese, removed the rind and washed the knife; in a small cupboard I found biscuits and a bag of pine nuts, I opened the bag and put everything together on one plate (if I opened a yoghurt it might go off). It was an absurd meal, a crazy mixture, but the important thing was that he should have something to eat if the person who looked after the flat was late in arriving. And to drink, I took a carton of fruit juice out of the fridge, filled a glass and placed it beside the plate, I put everything on the kitchen table, with a stool nearby, the child would easily be able to reach it, two-year-olds are great climbers. All of that would betray my presence, that is, someone's presence, but that didn't matter now.

There was nothing more to do, I couldn't do anything else. I glanced towards the bedroom, the idea of going back in there terrified me, luckily I didn't have to, there was nothing I needed to do in there. I went into the living room and put the television on for the boy, with the volume down low, at least that way he would be able to hear something; I left it on a channel where there was still something on, they were showing a film which I recognized at once, *Chimes at Midnight*, the whole world is in black and white in the early hours of the morning. I felt as if I were leaving that apartment in a state of devastation: lights and televisions left on, food taken out of the fridge and arranged on a plate, the tape removed from the answering machine, unironed clothes and unemptied ashtrays, a body, half-naked and covered up. Only the child's room remained in some sort of order, as if it had survived the disaster unscathed. I looked in again, I could hear his quiet breathing, and I stood on the threshold for some moments, thinking: "This child will not recognize me if he sees me again in the distant future; he will never know what happened, he will never know why his world has ended nor the circumstances in which his mother died; his father will hide it from him as will his aunt and his grandparents if he has any, the way such people always do with things they judge to be degrading or unpleasant; they will hide it not only from him, but from everyone, a horrible, ignominious death, a ridiculous death, one that offends us. In fact, it will be hidden from them too, by me – they weren't here – the only person who knows anything: no one will ever know what happened tonight, and the boy, who was here and saw me and was a witness to the preliminaries, will be the one who knows least of all; he won't remember it, just as he will forget about yesterday or the day before yesterday or the day after tomorrow, and soon he won't even remember this world or the mother he has lost today for ever or had already lost before, nothing of what happened in his life from the moment he was born, it's just useless time for him since his memory retains nothing of it for the future, his time until now has been useful only to his parents, who will be able to tell him later on how he was when he was a little boy – very, very little – how he talked and the things he said and the funny ideas he had (his father, not his mother now). So many things happen without anyone realizing or remembering. There is almost no record of anything, fleeting thoughts and actions, plans and desires, secret doubts, fantasies, acts of cruelty and insults, words said and heard and later denied or misunderstood or distorted, promises made and then overlooked, even by those to whom they were made, everything is forgotten or invalidated, whatever is done alone or not written down, along with everything that is done not alone but in company, how little remains of each individual, how little trace remains of anything, and how much of that little is never talked about and, afterwards, one remembers only a tiny fraction of what was said, and then only briefly, the individual memory is not passed on and is, anyway, of no interest to the person receiving it, who is busy forging his or her own memories.

All time is useless, not only that of the child, for all time is like that, however much happens, however much enthusiasm or pain one feels, it only lasts an instant, then it is lost and everything is as slippery as compacted snow, like the boy's dreams at this moment, at this very moment. Everything is to everyone else what I am to him now, a vaguely familiar figure observing him from his bedroom door without him realizing it, without him ever knowing or finding out and rendering him, therefore, for ever incapable of recalling it, the two of us slowly travelling towards our own dissolution. So much else goes on behind our backs, our capacity for knowledge is so limited, we cannot see what lies beyond a wall or anything happening at a distance, someone only has to whisper or move slightly away from us and we can no longer hear what he or she is saying, and our life might depend on it, all it takes is for us not to read a book and therefore not know about the principal danger, we cannot be in more than one place at once, and even then we often have no idea who might be watching us or thinking about us, who is about to dial our number, who is about to write to us, who is about to want us or seek us out, who is about to condemn us or murder us and thus put an end to our few evil days, who is going to hurl us over on to the reverse side of time, on to its dark back, just as I am standing here thinking about and contemplating this child, knowing more than he will ever know about what happened tonight. That is what I must be for him, the reverse side of his time, its dark back."

I emerged from these thoughts, and was again gripped by the need for haste. I moved away from his bedroom and went over to the front door, I again looked apprehensively around me, a pointless exercise, I put on my black gloves. I opened the front door very carefully, as one opens any door in the early hours of the morning, even if there's no risk of waking anyone up. I took two steps, went out on to the landing and, equally carefully, closed the door behind me. Without putting on the light, I felt for the lift button and pressed it, it lit up, indicating that the lift was on its way, it arrived at once, having come from a nearby floor. There was no one inside, no one had travelled up in it and I had not inadvertently brought someone up to my floor, fear believes in the most unlikely coincidences. I got in, pressed another button and the lift descended rapidly, and before opening the door on the ground floor, I stayed there absolutely still for a moment, listening, I didn't want to meet anyone in the hallway, the porter might be an insomniac or a very early riser. I heard nothing, I pushed open the door and stepped into the dark hallway, I walked over towards the street door that was my way out of all that, and then I saw a couple who had not yet come in, they were outside saying goodbye or having an argument, a man and a woman, possibly lovers, he was about thirty-five and she about twenty-five. When they heard my footsteps on the marble floor – one, two, three, or four – they stopped talking and turned round, they saw me; I had no option but to turn on the light and then look around for the button that would open the door for me automatically. I swung round, my hands performing an interrogative gesture from inside their hiding place in my overcoat pockets – the skirts of my coat lifting accordingly – I couldn't see where the button was. The woman, doubtless a resident, pointed one beige-gloved index finger through the glass, pointing to my left, just by the door. She didn't want to come in just yet, she wanted to continue their goodbyes or their argument, she wasn't prepared to use her key to help me and join me in the hall, that would force her to put an end to those kisses or to those bitter words, how long had they have been out there while I was upstairs? I pressed the button, and they stood to one side to let me pass. "Goodnight," I said and they replied in kind or, rather, she smiled and he looked startled and said nothing. A good-looking couple, they must be having problems, to stay out in the cold rather than going their separate ways. I noticed the cold at once, it hit me in the face as if it were a revelation or a reminder of my life and my world that had nothing to do with Marta or that apartment. I had to go on living – it was like a sudden realization – I had to busy myself with other things. I looked up from the street, I could tell which was the flat I had just left behind by the lights – on the fifth floor – and I started walking towards Avenida Reina Victoria and, as I was moving away, I just had time to overhear two remarks exchanged by the couple, for they had resumed the conversation interrupted by my poisonous footsteps. "Look, I can't take any more of this," he said, and she replied, without hesitation: "Well, piss off then."

But he didn't, because I didn't hear his footsteps following mine. I hurried off down Conde de la Cimera, I had to find a taxi, it was slightly foggy, there was hardly any traffic at all, not even along Reina Victoria, which is a wide street, there's a pedestrian area down the centre with kiosks selling drinks, and there's a hideous sculpture of the distorted head of that great poet, poor Vicente Aleixandre, who lived nearby. And I suddenly remembered that I hadn't checked that the windows and the balcony doors were all shut. "What if the child should have a fall tomorrow?" I thought. "Let me sit heavy on thy soul tomorrow! And fall thy edgeless sword." But there was nothing I could do now, I couldn't go back into that flat whose door had been opened to me hours before by someone who would never again open it to anyone, and for which, for a short while, I had felt responsible, as if I were its owner, everything seems as nothing once it is over. I couldn't even phone, no one would answer, not even the answering machine, I had the tape in my jacket pocket. In the middle of that yellowish, reddish night, I looked from one side of the street to the other, two cars passed, I couldn't decide whether to wait or to try another street, to walk on down General Rodrigo, the fog doesn't really tempt one to walk, I could see my breath in the air. I put my hands in my trouser pockets and pulled out something which I did not recognize by its touch as one does one's own things: a piece of clothing, a bra, a size smaller than it should be, I had shoved it in my pocket without thinking when I followed the boy to his room, after he had appeared in his mother's bedroom, I had put it away so that he wouldn't see it. I sniffed it briefly in the middle of the street, the crumpled white fabric in my stiff black glove, the smell of a good, but slightly acrid cologne. The smell of the dead lingers when nothing else remains of them. It lingers for as long as their bodies remain and afterwards too, once they are out of sight and buried and disappeared. It lingers in their homes as long as these remain unaired, and on their clothes which will not be washed again because they won't get dirty any more and because they become their repositories; it clings to dressing gowns, shawls, sheets, to the clothes that for days and sometimes months and weeks and years hang unmoving, ignorant, on their hangers, waiting in vain to be chosen, to come into contact with the one human skin they knew, so faithful. Those were the three things that remained of my fatal visit: that smell, the bra, the tape, and on the tape, voices. I looked around, the winter night lit by many street lamps, the kiosk in darkness, behind me the back of the poet's neck. No cars passed, there wasn't a soul to be seen. The cold air felt good.

I MET EDUARDO DEÁN a month later, although I had seen him before, not only with a moustache and in a photo and in his own home, but also without a moustache and in the flesh and at the cemetery, and not quite so young. A memorable face. We did not meet entirely by chance, chance had nothing to do with my presence at the funeral, which I had read about in the newspapers. For two days I watched for the dawn editions, leafing through magazines as I waited for the bundles of newspapers to arrive just after midnight, and I studied the way the newsagent sliced through the flat plastic ribbon securing them, and I was the first to take a paper from the pile and pay for it at the counter, before hurrying back to the café next to the kiosk and, having ordered a Coca-Cola, turning nervously to the page where you find the births and the weather reports, as well as the obituaries, birthdays, minor prizes, ridiculous honorary-degree ceremonies (no one can resist a mortar-board with a tassel), the lottery results, the chess problem, the crossword and even a complicated anagrammatic puzzle called the "revoltigrama", and, most important of all, the section entitled "Deaths in Madrid", an alphabetical list giving the full name (the person's given name and their two surnames) to which is appended a number, the person's age at the moment when they ceased to have an age, the age at which the deceased came to a halt, fixed in tiny print, for most people it is their first, insignificant and only appearance in the press, as if, apart from a random age and a name, they had never been anything. The list is fairly long – about sixty people – I'd never it read before and it's quite consoling to see that, generally speaking, most of those listed were quite advanced in years, people tend to live to a good age; 74, 90, 71, 60, 62, 80, 65, 81, 80, 84, 66, 91, 92, 90, almost all the nonagenarians are women, and fewer women than men die each day, or so it seems from the records. The first day only three of the deceased were under forty-five, they were all men and one of them was a foreigner called Reinhold Müller, 40, what could have happened to him? Marta didn't appear, so presumably she hadn't yet been found, or else the news hadn't arrived in time, newspapers go to press much earlier than people believe. By then, about twenty hours had elapsed since I had left the apartment. If someone had gone there in the morning, there would have been plenty of time to call a doctor, for the latter to fill out a death certificate, for someone to tell Deán in London, even for him to fly back, in times of misfortune, in cases of emergency, everything is made easy, if someone stands imploringly at an airline counter and says: "My wife has died, my son is all alone," the company will instantly find him a seat on the next flight out, in order not to be dubbed "hardhearted". But none of that had apparently happened, because Marta Téllez's name, along with her second surname which I did not know, and her age when she died – 33, 35, 32, 34? – did not appear in the list. Perhaps the shock, perhaps the sadness of it all had meant that no one had thought to comply with the formalities. But people always call a doctor, so that he can certify and confirm what everyone thinks (so that he can provide verification with his warm, infallible doctor's hand trained to recognize and identify death), to confirm what I both thought and knew when I lay at Marta's back, holding her in my arms. What if I had been mistaken and she hadn't died? I'm not a doctor. And what if she had merely lost consciousness and then recovered it in the morning and life had carried on as normal, her little boy packed off to nursery school and she back at her work, my night-time visit relegated to the world of mad escapades and bad dreams, everything tidied away and the sheets changed, even though I had never actually slipped between them? It's curious how easily one's thoughts are drawn to the improbable, allowing themselves that momentary lapse, finding rest or relief in fantasy and superstition, blithely capable of denying the facts and turning back the clock, even if only for an instant. It's curious how it all seems so like a dream.

It was nearly one o'clock in the cafeteria-cum-supermarket, the place was packed with people having supper and shopping, and in England it was still an hour earlier. I got up and went over to the telephone, luckily it was a card phone and I had a card on me, I took out the piece of paper with the number of the Wilbraham Hotel on it that I had kept in my wallet, and when I heard the porter's voice (the same one, he was obviously on permanent night duty) I asked him for Señor Ballesteros. This time he didn't hesitate, he said to me: "Just a moment please."

He didn't ask if I knew the room number or anything, instead he added it himself, as if broadcasting his actions and his thoughts ("Ballesteros. Fifty-Two. Right . . ." he said, pronouncing the surname as if it had only one "l"), and I suddenly heard the extension ringing, which took me by surprise, I wasn't prepared for that, nor, immediately afterwards, to hear a new voice saying: "Hello". I couldn't tell from that one word if the voice was Spanish or British (or, if it was Spanish, whether or not he had a good English accent), because I hung up as soon as I heard it. "Good God," I thought, "the man's still in England, he obviously doesn't know anything yet, but anyone who had gone to the house would have done exactly what I did, they would have looked for and found Deán's London address and phone number and he would, therefore, already have been informed. Presumably, then, he knows nothing about it, unless, that is, he's taken it all with remarkable calm. If the child is in good hands, he may have decided to fly back tomorrow. No, he can't possibly know, or perhaps he's only just been told and there's nothing he can do. Perhaps he's still sitting in tears in his foreign hotel room and will be unable to sleep tonight."

"Excuse me, have you done?"

I turned round and saw a man with very long teeth (so long that his mouth must have been permanently ajar) and well dressed, by conventional standards, in a camel coat: as is usual in these cases, he had a rather plebeian way of speaking. I removed my card and stood to one side, then I returned to my table, paid for my Coca-Cola and left; and that was when I returned to Conde de la Cimera in a taxi. It wasn't a long visit, but rather longer than I had envisaged. I asked the taxi driver to wait and I got out thinking that it would only take a matter of seconds, I stood by the side of the car and looked up, but what I saw did nothing to allay my fears: the lights I had left on were still lit, although it was hard to remember if they were exactly the same ones or if there had been some change. I had only glanced briefly up at them from that position when I left, I hadn't lingered, being then too shocked and fearful and tired; and if they were the same lights, it was very likely that no one had gone into that house all day and that the corpse was still there, undergoing its slow transformation, half-naked beneath the sheets, in the same position in which I had left it, or perhaps uncovered now, having been pulled about by an impatient, uncomprehending, desperate child ("I should have covered her face," I thought, "but it wouldn't have done any good"). And the child would still be there too, perhaps he had eaten everything I had left out for him and would be hungry again, no, for a small stomach I had left a fair amount of food, a mish-mash, a "revoltigrama". I didn't know what to do. I was standing there once more in my overcoat and my gloves, at my side sat a silent taxi driver who had decided to turn off the engine once he saw that my wait was going to be longer than planned. By then, more lights had gone on in the building, but my eyes were fixed on those of the apartment I knew, as if I were looking through a telescope. I felt more distressed than I had on the previous night, more than I had when I left there at dawn. I knew what had taken place and, at the same time, it seemed to me nonsensical and ridiculous that it should have taken place at all, nothing that happens has ever completely happened until you tell someone, until it is spoken about and known about, until then, it is still possible to convert those events into mere thought or memory – the slow journey towards unreality begun the very instant they occurred – and the consolation of uncertainty, which is itself also retrospective. I hadn't said anything, perhaps the boy had. Everything was as normal in the street, a group of drunken students passed by, garrulous and hideously dressed, one of them bumped against me with his shoulder, he didn't apologize. I was still gazing up at the fifth floor of that fourteen-storey building, trying to make sense of the light visible through the blinds on the balcony doors, the balcony on to which the living room opened, the glass doors were apparently closed, but it was impossible to know from below if it really was closed, or just pushed to.

"Why don't you use the entry phone and call up and tell them to come down?"

The taxi driver had assumed that I was there to pick somebody up and he was getting impatient, I had told him to keep the meter running, I wouldn't be long.

"No, it's too late, people will be sleeping," I said. "If no one comes down in the next five minutes, then they're obviously not coming. We'll just wait a little bit longer."

I knew that no one would come down, whoever the hypothetical subject of those sentences was, the taxi driver's and mine. The subject of his sentence was doubtless female, the subject of mine genderless, purely fictitious, although he would imagine it to be a young girl or an adulteress, someone who is dependent on others and who can never be sure that they will be free to come down. Marta would not come down nor would the child. I didn't have a very clear idea of where the rooms were (you rarely do from outside a building), but I imagined that Marta's bedroom corresponded to the window to the right of the balcony from where I was standing and where a light was still lit just as I had left it, assuming it was as I had left it. Suddenly, the taxi driver turned on the engine and I looked round at him, he had noticed before I had that someone was coming out of the front door, which was a few feet away from me, otherwise he would not have been able to see; he had just taken it for granted that the young woman coming out was the person I was expecting. She wasn't, although she was the same young woman with whom I had had an earlier late-night encounter, the one who could not be bothered to get out her key to open the door for me. I could get a better look at her now that I could see her from a distance and without a companion: she had brown hair and brown eyes, she was wearing a pearl necklace, high-heeled shoes, dark stockings, and she was walking gracefully along, despite the short, tight skirt visible beneath her leather coat which she wore unbuttoned, she was obviously in the habit of walking with her feet turned out, for she had a slightly centrifugal gait. She looked at the taxi, then she looked at me, she gave a slight nod of recognition, like a nod of agreement, then she crossed the street and – without removing the beige gloves, which did not match her coat – she took out of her handbag a key with which she opened the door of a parked car. I watched her throw her handbag on to the back seat and get in (she carried her bag in her hand as if it were a briefcase). As with most women drivers, there was a flash of leg as she got in and closed the door, then she wound down the window. The taxi driver switched off his engine again and automatically wound his window down too, in order to get a better look at the young woman. She turned on the ignition and, out of the corner of my eye, I watched her turning the steering wheel hard. I saw her stick her head out of the window to check that, as she drew away, she wasn't going to hit the car in front; her view was obstructed, so I made a beckoning gesture with my hand, twice, as if to say: "It's all right, you're clear." The car swung out and, as she passed me, the woman smiled and reciprocated with another gesture, halfway between goodbye and thank you. She was a pretty woman and not, apparently, in the least conceited, perhaps she wasn't the one with the key to the apartment, but the man whom I had heard her tell to piss off. Perhaps she had gone up with him to his apartment after that argument in the doorway and had not left until twenty hours later, until that moment when she met me again in the same spot – as if I had not moved during the long hours of wasted saliva, wasted on words and kisses, and the further hours of point-less, laborious dreams – although this time I was outside the build-ing and, to all appearances, waiting for someone, with a taxi at my orders. I couldn't tell if she was wearing the same clothes or not, the night before I had only noticed her gloves.

That was when I looked up again, first at the bedroom window, then at the balcony, then back again at the window, because behind the blinds of that window I saw the silhouetted figure of a woman taking off a jersey or a long-sleeved top or something, for at the moment I spotted her she was crossing her arms in order to grip the bottom edges of the jersey and pull it up over her head in a single movement – I caught a glimpse of her armpits – in such a way that she was left with only the inside-out sleeves on her arms or caught on her wrists. The silhouette remained there for a few seconds as if exhausted by the effort or by her day's work – the desolate gesture of someone who can't stop thinking and who gets undressed gradually and needs those pauses in order to ruminate or ponder between items of clothing – or as if she had looked out of the window and seen something or someone – perhaps me with my taxi behind me – only after emerging from the sweater that she had just taken off. Then she removed both sleeves from her wrists with a final tug, gave a half-turn and walked away, far enough off for me not to be able to see her any more, although I thought I could still make out her distorted shadow folding up the jersey, perhaps to change it for another cleaner, fresher one. Then she switched off the light and, assuming that was the bedroom I was familiar with, the light she had switched off must be the one on the bedside table which I had hesitated whether to leave on or not – I wanted to be able to see – and so it stayed on until after my departure. I wasn't completely sure, but when I saw the figure, I felt relief as well as shock, because someone was in the apartment and that someone might be Marta, Marta still alive. It couldn't be Marta, but again I allowed myself to think that, just for a moment. And if it wasn't her, why was that woman in her bedroom, more than that, why was she getting changed or undressed there as if she were about to go to bed, and where was Marta, where was her body, perhaps moved into another room for the wake, or removed from the apartment altogether and taken to the morgue. And in her bedroom there was a friend, a sister-in-law, a sister, who had stayed behind so that the child would not have to spend another night alone until Deán came back the following day, how could Deán not have come back once he knew about her death? Although it would make more sense to have taken the child to sleep somewhere else, what would his aunts have told him, they would have asked him to be patient, they would have deceived him ("Mama's gone on a journey, in a plane"). (And for ever after, the boy would view his miniature planes quite differently: for ever after, until he forgot.) Behind the balcony everything remained the same, and I was sure now that the light did belong to the apartment, to the living-cum-dining room where we had eaten supper and where the boy had watched his videos of Tintin and Haddock, only twenty-four hours ago according to the clocks. There was no point in my staying any longer.

"So, shall we go?"

I don't know why I felt I had to explain to the taxi driver:

"Yes, they won't be coming down now, they've gone to bed."

"Out of luck, eh?" he said, in understanding tones. What did he know about what was or wasn't lucky in this case?

I went back home with my early edition of the newspaper, feeling not in the least bit sleepy. The previous night I had gone to bed as soon as I got back, overcome by the need for temporary oblivion, stronger than any past or present distress and stronger than my concern for the child. I had left the apartment and there was nothing more I could do (or I had decided to do nothing more when I left), I slept for eight solid hours, I don't even remember dreaming, although my first thought when I woke up was simple and unequivocal: "The child," you always spend more time thinking about the living than you do about the dead, even when we hardly know the former and the latter were our whole life until only a month ago or the day before yesterday or tonight (but Marta Téllez wasn't my whole life, she might perhaps be Deán's). Now, on the other hand, the relative tranquillity of believing that there was a female personage who would take charge of the flat both cleared my head and left me incapable of thinking about anything else, or of distracting myself with books, television or videos, my backlog of work or my record player. Everything was in suspense but I didn't know until when, or what had to happen before life could start again: I wanted to know, and I wanted to know soon, if they had found the body and if the child was safe, that was all, in theory, I felt no curiosity beyond that, then. And yet I foresaw that once I had found that out, I would still not be able to get back to my daily life and activities, as if the link established between Marta Téllez and myself would never break, or might take a while to do so. At the same time, I didn't know in what way it might perpetuate itself, she would have nothing more to say, you can have no further contact with the dead. There is an English verb, "to haunt" and a French verb, "hanter" which are closely related and more or less untranslatable in Spanish, they both describe what ghosts do to the places and people they frequent or watch over or revisit; depending on the context, the first can also mean "to bewitch", in the magical sense of the word, in the sense of "enchantment", the etymology is uncertain, but it seems that both come from other verbs in

Anglo-Saxon and Old French meaning "to dwell", "to inhabit", "to live in" permanently (dictionaries are as distracting as maps). Perhaps the link was merely that, a kind of enchantment or haunting, which, when you think about it, is just another name for the curse of memory, for the fact that events and people recur and reappear indefinitely and never entirely go away, they may never completely leave or abandon us, and, after a certain point, they live in or inhabit our minds, awake and asleep, they lodge there for lack of anywhere more comfortable, struggling against their own dissolution and wanting to find embodiment in the one thing left to them that can preserve some validity and contact, the repetition or infinite resonance of what they once did or of one particular event: infinite, but increasingly weary and tenuous. I had become the connecting thread.

I switched on my answering machine and heard two anodyne, everyday messages, one from the woman who, until recently, had been my wife and the other from an awful actor I sometimes do work for (I'm a screenwriter for the movies, but I almost always end up writing television series instead; most of these never even get to the production stage, so it's a fairly pointless task, but television people are a profligate lot and they pay me for the scripts anyway). And that was when I remembered Marta's tape. If I had forgotten about it until then, it was because I hadn't made off with it out of indiscretion or curiosity or simply because I wanted to listen to it, I had taken it so that the man, whose imperative, condescending voice I had heard leaving a message that night, might come under suspicion. Suspicion of what? Not of anything particularly serious, not even of having slept with her at the time of her death or just before or just afterwards, I hadn't, nobody had, as far as I knew. The tape was the same size as the ones I use, which meant that I could listen to it. I removed mine and replaced it with hers, I rewound it back to the beginning and replayed it. The first thing I heard was that man's voice again ("Oh, for Christ's sake, pick up the bloody phone"), that tormenting, electric-shaver voice ("Are you stupid or something, why don't you pick up the phone?"), so sure of how far he could go with Marta ("Honestly, you're bloody useless you are"), the irritated clicks of the tongue. After the beep there were other messages, all of them pre-dating that last one and Marta would therefore already have heard them, the first was incomplete, the initial section erased by that man's words: ". . . so," a woman's voice began saying, "make sure you call me tomorrow and tell me all about it. The guy sounds rather nice, but you can never tell. Frankly, I don't know how you've got the nerve. Anyway, talk to you later, and good luck." Then came a man's voice, that of an older man, ironic, self-mocking: "Marta," he said, "tell Eduardo that it's common to say 'we'll get back to you', he ought to say 'we'll return your call', not that he's ever exactly been a man of letters, we've always known that, but then he's not an old pedant like myself either. Anyway, give me a call, I've got a bit of good news to tell you. Don't get too excited, it's nothing dramatic, but in a precarious existence like mine, a little bit of excitement goes a long way, *povero me*." He didn't say goodbye or say who he was, as if it were unnecessary, he could be someone's father, Deán's or Marta's, someone who needs an excuse to phone up even his nearest and dearest, an older man with little to do, fearful of appearing insistent, someone who had perhaps spent some time in Italy as a young man or was a fan of the opera. Then I heard: "Marta, it's Ferrán. I know Eduardo left for England today, but I've just realized that he hasn't left me a phone number or address or anything, I can't think why, I told him to be sure to let me have them, the way things are here, we can't afford not to be able to locate him. Perhaps you've got them, or else, if you speak to him, can you tell him to call me at once, at the office or at home. It's fairly urgent. Thanks." That was a neutral voice with a barely noticeable Catalan accent, a work colleague with whom continuous contact has become confused with friendship and trust, possibly non-existent. I didn't remember Marta giving Deán this message when she spoke to him during supper, but then I wasn't paying that much attention. This was followed by another incomplete message, just the end, which meant that it was fairly old, that is, not from that day or at least not from the part of the day during which Marta had been absent and a girlfriend or sister had phoned her, as well as her father or father-in-law and a colleague of her husband's. "So we'll do whatever you say, whatever you want. You decide," a woman's voice was saying, that was the end of the message, it seemed to me that it could be the same woman from before, the one who was so amazed at Marta's daring behaviour, it was hard to tell, even harder to know if she was saying it to Deán or to Marta, "You decide." And after that, there was yet another incomplete message, belonging therefore to an even older batch, in which a different man's voice was speaking in tones of feigned neutrality, that is, serious, polite, almost indifferent, as if wanting to pass himself off as a professional call, when it was almost certainly of a personal or even romantic nature, a voice that closed by saying: ". . . if that doesn't suit you, we could see each other on Monday or Tuesday. Otherwise, we'd have to leave it until next week; from Wednesday onwards, I'm up to my eyes. But anyway, there's no rush, get back to me and tell me what would be best for you, OK? See you." That was my voice, that was me some days ago, when I was still not sure whether Marta Téllez and I would be going out to supper and seeing each other for a third time, after our first conversation, standing up at a cocktail party on the evening we were introduced, and after the long talk we had over coffee a few days later, our intentions already far from honourable, any courtship looks pathetic when seen from outside or in retrospect, a mutually agreed manipulation, a laborious compliance with formalities, the social gift-wrapping around something that is pure instinct. The person speaking did not perhaps know then that this was something he was both seeking and wanting, but listening to him now, hearing his affected intonation, his barely suppressed excitement – that of someone who knows that his message might be heard by a husband, someone who, besides, considers dissembling to be a virtue – it was clear that I was seeking it and wanting it, what hypocrisy, what pretence, every word a lie, there's no doubt in my mind that the owner of that voice was in a great hurry, and it wasn't true that from Wednesday onwards I was "up to my eyes", how could I have used such an expression, I would never normally say that, it was the kind of thing a phoney would come out with, and I never usually say "see you" either, I simply say "goodbye", why had I said that, in order not to appear insistent when, in fact, I was, sometimes we weigh each word according to our secret intentions; and that "OK?", spoken in such unctuous, counterfeit tones, the blatant flimflam of someone wanting to seduce not only by flattery, but by appearing respectful and deferential too. It startled me to recognize not only my own voice, but also those few, transparent phrases, it frightened me to remember the day when I left that message, a message to which, later on, she replied, when, in reality, everything was already utterly predictable apart from what actually happened in the end or, rather, in the middle, everything else already both had and hadn't been consciously foreseen. It suddenly occurred to me that I must have given my name and surname at the beginning, I always do, in the part of the message that had been recorded over, and then I'd gone on to mention Monday or Tuesday, so Deán could have known about our date from the first, perhaps that was why Marta hadn't mentioned it to him on the phone in my presence, perhaps it was something he already knew about, not something hidden nor unspoken, and, in that case, my precautions would have been as vain as they were ineffectual, it was quite possible that, any day now, Deán would seek me out and find me and would ask me point-blank what had happened, how come his wife had died when she was with me, perhaps the only unpremeditated, hidden thing was the fact that the supper and the rendezvous had taken place in his own home. I rewound the tape and listened to my voice again, I found the sound of it repellent, it was Wednesday today and I wasn't up to my eyes at all, I was alone at home faffing about with dictionaries and a tape, how ridiculous. But I didn't have much time to be indignant with myself, because on the next message, I immediately recognized the electric-shaver voice again, except that on this occasion it was addressed to Deán and not to Marta and said: "Hi, Eduardo, it's me. Listen, don't wait for me to start supper, I'm going to be a bit late. A problem has come up which has rather complicated matters, I'll tell you both all about it later. Anyway, I shouldn't get there much after eleven, and please tell Inés. I can't get hold of her and she'll be going straight to the restaurant, just so that she doesn't worry. Anyway, could one of you save me a slice of ham? See you later." That man always had some tale to tell, or, which comes to the same thing, some titbit, postponed, probably some stupid incident that had happened that night – nights before, some incident that had "complicated matters" – on which two couples and perhaps other people too had arranged to have supper in a restaurant that served excellent ham. His voice was still despotic, although this time he didn't lard his speech with mild swearwords and insults, his was an irritating voice, he had said "It's me" as if he were so instantly recognizable that it wasn't necessary to clarify who that "me" was, which was doubtless the case at the apartment he was phoning – the house of a friend and the house of a lover, he was addressing Deán, but also Marta, "I'll tell you both", "Could one of you save me a bit of ham?" – but you should never take it for granted that your voice will be as unmistakable to others as it is to yourself. The beep sounded and, before the tape continued on in silence, traversing virgin territory – the messages at the beginning of the tape cutting each other off or cancelling each other out – a final voice emerged, a voice that said one thing only, the voice of someone crying; it was a child's voice, or that of a curiously infantilized woman, but then everyone becomes like a child when they cry, it's unavoidable, to the point where you can't even articulate or breathe, when the crying is strident, continuous and undisguised, beyond words or even thoughts, because it does not just replace them, it stops or excludes them – it impedes them – and that voice, whose distressing message, since it lacked a beginning, obviously pre-dated those in the previous batch – it pre-dated my mellifluous tones and that of the tyrant with the electric-shaver voice – was saying intermittently in the midst of the weeping, or incorporated into the weeping as if it were merely one of its many modalities: "Please . . . please . . . please . . . ," and it uttered those words in an oddly dehumanized way, it was not so much a genuine plea intended to have some effect as a conjuration, ritual, superstitious words, empty of meaning, spoken either to overcome or to fend off a threat. Again I was startled, I was on the point of stopping the tape, fearful lest that immodest, almost malign weeping might wake my neighbours and prompt them to come over in order to find out what brutal act I was committing: that hadn't happened with Marta, no neighbour had come to investigate, but then she had not cried out, she had not complained or pleaded, nor had I committed any brutal act. There was no need to stop the machine, however, once the minute allowed for each phone call was over –

again it wasn't the full minute – there was another beep and the tape ran on, as I said before, silent now; the voice crying childishly had used up its time without saying anything more and they had not rung again, perhaps knowing that the person the message was intended for, the cause of her torment, must be there, at home, by the telephone, listening to her crying and yet refusing to pick up the receiver, and that she would succeed only in continuing to record her grief that was now being listened to by a stranger.

The following night, I went back to the kiosk where they sell the early editions of the newspapers and waited there for a few minutes around midnight, then I hurriedly bought one bearing the date of the day that was officially beginning at that moment, especially in England, although, according to the clocks, it's always an hour earlier there. I didn't dare read it standing up in the midst of so many people, so I went into the café again and, this time, ordered a whisky before looking up the list of the recently deceased: although the list is alphabetical, I had sufficient self-control not to go straight to the end of the list and look at the Ts, but to start at the beginning and thus, for a few seconds more, prolong the agony and the uncertainty, that is, the hope that Marta's name would appear and would not appear; I wanted both things simultaneously, or, if you prefer, my desires were completely split: if her name appeared, I would know that she had been found and I would feel both relieved and cast down; if her name did not appear, I would be even more worried and would once again start to fiddle with the bit of paper bearing Deán's London number, or return to prowling around the block of flats, but also, for a few seconds, I would be able to savour the unbelievable possibility that it had all been a ghastly misunderstanding, a false alarm, an act of inconceivable haste on my part, she had merely lost consciousness or even gone into a coma, but was still alive. I looked at the surnames and their now abandoned ages: Almendros, 66, Aragón, 88, Armas, 48, Arrese, 64, Blanco, 77, Borlaff, 41, Casaldáliga, 93, but I couldn't keep reading them one by one and I jumped to L: Luengo, 59, Magallanes, 93, Marcelo, 48, Martín, 43, Medina, 28, Monte, 46, Morel, 61, a lot of fairly young people had died yesterday, Francisco Pérez Martínez, 59, but Marta had died the day before, in fact, she did not belong with these more premature dead but with the older dead of the previous day. There she was, Téllez, 33, Marta Téllez Angulo, aged 33, and that was more or less the age she looked, the penultimate on the list, after her, there was only Alberto Viana Torres, 55. Still terrified, I glanced quickly back at the Ds, in case there was a Deán, 1, Eugenio Deán Téllez, who was not yet two according to his mother, Coya, 50, Delgado, 81, no, he wasn't there, he couldn't be and wasn't, I had left him alive and asleep, left food for him on a plate.

I went back to the news kiosk and bought another paper, the most funeral-conscious of all the Madrid papers, I returned to my table and perused its abundance of death notices, and there was Marta's, giving an appearance of order to her disorderly death, it was a sober notice, beneath the black cross came her full name, the place and the exact date of her death (verified by the doctor's pressing, exploratory hand), then R.I.P., and after that, the usual list of shocked survivors, regretful and prayerful, I have appeared in some myself, "Her husband, Eduardo Deán Ballesteros; her son, Eugenio Deán Téllez; her father, *Excelentísimo* Señor Don Juan Téllez Orati; her brother and sister, Luisa and Guillermo; her sister-in-law María Fernández Vera; and other family members . . ." The names of a sister-in-law and a sister appeared, but not the name of a friend, and there was a father with an Italian mother, his was doubtless the voice I had heard on the tape, he of the precarious and pedantic existence who had a bit of good news to tell her, but why the *Excelentísimo*, it seemed rather presumptuous to include that in his daughter's death notice, a daughter who had recently died in such an unexpected manner, a shameful death, a horrible and, perhaps, ridiculous death. He must have written it himself, he was the kind of father who would know how one should word such things and who, besides, had nothing else to do, an old-fashioned sort of man, he had used the word "husband" rather than such mealymouthed terms as "beloved spouse", although it did seem overly pompous to give the full name of a child who was barely two years old – it was probably his first appearance in print, as it was for so many of the dead – as if he were a respectable gentleman, Master Eugenio. At least there was no mention of Marta having received the Holy

Sacrament, which is what they usually say about everyone, I would have been able to testify to the falsehood of that. "The burial will take place today, the 19th, at 11 o'clock, in the Cemetery of Nuestra Señora de la Almudena." And some days later, there would be a funeral service in a church whose name meant nothing to me, I've never known the names of churches in my own city; I tore out the page and folded it up in order to cut out that particular death notice, it joined the other bit of paper that was now, no doubt, useless, the one giving the number of the Wilbraham Hotel in London.

I reached the cemetery a little early, on a morning of cold, indifferent sunshine, so as not to miss the arrival of the funeral cortège or get lost somewhere in the cemetery. Some cemetery employees – not all of them gravediggers – showed me where the burial was to take place, I walked over there and waited for a few moments, reading the gravestones and epitaphs round about, rehearsing the act I would have to put on as soon as the Deán and Téllez families arrived with the coffin and their flowers and their black clothes. I was wearing dark glasses as has become customary on visits to cemeteries, not so much to conceal one's tears as to conceal their absence, when they are absent. I noticed that a gravestone had already been drawn aside – the hole or tomb or abyss open to view – as if in readiness to receive a new tenant, they only disturb the dead in order to bring them another dead person whom they surely loved in life, although there is no way of knowing if that gladdens them, seeing again someone they knew when they were younger, or if it saddens them even more to find that person reduced to the same state as themselves and to know that there is one less person in the world to remember them. I looked at the inscription and learned that there lay Marta's mother, Laura Angulo Hernández, and also her Italian grandmother, Bruna Orati Parenzan, possibly Venetian, and I learned too that Marta had another sister who had died years before – even before her mother and grandmother had died – when she was five years old, according to the dates inscribed there, Gloria Téllez Angulo, born two years before Marta, so the two girls would have known each other, although Marta would barely remember her older sister, just as her son, Eugenio, would barely remember her as he grew older. I realized that a death notice and a gravestone had taught me far more about Marta or her family than anything she had told me during our three preparatory meetings. Preparatory for what, for a modest party (Irish sirloin steak and wine, one guest) and for her farewell to the world, before my very eyes. In that tomb of women inaugurated by a little girl thirty-one years before, Marta was to occupy the fourth place, preempting her father, perhaps, who would have bought the plot when that first daughter died and would have assumed that he would be the next to lie next to his mother, wife and daughter, those tombs are usually made for four, but not always, sometimes they hold five, and, in that case, there would still be room for him, and when he arrived, he would know who all the inhabitants were. Marta's name had not yet been inscribed on the gravestone, that comes after the burial.

I left the graveside and whiled the time away reading a kind of riddle on a nearby tomb, dated 1914: "None that speak of me know me," it said in its ten brief lines (albeit of prose not poetry), "and when they do speak, they slander me; those who know me keep silent and in their silence do not defend me; thus, all speak ill of me until they meet me, but when they meet me they find rest, and they bring me salvation, for I never rest." It took several readings before I realized that it wasn't the dead person speaking (León Suárez Alday, 1890–1914, according to the inscription, a young man) but death itself, a strange death bemoaning its bad reputation and the lack of recognition given it by the insolent living, a death resentful of the slanderous remarks and desirous of salvation: weary, rather amicable and, ultimately, resigned. I was in the middle of memorizing the riddle, as if it were a telephone number or a few lines of poetry, when, in the distance, I saw thirty or so people getting out of their cars and slowly approaching behind the bearers, who were walking slightly faster because of the weight they were carrying, one of them had a spent cigarette between his lips which immediately prompted me to light one of my own. The people in the cortège gathered around the open grave, in a ragged semicircle, leaving room for the bearers to manoeuvre, and while a brief prayer was said, the coffin was lowered into the ground with the usual difficulties – squeaks and bumps and trial runs and hesitations, wood striking stone and the sort of grinding noises you might expect in a quarry, only shriller, like two bricks grating together or a nail that refuses to be driven home, and the occasional workman's voice giving orders under his breath; and the terrible fear of bruising the body that we will never again set eyes upon – I could see the people in the first row, standing closest to the upper part of the grave, six or seven of whom I could clearly make out from my 1914 tomb, where I stood with my hands folded in front of me, in one hand a cigarette which, from time to time, I raised to my lips; as if León Suárez Alday were an ancestor before whose ancient remains I could ponder and remember and even whisper the most uninhibited, and also the most comforting, words we can ever utter, words addressed to someone who cannot hear us. And although it is true that the first person I looked for was the boy – a pointless exercise, no one takes children of that age to funerals – the first one I noticed was not the man intoning a prayer – a robust, elderly gentleman whom I noticed subsequently – but a woman who bore an extraordinary resemblance to Marta Téllez, obviously her surviving sister, Luisa, who was wearing neither dark glasses nor a veil – you never see veils these days – but was weeping in a strident, continuous, undisguised fashion, although, in fact, she did try to disguise it by lowering her head and covering her face with her two hands, the way people do sometimes when they feel horror or shame and want not to see or be seen, or are the self-confessed victims of depression or malaise or fear or regret. And that gesture, which these victims usually make alone, sitting or lying down in their bedrooms – their face pressed into the pillow, perhaps, the pillow replacing their own two hands, something that hides and protects, or something in which they can find refuge – was being made by this woman standing up, in her immaculate clothes, her hands carefully manicured, in the middle of a cortège of people, and in a cemetery, with her rounded knees visible beneath her unbuttoned overcoat, with her black stockings and her polished high-heeled shoes; on her lips – to which she would automatically have applied make-up, a mechanical gesture performed every day before leaving the house – would be the sickly taste of lipstick mingled with her own salt tears, liquid, involuntary; occasionally she raised her head and bit her lip – those lips – in a vain attempt to suppress not her grief, but its overly frank manifestation, beyond words, and it was during those moments that I saw her, and although her face was distorted by grief, I could still see the similarity with Marta, because I had seen Marta's face distorted too, by a different kind of pain, but equally manifest; a younger woman, by two or three years, prettier perhaps or less dissatisfied with her lot, she was single, or a widow, according to the death notice. Perhaps she was crying too because she felt the kind of envy or sense of exile that afflicts children when they are separated from their siblings, when one of them is left alone with the grandparents while the others go off with their parents on a trip, or when one of them goes to a different school from the one the older children go to, or when they are ill in bed, nestling amongst the pillows with the comics and coloured prints and storybooks by which their world is configured (and above them, their model planes), and they see the others going off to the beach or the river or the park or the cinema and setting out on their bikes, and when they hear the first gusts of laughter and the summery sound of bicycle bells, they feel like a prisoner or perhaps an exile, this is largely because children lack any vision of the future, for them only the present exists – not the unwholesome, rugged, fragmented yesterday nor the diaphanous, flat tomorrow – in this, they resemble animals and certain women, and that child suddenly sees his bed as the place where he will have to stay for ever and from which he will, for an indefinite period, have to listen to the wheels moving off across the gravel and to the bright, superfluous ringing of bicycle bells by his brothers and sisters for whom time doesn't count, not even the present. Perhaps Luisa Téllez also felt that Gloria and Marta, the sister with whom she would never have played and the sister with whom she would have played, were reunited now in the earth with their mother and their grandmother, in a stable, feminine, kindly world where they would no longer worry over a yes or a no, where they would no longer weary themselves over a perhaps or a maybe, in a world in which time didn't count – a haunted or, perhaps, enchanted world – which it was not yet time for her to enter, a world from which she was literally exiled and in whose common dwelling place there would certainly be no room when her turn came; and while the earth fell symbolically once more upon that grave, she remained with her father and her brother amongst the inconstant living, and perhaps, one day, with a husband who has not yet appeared – the vague figure of a husband – in a world of men, a world configured by comics and coloured prints and storybooks (and, above them, their model planes), a world that is still, undeniably, the victim of time.

And there was the father, Juan Téllez, who had spoken a few brief, almost inaudible words, presumably a prayer in which he himself would not believe at his age, how difficult it is entirely to discard the superficial customs and beliefs of those who precede us, which we sometimes emulate throughout our whole life – another life – out of superstition and respect for them, the forms and effects of things take longer to disappear and be forgotten than do their causes and contents. He had been led stumbling to the grave, helped by his surviving daughter and his daughter-in-law as if he were a condemned man being led to the scaffold and lacking the strength to climb the steps or as if he were walking in snow, just managing to extricate one foot, only to plunge back in again at every step. But then he had recovered his composure and had puffed out his convex chest, taken a bluish handkerchief out of his breast pocket and wiped the sweat from his brow, not the tears from his eyes, for there were none, although he did also dab at one dry cheek and at his forehead, as if to soothe a rash. He had spoken his words with a mixture of gravity and reluctance, as if he were fully aware of the solemnity of the moment but, at the same time, wanted to have done with it as soon as possible and to go back home and lie down, perhaps there was a touch of shame mingled with his grief (that *was* a horrible death, a ridiculous death), although the likelihood was that no one had told him about the real circumstances, about his daughter's half-naked, dishevelled appearance when they found her, that there was clear evidence that a man had been in the apartment, not Deán or anyone, but me, who, for them, was no one. They would simply have told him: "Marta died while Eduardo was away." And he would have raised his mottled hands to his face, seeking refuge in them. "She would have died anyway, even if she hadn't been alone," they would have added in order not to alienate him still further from his son-in-law, or as if the knowledge that something was inevitable might make it easier to accept. (She hadn't been alone, I knew that and doubtless so did they.) They may not even have told him the cause, if they knew it, a cerebral embolism, a myocardial infarction, an aortic aneurysm, a meningococcal infection of the adrenal glands, an overdose of something, an internal haemorrhage, I don't quite know which ailments kill most swiftly and unerringly and I don't really care to know what killed Marta, he may not even have asked for explanations nor would it have occurred to anyone to think of having an autopsy done, he would simply have taken in the news and hidden his face and prepared himself for the burial of a second of his offspring and for a goodbye, goodbye laughter and goodbye scorn, life is unique and fragile. One assumes, though, that now, while earth fell for the fourth time upon a female person in that tomb, he would be remembering those who lay there and whom he had not seen for many years, his Italian mother, Bruna, who never quite mastered the harsher tongue of her adopted country and who taught her son Juan her own softer language; his wife Laura whom he had loved or not loved, whom he had idolized or hurt, or perhaps both things, first one and then the other or both at the same time, as is usually the case; and his daughter Gloria, who was the first to die, in an accident perhaps, drowned in a river or after breaking her neck in a fall one summer, or perhaps struck down by one of those swift, impatient illnesses that so effortlessly carry off the young – because the young put up no resistance – not even allowing them time to accumulate a few memories or desires or to learn about the strange workings of time, as if that were the way illnesses got their own back for the interminable struggle they have with all the adults who resist them so fiercely, though not so with Marta, who died as meekly as a child. And the father will already have begun to see that second daughter, whom he had seen only recently (and for whom he had later left a message), tinged with the colours of reminiscence and of the rugged past, and he would perhaps be thinking that his own existence had now become even more precarious. He had white hair and large blue eyes and arched, impish eyebrows and very smooth skin

for his age, whatever that was; he was a tall, robust man, an
excelentísimo, a figure who would fill a room and whose wavering
bulk immediately attracted one's attention, his voluminous thorax
making the women on either side of him seem smaller than they
were, the slenderness of his legs and the slight swaying that
afflicted him even when at rest reminding one rather of a spinning
top, he wore a black armband on the sleeve of his overcoat as
proof of his strong, old-fashioned sense of occasion, his black
shoes as polished and shiny as those of his surviving daughter,
small feet for a man of his height, the feet of a retired dancer
and the face of a gargoyle, his dry, astonished eyes staring down
into the grave or hole or abyss, watching as the symbolic earth
fell, and remembering, spellbound, his two girls, the one who
had never grown beyond childhood and the one who had at first
been younger but later much older, assimilated into the tomb now
by that other daughter whom they never saw grow up or grow
old or change or become disaffected or a source of anxiety, both
now shared the same sad fate, obedient and silent. I saw that
one of Juan Téllez's shoelaces had come undone and that he had
not noticed.

To his right was the woman who was, doubtless, his daughter-
in-law, María Fernández Vera by name, she *was* wearing dark
glasses and a look of social piety on her face, a look, that is, not so
much of grief as of irritation, not so much of contagious fear as of
annoyance at having her daily routine disrupted and her family
diminished, shorn of one of its members, and her husband, therefore, plunged into gloom, for who knows how intolerably long;
the person holding her arm as if begging her forgiveness or pleading for help – as if asking her to have pity on him – must be
Guillermo, Luisa and Marta's only brother and slightly less than a
brother to the child Gloria, whom he would not have known and
about whom perhaps he might never even have enquired. He too
was wearing dark glasses, his face was pale and gaunt and his
shoulders slumped, he looked very young – perhaps he was only
recently married – despite his visibly receding hair which he would
not have inherited from his father but from the men on his
mother's side of the family, the crania of uncles or older cousins
who might, in fact, be there in the second row. I couldn't see any

similarity with Marta nor for that matter with Luisa, as if parents always put less attention and effort into the engendering of their youngest children and grew more negligent when it came to transmitting family likenesses, leaving the task in the hands of some capricious ancestor who, spotting a chance to perpetuate his features on earth, intervenes and bestows them on the, as yet, unborn child, or, even better, at the very moment the child is being conceived. He seemed a pusillanimous young man, but it's foolish to say such a thing having seen someone only at the moment when their sister is being buried and when they have their eyes cast down; and yet he did seem lost, he really did seem frightened by the sudden revelation of his own death, doubtless for the first time in his life, clinging to the arm of his erect and more powerful wife the way little boys hang on to their mother's arm when they are crossing the road, and while the symbolic earth fell upon his dead female relatives, she did not squeeze his hand consolingly, she distantly, impatiently tolerated it – one elbow sticking out – perhaps she was simply bored. The newlywed's shoes were bespattered with mud, he must have stepped in a puddle in the cemetery.

And there too was Deán, whose memorable face I recognized at once, even though he no longer had a moustache as he had on his wedding day and even though the passing years had left their mark on him and had given him character and strength. He had his hands thrust in the pockets of the pale blue raincoat he had neglected to take with him to London and which I had seen hanging up in his house: it was a good-quality raincoat, but he must be cold. He wasn't wearing dark glasses, he wasn't crying and his eyes were not staring in astonishment. He was a very tall, thin man – or perhaps not, perhaps he just looked as if he were – with a long face in keeping with his height and the energetic jawline of a comic-strip hero or of some cleft-chinned actor, Cary Grant, Robert Mitchum or even Fred MacMurray, although Deán's face was anything but foolish, and he was utterly unlike either the prince of laughter or the prince of unadulterated evil, Grant and Mitchum. He had thin lips, visible albeit colourless, or of the same colour as his skin, his face marked with lines and threads which would, in time, become wrinkles – or perhaps they already had – like superficial cuts in a lump of wood (one day his face would be like the scarred surface of a school desk). His very straight brown hair was carefully parted on the left, perhaps simply combed through with water the way children did in days gone by, a child of his time which must have been more or less my time too, habits that are never lost and which remain unaffected by our age or by the years. At that moment – although I would have sworn it would be the same at any moment – it was a grave, meditative, serene face, that is, one of those all-accepting faces, a face from which one could expect anything, any transformation or contortion, as if his face were in a constant state of expectation and indecision, one moment expressing cruelty and the next pity, then derision and later melancholy, followed up by anger, yet without ever really expressing any of those emotions fully, the sort of face which, in normal circumstances, seems potent and enigmatic, due perhaps to the contradictory nature of the features rather than to any actual intention: raised, mocking eyebrows, candid eyes that indicate rectitude and good faith and a certain degree of introversion; a large, straight nose as if it were pure bone from bridge to tip, but with dilated nostrils suggesting vehemence, or even perhaps inclemency; the thin, tense mouth of the tireless plotter, of the anticipator – his lips like taut ribbons – but denoting also slowness and a capacity for surprise and an infinite capacity for understanding; his insubordinate chin now cast down, an edgeless sword; slightly pointed ears as if they were on permanent alert, tuned to hear what was left unspoken in the distance. They had picked up nothing from London, not the rustle of those sheets which I had not touched or the clatter of plates during our supper at home or the clink of glasses filled with Château Malartic, not the rattle of death or the boom of anxiety, the creak of malaise or depression or the buzz of fear and regret, or the sing-song hum of weary and much-maligned death, once known and encountered. Perhaps his ears had been filled by other London noises, by the rustle of sheets and the clatter of plates and the clink of glasses, by the shrillness of the traffic and the boom of the tall buses, the screech of the night-time bustle and the reverberating chatter in various languages at the Indian restaurant, by the echo of other, possibly mortal, sing-song voices. "I never sought it, I never wanted it," I said to him, though addressing only myself from my 1914 grave, and at that point, Deán glanced up for a moment and looked across at me standing there with my cigarette, watching him. Although he looked straight at me, his thoughtful expression remained unchanged, and I could see his eyes, the colour of beer, their gaze candid, but almond-shaped like a Tartar's eyes. I don't think he actually saw me then, his eyes looked at me, but did not rest on me, it was as if they merely skirted round or passed over me, and immediately returned to the grave or hole or abyss with what I judged to be anxiety, as if Deán, with his long, strange face, was feeling both serious and somewhat uncomfortable, as if he had landed up at a party that had nothing whatever to do with him because it was a purely female occasion, a necessary intruder but, ultimately, mere decoration, the husband of the new arrival in whose honour – or rather in whose memory, since he was the widower – everyone there was gathered together, no more than thirty, we do not, in fact, know that many people. Deán was someone who would remain for ever outside that tomb of blood relations, someone who would probably remarry and, then, those five years of marriage and cohabitation would be represented and recalled, above all, by the existence of the boy Eugenio, both now and later, when, with the passing of time, he was no longer a child, and less so by Marta Téllez, who would gradually diminish in importance and grow shadowy in her swift journey towards dissolution (how little remains of each individual, how little is recorded, and how much of that little is never talked about). Deán was so like the photo I had seen of him, he even began to bite his lower lip as he had on that nuptial occasion in black and white, when he looked at the camera. And while the symbolic earth fell upon his wife Marta Téllez, I saw him suddenly take his hands out of his raincoat pockets and raise them to his temples – his poor temples; his legs buckled and he seemed about to fall flat on his face, and he would have fallen – he staggered, skidded towards the grave for a moment – if several hands and the sound of alarmed voices had not sustained him: someone grabbed him by the back of his neck – the back of his neck – someone else plucked at his good-quality raincoat, and the woman by his side gripped his arm while he remained for a moment with one knee on the ground, all that remained of his equilibrium, his knee like a knife loosely impaled in a piece of wood and his hands clutching his temples, incapable of reaching out in order to break his fall had he fallen face forwards: "Let me sit heavy on thy soul tomorrow; and fall thy edgeless sword." He was helped to his feet, he brushed down his raincoat, rubbed his knee, smoothed back his hair a little with one hand, put his hands in his pockets again, and recovered his thoughtful expression which, now, seemed more like a look of bereavement or perhaps embarrassment. Seeing him falter, the gravedigger had paused with his spade in the air, already laden with earth, and for those few seconds during which the recent widower interrupted the silence of the ceremony, that figure remained there, paralysed, as if he were the statue of a worker or perhaps a miner, his spade aloft, his wide trousers, his short boots, a scarf round his neck and an old-fashioned cap on his head. He could have been mistaken for a stoker, although no one stokes boilers any more, his thick white socks had slipped down into his boots. And when Deán had recovered, the gravedigger finally tossed the spadeful of earth into the hole. But he had lost direction and rhythm during that moment of suspense and a few specks from that spadeful of earth besmirched Deán – his raincoat – who, since getting to his feet, was standing somewhat nearer the edge of the abyss and felt its touch. Juan Téllez gave a sideways glance, a look of evident annoyance, though whether it was directed at Deán or at the gravedigger, I don't know.

And that was when I also saw – or recognized, or noticed – the woman who had grasped Deán's arm with her beige glove, the neighbour whom I had seen twice already, once, when I was leaving the block of flats in Conde de la Cimera while she was arguing or kissing in the early hours of the morning and, again, when I was standing next to my taxi while she drove off, wearing her pearl necklace and tossing her handbag into the back of the car, and at that moment, I turned round in an impulse of pointless fear, since, if she had seen me and recognized me, it was too late (that was the third time I had seen her in three days). After those few seconds of reflex fear, I turned round again (after all, I had my dark glasses on, and it wasn't yet night) and although I felt observed and even scrutinized by her, as if she wanted to make sure that it really was me – no one – I saw in her brown eyes no trace of suspicion or fear or even bewilderment, possibly quite the opposite – perhaps she imagined that I too was a neighbour or a friend of the family, an old, distant or discreet friend – a friend, perhaps, of the dead woman only – who was attending the funeral but keeping his distance. That is what she must have thought, because when the gravestone was drawn up to cover the grave, just as I had covered Marta with the bedspread and the sheets, and everyone began to move away – although they only moved a short distance, too busy greeting each other or milling around and exchanging comments, as if they were not quite ready to abandon the place where their more or less beloved Marta would now remain – the young woman said hello to me with a sad half-smile as she passed me by, heading for the cars, and I responded using the same word and possibly the same smile, as I watched her pass and continue on by with her graceful, centrifugal gait (again I noticed her calves), accompanied, it seemed to me, by a woman friend or sister and a lady. That insignificant contact gave me the courage to leave my adopted grave ("and they bring me salva-tion") and to mingle with them, with the people in the funeral procession, not blatantly, but as if I too were on my way out. I saw that Marta's father had not yet left: he was standing with one foot resting on a nearby grave, he had noticed the untied lace on his shoe and he was pointing at it with his index finger as if in accusa-tion, but saying nothing; the excellent man was too unsteady on his feet and too heavy to bend or crouch down, and his daughter Luisa, one knee resting on the ground beside him (she wasn't crying now, she had something to occupy herself with), was tying it up for him as if he were a child and she his mother. Three or four other people had stayed behind to wait for them. And then I heard a voice behind me, the electric voice, it was saying: "Oh, bloody hell, don't tell me you haven't brought the car, *now* what are we going to do? Antonio gave me a lift here, but I told him not to wait because I assumed that you would come in your car." I didn't turn around, but I slowed my steps so that they could catch me up, the electric-shaver voice with its hidden knives and that of a woman who replied at once: "All right, it doesn't matter, we'll get a lift with someone else, and if not, there'll be taxis outside I expect." "What do you mean, taxis, for God's sake?" he said as he drew alongside and his profile came into view, he had a rather snub nose, or perhaps that was just the effect of his rather large dark glasses; "There aren't going to be any bloody taxis at the cemetery; what do you think this is, the Royal Palace? Only *you* would think of coming without your car." "I thought you would bring yours," she said as they overtook me. "Did I say I was going to bring it? Did I say that? Well then . . ." he replied threateningly, thus putting an end to the dispute. He was a man of medium height, but well built, the kind who frequents gymnasiums or swimming pools, doubtless rude and tyrannical. He obviously wasn't aware of funeral etiquette either, or else he didn't care, since he was wearing a light-coloured overcoat (not that Deán was wearing black either). He had long teeth like the chap, two nights before, who had stood behind me at the restaurant waiting for me to hang up, it wasn't the same man, just the same type: conventionally wealthy, conventionally dressed and with a wilfully plebeian vocabulary, there are thousands of them in Madrid, veritable waves of provincial self-made men who have been allowed to take over the city, a perpetual, centuries-old plague, and not one of them capable of pronouncing the final soft "d" in Madrid. He was about forty years old, and had fleshy lips, a firm jaw and a village complexion that betrayed his origins, an origin not so much remote as forgotten or, rather, erased. He used lacquer on his hair and wore it combed back as if he were a dandy, but talking like that, he was obviously not the genuine article. "Have they found out who the bloke was yet?" I heard him say in a quieter voice – he mumbled the question, and then his voice sounded like a hairdryer – while I walked a little behind them. And his wife, Inés, the magistrate or pharmacist or nurse, lowered her voice in turn and replied: "No, not yet, but they've only just started looking, but apparently Eduardo is determined to find him. But listen, Vicente, they don't want anyone to know, so would you please, just for once, be discreet and not go telling everyone about it." "So he's a loudmouth," I thought, "that's why he's always got some story to tell. For the moment, Vicente, I've done you an enormous favour, removing that tape from the answering machine. What a bit of luck for you that I was there with her."

"Everybody knows about it anyway," replied Vicente scornfully, "people like to talk; there's no such thing as discretion any more, it's died out, it isn't even considered a virtue. Poor Marta. They might manage to keep it from her father, but as for the others . . . They'll forget about it anyway, nothing lasts, that's the only form of discretion there is nowadays, I mean, everything's so quickly forgotten. Look, go and see who we can get a lift with, go and ask some people if they've got room for us," and with a swift shrug of the shoulders he readjusted his overcoat and stretched his neck. He probably used similar gestures to adjust his tackle when he felt uncomfortable. The people from the funeral had nearly reached their cars and I was there with them. Inés left Vicente's side to find out who could give them a lift to the centre, I hadn't got such a good look at her because she had been concealed by him while they were walking along, she had an unhurried gait, and her legs were rather on the muscular side, like those of a sportswoman or an American, the kind of calf that looks as if it's about to explode at any moment, some men find them a real turn-on, I'm not so keen myself. She was wearing high heels and she shouldn't. I imagined that she was probably a magistrate, rather than a policewoman or a pharmacist or a nurse. Perhaps hers was the infantalized, tearful voice on the answering machine and what she was asking Marta ("Please . . . please . . .") was for her to leave her husband alone. In that case, her wishes had been granted, how that death gladdens me, saddens me, pleases me. The man stood waiting with his arms folded, nodding from afar to people he knew as they got into their cars and whistling, not realizing that he was doing so and forgetting that he was still in a cemetery, he didn't seem either very affected or very worried, he had doubtless already heard about the disappearance of that tape on which he had described as "stupid" the person he was now calling "poor Marta". "I've got you," I thought, "I've got you, although that would also mean having to reveal myself. I would have to stop being no one." I saw that Inés, standing next to the door of a car, was gesturing repeatedly to him, beckoning him to join her, the magistrate had found a lift. I looked around then for Téllez and Deán and Luisa: the father and the sister had not yet arrived, they were walking along together, arm-in-arm, with some difficulty, he with his shoelaces now tied, María Fernández Vera and Guillermo following close behind them, ready in case the robust old man should suddenly stumble or fall, or else watching out for more puddles. Deán, however, had already reached the cars, he had opened the door of his own and was standing next to it, waiting, he was watching his in-laws who were advancing slowly towards him, advancing towards the tomb. He was actually looking back in the direction of the sealed grave and when his brother-in-law and his sister-in-law finally arrived, along with his brother-in-law's wife and his father-in-law, the four of them got into another car with Guillermo at the wheel, while Deán, on the other hand, remained a few seconds longer with his hand resting on the door, apparently not waiting for anyone, thoughtfully watching whatever it was he was watching, a haunted look. Then he got into his car, closed the door and started the engine. He was going home alone, he had plenty of room, he wasn't carrying any passengers, Inés and Vicente could easily have fitted in. "He could have given me a lift," I thought after a while, when they had all already driven off and I was getting set to leave, knowing all too well that this was not the Royal Palace. And then another thought occurred to me: "But then, if he'd given me a lift," I thought, "I would've had to stop being no one."

I N O N E S E N S E, I stopped being no one a month later, in another, it took me a little longer, in Deán's case a few days and in Luisa's a few hours. I mean that after a month, I became someone for Téllez and his son-in-law and his third and only daughter (the third to be born and now the only one left alive), I became a name and a face for them and I had lunch with them, but the man who had been present at Marta's death, though he had achieved little by that presence, continued to be no one throughout the whole of that lunch, even though I was that man, of that I was sure, for them, on the other hand, that man was only one of various suspects with or without a name, with or without a face: not for Téllez, though, from whom they had managed to hide the manner and the circumstances of the death, he had no need to suspect anyone.

I made the almost simultaneous acquaintance of his two children through their father, Téllez, and I tried to get to know him and did, in fact, meet him through a friend whom I have impersonated on more than one occasion, to whom I have often lent my voice and, in this instance, my physical presence, but unlike on those other occasions, this was precisely what I wanted. That friend's name is, or so he claims, Ruibérriz de Torres, a man of indecorous appearance. He is a hardworking writer with a good ear, average talent and rather bad luck (in the literary field), since other less hardworking people with a terrible ear and no talent at all are held to be great men and are praised and given prizes (literary prizes). When he was still a young man, some years ago now, he published three or four novels; he had some success with the first or the second, but that success never came to anything, it simply dribbled away, and although he's still not exactly old, his name is only known to older people, that is, he's forgotten as an author except by those who have already been in the profession for some time and never really keep up with all the changes and alternatives, they are rather inattentive people with entrenched views, the civil servants of literature, ancient critics, resentful professors, resting academics susceptible to flattery, and publishers who find in the endless complaints about the insensitivity of the modern reader the perfect excuse for simply loafing around and doing nothing, which they continue to do with each new wave of writers. Ruibérriz has not published anything for years now, I don't know if that is because he has given up or because he's waiting until he has been completely forgotten in order to begin again (he doesn't usually talk to me about his plans, he's neither confidential nor prone to fantasy). I know that he always has various shady deals on the go, I know that he's very much a night-bird, that he lives, in part, off various women, and that he's immensely likeable; he tones down his caustic comments in the company of people he knows can't take it, he flatters those who need to be flattered, he knows all kinds of people in all kinds of fields, and the majority of those who know him have no idea that he is or has been a writer, he's not boastful, neither is he given to attempts at salvaging what is lost. He only looks indecorous in certain places, though not all: he looks all right in cheap bars, in cafés at night, as long as they're not too trendy, and at open-air dances; he looks acceptable at private parties (preferably summer parties with a garden setting and a swimming pool) and he looks very good at bullfights (he usually has a season ticket for the bull-fighting festival of San Isidro); he can get by amongst people in film, television and the theatre, although he does look a touch old-fashioned; he cuts a plausible figure amongst coarse, surly journalists of the old Franco and anti-Franco schools (the former are coarser, the latter surlier), although he's obviously not one of them, since he's always immaculately turned out and even rather vain about his appearance. But amongst his true colleagues, other writers, he seems like an intruder and they treat him as such, he's too jokey and good-humoured, he tends to talk a lot and, with them, makes no attempt at tact. At official occasions or at a ministry, his presence causes genuine alarm, which presents him with a real problem, given that part of his income comes from that world of officialdom and ministries. His written style is as solemn as his talk is uninhibited, he is one of those people who feel such reverence for literature that, confronted by a blank sheet of paper, and regardless of his own scurrilous nature, he's incapable of transmitting one iota of that irreverence and cynicism to that venerable page, to which he will never commit a joke, a four-letter word, a deliberate mistake, let alone some bold, impertinent remark. He will never allow himself to give expression to his true personality, perhaps considering it unworthy of being recorded, and fearful of defiling such a high office, and it is there, in a manner of speaking, that the scoundrel finds his salvation. Ruibérriz de Torres, who has little respect for anything, sees writing as something sacred (and, doubtless, therein lies the reason for his lack of success). His grandiloquent style, combined with a sound background in the humanities, is perfect for the kind of speeches that no one listens to at the time and that no one reads when they're summarized in the press the next day, that is, the speeches and talks (including lectures) made by ministers, directors-general, bankers, prelates, presidents of foundations or professional bodies, much-talked-about or lazy academics, and other great men overly preoccupied with their image and their abilities as intellectuals, something which passes unnoticed by everyone else or which everyone assumes to be non-existent. Ruibérriz has no shortage of commissions and, although he doesn't publish anything, he writes constantly, or rather he used to, for recently, thanks to a stroke of genuine good fortune with one of his shady deals and to his assiduous cultivation of a wealthy woman who indulges and genuinely idolizes him, he has opted for a life of leisure and has allowed himself the luxury of rejecting most commissions or, rather, he accepts them and passes them on to me, along with seventy-five per cent of the profits, so that I am the one who carries them out in the shadows and in secrecy (though not in the utmost secrecy), my education being in no way inferior to his. He is what is known in the literary world as a ghostwriter and I have therefore become the ghost of a ghost, a double ghost, a double no one. There is nothing very unusual about this in my case, since the majority of the scripts I write (especially those for television series) rarely carry my name: the producer or director or actor or actress usually makes me a large additional payment in exchange for the removal of my name from the credits in favour of theirs (that way they feel they are the true creators of their films), which, I suppose, also makes me a ghost as regards what is my main current occupation and the source of considerable sums of money. This is not always the case though; there are occasions when my name does appear on the screen, in company with those of four or five other scriptwriters who, generally speaking, I have never seen amend or add a single line, I have never even seen their faces: they are usually relatives of the producer or the director or the actor or the actress who, by adding their names, are extricating themselves from a temporary difficulty or making up symbolically for some previous swindle that swallowed up all their savings. On a couple of jobs about which I was imprudent enough to feel anomalously proud, I refused the bribe and demanded that my name should appear separately, beneath the pompous rubric: "Additional Dialogue", as if I were Michel Audiard at the peak of his popularity. So I know that in the world of television and cinema and in that of speeches and perorations almost nobody writes what people think they write, although – and this is the most serious aspect, and not as rare as you might think – once these usurpers have read the speeches in public and received the polite or sparse applause, or have seen on television the scenes and dialogues to which they put their names, but which they did not themselves create, they become convinced that their borrowed or rather bought words truly are the product of their own pens or imaginations: they adopt them (especially if someone praises them, be it an usher or a bootlicking choir boy) and they will fight tooth and nail to defend them, which is rather sweet of them really and, from the ghostwriter's point of view, flattering. This conviction runs so deep that the ministers, directors-general, bankers, prelates and all the other habitual givers of speeches are the only citizens who actually listen to and take an interest in the speeches given by others, and they are as fierce and pernickety about other people's work as the more celebrated novelists can be about the work of their rivals. (Sometimes, without realizing it, they speak insultingly of a text written by the same person who writes their own speeches, attacking not only its content or ideas, which obviously vary, but the style as well.)

They take their oratorical side so seriously that they even demand exclusivity from their ghostwriters in exchange for an increase in fees and a bonus, or else they try to appropriate – or make off with – other people's ghostwriters, for example, if a minister felt jealous of the Deputy Governor of the Bank of Spain speaking at a charity supper, or if the president of a shareholders' meeting turned green with envy watching the television news on which a harangue delivered by some rabid military man was greeted with hurrahs. (This exclusivity, it should be said, is but a vain hope in a job based on secrecy and anonymity: all ghostwriters accept it and commit themselves to it; then, in double clandestinity, they happily work for the enemy.) Some people commission the services of famous, practising writers (almost all of them are for sale, or may even lend their services free in order to make contacts and gain influence and put across a particular message), in the belief that the style of these writers, in general, pretentious and florid, will enhance their speeches, embellish their slogans, not realizing that these famous, veteran writers are the least suitable people for this kind of abject task, in which the writer must not only erase his own personality, he must also interpret and embody the personality of the national hero he is serving, something which such writers are not usually prepared to do: that is, rather than trying to imagine what the current minister might say, they think what they would say if they were the minister, an idea they find not in the least displeasing and a hypothesis they have no difficulty whatsoever in accepting. Many dignitaries, however, understand the problem and feel extremely uncomfortable uttering crass, lofty phrases such as: "Man, that sad, unfortunate animal" or "Let us carry out our work with the forbearance of the world". It makes them blush. So writers like Ruibérriz de Torres or myself are the most suitable people for the task, cultivated and anonymous, with a knowledge of syntax, a wide vocabulary and a talent for simulation; as well as a capacity for getting out of the way when necessary. Neither overly ambitious, nor blessed with a great deal of luck. Although luck can change.

There are occasions when the famous man, who always acts and commissions such things through intermediaries (he usually remains a remote figure), wants to meet the ghostwriter to give

93

him direct instructions or to allow the writer to admire or feed off his illustrious personality, but also out of a rather ill-advised curiosity, and this is where Ruibérriz has run into problems. He is aware of his indecorous appearance and he knows that it is not merely a question of clothes or diction or manners, but of style and character, which is, of course, immutable. It isn't that he dresses badly or has a strange hairdo (a very low parting to conceal baldness, for example) or that he doesn't wash and therefore smells or has gold chains slung around his neck, nothing like that. It is simply that his essential scoundrel's nature is written all over his face, is evident in his every gesture, in the way that he walks, in his character and in his irrepressible gift of the gab. No reasonably observant person would ever be fooled by him, not because Ruibérriz lacks the desire or the ability, but because people can see him coming a mile off, even when his intentions are not fraudulent. Fortunately for him, there is never any shortage of scatterbrains and dupes, so he has deceived more than a few men and women in his time, and he hasn't finished yet; but he knows that he doesn't stand a chance with someone who errs on the side of suspicion or caution. (He therefore surrounds himself with charming people, perfect victims, proud men and innocent women.) His inability to disguise himself means that he does not even attempt to do so and trusts to his instincts and to the diaphanous nature of his fraudulent aims, and so on the few occasions on which a great man has asked to interview him for the purpose of lecturing or inspecting him or in order to ask him about some particular aspect of a speech or article, the great man has found himself confronted by someone overly groomed and flirtatious, too perfumed and too handsome and too athletic, with a smile that is too cordial and too continuous and full of extremely white, rectangular, healthy teeth, someone with attractive hair, which he wears combed back and wavy at the temples, rather thick but perfectly orthodox, yet his few grey hairs still fail to lend him respectability because they look as if they were dyed (it's the kind of hair a musician might have), someone amiable and excessively talkative, not in the least modest and uncommonly optimistic, a jovial person whose one aim is to please, someone full of plans and suggestions, constantly coming up with a welter of unasked-for ideas, someone altogether too active, too ebullient and who, inevitably, gives the impression that he is after rather more than he is actually being asked to provide, in short, a troublemaker. He has long, curly eyelashes, a sharp, straight, bony nose, and his top lip curls back when he smiles or laughs (and he laughs and smiles a lot) to reveal the moist inner surface, which lends his face a look of undeniable and apparently spontaneous salaciousness (it's no surprise that all sorts of women find him attractive). He always stands very erect in order to emphasize his washboard stomach and his well-defined pectorals and, when standing up, he usually folds his arms, his hands on either side gripping his biceps, as if he were stroking them or measuring them. Regardless of what he's actually wearing, he's just one of those people you always imagine in a polo shirt and high boots; enough said, I think. The fact is that when eminent people clap eyes on him, they usually react with shock and clutch their heads with their hands: "Ah, mais non!" a former ambassador in France is said to have exclaimed, a man for whom he was about to write a delicate international speech. "You've brought me a *marseillais*, a *maquereau*, a Pépé-le-Moko, I mean, you want me to put myself in the hands of a pimp!" he said, finally hitting on the exact word. The ambassador wouldn't listen to reason and refused to read anything Ruibérriz had written, he took the job away from him and punished the intermediary. After receiving him in his office one day, a Director-General of Culture for whom he had done some excellent work (three impeccable speeches, boring and vacuous as is the norm, but full of intriguing quotes from some quite unusual sources) decided not to commission anything else from him. The meeting had lasted only a matter of minutes but Ruibérriz, in order to ingratiate himself, mentioned the writers from whom he tended to quote on his behalf, which irritated the Director-General, because it reminded him that he was not the actual author of those competent speeches, as he had come to believe until that very moment, thanks to a remarkable process of dissociation (that is, despite having his ghostwriter there in front of him), it also meant that he could contribute nothing and was reduced to a few mumbled remarks, since, lacking all curiosity, he still knew absolutely nothing about the writers whose names had been on his lips and whose mention had brought him much applause, especially from his subordinates. Apparently, he remarked later to those same inferiors: "There's something fishy about that Rui Berry, I think he's a fraud" (and he pronounced the name "Berry" with an English accent), "I want nothing more to do with him, he's a namedropper, that's what he is; he does nothing but talk about obscure, insignificant authors that no one's heard of, he could be putting anything in those speeches just to make us look foolish. Tell Señor Berri" (and this time he pronounced it as if it were a French word, with an acute accent) "that his services are no longer required or necessary. Pay him enough to make sure that he keeps his mouth shut, and see if you can find me a ghostwriter who looks rather less like a beach boy." Ruibérriz had to wait for the subsequent removal of that Director-General before he received any further commissions from that particular ministry. He learned his lesson and, for some time now, he has avoided any interviews with his employers, or rather, he agrees to them, when there's nothing he can do about it, and has me go in his place with the connivance of the intermediaries who understand that a senator or nuncio might feel inhibited or irked to find themselves in the presence of a handsome chap who looks as if he should be wearing a bathrobe or a polo shirt (my appearance is more discreet and not in the least alarming). That is why, sometimes, I have been not only his voice, but also his physical presence, albeit reluctantly, since any encounters with people in power tend to be rather humiliating.

It was Ruibérriz, then, whom I asked about Juan Téllez Orati, since he is in the know about everything and everyone. Unfortunately, he didn't know him personally, but he did know who he was, that is, he gave me the rundown on him:

"He's an academician in the Academy of Fine Arts and of History too, I think," he said, "that's where the *excelentísimo* comes from, although he could have got the title for other reasons too, I suppose, indeed, before he dies, he may well be given some minor title of nobility, he has contacts at the Palace. He long ago retired, but they still use him, he's a good courtier, the way courtiers used to be twenty or more years ago. He hasn't written very much, I mean in the way of books, but he is or was fairly influential and still publishes the occasional article in a journal on some obscure, pedantic topic. With his other activities dwindling away, I imagine that he never misses a meeting at either of his Academies. He's on his way out, but, doubtless, like most people, he's a most reluctant has-been. What keeps him going is his contact with the Palace; from what I've heard, they'd give him pretty much anything he asked for, within reason. That's all I can tell you, is that enough? Why do you want to know?"

That's what Ruibérriz told me, when the two of us were sitting in a bar, the day after Marta Téllez's funeral. I made no mention of the death, it didn't seem appropriate. Given what he had told me, I was surprised that there had been only thirty or so people at the funeral and that I had seen no one whose face was familiar from the television or from the press. Perhaps, given the rather embarrassing circumstances of her death, the family had wanted a private ceremony, but, on the other hand, they had published a death notice, true, only on the morning of the service itself, people rarely read the newspaper in the morning and certainly not first thing: perhaps that way they felt they had done their social duty and, at the same time, avoided any potentially inquisitive or intrusive onlookers at the funeral itself.

"It's nothing I need tell you about now," I said. Not enough time had passed for my death to have become a mere anecdote (it was, of course, Marta's death and mine only in the sense that I had witnessed it, which is reason enough to make it mine, although much less of a reason than having caused it) and although I know that Ruibérriz is a loyal friend to his friends, I still can't entirely trust him. He has a pleasant face and I like him more and more as the years pass, but he still makes me feel uneasy, apprehensive: like everyone else, whatever clothes he has on, he always looks to me as if he were wearing a polo shirt. That's how I saw him on that particular day, even though we were both dressed for winter, perched uncomfortably on stools at the bar, his favourite place in cafés and bars, as if sitting there were a sign of continued youthfulness, it's also a way of keeping tabs on a place and, if necessary, can facilitate a fast getaway. I can just imagine him beating a hasty retreat from some dive or gambling den, in the early hours of the morning, with a flower in his lapel. Or even with a flower between his teeth. "And what about Deán? Do you know anything about him? Eduardo Deán." I noticed that Ruibérriz started as if it wasn't the first time he had heard the name. "Eduardo Deán Ballesteros," I said, giving him Deán's full name.

Ruibérriz passed his tongue briefly over his top lip, the one that curls back when he smiles (only now he was thoughtful). Then he shook his head.

"No."

"Are you sure?"

"No, I've never heard of him. For a moment, I thought I had, the name sounded familiar, but no, or if I do know him, I can't remember where from. Sometimes a name rings a bell simply because someone has just mentioned it and, for a second, the recent present seems like the remote past. I think that's what happened to me just then. Who is he?"

Ruibérriz couldn't resist asking the question. He did so less out of genuine indiscretion or historical curiosity as out of familiarity, knowing that if I didn't want to answer him, I wouldn't, and that I would make that clear, as again I did.

"I'm not sure, I only know his name." And that was true, I knew that he had been married and was now a widower, but I didn't know what he did for a living, Marta had – naturally and irritatingly – mentioned his first name several times, but only in the context of that conjugal, domestic world. She hadn't told me anything about him on the other two occasions either, as if she didn't want to hide the fact that she was married (she didn't), but nor did she want to make it too important either. "Do you know any of the other members of the family? Luisa Téllez? Guillermo Téllez?"

"He must be the son of William Tell, he's probably got an apple on his head with an arrow through it." Ruibérriz couldn't resist the joke. He jovially slapped the knee of one of his crossed legs. He never could resist making jokes, good or bad, even in the company of people who didn't appreciate them, and then they fell horribly flat, that was one of his problems. He waited for me to acknowledge the joke with a smile before going on. "There's a bloke on the radio," he added, "but his name's not Guillermo. Who are they, Téllez Orati's children?"

"Yes, they are." And I was about to add "his surviving children" but I didn't, that would only have provoked more questions from my friend. "Is there any way I could get to meet the father?"

Ruibérriz burst out laughing, with his lip curled back and his teeth flashing. He looked at me mockingly. He seized the ends of his scarf with both hands, despite being indoors in a heated environment, he had left the scarf on by way of adornment. (He grabbed it in order to check his short burst of laughter.) The scarf matched his trousers, both were cream-coloured: a nice colour, but more appropriate for the spring. The long, black leather coat he sometimes wears was draped over a nearby stool, the coat makes him look as if he had stepped out of a film about the SS, he enjoys that kind of nonchalant flamboyance.

"Why would you be interested in getting in touch with that old fogey? Don't tell me you've got business at the Palace."

"No, of course I haven't, I knew nothing about that until you told me just now," I said. "I'm not even sure if or why I do want to meet him; but he's the only one of the whole family that I know anything about. It may be that I want to meet his children, or the daughter, and the father could be a means to that end."

"And what about Deán, where does he fit in?" asked Ruibérriz.

"Could you get me an introduction to Téllez?" I asked, trying to extract an answer from him whilst, at the same time, avoiding replying to his question.

Ruibérriz likes doing people favours or, at least, showing that he is prepared to do so, that pleases everyone, he enjoys pondering, hesitating and then saying: "I'll see what I can do," or "I'll have a think about it," or "I'll sort something out for you," or "Leave it with me." He did ponder, but only for a few seconds (he's a man of action who thinks quickly or barely thinks at all), then he ordered another beer from the barman (Ruibérriz is one of the few men who can still get away with clapping his hands or clicking his fingers in bars or open-air cafés and I've never yet seen a waiter get angry with him or take offence, as if Ruibérriz had some sort of dispensation that allowed him to continue the abusive practices of the 1950s – things imitated and learned in childhood – and that his right to do this was so clearly irrefutable that the gesture seemed perfectly comprehensible. He snapped his fingers twice: middle finger and thumb, thumb and middle finger). He uncrossed his legs and stood up, that way he was taller than me; he turned towards me with his dazzling smile and a fresh glass of beer in his right hand.

"You could always pretend you were a journalist," he said. "I'm sure he'd be delighted to give you an interview. The older and more forgotten they feel, the keener they are to have someone pay them some attention. They get anxious, their time is running out."

"I'd prefer not to do it by deceit, the interview would never get published and he would be waiting for it to appear. Isn't there some other way?"

Ruibérriz de Torres folded his arms and placed his hands on his biceps, he was standing up, he seemed amused, an idea had occurred to him that tickled him, some machination, some artifice.

"There might be," he said. "It might mean a rather delicate little job."

"What delicate little job?"

"Don't worry, it's nothing you can't handle." He licked his lips again, looking even more like a scoundrel than usual, and gave a glance about him, a glance that combined the desires of both hunter and potential fugitive. "Give me a bit of time and I might just be able to hand it to you on a plate." He said the last part of the sentence in a rather agitated voice and the expression he used revealed his excitement, "I might just be able to hand it to you on a plate" was like saying "Leave it to me" or "Don't you worry about a thing." "You don't want to tell me what your intentions are, then?"

I wanted to tell him the truth and say: "I don't really have any intentions, something horrible and ridiculous happened to me, and I can't stop thinking about it, it's as if I were haunted; there's nothing I particularly want to find out because there's nothing to find out, there's no one I want to save because she's already dead, I don't even want to gain anything from it because there's nothing to be gained, apart from the reproaches or the unjustified hatred of someone, of Deán for example, of Téllez and his children, or even of a certain despotic, foulmouthed bloke called Vicente who, to put it bluntly, had been having it off with her, I didn't even manage to do it with her once, that one and only time. I don't want to supplant anyone or to harm them in any way, I don't want to usurp anything or to avenge myself on anyone, to atone for a sin or to protect or ease my conscience, to free myself from fear, there's no reason why I should, I didn't do anything, no one did anything to me, and the bad part or the worst part has already happened, and for no reason whatsoever, I'm not motivated by any of the things that usually motivate us, finding something out, saving someone, gaining something, supplanting, harming or usurping someone, avenging oneself, atoning for something, protecting or easing or freeing oneself from something; having it off with someone. But even if there's nothing, something moves us, it's impossible for us to remain still, in our place, as if vacuous resentments and desires, unnecessary torments, emanated from our very breath. And now, not only is there nothing that I want to know, I am the one who has to hide, I am the one whose every action and every step will be investigated, I am the one who will be forced to recount my story, each passive action, each poisonous step, 'They've only just started looking, but, apparently, Eduardo is determined to find him,' had heard someone say, and that 'him' referred to me and to no one else, not even to that man, Vicente, who would be at my mercy if I revealed myself and to whom the words were innocently addressed. I have no intentions. It's just that something horrible and ridiculous happened to me and I feel as if I were under a spell, haunted, watched, revisited, inhabited, my head and body inhabited and haunted by someone I only knew in death and by a few kisses we could just as easily not have exchanged." I would have liked to have told him all that, but even my opening words would have intrigued Ruibérriz more than the reply I gave him, which was more commonplace, simpler and easier to understand:

"Not at the moment."

It was nearly time for lunch, time for us to go our separate ways, an hour of the day when it still feels like morning; outside it was raining, we could see it through the large windows and on the people who came in through the revolving door, drenched and getting themselves entangled in their barely furled umbrellas. It was raining as it so often does in clear-skied Madrid, a weary, uniform rain, untroubled by any wind, as if it knew it was going to last for days and there was no need for anger or urgency. The morning was orangey-green and, a little way off, beyond the centre and beyond the suburbs, the rain would be falling with even less urgency on Marta Téllez's grave, raindrops falling on a gravestone that would be washed gratis until time or the stone ran out, although only infrequently in this place of bone-dry air, she was under cover, moreover, and there was no escape for her as there was for the passers-by on the Gran Vía, running across the road and keeping as far from the kerb as possible, seeking shelter under eaves and in shop doorways and in the entrance to the metro, as had their forebears, wearing hats and longer skirts, when they ran to find shelter from the bombing during the long siege, clutching their hats and with skirts flying, according to photos and documentaries I've seen about the Civil War: some of those who ran to avoid being killed are still alive, whilst others born later are dead, how odd: Téllez is alive but not his daughter Marta. The group of people who had taken refuge under the awning of our bar, a bar that was here in the 1930s and therefore saw the bombs fall and saw the fall of all those passers-by who did not manage to escape in the desolate Madrid of half a century or more ago, would block our path when we came to leave.

Ruibérriz ate a handful of nuts and looked apprehensively at his Nazi overcoat: it would get wet, what a nuisance. He excused himself and went to the toilet, he took more time than was necessary and, when he came back, it occurred to me that perhaps he had snorted some coke to help him face the rain and the inevitable drenching that his leather coat would get, as well as the lunch he was off to, where he would doubtless be discussing some important matter, nothing in which he is involved can be considered unimportant. I know that he occasionally takes cocaine in order to stay cheerful and to continue having fun and to continue dazzling people as long as possible, although that too has caused him a few problems with certain of his clients, especially those who show an interest in the merchandise and end up demanding a sample. He was still standing by the stool, looking momentarily melancholy and thoughtful, as if regretting his exclusion from an important project whose initial stages would, moreover, depend on him.

"Okay, if that's how you want it, don't tell me anything, we'll leave it like that," he said. "But you can't ask me anything just yet either. I can probably fix it, but it could prove delicate. Give me a bit of time and I'll be in touch when I've got some news."

Then he puffed out his chest to show off his perfect pectorals and, gripping his left wrist with his right hand, the way wrestlers do at the beginning of a bout, he began telling me or, rather, bringing me up to date on the latest profitable dealings he had had with various women.

I didn't ask him any questions during the short time I gave him, indeed, during the entire time he took, I didn't call him and I heard nothing from him for nearly a month, the time it took me to meet Téllez and Deán and Luisa, first the father and then the daughter and the son-in-law, the last two simultaneously. I asked him no questions, and after those four weeks, he called me and said:

"I hope you're still interested in Téllez Orati."

"I am," I said.

"Because I've got him for you: I'm going to introduce you or, rather, you're going to meet him on your own. But prepare yourself, my boy, he's not the only one you're going to meet."

"Okay. What's this delicate little job then?"

Ruibérriz delights in doing other people favours, but he can never resist emphasizing his part in it all, and will keep reminding you of this for months and years afterwards, he requires fulsome praise for his talents and his efforts.

"Don't imagine it was easy to get, without recourse to deception, as requested: endless phone calls, a lot of waiting about, a lot of intermediaries and a couple of meetings. Anyway, you're going to write a speech for the One and Only."

"The One and Only?"

"That's how his inner circle refer to him, the One and Only, Solo, Solus, Solitaire, even the Lone Ranger, Only the Lonely and Only You, they call him all sorts of names, the closer you get to someone grand the less you tend to use their name or title and, as I told you, Téllez is still quite close to him. It's all taken rather a long time, as you would expect, but now it's all set: I had heard from people at the Ministry that the One and Only wasn't happy with any of his recent speeches, it seems he never has been very happy, he's extremely fussy about them, he and his advisors have tried everything, civil servants, academicians, professors, notaries, Fascist columnists and pinko columnists, calumnious columnists, unctuous poets and mystical poets, precious novelists and traditional novelists, shy dramatists and vulgar dramatists, all terribly Spanish, and he's never been satisfied with any of them: not one of these temporary ghostwriters dares to be anything but impersonal and majestic, so the One and Only gets bored when he rehearses the speech in front of the mirror at home and when he reads the boring thing in public, and he's sick to death of the fact that, after all these speeches and all his years on the throne, his oratorical voice continues to lack any recognizable identity. He wants to have his own style, like everyone else, he senses that no one ever listens to him. Apparently, he wanted to write something himself, but they tried to put him off and, anyway, it didn't work out, he's got plenty of ideas but he finds it hard to put them in any kind of order. Through someone at the Ministry I managed to get some examples of our work sent to Téllez, or some of your more recent work, I should say, and they're prepared to give us a try, they had already noticed that lecture given by the President of the Chamber of Deputies and the speeches of welcome given to the Pope by the various 'Virgins' in Seville, they didn't pick up on any of the double entendres. Téllez is all in favour and he's delighted, he considers us to be his discovery and he's glad to be useful again, a good courtier. But the One and Only wants to meet you, he takes quite a bit of trouble over these things. Well, he wants to meet Ruibérriz de Torres, but, of course, there's no way I'm going to the Palace. Téllez understands that too, he knows about our methods and our limitations, he knows that you will be the one doing the writing and he knows that, when it comes to speech-writing, there are two Ruibérriz de Torres."

"You've met him, then?" I said.

"Yes, he arranged to meet me at the Academy of Fine Arts. The moment he saw me, I could sense that he was about to have the ushers grab me and throw me out, taking me for a pickpocket, a picklock, or whatever, the usual thing, he immediately raised his hand to his breast pocket like someone crossing paths with a possible thief. He's a bit of a bore, it's just his age, but he's pleasant enough, I knew his face, from the horse races rather than from photos in the press, he used to go to the races a lot and he doesn't often appear in the press any more. Once he'd calmed down, I think he quite liked me, he's a bit of an old fogey but very approachable. So prepare yourself: the day after tomorrow at nine o'clock, Téllez himself will come by and pick you up, you'll spend half an hour, maybe less, with him and the One and Only and possibly someone else, and if all goes well, you'll write the speech for him. I don't think this means that you would be obliged to do any more for him in the future, they probably won't be satisfied anyway, that's just the way he is. They don't pay much, as a business deal, I would rate it medium to crappy, the Palace is very tightfisted, they expect everyone to feel so overjoyed at being given the commission that they won't even charge them. Sometimes, if the ghostwriter is either very vain or very viperous, they send him a penknife inscribed with a capital R, or a shield, a special-issue coin, a signed photo in a heavy frame, or some such thing. I've made it clear that we charge the minimum fee, that we're professionals. But you don't mind, do you? You just wanted to meet Téllez, didn't you?"

"And you don't mind that your cut will be the minimum too?" I asked.

"No, of course not."

"What speech is it?"

"I don't know yet, Téllez or someone from the Ministry will explain later on, if they accept. It's for some foreign do, I think, in Strasbourg, Aachen, possibly London, or Berne, I'm not sure, he didn't say. Anyway, that's the least of it, isn't it? It'll be the usual vapid stuff. You just wanted to meet Téllez, didn't you?" Ruibérriz asked again. He wanted me to reward him by telling him why I wanted to meet the old fogey. He had been efficient, although, as usual, had taken the most complicated route possible, he always does more than you ask him to do, he always amplifies on what people propose to him, with his unsolicited ideas and his convolutions. He could have asked me to go with him to the Academy of Fine Arts, and then I could have decided if I wanted any further meetings or not, there was no need to involve the Lone Ranger. But it was done now.

"Yes, that was the idea." That was all I said at first, that is, on my own initiative; but I could tell by his silence that he felt that wasn't enough, I agreed, and so I added: "I owe you one, I'm really grateful."

"You owe me that story, when you're ready," he replied, and his tone of voice made me imagine his white smile at the other end of the phone; he wasn't demanding it of me, he wasn't pressing me.

"Yes, when I'm ready," I said, thinking that perhaps I already owed a lot of people that story, telling a story as payment of a debt, even if it's symbolic and not required of one, nobody can demand something they don't know exists and from someone they don't even know, something they don't know happened or is happening, and therefore can't demand that it be revealed to them or that it stop. I owed it to the busy, inquisitive Ruibérriz and to Deán, the husband, who had only just begun to look and who was determined to find me; perhaps to the idle, precarious Téllez and to his two surviving children, none of them would be pleased to hear it, but María Fernández Vera, a relative only by marriage, might be, and the irritable Vicente would doubtless want to know, Inés, on the other hand, would be horrified; perhaps I owed it to the young woman who had been standing at the entrance of the apartment block in Conde de la Cimera, I had interrupted her argument or her farewell or her kisses, although she would never have asked to hear such a story nor even asked after me; perhaps I even owed it to the night porter at the Wilbraham Hotel in London, I had bothered him late at night or in the early hours of the morning because of that story. I owed it to Eugenio, the boy, who, assuming they had taken him elsewhere that first night, would have returned to his home by now, to his bedroom, where he and his toy rabbit would once more be under threat, while they slept, from the peaceable aeroplanes dangling on threads – that inert oscillation – dreaming now of the weight of his absent mother growing ever lighter, a passenger in one of those planes, the child was also under a spell. Except that his was already journeying towards its own dissolution and would soon vanish.

TÉLLEZ AND I arrived early in what was, apparently, an official car, but, as befitted his rank and occupation, the One and Only kept us waiting, I imagine he's always slightly behind with his daily schedule and, as he gets later and later, he probably cancels one of his appointments at the last moment, thus returning at a stroke to punctuality and the timetable, I would find it a real curse, that continuous trail of activities and the hit-and-miss method used to curtail it, and I was only too aware that, even though we were near the start of the day, we might well be the ones to be cancelled, the ones to receive the formal apology and to be turned away, courtiers and ghostwriters can always be put off. During our wait in the rather chilly little room, Téllez took advantage of the wait to repeat yet again the advice he had given me on the way there, that is, not to interrupt but not to allow any silences either, only to speak when asked a question directly or when invited to make some contribution, to abstain from making any sudden gestures or raising my voice, since that could irk or disconcert Solo (that was the word he used, "irk", and it really did sound like something to be avoided), how I should address him both directly and when referring to him, how I should greet him, how I should say goodbye, that I was not to sit down until he had done so and had indicated that I too should sit down, that I should not, whatever happened, get up before he did, throughout the whole journey I had felt as I used to feel at school or on the eve of my first communion, not just because of the instructions themselves, but because of the manner and tone in which the old man spoke to me, a mixture of indulgence, reproval, pomposity and defeatism (unrest amongst his subjects, a lack of conviction), I was convinced by the end that he would be an expert writer of obituaries. When he saw me appear at the street door, he had scrutinized me from inside his car, as if my getting into the car or not depended entirely on my appearance (his mottled hand holding the back door open, his large, inquisitive face slightly on one side, his impish eyebrows sceptically arched, I felt like a prostitute being examined and evaluated by a client before being given the humiliating nod that means "Get in"); and having bestowed on me the approval that Ruibérriz had doubtless assured him I would merit, he beckoned rather urgently to me with the discreet handle of the stick he was carrying and with which he slightly shielded himself when I finally got in, the old live in constant fear of other people falling on top of them. Now he was playing with the stick while we were waiting, sometimes he rested it across his thighs like an edgeless sword, sometimes he made it spin between his legs, its point on the floor, as if it were a closed pair of compasses. We were not alone: ever since we had been ushered into the room (after the security checks) by a plain-clothes *camerlengo* or chamberlain or whatever he was, a servant or factotum in an old-fashioned uniform had stood there, unmoving (I couldn't make out what period he was from, but he was dressed in melon-green livery, with black calf-length breeches, white stockings and patent-leather slippers, but no wig of any kind), he was a very ancient man next to whom Téllez seemed like a mere youth. Téllez had greeted him saying: "Hello, Segarra", and he, in turn, had replied brightly: "Good morning, Señor Tello", they were doubtless old acquaintances from harder times. The old man had very white hair brushed forward in the style of the Roman emperors and he was standing to attention in an altogether unmilitary fashion next to an empty fireplace above which hung a large, tarnished mirror; he only changed position to put his weight first on one foot and then on the other or to remove from his gloved hand some fleck or piece of fluff on the other glove which was thus inevitably transferred to the first glove (both gloves were white, like his stockings, which were reminiscent of the seamed stockings worn by nurses); and although, at first, I was concerned about his stamina and his ability to remain upright, I imagined that he must have spent so many years standing up that this would now be his natural state and he would be immune to tiredness (besides, there was a small palace armchair next to him, perhaps he sat down on it when there was no one else around). Some way away from us, in a corner, there was a senescent painter holding a palette in his hand, before him stood a rather large canvas, of which we could only see the back, mounted on an easel that was too small for it and which made one fear for its stability: he took no notice of our presence, he did not greet us, he seemed to be concentrating on his unfinished work, he must be doing so in order to take maximum advantage of the imminent arrival of his model. He wasn't wearing a beret, but he was wearing a kind of overall or indigo blue smock. The palette trembled in his hand, as did his brush when he made a stroke (he must have been painting from memory), his hand didn't seem at all steady.

Téllez looked at him from time to time in a rather offhand, awkward manner, and, after a few moments, he addressed him, wielding a pipe that he had just produced from his jacket pocket, and asked:

"I say, maestro! Do you mind if I smoke?" It didn't occur to him to consult me or Segarra.

The painter didn't react, which caused Téllez to pull an even more scornful face (the meaning of which was more or less: "Well, go to hell, then") and he began to prepare his pipe. As he was gathering up the tobacco into the bowl of his pipe and pressing it in with his index finger, a few strands fell to the floor. "He's going to smoke a pipe," I thought, "this could take some time, unless, of course, he really does know Solus well and won't put it out even when he arrives." I didn't dare light a cigarette though. The ancient liveried servant disguised as an antique tottered over bearing an elaborate and extremely heavy ashtray which he had taken from the mantelpiece above the fireplace.

"Here you are, sir," he said, moving in slow motion to place it on the low table by our side, in case he should miscalculate the distance and drop it, smashing the table.

"How are things, Segarra?" Téllez asked him.

"I don't know, Señor Tello. When you arrived he was still fletcherizing his cereal."

"He was what?" asked Téllez, terrified (and dropping more threads of tobacco on the floor), although Segarra had said it perfectly naturally and confidently. This must be the waiting room reserved for dependable or perhaps insignificant visitors (when it came to it, we were all of us servants), he probably gathered them all there together, the way rock stars do with journalists.

Segarra, the steward or seneschal (I am not versed in the different names of the various posts) seemed pleased to have provoked intrigue or alarm and to be able to offer a piece of information which was, at once, useful and eccentric. He had the optimistic, lively eyes of one who has witnessed many unusual things, though without comprehending them, thus preserving intact his capacity for enthusiasm and celebration and surprise, as well as his curiosity.

"'Fletcherizing', sir," he said, and this time he placed it in quotation marks at the same time raising one gloved finger. "It's an old and extremely healthy method of chewing food, it converts solids into liquids, it was invented by a Mr Fletcher, thence its name, and a lot of people nowadays are rediscovering it. The only problem is, it is a bit rough on your gums and rather time-consuming. He only practises it at breakfast, with his cereal and poached egg."

Téllez looked round for a moment at the court painter, to see if he had pricked up his ears and was listening, but the man in the smock was entirely occupied at that moment trying to reposition on his easel (his arms weren't quite long enough) the rickety canvas that we could not see. I began to long to have a look at it.

"Do you mean that it's one's own jaws that liquefy the food?" asked Téllez, addressing Segarra and, at the same time, pressing down the tobacco with his thumb, the tobacco that he hadn't spilled. I would have said the tobacco was overly scented with whisky and, perhaps, piquant spices, some effeminate Dutch product.

"Precisely, sir; apparently, it's much healthier than any mechanical method. They call it anatomical liquefaction, that's an alternative name for it, as well as the other term I used." The servant was apologizing for his involuntary acquisition of knowledge.

"I see," answered Téllez. "Do you think you could go and find out how this fletcherization is going along? Not that we're in any hurry, but just to get an idea."

"Of course, Señor Tello, delighted I'm sure. I'll go at once to see what I can find out."

With infinitesimal steps (although not quite as infinitesimal as when the weight of the ashtray threatened to bring him low), the lackey Segarra went over to one of the three doors in the rather chilly room (the longer you were in the room the chillier it felt), not of course towards the door through which we had entered, but towards the door nearest him, on the other side of the disused fireplace. (The only wall without a door was filled by a large rectangular landscape window, providing excellent light for painting, for example.) I do not wish to be disrespectful nor to affirm or imply anything, but the fact is that during the long seconds in which the slow figure of Segarra held that door open, I heard the unmistakable clack of someone playing table football in the next room. Téllez, on the other hand, didn't seem to notice, although he may have been slightly hard of hearing when it came to certain noises, either that, or he was simply not familiar with that particular vulgar sound. The painter did hear and he looked up and turned his head twice, like a bird, only to dismiss the sound at once (it didn't concern him) and position the palette more firmly in his hand, the palette trembled at the least unexpected or ill-prepared movement. It was as if he were the one about to have his portrait painted.

Téllez didn't seem very interested in me, nor was he particularly impatient. He probably got satisfaction merely from being of service, taking me there, discovering me, finding a recommended candidate and being congratulated if that candidate were found to be acceptable and did the job well, nothing more, and, if necessary, spending the morning at the Palace occupied in that rather uncertain manner. While he lit his pipe with a match, he looked at me out of the corner of his eye, as if to make sure I had not removed my tie or dirtied my trousers during the wait, that was the feeling I got (indeed he leaned forward slightly to inspect my shoes with a critical eye). I had taken great care over my appearance, and may even have overdone all the pressing and ironing, I thought I looked immaculate, almost gift-wrapped.

After several minutes of very perfumed pipe-smoking (even more perfumed now that it was lit), Segarra reappeared, his

Roman hairstyle looking slightly dishevelled as if some taller person had lightheartedly ruffled his hair, and this time, when the door opened again and took a while to shut, I heard the instantly identifiable sound of a pinball machine, I know it well from my adolescence and, besides, there are hardly any left, it's more or less a sound from the past, more fixed and recognizable than sounds that are still current and therefore subject to change. I heard the wild trajectory of a ball, racking up the points, I trusted that the machine was not one that gave the player a bonus game. Instead of delivering his message from the doorway and thus saving himself a journey, Segarra approached slowly – provoking in us the expectation and some concern that he might never reach us at all – and did not speak to us until he was by our side, a dutiful manservant:

"Don't worry, Señor Tello, the process I mentioned was successfully concluded some time ago," he said. "He had to receive a group of trade unionists, but they're leaving now and he'll be here any moment, he's on his way."

And indeed, Segarra had barely finished speaking when the third door opened and Solitaire strode energetically in, followed by a young woman struggling to keep up, her short, tight skirt forcing her to break into a run, her feet slightly turned out and her high heels scratching the doubtless, fine, wooden floor encrusted with tiny, rectangular pieces of marble, real or imitation. I got up at once, much more quickly than the heavily-built Téllez, whose shoelace (I noticed just at that moment) had again come untied, and his daughter wasn't there to tie it up for him. The painter was already standing up, but when he saw the Lone Ranger come in, he reached out his arms like a hysterical fifteen-year-old at the appearance of her idol (or perhaps – a more virile image – like a wrestler in his corner placing himself on guard), that only made him look even more like a person engaged on some artistic endeavour. I was the first to greet the Lone Ranger, mumbling my false name (and adding clumsily and insincerely: "at your service") and so could not imitate Téllez as I had planned, and, of course, I forgot to make the recommended bow; Téllez, on the other hand, once he was up, bowed as low as his voluminous chest would allow and, with great reverence, he clasped one of Only the

Lonely's hands in his, despite the fact that his left hand was still holding his lit pipe, and narrowly missed burning him. It would clearly not have mattered very much, though, for one of the first things I noticed was that Only You had band-aids on each of his index fingers, a blister from a burn would merely have spoiled the symmetry. These effusions very nearly did for Segarra, who found himself caught in the middle, as he was beginning his retreat with his usual paralytic slowness. Only You sat down on my right-hand side, in an armchair, as did the young lady, who sat between us but on the same sofa as myself (in her hands she carried a notebook, a pencil and a pocket calculator, and a portable phone peeked out of her jacket pocket); Téllez, after swaying around for a moment, dropped down heavily into the armchair he had chosen before, opposite me and almost with his back to the painter, whom Only You greeted from afar with a wave of the hand, saying: "How are you, Segurola?", but not waiting for a reply: he must see him every day, he probably found the painter irritating and did his best to keep him at a distance. Solus had very long, thin legs which he confidently crossed (the young woman immediately crossed hers in imitation, she had a ladder in one stocking that gave her a rather dissolute air, perhaps it had happened while struggling with the trade unionists or partnering Solus at table football); I noticed that he was wearing so-called executive socks, too transparent for my taste, you can see the hairs on the legs flattened against the calves: otherwise, he was dressed like any other man of the world, his trousers a little creased around the thighs.

"Juanito," he said to Téllez, "one of your shoelaces has come untied." And he pointed to the shoe with one band-aided finger.

Téllez looked straight down – again his head looked like that of a gargoyle – first horrified and then resigned, like someone finding himself before an insoluble problem. He bit on his pipe stem.

"I'll tie it up later on, when I get up. As long as I'm sitting down, there's no risk of my tripping over it."

Solitaire leaned towards him, then, to whisper something – resting his whole chest on the arm of the chair, I was afraid it might give way – but he didn't lower his voice quite enough or else the distance was insufficient for me not to hear.

"Tell me, who *is* this?" he asked, indicating me with the slightest lift of his eyebrows and wriggling two restless fingers in the air – "I've completely forgotten why it is you've come today."

"It's Ruibérriz de Torres: the new speech," muttered my patron, biting even harder on his pipe stem.

"Ah yes, Ruibérriz de Torres," said the Lone Ranger calmly, this time out loud; and he turned towards me. "Now I wonder what you're going to write for me, you'd better watch your step."

There was nothing threatening about his tone of voice, rather a tendency to jokiness. He addressed me using the informal "*tú*", it being the prerogative of Only the Lonely to address anyone he meets in this way, even if he doesn't know that person and independent of their age, condition or title, rank or sex. The fact is it creates a very bad impression and, if I were him, I would give up that particular privilege. I had decided to address him using the formal "*usted*". That seemed to me sufficiently respectful and that way I wouldn't get confused, I really didn't care if Téllez told me off afterwards.

"I certainly will, sir," I said. "I will follow to the letter any instructions you care to give me. You have only to say the word." I had said this, I thought, in a fairly serene, circumspect manner, although he seemed neither pompous nor particularly cere-monious. I could, I thought, perhaps have omitted the last two remarks, they grated on me, they were too explicit.

Only You sat more upright in his chair (he had remained leaning to one side after whispering to his courtier), as if he had, at last, managed to focus on what it was we were there to discuss. He interlaced his fingers and clasped his crossed knees (he had no difficulty in doing this, for he had very long arms) and he said thoughtfully, though cheerfully:

"Look, Ruibérriz, let's get straight to the point: the thing is I'm tired of the fact that, after twenty years, people still don't know who I am. Not that I think people read or pay much attention to my speeches, but you have to start somewhere, there aren't many other ways I can get myself known without making a fool of myself, most other methods are barred to me. The fact is that, for yonks now, I've been aware that people just can't stick the speeches I give and, frankly, I don't blame them, they even make me yawn." He used the expression "for yonks" which certainly didn't strike me as being particularly highflown; I suppose "stick", on the other hand, was a word that one could stick when spoken by him. "The government are always very willing, so are the writers, too willing, really, and when they do a job for me they clothe themselves in royalty, or what they imagine to be royalty, like peacocks. Some take their inspiration from others, when they take on the job, they all ask to see a few of the previous speeches and so they create, what's that expression, Juanito?"

"A vicious circle?" suggested Téllez.

"No, no, that's not a phrase I'd be likely to forget," replied the Only One. "There's another expression. What's that thing that spins repeatedly on its own axis, but always returns to its original position."

"The eternal return? A ship's compass?" suggested Téllez, more doubtfully this time.

"A gyro compass?" put in the young lady, rather opportunistically. We had not been introduced. She had nice legs with plump thighs, one of them adorned with a tiny ladder, though, with legs like that, it was hardly surprising her stockings should ladder.

"No, what are you talking about, not that, what possible relevance could that have? Something else, something that turns right round and leaves us back where we started."

I saw that the painter Segurola had raised the same arm he was holding his brush in, like a good student in class who knows the answer. That meant that he was listening now, perhaps because he was staring intently and fixedly at the Only One – a look of fire – inspired, one hopes, only by a desire to paint him. Solus saw him too and tilted his chin towards him with a look of tedium and with little confidence, as if to say: "All right, let's hear it, what's your contribution?"

"The wheel of fortune?" Segurola said hopefully, in a slightly Renaissance vein.

Solitaire sliced the air with one hand, giving up the artist as a lost cause. "Yes, of course, and Russian roulette, and satellites, but the thing I mean . . . ," he began, "oh well, it doesn't matter, now where was I? I realize that people don't know what kind of person I am, what I'm like, and maybe that's the way it will have to stay as long as I'm alive; but while I'm alive, I can't help thinking that the way things are, I'm going to pass into history with no personal attributes at all, or worse, without even one attribute, which is tantamount to saying with no character, with no clear, recognizable image. I wouldn't want people to talk about me using phrases like "He was terribly decent" or "He did a lot for the country", though that would be no bad thing, I'm not complaining, a lot of others never even got that, and I hope I still deserve those words of praise when my time comes. But it isn't enough if there's some way I could change it, I've been pondering the matter for some time now and I don't really know what to do, it's not easy after all these years. I wouldn't want to blot my copybook, as people used to say, but it hasn't escaped my notice that those who are remembered are those who were most riven with indecision or who were traitors, those who committed crimes or were cruel, those who suffered from delusions or led dissolute lives, those who were endlessly tolerant or out-and-out tyrants, those who abused their power and behaved outrageously and those who were wretched, crazed, even those who were cowardly, even the Bluebeards. In short, all the ones who were complete and utter bastards." That was the word he used, but it wasn't, in fact, shocking in context and was actually rather convincing, rhetorically speaking. "It's the same everywhere, you just have to look at the histories of different countries: the more reviled the person, the more memorable they are. I wouldn't want to be seen merely as a focus for nostalgia, I couldn't possibly play a dirty trick like that on those who come after."

He remained silent for a moment, as if contemplating his own funeral and imagining the future that awaited his various successors. He was still clasping his right knee, but his expression had grown almost nostalgic, perhaps he was feeling a kind of advance nostalgia for himself. I didn't want to interrupt, but I didn't want to leave room for any silences either, Téllez had advised me to avoid them. I waited for a while. Then I waited another while. I had a phrase on the tip of my tongue, when Téllez got in before me:

"But Your Majesty cannot, for that reason, commit knavish acts or call down misfortunes upon yourself," he said in a slightly anxious voice. "I mean, Your Majesty cannot deliberately commit outrages," he said, swiftly correcting himself, in case "knavish" seemed an inappropriate word.

"Good grief, he really does call him 'Your Majesty'," I thought, "he's clearly a genuine enthusiast."

"Don't worry, Juanito, I wasn't thinking of doing so," replied the Lone Ranger, gently tapping Téllez's hand with one of his band-aided fingers: he tapped the limp hand holding the pipe rather too hard, however, and the still-smoking pipe flew through the air. I saw Segarra watch it fly past with a look of unspeakable apprehension (two gloved fingers poised upon his lips), fearful lest it land on Only the Lonely's head or on his lounge suit (had he been younger he would have tried to catch it on the wing). Luckily, it crashlanded in the ashtray, and there one saw the advantage of the ashtray's enormous size; the pipe bounced twice and, with great good fortune, did not break, so that Téllez was able merely to pick it up as one might a rebellious ping-pong ball and, without a pause, take out a match and light it again, whilst he and Only You, the young lady and myself, and Segurola and Segarra from a distance, all laughed briefly in unison. The young woman laughed the loudest: her mobile phone nearly leapt out of her jacket pocket with the rather hysterical quakings of her body and I was afraid she might irk the Only One with her rather brusque movements. Then the Only One continued, he was one of those men who never lose the thread, they tend to be rather terrifying: "But that doesn't mean that on the few occasions when I do address people I don't want them to get a clearer idea of me, to recognize me. Of course, no one believes that I write those speeches myself, in fact, the whole thing is rather ludicrous: everyone knows that I don't write them, and yet everyone listens to them and talks about them as if they were my own words and reflected my innermost thoughts. In the newspapers and on television they gaily report that I said such and such and that I neglected to mention such and such and they pretend to lend deep significance and a degree of importance to that, they pretend to read between the lines and to see dark allusions or even reproaches, when they know better than anyone that I am in no way directly or genuinely responsible for any of the things I've read out over the years, at most, I've given them my approval, sometimes not even that, sometimes the Palace approves them for me; so all I do is subscribe to or make mine (a mere *nihil obstat*, nothing more) a few words that never are mine, they belong to someone else or to several different people or to that vague thing called the Monarchy, in fact, to no one. All this is a fantastic pretence to which we all adhere, from myself to the politicians and the press to a few readers or viewers, those few citizens innocent and goodhearted enough to pay attention to what they imagine I'm actually saying and thinking."

Solus paused or, rather, he again fell silent while he meditatively stroked one temple. I noticed that the band-aid on his right index finger was coming unstuck due to those absorbed caresses, and I wondered what would be revealed if it came away: a cut, a burn, a wound, Mercurochrome, a boil, a callus from playing too much table football or pinball? I scolded myself for having such thoughts, you would have to be a real addict of those games to get a callus from them. I myself still find them enjoyable and relaxing, but if *I* don't have time to do so, how could Solus, always so busy, so institutionalized, in the unlikely event of him actually enjoying such pastimes. I dismissed the irreverent idea, he must have done whatever it was he had done whilst skiing or by shaking too many hands. I again wondered if we should allow such a long silence. But this time it was the young lady who prevented me from falling into temptation (the ladder in her tights was growing, and from looking slightly dissolute, she was now beginning to look positively degenerate):

"Well, Your Majesty, I am one of those people who pays attention to anything Your Majesty has to say, whether in the press or on the television news. Even though you don't actually write those speeches yourself, they have a big impact because it's Your Majesty giving the speech; I see you every day in private and I know what you do and I know your views on a lot of things, but even I find it hard not to take those words literally when I see Your Majesty on screen, not that I always quite understand what the speech is about."

She too called him "Your Majesty", whether that was normal or just Téllez's temporary influence, I don't know.

"You're very good and loyal, Anita," replied the Only One, without actually taking much notice of what she had said.

"I take an interest too, Your Majesty, and I often record you on video when you appear on television, in order to study Your Majesty's expressions when Your Majesty is thinking out loud," said the painter from the punishment corner, imitating the others' form of address.

"What would you know, Segurola?" replied the Lone Ranger, but he said it under his breath and the painter did not quite hear: in fact, he cupped his ear with one hand, forgetting that he had a brush in that hand, smearing his ear slightly with paint and having to wipe it off with a dirty rag. We all tittered, apart from him, but we did so surreptitiously this time. He obviously drove his model mad. "Anyway, as I was saying: I have nothing against this whole, doubtless necessary farce; it has always been like that and now it's even more so, when people with a high public profile have the eyes and ears of the world trained on them all the time, multiplied by a thousand cameras and microphones, apparent and concealed, it's a real nightmare, I don't know why we don't all just commit suicide. Sometimes I feel like a . . . what's that thing called, Juanito? You know, those things you see under the microscope."

And he made a tiny circle with his thumb and index finger and bent over it, peering through it at the ashtray full of matches and strands of tobacco.

"A strand of something?" said Téllez, not using his imagination at all.

"No, no, that's what I'm looking at now."

"An insect?" Téllez tried again.

"No, what do you mean, 'an insect'?"

"A molecule?" ventured Señorita Anita.

"Similar, but not quite."

"A virus?" said the majordomo Segarra from his post by the fireplace. He had respectfully raised one white glove.

"No, not that either."

"A hair?" offered Segurola from his easel, doubtless dredging up memories of childhood.

"What do you mean 'a hair'? Honestly."

"A bacterium?" I finally dared to speak.

Only the Lonely hesitated, but he seemed wearied by our ineptitude.

"Well, that might be it. Like a bacterium under a microscope, it doesn't matter. And that's what's so paradoxical, that despite all this vigilance and study, they still don't really know me, my personality is still as vague as ever; and since it's all such a farce anyway, I don't see why we shouldn't try to influence it a little more and make it more to our taste, and present to the current generation some clearer and more recognizable qualities, qualities that will prove memorable to future generations too" – I wondered if now he was using the royal "we" or if, in a friendly manner, he was including us in his words and in his plans: any doubts were soon dispelled – "I still have no idea how people perceive me, what their predominant image of me is, which means, alas, let's not kid ourselves, that I simply do not have an image. How can I put it, I have no artistic image and, again, let us not deceive ourselves, that is the image that counts, in life too, yes, in life too. Anyway, an initial step in that direction could be through my speeches, I don't see why the vague and vacuous things which, institutionally, I am obliged to say could not, nonetheless, be said in a more personal manner, how can I put it, yes, in a less bureaucratic and more artistic manner, a manner that would make people sit up and take notice, that would surprise them, and that would give them a sense that behind it all there is a good deal going on, I mean, that there's a man who also has his problems, a slightly tormented man, acting out his own drama, even though that drama is hidden. Let's be quite frank, there's no drama in my current public image, and I want people at least to glimpse that, a bit of artistic enigma. That, I think, is what I want, do you understand, Ruibérriz? That's how I see it."

Now I was absolutely certain that it was my turn to speak, he had addressed me by my name which was also not my name.

"I think I do, sir," I said. "And what image would you like to have or to reveal? What image, if I may ask, would you choose?"

I saw a slight look of censure in Téllez's pale eyes, doubtless due to my use of a mere "sir" which, after the "Your Majesty" used by the others, even grated a little on me, we are so easily influenced, we can be convinced of anything. The pipe Téllez was smoking seemed eternal, as if the burned tobacco regenerated itself and was consumed several times.

"I don't quite know," replied Only You, stroking his other temple now. "What do you think, Juanito? There are so many to choose from, I'd prefer this farce of ours to have at least a degree of authenticity, I mean a certain correspondence with my true character and deeds. For example, few people know how full of doubts I am. I have a lot of doubts about everything, as you well know, Anita. I often feel glad that most decisions are made for me, in another time, my life would have been all hesitation, all confusion, my spirits in a state of perpetual flux. I even doubt the justice of the institution I represent, not, I'm sure, that anyone would suspect it."

"What do you mean by that, sir?" I couldn't help but ask, in my eagerness not to allow any silences, that is, in order to get in before Téllez, who probably disapproved of my last question: indeed, he sat up in his chair and bit harder on his poor pipe.

"Yes, you see, I do not entirely believe in its raison d'être, perhaps I used the word 'justice' too lightly, it's such a difficult concept, and utterly subjective, depending on what you want or intend, and, of course, justice never prevails, not in this world anyway, for that to happen the man sentenced by justice would have to be in absolute accord with his own sentence, and that rarely happens, except in extreme, rather unconvincing cases of contrition and repentance. I would even go so far as to say that when it does happen, it is because the condemned man has abdicated his own idea of justice, he has been convinced by threats or arguments or whatever, and has been persuaded to adopt the other's point of view, that of his opponent, that favoured by the judge's ruling or, rather, the common view, that of the society of his time and, let us not deceive ourselves, society's view is never that of the individual, it is only the view of the time: the point of view common to everyone, or to the majority, is never an individual point of view, at least only insofar as the individuals in the group give in to the group view because they do not want to become marginalized. Let us say that it is merely a concession to subjectivity, a sop. No condemned man is going to exclaim with relief and satisfaction: 'Justice has prevailed.' That always means: 'Justice agrees with me and with my views.' The most a condemned man would say is: 'I abide by the sentence,' or 'I accept the verdict.' But that isn't the same as being fully in accord, indeed, if such a thing as objective justice really existed, there would be no need for judgements, the condemned men themselves would demand to be sentenced, in fact, there would be no crime. Crimes would not be committed or, rather, the concept of crime would not exist, there would be no such thing, because no one does anything convinced of its injustice, not, at least, at the moment of doing it, our idea of justice changes according to our needs, and we always think that what we need is equivalent to what is just. And that, however strange that may sound to you, is how I see it."

I had to agree with what the real Ruibérriz de Torres had told me: the One and Only did have ideas, but he found it hard to put them in any kind of order. I had followed his argument up until his penultimate sentences but there he had lost me.

"Hmm, Your Majesty," said Téllez, taking advantage of the breathing space, he was probably going to say more, but Solo went on talking, without a pause now, he seemed to have hit his stride, and though everyone else present had lost the thread, he had not:

"But, as I was saying, I'm not convinced that a man or woman should have their profession fixed from birth and from even before that, or their destiny if you prefer, I have no objection to using that word" – now it was clear that he was addressing all of us – "I don't think it's fair to him, and certainly not to the citizens who, normally, have no say in the matter. That doesn't concern me quite so much, those same citizens can, if they want to and if they insist, cut off our heads, there's nothing to stop them. It's true that no one is asked whether or not they want to be born, people have no option but to be born. It's true that no one asks us if we want to belong to the country we're born in, or if we want to speak the language we speak, or to go to school, or to have the brothers and sisters and parents that fate gives us. Everyone has things imposed on them right from the start and, until a relatively advanced age, people are interpreted by other people, mothers, in particular, are constantly interpreting the needs and wants of their small children and, for years, they decide things for them according to their own interpretative criterion" – "Who will be doing the interpreting for Eugenio now, who will decide things for him," the thought came to me in a flash – "That's all very well, that's all perfectly normal, because that's the way things are and there's nothing one can do about it, we aren't born with an opinion, although we are born with desires, or so it seems (primary desires, I mean). But I wonder if, beyond that, anyone can map out another person's life, especially in extreme cases like ours. It's a serious business, you know. Representing this institution implies, first off, an enormous loss of personal liberty, and, secondly, an even greater loss, the time one could spend thinking about things one isn't obliged to think about, and being able to think about things one isn't obliged to think about is crucial to anyone's life, whoever they may be, at least I find it so, to be able to think about irrelevancies, just to let one's thoughts drift. It means, too, becoming the main target for gangs of murderers and solitary assassins, who want to kill one because of one's position, just like that, in the abstract, and not because of anything one has done or failed to do; and that, quite apart from the risk, to which one becomes accustomed, seems to me a real personal calamity: it doesn't matter what one does and how one does it and the amount of care one puts into doing it, there will always be someone who wants to kill one, some megalomaniac, some madman, some hired killer, people who don't even bear us any particular grudge perhaps. To die like that, an undeserved, unwarranted death, simply because of one's name, that would be a ridiculous death." – Solus's face had grown sombre, although he hadn't changed his posture, he was still clasping one crossed leg, merely raising his hand now and again to stroke his temples, first one then the other, his poor temples – "The dying man's scorn for his own death," the thought flared up in my mind. The lines on his forehead were growing deeper – "It also means that one is continually surrounded by a group of potential homicides who, more because you pay them than out of any loyalty or conviction, will do their best to protect your life instead of making an attempt on it, and they may kill others in their well-remunerated mission, it will be our life against the lives of others, but sometimes those who guard us act precipitately, they have orders to do so and they can always justify it. It also means that one cannot choose with whom one deals and with whom one does not, it means having to shake hands with people who fill one with disgust, having to reach agreements with them and feign ignorance about what they have done or what they propose to do with their governments or with their equals. It means having to forgive the unforgivable. And having to pretend, of course, all the time: and while one is pretending one has to shake hands that are stained with blood and thus ours become a little stained too, if they were not already stained from the beginning, from our birth and even before that. I don't know if, in certain positions of power, it is possible for one not to have bloodstained hands, sometimes I think it isn't, throughout history there hasn't been a single governor or king who has not been responsible for at least some deaths, mostly they have been directly responsible, but also indirectly, it has always been like that, everywhere. Sometimes it has simply been a case of not having tried hard enough to prevent those deaths or of having chosen not to know about them. But that is not enough to save one."

Solitaire fell silent. Anita knit her brows in unconscious imitation of her boss, she clenched her jaw and lines appeared above her lips. Segurola's palette was trembling even more than usual, fortunately, the Lone Ranger did not notice and so could not feel irked, although he had perhaps irked himself with his errant, non-obligatory thoughts. Segarra's bright, optimistic eyes were still very wide, the eyes of one who never quite understands things, and he was growing a little unsteady now, resting one gloved hand on the back of the armchair at his side. Téllez was finally emptying his exhausted pipe, tapping it on the ashtray, and mumbling stiffly:

"Things aren't that bad, it's just an excess of scruples, there's no need to torment yourself, Your Majesty, over hypothetical, improbable things like that. Besides, Your Majesty can't be held responsible for something you know nothing of or for something you only find out about later, they don't tell Your Majesty everything after all."

"I should think not," intervened Anita zealously, "he's already got far too much on his mind."

"Really?" said Only the Lonely quickly (although not quickly enough to prevent the young lady's motherly intervention). "Are you sure of that, Juanito? A hunter can go out hunting and shoot at a vague shape in the distance. He inadvertently kills a boy sleeping amongst the bushes in the woods, who does not even cry out when the bullet hits him, he dies in his dreams: the hunter does not know what he has done, he may never find out, but it is done all the same: the boy did not just die of his own accord. A driver knocks down a pedestrian one night, he bumps into him, but he's in a hurry or he's afraid or he's drunk, even so, he brakes, slightly uncertain what to do; in his rear-view mirror, he sees his victim stumbling to his feet, it was obviously nothing very serious, he breathes easily again and drives on. After a few days, an internal haemorrhage carries the pedestrian off to his grave, the driver is not told, he may never find out, but the deed is done: the pedestrian did not just die of his own accord. But take another example, even more problematic, more unintended: a doctor phones a sick woman, she's not at home, but her answering machine is on, he leaves a trivial message, then forgets to press the button that switches off these modern phones" – Only You pointed to the one Anita had in her pocket, and she immediately got it out as if ready to give a demonstration if called upon – "immediately after that (his mind still on the woman), the doctor discusses with his nurse the woman's terminal condition, although, for the moment, he has decided either to give her new hope or else to say nothing. His kind remarks and those of the nurse are recorded on the patient's tape, who, when she hears them, chooses not to wait for the pain and for her own slow decline, and takes her life that same night. The doctor may never find out, especially if the woman lives alone and it doesn't occur to anyone else to listen to the tape. But the deed is done: the sick woman did not die of her illness, she did not die of her own accord."

"Unless someone takes the tape," I thought, and this time the thought came much more slowly, "unless someone steals it, the doctor himself or the nurse realizing too late what has happened. Unless their remarks were not made innocently and they were merely feigning pity, unless both of them knew the patient and had something against her, or she was somehow in their way."

"But the same thing happens to all of us," protested Téllez, "and not just to those in the ruling classes, your own examples are proof of that. The only safe option would be never to say or do anything, and even then, inactivity and silence might have the same effects, produce identical results, or, who knows, even worse ones."

"It does not console me, Juanito, to know that things are just like that, that responsibility can never be clearly assigned," replied the One and Only, his face betraying clear signs of grief, his mouth suddenly gone dry. "It's as if you were to say after the death of a friend: 'Oh well, that's the way things are, everyone dies in the end,' that wouldn't console me either. That doesn't make a friend's death bearable, it is quite simply unbearable that one's friends should die. You recently lost a daughter, forgive me for reminding you of it, and knowing that things are just like that will have been of little comfort to you, of little relief. In my case, what I do or don't do has more repercussions than what other people do or don't do, it's more serious, my errors and mistakes could affect many people, not just a sleeping boy or a pedestrian or a woman under sentence of death. Each one of my acts could set off a chain reaction, have massive consequences, that's why I'm so filled by doubt. Everything you do affects individuals, whereas I do not deal with people on an individual basis. I am aware, though, that each life is unique and fragile." He turned towards me, and sat looking at me for a moment without really seeing me, and then added: "It's unbearable that the people we know should suddenly be relegated to the past."

Téllez took out his pouch of perfumed tobacco and started to prepare a second pipe as if to conceal his faltering voice by some physical activity. (Perhaps, too, he needed an excuse to lower his eyes.) While he was doing this, he said very slowly, almost languidly:

"There's no need to apologize, Your Majesty. That's all I think about all the time, you haven't reminded me of anything. What is truly unbearable is that the person one recalls as part of the future should suddenly become the past. But the only solution to what Your Majesty says is for everything to end and for there to be nothing."

"Sometimes that doesn't seem such a bad solution," replied Solo, and Téllez must have judged that to be too nihilistic a response for witnesses to hear from such illustrious lips, for he reacted, at once, by trying to change the subject and said:

"But let's return to the business in hand, Your Majesty, if you don't mind. What aspect of Your Majesty's real personality would you like to have reflected, apart from these doubts of yours, which I'm not sure would be terribly acceptable? Your Majesty must give Ruibérriz instructions."

Then the door through which Solus and Anita had entered was flung open, and in came an elderly cleaning woman, somewhat surly and ill-tempered in appearance. She was carrying a feather duster and a broom and was sliding along, rather hunched, on the two dusters on her feet in order not to tread on the floor with the soles of her slippers, so that she advanced very slowly as if she were a skier crossing firm snow with one very long ski pole and one very short. Astonished, we all turned to watch her interminable passing, she had that loose, white hair that makes old women look even older, and conversation was suspended for a minute or two, because she was singing tunelessly under her breath as she continued her rapt progress; until, at last, when the cleaning lady reached his side, Segarra grabbed her arm with one white gloved hand – which seemed suddenly like a claw – and said something to her in a low voice, at the same time pointing to us. The woman jumped, looked at us, raised one hand to her mouth to stifle a silent cry and hurried as quickly as she could over to the first door, the one Téllez and I had entered some time ago. "She looked like a witch," I thought, "or perhaps a banshee": that supernatural female figure from Ireland who warns families of the imminent death of one of their members. They say that sometimes she sings a funeral lament while she combs her hair, but more often, one or two nights before the death she is warning them of is to take place, she shouts or moans beneath the windows of the threatened house. The cleaning woman had been humming some unrecognizable tune, she had uttered no cry or moan, neither was it night-time. I thought: "I don't believe this house is under threat, Téllez and I are the ones who suffered a bereavement a month ago, he lost a member of his family and I one of my lovers. A prediction of the past." She closed the door behind her, and the last thing we saw was the feather duster that got hooked on the door handle for a moment.

"One night, about a month ago, I couldn't sleep," said Solitaire, taking very little notice of the sudden appearance of the banshee. "I got up and I went into another room so as not to bother anyone, I turned the television on and I started watching an old film that had already started, what it was called I don't know, afterwards, I went to look for that day's newspaper, but it had already been thrown out, they always throw things away before I've finished with them. It was in black and white and featured a very old, very fat Orson Welles, I'm sure you know him, he's buried in Spain. In fact, it was filmed in Spain, I recognized the walls of Ávila and Calatañazor and Lecumberri and Soria, the church of Santo Domingo, but the action took place in England, and one believed it too, despite seeing all those familiar places, even the Casa de Campo appeared and that fooled one too, it all looked like England, it was very odd, seeing what one knew to be one's own country and yet believing that it was England on the screen. The film was about two kings, Henry IV and Henry V, the latter when he was still the Prince of Wales, Prince Hal they called him sometimes, a good-for-nothing, a rake, who, while his father lies dying, spends all day drinking, or hanging around whorehouses and taverns with prostitutes and his vile friends, the fat Welles, the oldest of the corrupters, and another man his own age, a man called Poins, with an unpleasant, cynical face, who takes too many liberties with him, he clearly doesn't know where to draw the line, and the Prince again and again puts Poins in his place as he himself begins to change. The old King is sick and anxious, in one scene, he asks them to place the crown on his pillow and the son, believing that the King has already died, prematurely puts it on his own head. In between there's another scene in which the King cannot sleep, as was happening to me that same night, luckily in my case it was just a one-off. He hasn't been able to sleep for days, he stares at the sky out of the window and rebukes sleep, which he reproaches for visiting much poorer homes than his, even the homes of murderers, but scorning his more noble house. "Oh partial sleep," he says bitterly, and I couldn't help but identify with him at that moment, watching television in my dressing gown while everyone else was asleep, although I did sometimes identify with the Prince too. In fact, the

King doesn't appear much in the film at all, at least not in the bit I saw, but it was enough to get an idea of what he's like, or what he was like. You see how the Prince changes when his father does at last die and he is crowned king, he abjures his past life (his immediately past life, you see, it was the day before yesterday, even yesterday) and he dismisses his companions, he sends poor Welles into exile despite the fact that the old man calls him 'my sweet boy', kneeling before him at the coronation ceremony itself, waiting for the promised favours and the postponed joys, postponed until his final decrepitude. "I am not the thing I was," the new King says to him, when only a few days before he had shared adventures and jokes with him. He disappoints everyone, the old King Henry senses his changed son's haste, "I stay too long by you, I weary you," says the dying man. Even so he gives him advice and tells him secrets, he says to him just before he dies: "God knows, my son, by what by-paths and indirect crooked ways I met this crown; how I came by the crown, O God, forgive!" His hands are stained with blood and he has not forgotten it, he was perhaps poor and doubtless a conspirator or a murderer, although, with the years, the dignity of his position has dignified him and, seemingly and superficially, erased all that, just as the Prince ceases to be a dissolute once he becomes a king, as if our actions and personalities were in part determined by people's perception of us, as if we came to believe that we are different from what we thought we were because chance and the heedless passing of time change our external circumstances and our clothes. Or else it is the by-paths and the indirect crooked ways of our own efforts that change us and we end up believing that it is fate, we end up seeing our life in the light of the latest or most recent event, as if the past had been only a preparation and we only understood it as it moved away from us, as if we understood it all completely at the end. The mother believes she was born to be a mother and the spinster to be single, the murderer to be a murderer and the victim a victim, just as the leader believes that his steps led him from the very beginning to hold sway over other people's wills, just as one traces the genius back to the child once one knows he is a genius; if he comes to the throne, the king persuades himself that it was his rôle to be king and, if he doesn't, that it was his rôle to be the martyr of the family, and the man who reaches old age ends up seeing his whole life as a slow progress towards that old age: one sees one's past life as if it were a plot or a mere piece of circumstantial evidence, and then one falsifies and distorts it. Welles doesn't change in the film, he dies faithful to himself, seeing all the favours and joys postponed once more until beyond death, betrayed and with his heart broken by his sweet boy. ("Goodbye laughter and goodbye scorn. I will never see you again nor will you see me. Goodbye ardour, goodbye memories.") Both his face and those of the kings glimpsed during that hour and a half are clear and recognizable, I will always see those faces and hear those words whenever I think of Henry IV and Henry V of England, if I ever do think about them again. I'm not like that, my face and my words mean nothing to anyone, and it's time for that to change." The Lone Ranger stopped short as if he had suddenly stopped reading a book, he looked up and added in another tone of voice: "That, I suppose, is the sheer power of the performance, I must see the whole film one day."

"If you're interested, sir, it was *Chimes at Midnight*," I said.

"I'm sorry?"

"The title of the film you saw, sir. It's *Chimes at Midnight*." Only the Lonely looked at me surprised and a touch wary:

"And how do you know? Did you see it that night?"

"No, I was watching another film on the other side, but when I changed channels, I saw that they were showing that too. I recognized it at once, I saw it years ago in the cinema."

"Ah well, I'll have to have them show it to me or lend me the video. Note it down, Anita. And what film were you watching? Couldn't you sleep either? It was about a month ago, as I said."

I looked at Téllez, but I noticed no particular reaction on his part, doubtless he was sleeping that night and could not identify it by the television programmes being shown. He had recovered from his moment of grief, he had lit his second pipe and seemed comfortable there, pleased to pass the morning like that, although it was growing steadily colder. It was a bit like being at school, like when the boys got together in the playground during break when

I was a child, and the one who had seen a film would describe it to the others and make them want to see it or, rather, his telling of the story made it up to them for not having seen it, it's a kind of act of generosity, telling someone something. Only You was the leader of the class.

"I don't know the name of the film I saw, I turned on when it had already started and I didn't have a newspaper to hand. I wasn't at home." And I don't know why I added that, I could easily not have said it, perhaps I wanted to be generous. I didn't say that I had watched it with the sound turned down.

"Well, it seems rather late not to be at home," said the Only One, half-smiling. "What do you make of our friend here, Anita? A bit of a nightbird, eh?"

Anita instinctively touched the ladder in her stocking as if to cover the flesh that it revealed. She caught a thread with her nail and made the ladder even worse, that stocking was ready to become a cast-off. We all pretended that we hadn't noticed, and she said:

"Oh, good heavens," though it wasn't clear if this was a comment on her ruined silk stockings or on the euphemistic insinuation that I was a nightbird.

"Anyway, as I was saying," Solo went on, "I think I've made myself pretty clear, eh, Ruibérriz? You will work over the next few days in constant contact with Juanito, in his apartment if that suits, so that he can watch over and control everything and give you instructions, he's known me since for ever. And if we're happy with the work, you can be sure that you'll get more," he added, as if he were offering me a really cushy number. He was doubtless ignorant of the low fees paid by the Palace. He stood up and those of us still sitting immediately copied him, Anita and I swiftly, Téllez slowly or with difficulty; Segarra again stood to attention and Segurola laid down his tools, holding his paint brush and palette in his fallen hands, any possibility of being able to continue his work being over. Solus was leaving, but first, he indicated Juanito's foot: "Juanito," he said, "don't forget that shoelace, you'll trip over."

Téllez looked down again, this time a touch despairingly, he would clearly be incapable of tying it himself, not even with his foot raised. I grasped the situation in an instant: it would take Segarra ages to reach us and he was even less capable of bending down than Téllez was; you couldn't rely on Segurola, perhaps he didn't even have permission to leave his corner and approach Solitaire, he looked like a man in exile or immured; young, conscientious Anita would have been perfect for the job, but if she crouched or knelt down the buttons of her jacket might pop off and her stockings fall down. It was up to the Lone Ranger or myself. I looked at him out of the corner of my eye and I saw that he made no move to help. That was to be expected. I didn't hesitate.

"Don't worry, I'll tie it," I said and although I seemed to be saying it to Téllez, I was really saying it to Only the Lonely, as if there had been a genuine chance that he might take on the job.

"No, no," protested Téllez, with relief or possibly gratitude. There was no need for me to speak to him, I won him over with my own unsolicited gesture.

I knelt down and picked up the two ends of the shoelace which were of uneven length; I tied it using a double knot, as if he were a child and I were Luisa, his daughter, in the cemetery, with whom I felt identified for a moment, or perhaps twinned. Everyone watched the brief operation while it was being carried out, like a group of surgeons watching the master surgeon as he removes the bullet. I knelt down before Marta Téllez's old father just as the old Orson Welles or, rather, Falstaff had fallen on his knees before the new King, who because he was now king had ceased to be what he had always been until then, his sweet boy.

"There you are," I said, getting up and instinctively blowing on my fingers. Téllez stood looking down at the neatly tied shoelace for a moment.

"It might be a bit tight now," he said, "but it's better like that."

In a reflex act of imitation Only You also blew on his band-aided fingers. And then I couldn't help asking him, even at the risk of proving irksome at the very last:

"What are those band-aids for, sir?" I asked him.

The One and Only raised his two index fingers as if he were about to give the signal for the music to start, and he looked at them, amused, as if recalling some past joke. The half-smile returned to his lips and he said:

"Now that would be telling."

And again we all briefly laughed.

NEEDLESS TO SAY, Solo's vague desires not only exceeded my provisional powers, they were doubtless also only a passing fancy provoked, quite randomly, by "partial sleep" who does not always elude or visit the same houses, and by the late-night television schedule. He had seen only part of that film and had experienced a feeling of instantaneous, primitive jealousy, forgetting or not realizing that the two medieval Henries of Lancaster had benefited from the passing of the centuries which had, by itself, made them into fictitious beings, objects of representation, nothing more, not even objects of investigation or study, leaving them clear and recognizable in a way that a person never is, but in a way that personages can be. He was still a person, although, unlike most mortals, he could be almost certain that, posthumously, he would cross that frontier that almost no one crosses: and people are voluble and unstable and fragile and easily distracted from their own affairs, thus betraying or blurring their character, they have only to glance in the other direction and the portrait is ruined, or rather you have to falsify it and anticipate the death of the person being painted, painting him as if he could no longer change because he was no longer alive and would never again grumble about anything, like Marta Téllez, whom I perceived more and more as someone who had always been dead, she has been dead so much longer than the time that I knew her when she was alive, when I saw her and talked to her and kissed her: for me, she was only alive for three days, and I was a witness to her breathing during a few hours of those three days. And even though that wasn't actually true: any dead life lasts longer than an inconstant lived life, and that applies not only to her dead life, which arrived prematurely, but to all the living who have been in the world and who endure longer as dead people, once they are part of the past, providing there is still someone alive to remember them. And when she said "Hold me", she must have believed that she had been born to die rather young and married and a mother, perhaps she saw all her steps up until that moment, all her early days, as an itinerary that was at last comprehensible, that led to that night with me, a night of unconsummated infidelity. And I, in turn, would see her as someone who had appeared in my life merely in order to die by my side and to provoke in me this state of enchantment, what a strange mission or task that was, to appear and disappear just so that I would take different steps than those I would otherwise have taken – the thread of continuity uninterrupted, my silken thread still intact but with no guide – so that I would feel concerned about a child and look for a death notice and attend a funeral, pretending I was visiting a tomb dated 1914 and listen again and again to a tape ("You can't be that keen to see me, if you want, I could still come over for a while, the guy sounds rather nice, he's never exactly been a man of letters, don't get too excited, *povero me*, we can't afford not to be able to locate him, so we'll do whatever you say, we could see each other on Monday or Tuesday, hi, it's me, could one of you save me a slice of ham, please, please"; and that crying), so that I would become involved aimlessly and surreptitiously in the lives of strangers, as if I were a spy who doesn't even know what it is he has to find out – if there is anything to find out – and, at the same time, risks exposing his own secret to the very people he should conceal it from, not that they are aware he has a secret that affects them; so that I can keep my secret for a while longer and write the words that Solus will say to the world even though I am no one, even though I barely belong to the world, although perhaps that is entirely appropriate, that those words attributable to his person should come from the most obscure and anonymous subject in his kingdom, so that they can truly become his words; or, rather, from his most obscure and pseudonymous subject, since he believed me to be Ruibérriz de Torres, that was my name. What a strange mission or task Marta Téllez's was, to appear and disappear just so that I would take those steps towards her old father's apartment and make his existence a little less precarious, make him feel useful, even, for a week or so, like someone with responsibilities of state, so that I would breathe life into one of the soon-to-be-dead who nevertheless survives his own children. If Marta were alive, I would not be going through the vast, old-fashioned portals of a house in the Salamanca district of Madrid, nor would I be going up in a lift with pretentious, ancient, wooden doors and an anachronistic bench on which to sit, nor ringing the doorbell on several successive days, I would not be spending the mornings in a large study full of books and pictures, jumbled and alive, sitting at a borrowed table before my own portable typewriter which I had transported there on the first day, a typewriter I rarely use now, with an older man who keeps hopeful guard in the room next door, an affable man, glad perhaps to have another presence in the house besides that of a maid of a kind one no longer sees, in uniform with an apron, but no cap, and who is doubtless the person who ties his rebellious shoelaces each morning. I would not be on the receiving end of the trumped-up visits or pretences at supervision of that old man who, on the pretext of fetching a book or looking for a letter, prowls around the study whistling a tune and invariably asks me: "So, how's it going? Getting on all right? Do you need anything?" in the hope that I will ask him a question or let him read the last lines of the speech I have written so that he can give his approval or suggest emendations in his rôle as an old and privileged connoisseur of the Lone Ranger's psyche. (And then, from time to time, he goes into the kitchen to grind some coffee.) And I would not be meeting Luisa, Luisa Téllez, the surviving daughter and sister, who arrived late on the second morning of whistling and work in order to pick up her father, nor Eduardo Deán, the son-in-law, the husband, the widower, who arrived shortly afterwards to go out and have lunch with them, that is, with us, or else, I would have met them in other circumstances ("Would you like to join us?", it had been Téllez's suggestion, and I said "Yes, why not," not waiting to be asked again, not making them insist, which they might not have done anyway). Nor would I be going into a restaurant with them, the father the first to go through the door, as fathers and Italian men always are, they won't let a woman go into any public place ahead of them because, first, they have to test the water (at that moment, bottles might fly or knives flash, men fight even in the most unsuitable places for a brawl), then Luisa Téllez, then me, to whom Deán gave way with a gesture that was half-paternalistic and half an indication of vague social superiority (or perhaps it was the false deference with which such people treat mere wageslaves), you fool – I thought, addressing him mentally as "tú" (any mental insult demands the use of the informal "tú") – you don't know that your wife died in my arms while you were in London, you fool, you still don't know, and then, ashamed, I corrected myself: sometimes my mental reactions are too aggressive, too masculine.

Deán was rather a handsome man, he had improved a lot with the years, now that I saw him close to, and now that his face no longer had the pallor I had seen at the cemetery a month before, his hands clutching his temples. I don't know if it is fair to say what I'm going to say, since, from the very start, I already knew quite a lot about him and had been present at his change of marital status when he still knew nothing about it, but the fact is that he had the face of a widower, though it was difficult to know if he had acquired that face in the last month or if he'd had it for a long time before becoming a widower. (Widows and widowers seem very calm even underneath their despair or sadness, when they feel despair or sadness.) He offered me his left hand, although he wasn't left-handed and his right hand wasn't bandaged or immobilized in any way, an idiosyncrasy, a quirk, which made that first contact with him slightly clumsy and difficult and odd, as if that were part of his character, his ever mutable face, the mocking eyebrows, the grave, almond eyes, the cleft chin like that of Cary Grant and Robert Mitchum and Fred MacMurray (though he was thinner than any of them). During the introductions at Téllez's apartment I was certain that neither he nor his sister-in-law Luisa had noticed me at the funeral and could not therefore recognize me; however, during lunch or while we were waiting for it, I had a sudden moment of doubt while Téllez and his daughter were resolving some domestic matter that was of no interest to Deán or to me and so we sat listening, not saying anything: during those two or three minutes, he looked at me both directly and indirectly as if he knew something about me or, rather, as if one could have no secrets from him, he had the sort of incredulous, expectant eyes that oblige one to go on talking even though no questions have been asked and there is only silence, to explain more than has been asked for, to prove with new arguments something that has not been put in doubt or verbally refuted by anyone, but which one feels to be invalid or that simply won't wash, all because the other person doesn't answer, but goes on waiting, like someone at a show who does not participate and wants to be entertained right up until the end. And you are that show, although during the two or three minutes when he looked at me, I was a dumb show at which he cast only the occasional glance, as one does at a television with the sound off. "I can't understand how Marta could ever have had a lover," I thought, "especially not that loudmouth Vicente who, according to his own wife Inés, is never discreet, the kind of loudmouth who always ends up spilling the beans, even revealing things that might prejudice or ruin himself. I don't understand how such a thing could be possible given this husband and his comminatory eyes, from whom no one could hide anything of that nature for very long, unless the relationship between Marta and Vicente was a recent one, a new one, despite the recorded confidences and the verbal, not merely mental, insults, the flesh makes people over-confident and invites abuse, everything becomes creased or stained or crumpled, I would have to listen to that tape again, perhaps I would hear in that man's voice the impatience that newness brings with it, when what is new fills you with enthusiasm and you can't do without it. Deán is very sharp and doubtless vengeful, according to Inés, he's determined to find me and he doesn't seem the kind of man who would just accept what is given to him or who would not take steps, he seems more the active sort, a schemer, manipulative, persuasive, he's probably the type to force and bend both events and wills, that look denotes attitudes which, once adopted, become rigid, as well as a wealth of acquired conviction, those incipient, multiple lines that will make his face as craggy as tree bark when he's older, that slowness and that joint capacity for surprise and for infinite understanding that I now feel and see close to, on the other side of the table, he is the kind of person who knows and measures the consequences of his actions and who knows that everything is possible and, therefore, any wonderment we might feel should last no more than an instant – the instant that precedes infinite comprehension – not even what we might think or do ourselves, cruelty, pity, scorn, melancholy and rage; mockery, rectitude, good faith and self-absorption; vehemence, or perhaps inclemency, everything stripped of the justifications that anyone who paused to think a little would reject or ignore, and then act. This man is far-sighted and prescient, he is alert and takes account of what almost no one takes account of: he takes account of the future and he sees what will happen later on, and that is why when he does something, he believes it to be right. Or perhaps he isn't like that at all, but quite the opposite, perhaps he has a good sense of mental and verbal rhetoric and, on all occasions, acts without thinking, knowing that, later on, he will find the right argument or judgement to justify what his taste and instinct will have improvised, that is, to explain his actions and his words, knowing that everything can be defended and that any opposing conviction can be refuted, we can always prove ourselves to be right and everything can be told if accompanied by some justification, some excuse or by some attenuating circumstance or even by its mere representation, telling is a form of generosity, anything can happen and be said and be accepted, you can emerge from anything unharmed, or more than that, unscathed, no codes or commandments or laws can be made to stand up, they are always convertible into so much scrap paper, there will always be someone who can say: 'They don't apply to me, or not in my case, or not this time, although perhaps the next, if there is a next time.' Someone who will manage to maintain that and to convince others of it." His voice was very deep, rusty and hoarse as if it emerged from behind a helmet or had spent centuries meditating upon and storing up each word, he spoke very slowly and that was how he spoke when we were on the second course and he finally made a reference to Marta, to his wife who had died a month before without the benefit of his presence:

"I don't know if you've realized, but in a week's time, it's Marta's birthday," he said. "She would have been thirty-three, she didn't even manage to make it that far."

He said this with his Tartar eyes the colour of beer fixed on Luisa, whose previous words had given rise to his, or had at least meant that his did not seem extemporaneous and merely the product of meditations unrelated to the general conversation which, until that moment, had flowed in a desultory, stop-start fashion with the occasional brief pause, influenced perhaps by my awkward presence and perhaps, too, by the domestic matter that Luisa and her father had begun discussing as soon as we sat down, a matter of a purchase to be made. Or maybe it was a way of trying to avoid or rather postpone what the three of them would doubtless experience as an incessant beating in their thoughts, especially when they got together, and which Deán had no longer been able to avoid mentioning, he had waited until we had ordered and had eaten our first course, and until they had brought us the second (he was eating sole and drinking wine). Up until then, they had not paid me much attention, that is, they had not treated me like a new person in whom it would only be polite to take a minimal interest, not like an equal, but like an employee who has simply joined his paymasters for lunch, because otherwise he would have no lunch, except that they were not going to pay me anything, nor was Téllez, and I would have been perfectly capable of having lunch alone without feeling that it showed any lack of consideration on their part. Perhaps, too, they were overly self-absorbed and too accustomed to talking about their own affairs (it happens in all families) to vary the programme and the tone and the usual erratic agenda of their meetings, perhaps more frequent now than they had ever been, the death of someone temporarily brings together those who are left behind. Luisa had asked her father how much money he wanted to spend on the present he would give – but which she would buy for him that afternoon – to the daughter-in-law and sister-in-law María (María Fernández Vera, I remember all the names), whose birthday it was the following day, that was the kind of conversation they were having, and it was then that Deán said what I have said he said, with his understandable confusion of tenses, first he spoke as if Marta were still alive ("it's Marta's birthday"), then he corrected himself when he mentioned how old she would have been, the dead abandon their age and thus end up being the youngest if we who go on living and remembering them last a long time, so far only a month longer in this case. Luisa must have had a similar thought, because she was the one who answered first after a silence that acknowledged the pointlessness of avoiding talking about what three people are simultaneously thinking, three people who are in fact four and that fourth a haunted person, although the other three knew nothing about this for they too had perhaps been under a spell ever since they had watched the symbolic earth falling. Téllez left his fish knife and fork crossed on his plate (grilled fish which he had eaten, up until then, with a good appetite); Luisa raised her napkin to her lips and held it there for a few seconds as if she were using it to hold back her tears – rather than anything the mouth itself might emit, vomit or words – before replacing it on her lap, the napkin stained now with lipstick and saliva and the juice from her rare steak (definitely not Irish); first spearing a roast potato with his fork, Deán himself raised his right hand to his forehead and rested his right elbow ostentatiously on the table, as if he had suddenly forgotten all his manners. And when Luisa finally replaced her napkin on her lap – I had a glimpse of her thighs across the table while they remained uncovered, though her skirt was not as short as her sister's had been, the white napkin covering her open mouth – what she said was this, echoing my own thoughts:

"I never imagined that one day I would be older than Marta, that's one of the things that you know to be impossible from childhood on, even though you might want it sometimes, when your older sister takes your toy away from you or you have a fight with her, and you always lose because you're the youngest. And yet it is possible. In two years' time, I'll already be older than her, if I live that long. It seems incredible."

She was still holding her knife in her right hand, a sharp serrated knife with a wooden handle, the sort they sometimes give you in restaurants so that you can cut your meat more easily. She had placed her fork on the plate in order to take up her napkin, and hadn't picked it up again. She looked like a frightened woman ready to defend herself, wielding that knife with its cutting, serrated edge.

"Don't talk such nonsense, my dear, and touch wood," Téllez said apprehensively. "'If I live that long, if I live that long', honestly. Haven't we suffered enough misfortunes?" And turning to me, he added as an explanation (he may have been superstitious, but he was the one who was most conscious of my presence), also hovering between tenses: "Marta is my eldest daughter, Eduardo's wife. She died very suddenly, just over a month ago." Despite everything, he believed in luck and that things do not necessarily repeat themselves.

"I thought I heard something of the sort at the Palace," I replied, I was the only one who still had both knife and fork in my hands, although, by then, I wasn't eating either. "I'm so terribly sorry." And in my mouth that cliché was only too exact and too right ("how that death gladdens me, saddens me, pleases me"). Then I fell silent, I didn't even ask what she had died of (it had never mattered much to me, and it mattered less all the time), I wanted to say only enough to allow them to go on talking as they had done until then, as if I wasn't there, as if I were no one, although I had been duly introduced to them, and by my real name which never appears anywhere.

Deán finished the white wine in his glass and refilled it, still with his elbow leaning on the table and his forehead resting on his hand. But it was Luisa who spoke again, and she said (not without first touching wood as her father had recommended: I noticed her mechanically touch the table beneath the cloth like someone linking a word to an action, it was a normal gesture, customary in her, she was superstitious too, perhaps it was her Italian inheritance, although, in Italy, people tend to touch iron).

"I still remember the parties we went to as adolescents, where I always had a terrible time and all because of her: she would forbid me to like any boy until she had chosen one. 'Just wait until I've decided,' she would say to me as we stood outside the front door of the house where the party was being held. 'You just wait, all right? Otherwise, we don't go in,' she used to say, and only when I'd said: 'Yes, all right, but be quick' would we ring the doorbell. Because she was the eldest she had a kind of right to first refusal, and I let her get away with it. Then, during the party, she would take her time deciding, she would dance with a few boys before telling me which one she had chosen, and I would be on tenter-hooks, afraid that what nearly always happened would happen, that she would end up choosing the boy I most liked. I'm con-vinced that she often tried to guess who I liked just so that she could choose him and then, when I protested, she would accuse me of being a copycat, of always choosing the boys that she liked best. And then she would dance with him all evening. I tried hard to hide my preferences, but it was no good, she knew me too well, she always homed in on the right one, and so, when we were older, we stopped going to the same parties. That's the way she was," said Luisa, a distant look in her eyes, the eyes of someone plunging effortlessly into her memory, "although the fact is she would have had first choice anyway, she had a bigger bust than me then and had much more success with boys than I had."

I couldn't help glancing swiftly at Luisa Téllez's bust, calculating its size. Perhaps her sister Marta's bra had not been a size too small, perhaps her breasts had always been on the large side. "How can I possibly be ogling Luisa Téllez's bust and thighs?" I thought. I know it's normal behaviour for me and for many other men, regardless of the circumstances, however sad or even tragic, we can't resist looking at something that is visually attractive, not without making a superhuman effort, but just then it made me feel like a complete scoundrel – in adolescent-speak: a "perv" – yet, nevertheless, I continued visually to measure her bust – surreptitiously, it was a matter of moments – with such veiled, hypocritical eyes that I immediately lowered them to my plate and ate another mouthful, the first at the table to eat since Deán's mention of the approaching birthday of someone who would not in fact be there to celebrate. She hadn't had the chance to decide whether or not she liked me first, Luisa hadn't seen me before, her voice did not strike me as being the same one which, for all eternity, would say on my answering machine, unless I erased the tape: " . . . so, make sure you call me tomorrow and tell me all about it. The guy sounds rather nice, but you can never tell. Frankly, I don't know how you've got the nerve. Anyway, talk to you later, and good luck." I hadn't really wanted to think about it, but perhaps I was "the guy", that message must have been the penultimate or rather the last (the penultimate would have been erased by the superimposition of the electric voice that I had heard directly and which Marta never heard) before I rang the doorbell and came through the door; it's possible that having finally decided that she was going to see me, Marta had had time to talk to a friend or to her sister about it: "I've got a date with a guy I hardly know, and he's coming over for supper; Eduardo's in London, I don't quite know what will happen, but you never know" with the same excitement she used to feel as an adolescent, before a party ("Just wait until I've decided" and only then ring the doorbell), perhaps Marta had, in turn, left that message on her friend's or sister's answering machine, a message that had, in turn, been replied to while she dashed out, at the last minute, to a nearby supermarket, leaving the child alone for a moment as I had left him alone most of one night, in order to buy the Häagen-Dazs ice cream for dessert: perhaps, for example. She might not have said "the guy" but my name, even my surname, she might have managed to speak to the friend or the sister without any intervening answering machine and to have talked about me (but then they would have known my name, and Luisa clearly didn't recognize it when her father introduced us, perhaps she wouldn't even remember it now), to have speculated and commented, I met him at a cocktail party and we arranged to meet for coffee the next day, he knows all kinds of people, he's divorced, he writes scripts and things, that's what I usually say I do and, at first, I don't say anything about my rôle as ghostwriter, although I don't conceal the fact if the subject happens to come up, I know that people find my stories about it amusing. That night, too, Marta had hesitated or exercised her right of first refusal, she had called Vicente but he hadn't been in, she had certainly called him and possibly someone else, I had probably been an ill-fated second best, and that was the only reason she had died before my eyes and in my arms. I've already said that I don't care about the medical causes of her death, nor was I interested in reconstructing what had happened the day before our meeting nor the process that had brought us together, nor to find out about her history or that of her family or that of her jaded marriage, nor to relive vicariously what had been interrupted or, rather, cancelled, I'm a passive kind of person who almost never seeks or wants anything or isn't aware that he's seeking or wanting anything, the sort of person things just happen to, you don't even have to move for everything to become horribly complicated, for things to happen, for there to be anger and litigation, you only have to breathe in this world, the slightest in-breath or out-breath like the minimal swaying inevitable in all light objects hanging by a thread, our veiled and neutral gaze like the inert oscillation of toy aeroplanes suspended from a ceiling, and that always end up going into battle because of that minimal tremor or pulsation. And if, now, I was taking a few steps, it was with no very definite aim, I didn't even want to decipher that tape which I had listened to so often, because it simply wasn't possible: that message could have been for Deán and not for Marta, perhaps "the guy" was someone with whom Deán was going to do a deal that required great daring and perhaps she hadn't spoken about me to anyone and no one in the world knew that I had been chosen for that night, not to go to bed with her, but to accompany her in her death. What I was seeking perhaps – this occurred to me while I was chewing the mouthful of food and dragging my hypocritical gaze away from Luisa's bust – what I wanted perhaps was something absurd but understandable, perhaps I wanted to convert my unjustified presence that night into something more deserved and formal, even though it was after the fact and I was, therefore, playing dirty, a more plausible way of altering the facts than any other, seeing one's past life as if it were a plot or a mere piece of circumstantial evidence, as if the past had been only a preparation and we only understood it as it moved away from us, as if we understood it all completely at the end: as if I thought that it wasn't right or fair that she should have said her goodbyes beside someone she barely knew, who was there merely in order not to let the opportunity of a romantic evening slip by, and that it would be fairer if that no one eventually ended up becoming *someone* to those who were close to her, if, in virtue of her death and what it brought in its train, I ended up being indispensable or important or even useful in the life of one of her loved ones, or else saved them from something. And yet I had had an initial opportunity at the time, I thought, had I stayed in the apartment in Conde de la Cimera, I could have guaranteed the safety of Eugenio who was left there alone with a corpse, but I had not done so. I could also have phoned again, I could have persisted with the melodious night porter at the Wilbraham Hotel in London and warned Mr Ballesteros, I could have let him know what she would have wanted him to know the moment she realized that she was dying, we can't bear those close to us not to know about our troubles, there are four or five people in everybody's life who must be informed immediately of whatever is happening to us, we can't bear them to think us still alive when we are dead. I had not done that either, to protect myself from possible anger and to protect her, who had said to me at the start: "You're mad, how can I possibly phone him, he'd kill me," but it doesn't make much sense protecting a dead woman from being killed when she's already dead and, besides, I hadn't even managed to save her reputation, they knew that I had been there that night, that is, that a man had been there. I had not done so. Filling the father's empty days for a while wasn't much of a contribution, but it was all I had managed up until then.

"Honestly, the things you girls come out with," said Téllez, and he too took another furtive mouthful of his fish, he was still hungry, but then he crossed his knife and fork on his plate again as if he did not dare to go on eating. He obviously didn't like his daughters to talk about their busts, even though they were adolescent busts that belonged firmly in the past now and could therefore easily be made the subject of a joke: doubtless, for him, his daughters did not have such things as breasts, no more than had the daughter called Gloria who had lived so briefly, I think he blushed a little, although in older people it is difficult to distinguish blushing from overheating, not that they often blush. He had said "you girls" as if Luisa were a chance individual representative at the table of what had always been a collective, his daughters, as if Luisa's remark could easily have been made or subscribed to by her sister, it's hard to get used to the idea that someone will never again comment on anything. "You all have such a coarse vision of things. Coffee, please," he added, raising a finger at a passing waiter laden with trays who took no notice of him. "Do any of you want pudding? I'm going to skip it." That plural "you" was different: it included me, the two other men at the table.

We were in a restaurant where he was a familiar face, it was close to where he lived, he was used to getting prompt service. He shot a look of irritation at the waiter, took out his pipe and tapped it on the palm of his hand; as soon as the head waiter saw that gesture, he approached solicitously, addressing him as "Don Juan":

"Didn't you enjoy the fish, Don Juan?" he said.

"Yes, yes, but I haven't much appetite, and I don't think the others have either, you can clear all this away now. I'd like a coffee. What about you?" I noticed that he used the informal plural "vosotros" which included me, he would soon be addressing me as "tú".

Just then, the head waiter turned towards the window, a moment before there was a loud clap of thunder – as if he had sensed it – and it began to rain heavily just as it had a month or more before, although not quite as it had then, this time it was raining faster and more furiously, as if the rain had to make the most of the brief time allotted to it or as if it were an air raid being fought off by artillery. In the space of about half a minute, people from the street had crammed into the doorway of the restaurant, men and women and children were running to find shelter from what was falling from the sky, again, like the men, women and children of the 1930s in this same city which was, at the time, under siege, who were also running to find shelter from what was falling from the sky and from the shells fired from the outskirts, from Ángeles or Garabitas hill, the so-called "*obuses*" or mortar bombs that traced a parabola and fell on the main telephone exchange or on the square alongside when their aim went wrong (in the quirky black humour of the time, the place was renamed Ouch Square), or on the vast Café Negresco that was completely destroyed and strewn with corpses, yet the next day, people, simultaneously unperturbed and resigned, went and ordered their glass of hot malted milk at the neighbouring café, La Granja del Henar, in Calle de Alcalá opposite the start of the Gran Vía, knowing that the same thing could easily happen there, the suburbs and the sky became the biggest threat to pedestrians, who consequently sought out the pavements that were not in the firing line, just as those caught in the storm did now, for the wind was driving the rain hard, and the shells were more likely to hit one or other pavement according to which hill they were being fired from, two and a half years in the life of those besieging and those besieged, two and a half years of running down these streets, hands clutching hats and berets and caps, skirts flying and stockings laddered or no stockings at all, in this city which, ever since, has never lost that sense of living and being like an island.

The head waiter took a personal note of the order; tied around his waist, in the manner of French waiters, he wore a kind of white sheet (rather than an apron) that almost reached his feet, a white cloth over his black uniform, that way it didn't matter if he got dirty. The four of us sat watching the rain for a moment.

"It won't last, but we might as well order a dessert," said Deán, "though I'll have to rush off afterwards."

"Don't be in such a hurry," said Luisa, "we haven't discussed Eugenio yet."

"I know, perhaps we should put it off for another occasion," replied Deán in his slow way, shooting me an angry glance – either deliberately or involuntarily – like a finger pointing, then another more tempered glance at Téllez, who understood what was meant and looked away and stroked his, as yet, unlit pipe. Maybe that was the reason they had arranged to have lunch, to talk about the boy, whatever that meant (another domestic matter) and Téllez's invitation, and especially my acceptance of it, had made the meeting pointless. Téllez looked like someone who knows he has put his foot in it and would prefer not to have his attention drawn to it, I kept my gaze neutral as if none of it had anything to do with me.

"It's very simple, Eduardo," replied Luisa, "now that Papa is here, just tell me what you've decided and then he can say what he thinks too, I'd rather we all talked about it together so that there are no misunderstandings. I can't spend my whole life going back and forth from my apartment to yours, and neglecting both. If you want me to have him for the moment, tell me and be done with it, or if you'd prefer to have him, then I'll help you to get that organized, although it won't be easy with your workload and with all the travelling you do. What I can't do is to keep coming and going like some sort of messenger, I've been doing that for more than a month now."

"Or like one of these modern-day girlfriends," intervened Téllez, thinking he would not now be punished for a *faux pas* committed out of courtesy. "Isn't that why people get married nowadays, because they get tired of getting up in one apartment and having to cross the city and pretend that they've just got up in their own? That's what I've heard, anyway, that marriage survives as an institution thanks to people constantly forgetting their toothbrush or being too lazy to buy a second one, people never used to sleep in other people's houses, it's not at all a good thing." And he wagged his index finger from side to side as if he knew for certain that all three of us were in the habit of doing just that. "Luisa's right, Eduardo. Let her take care of things, it will be easier for her to organize it all from her own apartment and according to her timetable. At least for now, until you see how the land lies, until you sort yourself out, or decide to get married again, you're still young and maybe, one day, someone will tire of staying over at your place and not having their own toothbrush to hand in the morning." And again it was Téllez who noticed my presence or took it into account, for he added politely, so that I could understand what they were talking about: "My daughter Marta left a son, my grandson Eugenio. He's only little, two years old. Eduardo has a very hectic lifestyle and Luisa is offering to look after the boy. Eduardo travels a lot and often at the wrong time too."

There was no reason why I should have understood that last malevolent remark, but I did understand it and it was, perhaps, strange that I did not ask what was meant. Or perhaps not. I was being discreet to the point of invisibility, being accustomed to disappearing into the background, accustomed to ceasing to be someone comes in handy sometimes, it's a form of flattery: the withdrawal of one person leaves the remaining members of the group feeling more relaxed, feeling that they have taken his place and thereby profited. "So," I thought, "Téllez can be spiteful – with Deán anyway – beneath that peaceable, absent-minded, slightly boring and ingenuous exterior, a figure who would fill a room." Perhaps it was that false ingenuousness so common amongst old people, which allows them to say or do whatever they like without anyone reproaching them or taking any notice, they pretend to be a member of the "soon-to-be-dead" so as to appear unthreatening, as if they had no desires, no expectations, when the truth is that no one ever ceases to be immersed in life as long as they have a consciousness and a few memories to ponder, more than that, it is a person's memories that make every living being dangerous and full of desires and expectations, it's impossible not to relocate your memories in the future, that is, not merely to note them down in the credit column, in the past, but also in the debit column, in what is still to come, there are certain things that one simply cannot believe will not reoccur, you can never discount the possibility that what once was will be again, if you were absolutely certain that you had made love for the very last time, you would put an end to your consciousness and to your memories, and commit suicide: perhaps, for example, immediately after making love for that last time. The living also believe that what has never happened can still happen, they believe in the most dramatic and most unlikely reversals of fortune, the sort of thing that happens in history and in stories, they believe that a traitor or beggar or murderer can become king and the head of the emperor fall beneath the blade, that a great beauty can love a monster or that the man who killed her beloved and brought about her ruin can succeed in seducing her, they believe that lost battles can be won, that the dead never really leave but watch over us or appear to us as ghosts who can influence events, that the youngest of three sisters could, one day, be the eldest: perhaps, for example. With whom would Marta Téllez have made love for the last time, with Deán the uptight or with Vicente the exasperated, not with me, at any rate, not that she would have known that it was the last time, it would never have occurred to her, whoever it was, she would not have endowed it with any particular significance or solemnity or even passion or affection, when she was alone again, dazed or sleepy, she would have showered if she had been with Vicente in a hotel or in the car, to rid herself of the smell of obscenity left by the other person, just as it took time to get rid of Marta's smell from my shirt and my body, even though I had a bath in the morning, hers was a smell of metamorphosis; and she would have simply washed herself in the bidet and then, back in bed, turned over, thinking only that she had lost half an hour's sleep, if she was with Deán in that bedroom that I now knew, the full-length mirror, the television on, the tube of Redoxon and an eye mask from some plane trip, the trousers and skirts draped over the chair and left unironed that night or any other night. And in both cases, she would have gone to sleep a little later with all thought finally banished, her mind a blank, whilst if she had known what one almost never knows and what she did not know, she would never have been able to get to sleep, indeed, she would have urged her husband or her lover to continue, to overturn that verdict without delay and to prove at once that it was not the last time, but had she managed to persuade one or the other, had she forced them to stay awake and to take her in their arms again, after a while, she would have found that that last time had come round again and had passed, and that is how time passes, constantly subjected to these ineffectual and contradictory struggles of ours, we allow ourselves to be impatient and to wish that the things we long for, but which are postponed or delayed, would happen at once, even though everything seems as nothing and to have happened too fast once it does happen and is over, repeating each beloved act brings us a little nearer to its end, and the worst thing is that not repeating it brings us closer too, everything is travelling slowly towards its own dissolution in the midst of our vain accelerations and our fictitious delays and only the last time is the last time. On the night that she entertained me, Marta Téllez must have thought that she would sleep with at least one other man during her lifetime, certainly while we were walking together towards the bedroom (she leading me by the hand, both of us slightly unsteady on our feet, the Château Malartic) and when I began to undress her and, mechanically, to explore her with my fingers and we gave each other kisses that we might just as well have spared ourselves, for then I would have no need to remember them. She would have been almost certain what was going to happen, she would in fact have gone to bed with me, I think (she would have made it in time), if the boy had gone to sleep earlier and I had made my first move less hesitantly or less tardily – that first gesture that you can sense in the air and that can undeniably speed things up or slow them down, like clouds condensing just before the peal of thunder: the fury and then the haste – there had been no sense of significance or solemnity or passion between us either, perhaps a slight touch of obscenity and some incipient affection, there wasn't time for anything more, but what was going to happen did not happen, what took place instead was her metamorphosis. And if the boy had taken even longer to get to sleep or if hesitation had won the day and I had not dared to make that move that can so easily not be made, even though you have long since sensed its presence, then I would have left Conde de la Cimera after a little more conversation and a liqueur and a few jokes and she would have been left alone to take a shower to wash away the smell of expectation. She would have sat down at the foot of the bed, neither smiling nor laughing, after putting away the plates and putting to bed the child who would have calmed down as soon as I had disappeared, she would have removed the elegant Armani top, pulling it over her head, and she would have been left with the inside-out sleeves caught on her wrists, and would have sat like that for a few seconds as if exhausted by the effort or by her day's work – the desolate gesture of someone who can't stop thinking and who gets undressed gradually in order to think or ponder between items of clothing, and needs those pauses – or perhaps because of the smell of frustrated expectations that she can still smell on herself; she would have taken off the cream-coloured top, which I had helped her take off, with the television turned on, staring indifferently at Fred MacMurray's coarse, salacious face or she would perhaps have turned to the channel that the Lone Ranger chanced upon during his sleepless night, the channel showing *Chimes at Midnight*, with Spain pretending to be England, in the early hours the whole world is in black and white; later she would have stood under the shower perhaps wondering whether she should call Vicente again and leave him another message: "If I'd managed to get in touch with you, you could have come over for a bit, instead of me wasting the whole bloody night. If you come back soon, say, before half past two or quarter to three, call me if you like, I'm not going to bed just yet and you could still come over for a while if you wanted to, I've had the most ridiculous night, disastrous, I'll tell you later about the mess I've got myself into, I don't mind going to bed a bit later still, I'll be wrecked tomorrow anyway. I should have remembered before; honestly, I'm useless." No, she wouldn't have said that, only a man is capable of describing as "disastrous" a night that has not come up to expectations, a night when he had expected to have a fuck, but hadn't, when he didn't get his rocks off or dip his wick, as Ruibérriz de Torres would say, standing at some bar. She wouldn't confess to him that she had invited someone else to the apartment, someone to replace him since he wasn't in when she had phoned, on the contrary, she would have immediately erased all trace of my presence and of the supper, and her night-time message intended for Vicente's ears would have been (she would have thought it out while she was in the shower): "I can't sleep, I don't know what's wrong. Since you weren't in, I went to bed early and I just can't get off, I even had some wine to make me sleepy, it must be because I'm so angry with myself for not having remembered before today that Eduardo wouldn't be here. Call me when you get in, even if it's late. I want to see you. Besides, at this rate, you won't be waking me up. If you're not too tired, come over." But who knows, perhaps she would never have made that call after her shower, in her dressing gown or towel, perhaps she would not have emerged from the shower at all, but would have slipped over out of frustration or too much thinking or over-tiredness and would have struck the back of her neck whilst still having time, as she fell, to turn off the tap in one last instinctive or desperate movement, to lie on the tiles, drenched and crumpled, drenched and naked, with her neck broken, the back of her neck, which would look, after a while, as if stained with half-dried blood, like striations or strands of black, sticky hair or mud, although no one would have seen it, because I would not have been there: now this *is* a horrible death, unable to call for help all night, the boy at last deep asleep and the telephone too far away, if only I'd bought a mobile; this *is* a ridiculous death, there could be nothing more ridiculous than having an accident in my own house on a night when my husband is away on a trip and when the guest who might have saved me has gone, such bad luck, and naked too, so unfortunate, everything can be ridiculous or tragic according to who is doing the telling or how they tell it, and who will tell others about my death or will it be retold several times by everyone who knows me, one to the other, in every possible manner. And she would have had those rapid thoughts only as she was falling, because perhaps Marta Téllez would have died anyway and would have died immediately with no time for feelings of malaise or fear or depression or regret. That did not happen, but a different death, no less horrible and no less ridiculous, with a stranger beside me, just as we were about to have it off, how awful, how embarrassing, how can I describe it in those terms, what isn't coarse or elevated or funny or sad when it happens can be sad or funny or elevated or coarse when you tell it, the world depends on its storytellers and I have a witness to my own death and I don't know how he will have taken it; but perhaps he won't talk, perhaps he won't tell the story, in fact, it doesn't matter how he does it – the first one, the source – stories do not belong only to those who were present or to those who invent them, once a story has been told, it's anyone's, it becomes common currency, it gets twisted and distorted, no story is told the same way twice or in quite the same words, not even if the same person tells the story twice, not even if there is only ever one storyteller, and what will my narrator or witness have thought of my own inopportune death, the fact is he didn't save me despite not having left me, despite remaining by my side, he didn't save me even though he was here, no one can save me.

No, none of that happened, and thinking about what didn't happen must be part of my bewitchment, there's no reason why I should try and shake off these voices and thoughts, I should, instead, get used to them, for as long as I remain watched or haunted or revisited. Deán shot me another rapid, impatient glance as he replied to Téllez with his voice like a rusty sword or lance or suit of armour:

"That's quite enough, this is not the right moment to talk about it. Let's just leave it, shall we?" And this time there was curiosity in that glance too, as if he had paused to wonder whether this really was the wrong moment. As if he were suddenly considering doing precisely the opposite of what he had just said, because it might suit his purposes to use the presence of a stranger to block or thwart his interlocutors.

"Just tell me one thing, Eduardo. I need to know where I stand," said Luisa even more impatiently. "There's quite a difference between living on your own and living with a child, it's not something you can just make up as you go along."

"Give me a little more time, a few more days won't hurt you. Perhaps I can arrange it so that I don't have to travel any more or so that I travel less, I have to discuss it further with Ferrán, I don't know yet. And I don't know either if I can live with the child on my own, the child belonged to both of us, you see."

"Travel, travel . . . and at the wrong time too," repeated Téllez, making his dislike of his son-in-law patently obvious. When he said it, he raised one finger as if he were a prophet.

"Look, Juan," Deán said to him then, "the fact that I wasn't at home has nothing to do with it, you know that. No one could have done anything."

I had made no effort to find out, but I confess that when I heard that, I felt greatly relieved: I was extremely glad to know that no one could have done anything, since I hadn't. It was a feeling of retrospective, conditional joy.

Téllez was sitting with his coffee before him now, he lit his pipe and looked at Deán through the fluctuating flame of the match. It took him time to extinguish it (he didn't blow on it, he waved it rather feebly in the air) and, meanwhile, he said, without looking at Deán and with his pipe in his mouth, perhaps making an attempt at unintelligibility (he was looking at the disobedient flame, but it was his arched, impish eyebrows that did the looking, rather than his large blue eyes):

"That isn't what I'm reproaching you with, Eduardo, I'm not so unreasonable as to blame you for not having saved her when no salvation was possible, I blame you for the fact that Marta died alone. You don't even know if you could live alone with the boy, she died alone, with the boy asleep. And the boy was left completely alone, with his mother dead and his father away travelling, just like that. It's lucky he's so young."

The flame singed his nails just as it went out. As I had thought, Téllez did not know about the circumstances of Marta's death.

Deán mumbled something inaudible, perhaps he was counting up to ten as they say people do to postpone their anger and thus diminish it, I've never done it, there are some things, on the other hand, that grow worse if postponed. Perhaps he was wondering whether or not to say to his hurtful father-in-law: "Your daughter wasn't alone, you old fool, nor was your grandson either, Marta made the most of my absence, it suited her down to the ground, who knows how many other times she did just that. But there's one thing you're right about, you old fool: all that travelling, and at the wrong time too." Luisa had lowered her eyes and had smothered any feelings of impatience or urgency, she regretted the impolitic or unwanted turn the conversation had taken because of her, she would know about her sister's end, her unsolitary end. I knew too, I felt a wave of heat rush over me, I must have blushed a little, I crossed my fingers, luckily no one was looking at me just then, although my blushes could have a reason: it could have been a response to my increasingly obtrusive presence there, indeed, it was due to that in part. Deán did not succumb to temptation, now he too was hiding something from someone and to his own disadvantage, out of pity for the old fool; he gave the sensible or expected reply based on the assumption that Marta had died as her father believed:

"No one could have foreseen that, how could any of us have known? She was in perfect health when I left her, I phoned her and I talked to her from London after supper and she was fine then, she didn't say anything to me, she was just about to put the child to bed, I've told you that already. Are you suggesting that I should never ever have gone anywhere, just in case? I imagine that before this happened, you didn't find it odd or wrong of me to go away, as I did on so many other occasions. Did you never leave your family alone for a few days? Don't be so absurd. Don't be so unfair."

"I didn't think anything of it because I didn't know you had gone."

"Well, I doubt very much if, over the last few years, you have been kept informed of all my movements. There was no reason why you should know."

"There was no reason why *I* should know, but she should have known. She couldn't ask you for help, she couldn't phone you, could she? You left your London phone number, but we couldn't find it anywhere, there was no sign of it in the apartment, we looked for it all over, no one could get in touch with you until the following night, that's one thing, but you hadn't left it with your friend Ferrán either, why should we believe that you left it with her? You didn't even bother." Téllez had used the plural in order to include Luisa, and doubtless Guillermo and María Fernández Vera and the whole Téllez family, who would nevertheless feel sorry for Deán, knowing what they knew, they would never have dreamed of reproaching him. Deán had also resorted to the plural so as not to feel excluded and to feel that he was one of them: "How could any of us have known?" he had said. Téllez paused for a second and then added in a harsh voice, biting on his pipe stem, through gritted teeth: "I dread to think how you spent that day, with your wife dead and you not knowing. I imagine you see those hours of indifference and ignorance in a different light now, I wouldn't want to be in your shoes, it must recur again and again in your nightmares." He stopped, removed his pipe from his mouth and said point-blank and even more scornfully: "Although, of course, you probably weren't even in London."

They had by now completely forgotten about me, at least Téllez had, for he no longer thought it necessary to bring me up to date on earlier events, old people don't make many distinctions, that is, they don't tend to consider all the elements of a situation, especially if the situation is an awkward one, only the main ones, and what mattered to him were Deán and Luisa, I was just part of the décor, I had no more reality or importance than the maître d'hotel or the waiters and customers or the crowd of people sheltering from the rain in the restaurant doorway, or the present storm (out of the window I noticed that several people were sheltering beneath a newspaper). And it was only then, when no one was taking any notice of me, not even to give me a sideways glance, that I realized that when I left Conde de la Cimera, I had taken with me not three things but four: the smell, Marta's bra, the tape from the answering machine and a yellow post-it, doubtless in Deán's handwriting and not Marta's, and which I still had in my wallet, in my pocket. And I thought: "Deán won't put up with this, this time he'll succumb, he'll tell him what happened, he won't stand for someone doubting that he even went to London, he's going to say: 'Someone took the piece of paper on which I'd noted down the name of my hotel and the phone number, the same person who was with her all night and who watched her die with his own eyes without telling anyone, the same person who took that piece of paper that you all looked for so eagerly, and who used it twenty-four hours later, the following night, he called me in my hotel room in London and he asked for me, but didn't dare speak to me when I picked up the phone, what did he want to tell me, what could he tell me then, it came too late to change anything, as did the message I received shortly afterwards when the voice of Ferrán and the voice of Luisa told me that Marta had been dead all that day and the night before or part of it, because the rest of that night she was alive and had company. Luisa knows, she can tell you, you're the only one who doesn't know, Marta's death wasn't just horrible, it was ridiculous, they found her half-undressed under the sheets and with her make-up smudged not just by her tears but by someone's kisses, the man who gave her those kisses must have been horrified, stunned, perplexed, frustrated. Imagining that man's horror is the one thing that gladdens me.' That's what he's going to say," I thought, "and I'll have to get up and go to the toilet with my napkin pressed to my mouth because I can't bear for him to say it." I had been on the point of copying down the name of the hotel (the Wilbraham Hotel) and that phone number, I had thought of doing it and had even picked up another post-it for that purpose, I had got my pen out of my jacket pocket and taken the opportunity to put my jacket on and thus prepare myself to leave, but, in the end, I hadn't written anything down, I had instead kept the post-it, unconsciously, unwittingly, I had stolen it unintentionally, without realizing what I was doing – I had so many other things to think about – when you first get hold of a telephone number, you always feel tempted to dial it at once, and that was why, the following day, no one would have found it, Luisa and Guillermo and María Fernández Vera and, who knows, perhaps the woman with the beige gloves, whom I had met downstairs at the front door, would have looked and searched everywhere, worried sick that they were unable to give this worst and gravest piece of news to Deán, the worst thing that could possibly happen and had happened. They would have spoken several times with Ferrán and it was true that he had no idea where his associate was, I had the proof of that too on my tape, before anything had happened he had left a message for Marta, I know it by heart now like all the others: "Marta, it's Ferrán. I know Eduardo left for England today, but I've just realized that he hasn't left me a phone number or address or anything, I can't think why, I told him to be sure to leave it, and the way things are here, we can't afford not to be able to locate him. Perhaps you've got them, or else, if you speak to him, can you tell him to call me at once, at the office or at home. It's fairly urgent. Thanks." And she hadn't called him to give him the phone number that *was* there then and she hadn't passed on the message to Deán when he phoned after his excellent supper at the Bombay Brasserie next to the tube station in Gloucester Road – I know it myself – or at least I can't remember her doing so. Doubtless she had a lot of things to think about too – she was still thinking then – or perhaps, on the contrary, the two mutually incompatible presences, mine and the boy's, did not allow her to think about anything apart from us, him and me, and getting rid of the boy just for a moment and using that moment to pay me some attention, hoping that the phone wouldn't ring again, that her son wouldn't have a tantrum and kick up a fuss, drinking enough wine to seek and to want what she still wasn't even sure she was seeking or wanting. And all day Deán had been just that, unlocatable, Téllez was right, he was very acute and he knew just where to put the knife in, what would Deán have done during those hours of neglect and ignorance in London, how would he have spent that day believing that someone who was dead was, in fact, alive, he would have spent the early part of the day in meetings, the object of the trip, then he might have gone for a walk in St James's Park or around Hampstead or Chelsea, perhaps in his free time, he would have bought a present for Marta, if so, she would never have got that present or souvenir or known what journey or absence brought it, if it was a reward for waiting or a message from some new conquest or intended to ease a guilty conscience: it came too late; and so that present never even became a souvenir, it had neither past nor origin, or only in another consciousness and another memory if Deán had decided to give it to someone else when he learned of the death of its intended recipient, to his sister-in-law Luisa or to his brother-in-law's wife María or perhaps to the woman at the cemetery, the one with the beige gloves, or perhaps to none of them – a brooch, a dress, earrings, a headscarf, a handbag, Eau de Guerlain, who knows what the chosen object was. Deán would perhaps have dined in Sloane Square, close to his hotel, in order not to have to go too far after a tiring day, either alone or in company with colleagues or acquaintances or friends, who knows, then he would have gone back to his room with its sash window and would have looked out at the veteran dark of the London night, at the buildings opposite or at other rooms in the same hotel, most in darkness, staring at the attic bedroom of a black maid getting undressed after her day's work, removing her cap and her shoes and her stockings and her apron and her uniform, then standing at the sink and washing her face and under her arms, British-fashion. He can't smell her, but he may already know her smell, perhaps he has already passed her in a corridor or on the stairs, and then the phone would have rung at an hour considered unsuitable in that city, and when Deán picked it up and said "Hello", I hung up, frightened, standing at a public phone in a self-service restaurant in Madrid, with a guy with long teeth waiting for me to finish. The ringing of the phone in Deán's hotel room echoes and bounces out across the night to the half-dressed, half-naked maid, and alerts her to the fact that she can be seen, in bra and pants, she takes a few steps over to her window, opens it and peers out for a moment as if to make sure that no one is climbing up towards her – no burglar, for in English there's a specific word for house thieves, for the intruder I had been the previous night in Marta's home, in her husband's home, although I had not entered surreptitiously – and then she closes it and very carefully draws the curtains, no one must see her in the midst of her desolation or fatigue or dejection, or half-dressed or half-naked or sitting at the foot of the bed with the inside-out sleeves of her uniform caught on her wrists, perhaps she had already been seen like that without her realizing it. "And Deán will say more," I thought, "he'll say: 'But his stupefaction and anxiety and panic and bad luck are not enough for me, nor is his momentary horror which will already have passed, I want to meet that man and talk to him and call him to account and tell him what happened because of him, in particular, I want to tell him exactly how I spent that whole day when I thought Marta was still alive and when she was, in fact, dead, and how I feel about that day now when it's repeated in my nightmares and I hear the voice that says: Tomorrow in the battle think on me, and fall thy edgeless sword. Tomorrow in the battle think on me, when I was mortal, and let fall thy pointless lance. Let me sit heavy on thy soul tomorrow, let me be lead within thy bosom and at a bloody battle end thy days. Tomorrow in the battle think on me, despair and die.' That's what he's going to say and, if he does say it, I'll raise both hands to my ears and drop to the floor, or perhaps I'll raise both hands to my temples, my poor temples, that feel as if they are about to explode, because I won't be able to bear to hear him say it and to be forced to listen to him."

But Deán did not succumb to temptation then either, he said nothing about that, but remained silent or briefly resumed his inaudible mumbling, as if he were counting up to twenty this time, and then he replied in his calm, rusty voice, or perhaps with the infinite patience we owe to those whom our dead have loved:

"Look, Juan, you've got it into your head that I'm to blame for what happened. Fine, maybe I am, probably I am partly to blame and anyway there's no way I could convince you otherwise. I can show you my plane ticket and my receipts from the hotel and from restaurants and from the things I bought in London, but if you prefer to believe that I wasn't even there and you find that useful, fine, believe it, it's not going to change anything, except that you'll have even less respect for me than ever, it doesn't matter, we probably won't see much of each other from now on, there won't be much reason to. *I* don't matter. I have no idea where Marta put the bit of paper with my address and telephone number on it, perhaps she put it in her handbag and then lost it in the street, perhaps it blew out of the open window and the streetcleaners swept it up, I don't know. All I know is that I left it with her, but I can't prove it and there's no reason why you should believe me, and it's true that I did forget to leave it with my friend Ferrán. You're right about one thing though: I won't forget those hours you talked about. There are certain things that we should be told about immediately so that we do not, for a single second, walk about the world believing something that is utterly mistaken, when the world has utterly changed because of them. It is simply unacceptable to think that everything is carrying on as it was, when, in fact, everything is different, turned upside down, and it's true that, afterwards, the time we spent in error becomes unbearable to us. How stupid I was, we think, and yet we shouldn't find that so very painful. It's so easy to live in a state of delusion, or to be deceived, indeed, it's our natural condition: no one is free of it and it certainly doesn't mean that one is stupid, we should not struggle so hard against it nor should we let it embitter us. And yet, when we do learn the truth, we find it unbearable. The worst thing, what we find hardest, is that the time during which we believed what was not, in fact, true becomes something strange, floating and fictitious, a kind of enchantment or dream that must be suppressed in our memories; suddenly, it's as if we had not really lived that period of time, as if we had to re-tell the story or re-read a book, and then we think that we would have behaved otherwise or that we would have used the time differently, the time which now passes into a kind of limbo. That can be a source of despair. Besides, sometimes that time doesn't pass into limbo, but into hell." ("It's rather like when we used to go to the cinema as children, to see a double bill with continuous showings," I thought, "and we'd go into the darkness and start watching a film that was already halfway through and we'd watch it to the end trying to deduce what had happened before, what had brought those characters to the terrible situation in which they found themselves, what offences they had committed that they should end up as enemies, hating each other; then another film would come on and, only afterwards, when the first film was shown again and we saw the beginning that we had missed, did we understand that what we had imagined had no foundation and bore no relation to the missing half. Then we had to erase from our minds not only what we had imagined, but also what we had seen with our own eyes according to our guesswork, a non-existent film or, rather, a distorted version of it. They don't have cinemas like that any more, but the same thing often happens when we switch on the television at random, except that the beginning doesn't get shown again and we are left with our partial vision based on surmise and imagination, although we do see the outcome, what would Only You have made of the story of Poins and Falstaff and the Lancastrian Henries, the King and the Prince, what was the strange interpretation or story he came up with that so troubled him during his lonely night of insomnia. I, on the other hand, didn't see the beginning or the end of the film starring Fred

MacMurray and Barbara Stanwyck, nor did I hear what they were saying, during that wakeful night, I only saw their words in ghostly subtitles and I paid them no attention, I had to attend to my own story that had only just begun.") Deán breathed deeply as if to catch his breath or, rather, as if to regulate it again after the almost vehement speech which he had been drawn into after his initial calm, as if his thoughts had served as an antidote to his rage, or a substitute. "So you're right to think that that day will keep coming back to me, you need have no worries on that score," he said, "it already does."

Téllez was smoking his pipe in silence and now he held his son-in-law's gaze, but Deán could not sustain it once he had stopped speaking: he glanced to one side, his Asiatic eyes searching for the head waiter to ask for the bill – he made the customary gesture of writing in the air – as if he wanted to break up the party or at least pass on to another subject. "He must be biting his tongue," I thought, "perhaps he's hoping he can be on his own with Luisa later and unburden himself, since she knows the truth." Luisa had completely changed her attitude, she seemed remorseful, she didn't interrupt now or try to make Deán come to a decision, a few more days wouldn't hurt. It seemed as if Deán's words had had an effect on Téllez too, he was smoking his pipe meditatively. But his obsession was greater than his understanding: in fact, he was only waiting for the effect of doubt and consideration and, possibly, surprise to dissipate slightly, in order to return to his earlier posture of accusation and resentment, this time even more acerbically. When he saw that Deán was upset and had looked away, he took courage and said:

"What matters is that you weren't there. What matters is that she couldn't call you, although she probably decided not to bother. She might have met with your frivolity and your indifference. You might have told her that she was being alarmist or was exaggerating and you wouldn't have lifted a finger, not even to tell us, or a doctor. Who knows? But she knew you. What we do know is that you can't be relied on," and he again used the familial plural that excluded the widower, his son-in-law, "There will be little reason to see each other now, that much is true. When my turn comes, you might be in London or in Tampico or in the

Peloponnese, I know that you won't be anywhere near me. And, please, don't even consider paying for lunch, they know me here."

Deán put away the wallet he had got out after gesturing to the waiter. I imagine he'd had enough, sometimes the only way of keeping one's patience is to withdraw, to stop listening. His sombre expression made the incisions in his woody skin seem deeper, his face would be set like that when he was older. His energetic chin seemed ready for flight, his beer-coloured eyes had a devilish glint in them, the effect, perhaps, of the greenish light from the storm: his eyes were very open, out of dryness or grief. He stood up then, retrieved his raincoat from where he had left it, in the rack above, put it on and plunged his hands into his pockets.

"Since I'm not going to be paying the bill, I see no reason why I should wait. I'm in a hurry. Goodbye, Juan. We'll talk later, Luisa. Goodbye."

He had not drunk his coffee, the last phrase had been addressed to me (just barely sufficient not to be considered rude, and I said: "See you"), he kissed Luisa on the cheek (she said: "I'll see you later on at home" as if that home belonged to both of them now, Téllez said nothing). Deán got as far as the door and said goodbye to the head waiter who had accompanied him there and opened it for him, any relation of Juan Téllez was worth a bit of trouble. Deán turned up the collar of his raincoat before going out into the rain, the people standing there blocked his path, he was obliged to make his way round them. I thought that, had I wanted to, I would not have been able to follow him after lunch, if I decided to follow anyone, I had no alternative but to follow Luisa when we left the restaurant, I didn't have much to do, I had set aside that week to work with Téllez on the speech for Only the Lonely, the scripts for a television series that I was working on could wait, they probably wouldn't make the series anyway, but they would still pay me. Téllez had drunk his coffee, cold by now no doubt: he downed it in one, as if it were a shot of vodka. Then he remembered my presence again and offered me a sort of indirect apology:

"My daughter was unable to ask for help," he explained, as if I might not have understood. "The doctors say she could not have been saved. But it breaks my heart to think of her alone in her bed, dying unconsoled and worried about the boy, who would be left on his own with no one to look after him." All his malice had vanished along with Deán, as if it were something that had been forced on him. "I just can't bear it," he added.

"The odd thing is, Papa (as I've told him several times)," said Luisa (this was the first time she had addressed me, she was explaining the situation to me in parenthesis), "she didn't warn us either. She probably couldn't call Eduardo in London, but she could have called us, and she didn't." It seemed to me that with those words she was trying to throw a lifeline to Deán without betraying her dead sister, doubtless she felt sorry for him. She remained thoughtful and added: "Perhaps she didn't think she was going to die, perhaps she thought it would simply pass off and she didn't want to bother anyone so late. Perhaps she didn't realize, and then it wouldn't have been so frightening for her. What would be frightening would be to think it and to know it."

I felt like saying to Téllez: "Believe me, she wasn't alone in bed, I know. She didn't die alone, it wasn't so very horrible because it took her a long time to realize that she was dying and, when she did, she said to me 'Hold me, hold me, please, hold me' and I held her, I put my arms around her from behind because she didn't want me to do anything else, she said 'Don't do anything yet, just wait,' she didn't want me to move her an inch or to phone anyone. I held her in my arms and I embraced her and at least she was lying against me when she died, close to me, she died protected, supported. Don't torment yourself so much."

But I couldn't say it. Instead I said:

"I'm really sorry, I shouldn't have come to lunch with you."

"No, it's not your fault," replied Téllez. "We're the ones who invited you. The fact is I didn't have any intention of talking about all that again." And leaving his smoking pipe in the ashtray, he put his hands to his head. "My poor child," he said, as if he were Falstaff, and exhaled the smoke from his pipe.

The storm had suddenly stopped. The restaurant doorway was clear.

WHAT A DISGRACE it is to me to remember your name, though I may not know your face tomorrow, names don't change and, when they become fixed in the memory, they are fixed for ever, and nothing and no one can remove them. My head is full of names whose faces I have forgotten or which are merely a blur floating in a landscape, a street, a house, a particular time or screen. Or else, they are the names of places and establishments that seemed to us eternal because they were there when we arrived or were born, a fruiterer's called La Flor Sevillana, all those cinemas, the Príncipe Alfonso, the María Cristina, the Voy and Cinema X, the Buchholz bookshop near Plaza de la Cibeles or the grocer's shop that has kept its old sign: Viena Capellanes, the Patisserie Hermanas Liso and the Hotel Atlantic and all those other hotels, the Hotel Londres y de Inglaterra, Oriel, San Trovaso, le Zattere and Halifax, countless names of streets and shops and towns – Calatañazor, Sils, Colmar, Melk and Medina del Campo – the names of the infinite number of actors and actresses seen since childhood and that echo for ever in our memory without our being able to recall their features: Eduardo Ciannelli, Diane Varsi and Bella Darvi, Ivan Triesault and Leora Dana, Guy Delorme, Frank De Kova and Brigid Bazlen, and through them, we can refresh our memory if we happen to see them again on screen, where, years and years ago, we first saw them in those unfading films. Places, on the other hand, have changed, shops have disappeared or have been replaced by banks, and sometimes those that remain are only the slow shadow of their former selves, we look at them from the street, not daring to go in, and, through the window, we vaguely recognize the ancient employees or owners who, when we were children, used to give us sweets and joke with us, we suddenly see them bent and diminished and ruined, with a life behind them, a life we did not witness, standing at their wooden or marble counters, they make the same gestures only less confidently, more ponderously: they get confused when giving change, their fingers fumble when wrapping things up. I can barely recall the face of a young, blonde maid who I tickled after cunningly pulling her down on to the bed when I was nine or ten and my parents were out, but her name returns instantly: Cati. I can scarcely remember the expression on the face of the cripple who used to get about in a little wheeled cart that he operated with a handle, selling tobacco and chewing-gum and matches at the place where we spent our summer holidays – half a man, his expression was proud and innocent – but his name is still there, crystal-clear, Eliseo. The childish faces, which will no longer be childish, of my more nondescript classmates, or the ones I was never particularly friendly with, are just dim shapes to me, but I can summon up their surnames as if I were hearing Señorita Bernis calling the register: Lambea, Lantero, Reyna, Tatay, Teulón, Vidal. I have no visual memory at all of another, less constant group of boys with whom I was always getting into fights in the summer in the park, but I still remember their long, sonorous surnames: Casalduero, Mazariegos, Villuendas and Ochotorena. I don't know what the barber looked like who used to go to my grand-father the doctor's house to give him a shave and to trim his thinning hair, but I know he was called Remigio, I know that for certain. That fierce, bald shoeshine with the huge moustache and sideburns, sitting, watchful, on his box, all dressed in black and with a red scarf round his neck, I know what he was called: Manolete. I don't recall the name of that small man with the neat little moustache, the owner of a stationer's, but I do remember his nickname: my brothers and I used to call him "Willem Dekker" after the unctuous, cowardly character whom he resembled, a character in the film *The House of the Seven Hawks*, we used to send him threatening messages signed "The Black Hand" on bits of paper scorched with a magnifying glass: "Your days are numbered, Willem Dekker." I failed maths one year and the teacher who taught me that summer, of whom I can now see only his striking cranium with the scar he got in the war, his hair carefully combed over it with water from the river, but I can remember his name perfectly, Victorino, old-fashioned names that no longer exist or are no longer used, names from another age. I can see the face of that other tall, patient, smiling man who used to sell records, the name conjures it up for me: Vicen Vila, which was also the name of his shop. And I can barely recall the ancient porter who every morning for years used to greet me from his lodge with a cheery wave of his hand: but his name was Tom, I remember that.

What a disgrace it is to me to remember your name, though I may not know your face tomorrow, the face that we will one day cease to see will, meanwhile, betray itself and betray us in the time allotted to it, in the time remaining, it will distance itself from our fixed image of it in order to lead a life of its own during our voluntary or unhappy absence. The faces of those who have gone for ever because we did not hold on to them or because they have died will grow vaguer in our memory, which is not a visual faculty, although sometimes we deceive ourselves and think we can still see what we no longer have before us and which we can only evoke swathed in mists, the vague figure conjured up by our illusions or our nostalgia or, occasionally, our ill luck is called the inner eye, or the mind's eye. I could easily believe that I had never met you if I did not know your name, which remains immutable, unaltered, its brilliance undimmed, and so it will be even if you disappear completely, even if you die. It is what remains and there is no difference between the living name and the dead name, not only that, it is the only thing by which we can recognize ourselves, with which we can hold on to our sanity, because if someone denies our name and says to us: "I may be able to see you, but you are not you, even though you look like you," then we would effectively cease to be ourselves in the eyes of the person saying that and denying us, and we would not become ourselves again until they returned to us the name that has hitherto accompanied us as surely as the air. "I know you not, old man," said Prince Hal to his friend Falstaff, the moment he became Henry V, "I know not who you are, nor have I ever seen you before, do not come asking favours or calling me sweet names. I have turned away my former self. When you hear that I am as I have been, approach, and you will be as you were." And if that happened to us, we would think, horrified: "How is it possible that he doesn't recognize me and call me by my name?" But sometimes we might also think with some relief: "Thank heavens he doesn't call me by my name now or recognize me, that he doesn't admit that I am the person doing or saying these terrible things, and that precisely because he sees these things happening and hears me saying them and cannot deny them, he charitably denies knowing me so that I can continue to be the person I once was in his eyes, and so saves me."

Something similar happened to me one night some time ago, long before I knew the names of Marta Téllez and of her father and of Deán and Luisa and Eugenio, and, on that occasion, the denial was mutual, if that is what it was, if there was a moment of recognition. I was driving home late in my car, when I saw a woman standing in Hermanos Bécquer, a short road that curves steeply uphill and emerges into the Paseo de la Castellana, so curved and steep is it that it seems like two separate streets set on different levels at right angles to each other, as if the upper section were a partial bridge connected to the lower section, it's a very posh street along which prostitutes and transvestites often take up their posts, though normally only one man or woman at a time, usually a lone woman waiting on the corner at the bottom of the hill, while a few streets away in either direction, on the other side of the Castellana and beyond María de Molina, the numbers proliferate, the prostitutes stick together more and keep each other company and make each other jealous while they wait in their flimsy clothes that belie the winter and the autumn too. There's always a different woman on that corner, a corner I often pass, at least it never seems to be the same one, and she has the look of an explorer or an exile, or perhaps they draw lots for that place each night because, while it's discreet and isolated, there's also a fair amount of traffic and there are security guards nearby (the American embassy is close at hand), a good place for her itinerant clientele. That night I stopped at the traffic lights as usual and, from my car, I looked across at the prostitute with the mixture of curiosity and fantasy and superiority and pity with which we men who don't frequent prostitutes always look at them – or perhaps that's just bravado. And when the lights changed, instead of driving on, I continued looking at her through my car window, because – I saw at once that she really was a woman and not some artful simulacrum – I thought I knew her name. She was wearing a short raincoat that revealed half of her black-stockinged thighs, she had her arms folded against the still bearable cold, and when she saw that my car had remained where it was when the lights changed, she perked up and uncrossed her arms to let me have a better look – to let the driver have a better look, she couldn't yet see me – at her skirt which was even shorter than the raincoat and at the body she was wearing – that's what they're called, bodies – doubtless to emphasize her breasts. She took her hands out of her pockets and thus opened or half-opened her raincoat in a lacklustre gesture of exhibitionism. I stayed there, leaving enough space to my right for any cars that might be coming from the same direction I had come from, but without actually having to move, without having to mount the pavement, that would have been too definite a step and would have shown an evident interest that would have obliged me to talk to her, or at least exchange a few words. And the fact is that although, during a matter of seconds, my interest had grown to enormous, indeed, alarming proportions, I wasn't sure if I did want to speak to her or get a better look at her, because I was afraid that I knew her name and recognized her, and the name I thought I knew was Celia, Celia Ruiz Comendador, because she used her whole name, including both her family names, and that was the name I had married some years before and from which I had later separated and, not long since, divorced.

Besides, I had heard something and I had heard it from someone who knows everything and whose information is usually reliable and exact when he is not in the business of trying to deceive someone or commit a fraud: I had heard it from Ruibérriz de Torres, although at the time I didn't believe him. My marriage, while it lasted, didn't do too badly, given the impatient times we live in, and it lasted three years, which is quite a long time for such a young bride, eleven years younger than me when she donned a bridal gown, perhaps less now, for certain facts and certain ways of looking at things can alter and confound ages. She was twenty-two and I was thirty-three when we got married on her insistence, the insistence of someone who is not thinking much beyond two or three years when she says "for ever" or, if you prefer, "for good" (and it therefore seems to her a desirable and friendly thing to do) childhood being still too recent for her to be able to imagine a future that is any different from the present, genuine impetuosity has deeper roots, doubtless a personal characteristic. I agreed, in a moment of weakness or enthusiasm, both of which prevailed during the first year, I find it hard to remember now; the young woman made me laugh, which is all one requires of a young woman and is therefore more than sufficient; later, I merely tolerated her and soon we simply found each other irritating, we had to sit out the storms in silence before the kisses could begin again, warm, sexual reconciliations are very useful where possible, even necessary sometimes: they prolong a relationship that is already over, but not for ever. As usually happens, I was the one who left the matrimonial home, about three years ago, and I came to live where I still live now. Being so much younger than me, her feelings of irritation were more transient and she tended not to let them fester, they simply dissolved, for her, each minor irritation was no more serious or onerous than the first, she was quite devoid of malice and her continual re-offences were not intended to offend, they had to be pointed out to her and even explained before she realized what she had done. I had to provide glosses for her. I, on the other hand, did let my feelings of irritation fester and I was as impatient as the times we live in. I mean that she did not understand and so grew desperate and opposed my wishes, which was why it ended badly later on, after we had called a halt to our life together. During a temporary truce, we decided or chose not to see each other, at least for a few months, to wait until we could see each other slightly differently, different in all but name that is. I gave her money via a monthly cheque delivered by courier (we both saw his face, but not each other's), not only because I was the one who had left and had the larger salary, but because the more experienced partner tends to feel responsible for the less experienced one, even when they are apart, they still fear for them. Now I still send her a cheque, legally, and I sometimes give her money in person, a helping hand when she needs it, like someone giving pocket money to a child, though she may not need it for very much longer. I don't usually like talking about Celia.

I found out what one usually finds out in a city in which everyone meets everyone else and in which phones ring at all hours, phone calls in the middle of the night are commonplace, and there is a section of the population that does not sleep and will not allow those trying to sleep to sleep either. Someone would tell me that they had seen Celia here or there with such and such a person, either someone quite predictable or a stranger, she did not lack for admirers. From this information I deduced that she was not really using her imagination and was merely going through the motions expected of abandoned lovers in the big city: she went out a lot and stayed up late, she drank and pretended to be enjoying herself, she danced, she got bored, she didn't want to go home to bed and sometimes she would burst into tears at the end of the evening or perhaps even in the early hours; she made sure that this news reached my ears and she would ask after me like someone asking after a distant acquaintance, I've done it myself, your lips tremble and betray you, your voice falters. My phone would sometimes ring at odd hours and when I picked it up, no one was there, she just wanted to know if I was home, or perhaps her aim was less ignoble, perhaps she just wanted to hear my voice, even for a moment, even if all she heard was a question repeated back at her. Once, before going to sleep, while I was sitting at the foot of the bed getting undressed, I dialled my old number, but I didn't say anything when she answered, for it suddenly occurred to me that she might not be alone. And another time, Celia left me three messages one after the other on my answering machine, she said a lot of things, feverish and grotesque and sarcastic and threatening, but before the tape ran out for the last message, she began pleading with me, saying: "Please . . . please . . . please . . ." I had heard that before, years before, on my own tape. I didn't dare return her call. It was best not to.

Later on, I was given some information which I ignored at first, even though it was Ruibérriz de Torres who took it on himself to tell me, first through hints and as if sounding me out, then more bluntly. One day, he asked me if I knew what Celia had been up to lately, and when I said that I hadn't heard anything from her for some months, he affected a look of concern, for I could see that, deep down, he found it all faintly amusing. "Perhaps you should take more of an interest in her life, keep an eye on her from time to time," he said. "No, it's best if I don't," I said, "I need to let more time pass, I don't want her to get back into the habit of relying on me to solve all her problems or to listen to them and give her advice. That always establishes a link and a good excuse and it's been hard enough breaking off all communication with her, apart, that is, from the cheques I send her." "Well, perhaps you should make that communication more frequent or more generous," he replied. And when I asked why, or what it was that he knew, he told me rather primly and almost gleefully something that struck me at the time as absurd: someone had seen Celia in a late-night bar frequented by prostitutes, with two rather unusual drinking companions, men who looked like ordinary businessmen from Bilbao or Barcelona or Valencia, people passing through, people who weren't at all her type and with whom it seemed unlikely she would have arrived. "So what? What conclusions do you draw from that?" I said rather angrily. "Well, it just looks odd. It is a bit worrying, don't you think? If I were you, I'd have a word with her." "Don't be stupid," I replied, "Celia has always enjoyed going out and about, the more exotic and bizarre the place the better, it makes her feel adventurous, she's very young. When she was married to me, she went to a lesbian bar a couple of times with some girlfriends, but that didn't make me think she was a lesbian." "All right, all right," said Ruibérriz, "but this is different." "Why is it different?" "One, she's no longer married to you; two, she wasn't with any girlfriends; three, she's been seen there more than once and in two different bars that are known haunts for prostitutes," and, as he counted, Ruibérriz held out first, the little finger, then, the ring finger and, finally, the middle finger of his right hand. "Well, your friends certainly get around," I replied, "they must be awfully keen on prostitutes to go to these places all the time. Have they also seen her stuffing money down her cleavage? People invent the weirdest things. Celia goes through phases: suddenly she finds a certain kind of person amusing and she goes out with them all the time, or she goes to one or two places every night on the trot, then, after a fortnight, she's sick to death both of them and of her new friends and, for the next fortnight, she stays at home. That's what she was like when I met her and that's what she'll continue to be like until she finds some stability and can put her life in order. Besides, I send her quite enough money and I'm sure her parents in Santander help her out too. She gets jobs occasionally, I don't think she's got any money problems." "Whether or not the money you give her is enough depends on her needs and the kind of life she leads, it depends on how she spends it. She goes out a lot. She's probably on something." "No, she's always been terrified of drugs, apart from alcohol and tobacco, she's never even wanted to try marihuana; and plenty of people have asked her when she's been out," I replied, "but, you know, there's a big difference between that and becoming a prostitute. Why are you telling me these ridiculous, malicious stories?" Ruibérriz fell silent for a moment and, with one hand, smoothed back his wavy, musician's hair, while he stared down at the floor, as if he wasn't sure whether to provide still further proof or to leave it be. "Well, it's up to you," he said, "I've told you what other people have seen and told me, I thought you should know." "All right, what else have they seen, tell me everything, what else do you know?" I said impatiently. He couldn't help smiling, flashing his white teeth, his upper lip curled back to reveal his gums, like someone amused to have been caught out. "There isn't anything else, that's it. It seems quite enough to me, but you think it's just a rumour. Anyway, let's forget it, I don't want you getting angry with me." A suspicion suddenly crossed my mind. "Have you seen her?" I asked. "Have you seen her with your own eyes?" He took a deep breath, puffing out his chest, perhaps like someone taking a breath in order to lie more fluently without his voice giving him away (but I didn't think that then, only three weeks later, when I stopped at the traffic lights in Hermanos Bécquer, at the bottom of the lower section which is, in fact, the beginning of General Oraa, as I realized when I saw the street name, but which I have always seen as being part of Hermanos Bécquer, as do taxi drivers and other people in Madrid). "No, if I'd seen her, I would have said so, in order to convince you that you should, at least, talk to her. You might as well check out whether or not it's true, talk to her."

I didn't talk to her, I didn't believe what he had told me, I didn't want to phone Celia and break the silence that had been built up so slowly and tenaciously and which needed to last a while longer. But I did speak to a friend of hers who used to see her and I told her what I had learned through Ruibérriz. I was going to ask her to talk to Celia and find out the possible motive or origin of that malicious rumour, but I didn't need to. Before I could ask her, she said exactly what I had said and that made me think that there probably was no motive or origin: "What a stupid, horrible thing to say, haven't people got anything better to do than invent vile rumours like that? Poor Celia." I asked her not to tell Celia that I had called, but I imagine I asked in vain, alliances between girlfriends always prevail, they tell each other everything that might be of interest, although perhaps on that occasion she didn't in the end tell her, not because of me, but to save her any unpleasantness. Anyway, I felt reassured, I did nothing further and I forgot about it.

And now I was there at the traffic lights which had turned red again, looking at the gnarled trees along the Castellana – although it was autumn, they still had their leaves, and were perhaps gnarled by decades of storms – and at the prostitute who was standing guard outside the pink and green building of an insurance company, and, as I peered at that woman whose name I thought might be Celia Ruiz Comendador, I suddenly found myself giving credence to a purely hypothetical situation and the hypothesis that occurred to me was that, if the information was correct and one night Ruibérriz had, with his own eyes, seen Celia working as a prostitute, he would have been quite capable of hiring her for the night and would have done so confidently and blithely. Only afterwards would he have felt some concern, as sincere as it was insincere, Ruibérriz doesn't take anything very seriously, nothing matters very much to him, or perhaps it is simply that he sees life as a comedy. And if it was her and she bore the same name – because a face is not enough, it grows old and can change and can be made up to look different – if it was Celia and Ruibérriz had hired her and had spent the night with her, then there would have been established between the two men – between him and me, between us – a relationship that our languages no longer reflect, but that certain dead languages do. Whenever I learn of sexual infidelities or I am a witness to changes of partner or to second marriages – also when I see prostitutes in the street as I pass in my car or in a taxi or walking – I always remember my time as a student of English, when I learned of the existence of an ancient verb, no longer in use, an Anglo-Saxon verb that has not survived and which, besides, I cannot quite remember, I heard a teacher mention it once in class, and its meaning, which I do remember, remained fixed in my mind for ever, although not its form. The word describes the relationship or kinship acquired by two or more men who have lain with or slept with the same woman, even if that happened at different times and bearing in mind the different faces of that woman whose name remains the same through all time. The verb probably bore the prefix *ǧe·*, which originally meant "together" and, in Anglo-Saxon, can denote "comradeship" or "conjunction" or "companionship", as in certain nouns which I haven't forgotten, *ǧe·fēra*, "travelling companion", or *ǧe·sweoster*, "sisters". I suppose it must be something like our own common prefixes "co-", "com-" or "con-" that appear so often in, for example, "co-worker", "companion", "consort", "compatriot", "co-conspirator" and "confidant", and that verb, which has now disappeared and which I no longer remember, was perhaps *ǧe·licgan*, since *licgan* means "to lie" in the sense of "to lie with someone", "to fornicate", and thus the translation and the idea would, therefore, be something like "co-fornicate" or, rather, "co-fuck", if the word were rather cruder. Although it may be that the word used to convey the idea was not a verb but a noun, perhaps *ǧe·brȳd-guma*, which would translate as "co-bridegroom", or perhaps *ǧe·for·liǧer*, "co-fornication", who knows, and I'm afraid I never will know now, since when I wanted to confirm my memory and recover the word as well as the idea and I phoned my former teacher to ask him, he claimed he couldn't remember; I consulted my old Anglo-Saxon grammar and found nothing in it nor in the glossary attached, perhaps my memory invented it; and so, whenever the occasion arises, I merely ponder on the possibilities that come to mind. Whether it existed or not, though, that mediaeval verb or noun was useful and interesting, dizzying too in a way, and dizzy was what I felt when I saw the prostitute and it occurred to me that, if her name was Celia Ruiz Comendador and if the hypothesis were correct, I would be related Anglo-Saxon-style to a lot of other men besides Ruibérriz de Torres. Both men and women are often ignorant of that relationship or link, and its most tangible, visible manifestation is disease, to which those who come afterwards are more exposed, the later they come, the more exposed they are, perhaps that is why virgins were so highly prized in the rather remote past. And that unwanted relationship can prove troublesome or humiliating or hateful when you suspect or know of its existence, having that relationship with someone often leads people to hate each other and even kill each other, it is both rare and commonplace, perhaps the verb described what was principally a bond of hatred, which is why it has not survived in the language that developed from it nor in any others, a connection based on rivalry and unease and jealousy and drops of blood, a network with multiple spurs or tributaries that might lead on into infinity and which we no longer wish to designate or give house-room to in our language, even though we conceive of it in our thoughts and in our actions, another bothersome reminder, the co-fornicators or co-fuckers; of course, the opposite is also possible and there may be certain sexual relationships with another man or woman that provide a certain degree of prestige and ennoble those who begin or contract or acquire those relationships, those who come *afterwards*, who receive not only the disease but also the aura, probably more nowadays than at any other time, or at least more publicly, I did not feel ennobled by that hypothesis, but then I had come *before*.

The woman took a few expectant, incredulous steps towards the kerb when she saw me stop at the traffic lights, with the lights on green again and my engine running (she couldn't see me or know how dizzy I felt), doubtless she thought she should come a little closer and allow me to have a better look before I decided, perhaps during the whole of that cold Tuesday night she had not yet made a single visit to a flat or to a car, her footsteps and her visits destined to leave no mark on anyone, or to become super-imposed one on the other in her confused, fatalistic, fragile memory. And then I felt it was unfair – how can I put it, humiliat-ing – to make her risk stepping out into the road to reach my car window. I checked that no one was coming up on my right and I parked the car by the pavement, just beyond the bus shelter beneath which she or the colleagues she alternated with would stand when it rained – number 16 and number 61 – almost turning into the nearside lane of the Paseo de la Castellana, stopping right on the corner; and before realizing what my intention was, she quickened her step and raised one arm as if to detain me with that gesture, as if fearful of losing a client out of indecision or pride or as if that were her usual way of hailing a taxi. I still kept the engine running, although I wasn't sure whether or not I would say anything to her or invite her to get into the car, it didn't just depend on her name. I watched the approach of her strong, gleaming, silky legs and automatically wound down the passenger window. Then she bent over to see my face and to talk to me, she bent over and immediately leaned an elbow on the lowered window, perhaps a trick to stop you immediately winding it up again if you changed your mind. She looked at me unblinking, as if she had never seen me before, although it seemed to me that she was holding her breath: if it was Celia, she was perhaps preparing her first sentence or reply as well as a distorted tone of voice, or a different way of speaking from her normal one, she was playing for time. The face was Celia's face, which I know so well, and at the same time it wasn't, I mean, she wore her hair in a calculatedly dishevelled style, with artificial curls and blonde highlights, that Celia would never have dreamed of adopting and I had never seen her wear make-up like that either, her lips were painted blood-red and outlined rather too boldly, her eyelashes were undeniably false and she had extended her eyeliner right into the corners of her eyes, making them look more almond-shaped, more striking. Her clothes weren't Celia's clothes either, the too-short skirt, the too-tight top, only the raincoat could have been hers because, when I saw it in a better light and closer to, I saw that it wasn't a raincoat but a mac like the one Celia used to wear sometimes, the high heels could have been Celia's too on the nights we used to go out partying. Still leaning on my window, she shot a couple of rapid glances to her right to check on two other prostitutes, whom we could both now see from the corner, standing on the steps of an imposing doorway in the Castellana, doubtless awaiting the result of our transaction, if we didn't reach an agreement, they might be in with a chance, or so they thought. One of them was gazing up at the trees in the avenue – the foliage – as if she were attracted by the gentle, unchoreographed swaying of the branches or rather of the leaves, there was nothing but breeze and clouds. From that distance, they looked less pretty or less colourful.

"Get in," I said and opened the door, forcing her to move away from the window for a moment. I didn't quite know how to address her, so I just said what I would have said to Celia if I had met her alone in the street at that hour. I was the driver or the man with the large hands and hard, clumsy fingers on the wheel – my fingers are like piano keys – who was inviting her to get into the car from my seat, the passenger door flung open, I was the one who was telling her what she should do, I was the one giving the orders, it wasn't like that with Celia. But a deal had not yet been reached.

"Hey, hang on, hang on. First, where are we going and, second, have you got the readies?" she said, taking a step back – one of her heels dragged along the ground – and placing one hand on her hip. I heard the jangle of bracelets when she made that gesture, it was a noise that Celia had made sometimes, only less obtrusively, she never used to wear quite so many, or perhaps they just fitted more tightly.

"Let's take a drive around here to begin with, and don't worry, I'm ready for anything. Go on, take a few, perhaps you'll be nicer to me then," I replied, and I took out a few notes from my trouser pocket, I had quite a lot of cash on me. There would be no worries on that score, that's what I meant to say and that is what she understood. As I reached out my hand holding the fan of notes, it occurred to me that, if she wasn't Celia, I was being rather imprudent: it was like inviting her to rob me somehow – what people call the "the kiss of sleep" – we want to have whatever we can see and is within our grasp. But she still looked too much like Celia for me to feel distrustful or to decide that it wasn't her. Anyway, it was her, even if it wasn't.

"Well, I'll just take this and this for the moment, for the drive, all right?" she said, selecting two notes as if they were playing cards, she did so very carefully and as if asking my permission. She put them in her handbag. "Then we'll talk about it, if you want to go any further, well, Barajas Airport is one thing, Guadalajara is quite another. And if you want to go to Barcelona, then you'd better stop off at a cashpoint first."

"Come on, get in," I said, patting the empty seat on my right. A cloud of dust flew up.

She got in and closed the door, as we drove off, I saw that the other two prostitutes were sitting on the steps, their opportunity lost, it would be cold on the stone steps, waiting there in their short short skirts, it had rained earlier on and the ground wasn't quite dry. Celia's skirt was so short that, once she was seated by my side, it looked as if she wasn't wearing one, I saw the part of her thighs not covered by her black elasticated stockings – she wasn't wearing a suspender belt – I saw a fringe of very white skin, too white for my taste, it was autumn. I began to drive away from the area, up the Castellana.

"Hey, where are you going?" she said. "It's best if we go up one of the back streets." She meant Fortuny and Marqués de Riscal and Monte Esquinza and Jenner and Fernando el Santo, quiet streets with hardly any traffic, streets occupied by the embassies of rich countries, surrounded by black railings and private gardens with smooth, well-mown lawns, streets lined with trees, peaceful night and day, near where I spent my childhood, when the two buses, which are now long and red, the 16 and the 61 – I had picked up the false Celia or Celia herself at that very bus stop – were, respectively, a double decker and a tram running on rails, sections of which you can still see, like fragments of fossils in the asphalt along its old route, both were blue, the tram and the double decker that I used to catch to and from school: they still have the same number, that is, the same name, the 16 and the 61. A car can stop and switch off its engine for a while in those streets without the lights from other cars constantly dazzling its occupants, you can sniff and chat and lick, and boys can snatch a cigarette before going into class, they are the most foreign of streets and the freest.

"Don't worry, we won't be long. And I'll drop you back on your corner or wherever you want, you won't have to get a taxi. I imagine taxis don't always want to pick you up." It was a rather old-fashioned remark, potentially offensive if she wasn't Celia. "I just fancy driving for a while without any traffic."

"Fine, you're in charge," she said, "Tell me when you get tired, but don't take too long or I'll start feeling like a taxi-driver's girlfriend being taken for a ride, only with the meter running."

Her last words made me laugh a little the way Celia used to make me laugh once I'd got over my fit of enthusiasm or weakness and I merely found her amusing. It's true, some young taxi drivers on Friday and Saturday nights do have their girlfriend by their side, they have to work and it's the only way they can go out together and see each other, the girls have enormous patience, either that or they're terribly in love or desperate. They can't even talk very much, with a passenger always behind them, watching the backs of their necks – especially hers if the passenger is a lonely, desperate man – and possibly listening to their conversation.

I drove in silence down the familiar Paseo de la Castellana, some places are just as they were, though not many, the Castellana Hilton isn't called that any more, but for me it's still the Hilton, there's the brash sign for the House of Ming, both the place and the name were mysterious, forbidden things to me when I was a child, and then Chamartín, the Real Madrid stadium that also evokes names that have not been erased and never will be, whole line-ups that I still know by heart, and sometimes the faces that I knew from the cigarette cards I used as swaps in the game of heads or tails I played daily with one of my brothers: Molowny, Lesmes, Rial and Kopa, the fat man Puskas, Velázquez, Santisteban and Zárraga, players whose faces I wouldn't recognize now if ever I saw them, but their names persist, and Velázquez was a genius.

I drove in silence because I was looking at the prostitute out of the corner of my eye to see if I had the same feeling I would have had when I used to drive a tired Celia home, as I had on so many nights when we went home together. I wanted to see her full face, to get a good look at her and to study her features, but there would be time for that and, besides, faces are deceptive, sometimes you can rely more on the emotions and feelings provoked by those faces, as well as on the involuntary gestures made by the other person, the rhythm of their breathing, the way they clear their throat or make a certain gesture or mispronounce a certain word, a particular cliché they use, their smell – the smell of the dead lingers when nothing else remains of them – the way they walk or the way they cross their legs, their impatiently drumming fingers or the way they rub their thumb back and forth beneath their lower lip; and their laugh, that would certainly unmask anyone who was pretending to be someone else, a person's laugh is almost unmistakable, and I wondered if I should run the risk of trying to provoke into laughter the prostitute I had picked up in my car, because that might force me to decide if I was right or wrong.

I drove in silence, too, because I was wondering why, if it was Celia, she would be walking the streets, she couldn't need the money that badly, perhaps she was frivolous enough and enough of an adventurist – an eminently Soviet word that, "adventurist", someone who always wants to be able to say: "I've tried that" – or perhaps it was revenge, a reprisal that would have begun to take shape when Ruibérriz's friends had seen her in those two different bars or when Ruibérriz himself had hired her that night he saw her, a vengeance that could be fully realized now, if I was I and she was she, she might have her doubts about me too, we barely notice the changes that take place in ourselves, I'm not aware of it in myself, even though those changes might be profound and serious ones. And what other form could that revenge take, I asked myself silently, but that of plunging me tumultuously into relationships with strangers I would never know about – I would never know who they were or how many – nor would she, unless she kept count and noted them down in her diary and asked them their names, which they would refuse to give her.

"What's your name?" I asked the prostitute when we reached the end of the Castellana, as I was turning round to drive back in the opposite direction.

"Victoria," she lied, assuming she was Celia and perhaps even if she wasn't. But if she was Celia, then she lied deliberately, ironically, maliciously, even mockingly, because that is the female version of my own name. She took some chewing-gum out of her handbag, the car smelled of mint. "And you?"

"Javier," I lied in turn, realizing that I would have done so either way, whether she was Victoria or my Celia who was no longer mine.

"Not another Javier," she remarked, "Madrid's full of them or perhaps it's just the name you'd all like to have, I don't know what's got into you all."

"All who?" I asked. "Your customers?"

"Blokes in general, blokes, or do you think the only men I know are customers?"

She had a surliness that Celia neither had nor has, if it was her, she was putting on a pretty good act, or perhaps she had been working for a long enough period of time – possibly more than a month or two months, I had managed not to see or speak to her for about four or five – to pick up a few of the mannerisms. It also occurred to me that she might be irritated by my prompt payment, paying in advance as well: she might be wondering if I had picked her up because of the resemblance and as a one-off or if I had always gone with prostitutes and she had known nothing about it while we were married.

"Not at all, no, I'm sorry. I imagine you have a family too."

"Somewhere around, I never see them, so don't ask me about them." And she went on in a resentful tone, her eyes still wearing the dusky night: "Listen, I know lots of people."

"I'm sure you do, I'm sorry," I said.

Conversation was not easy, perhaps it would be best to remain silent. One moment, I would feel certain that she was Celia and that we could, therefore, cut the pretence and talk about everything or simply about what we always used to talk about or could question each other openly, and the next I would be sure that it couldn't possibly be her and that it was just one of those extraordinary resemblances which nevertheless do sometimes happen, as if it was Celia but with another life or history, the same person who had been swapped while in her cradle, as occurs in children's stories or in the tragedies of kings, the same physical appearance but with a different memory and a different name and a different past in which I would not have existed, perhaps the past of a gypsy child perched on top of a pile of shabby, useless objects on a cart drawn by a mule, Our Lady of the rag-and-bone men, bumping against the branches of the gnarled trees and watching the bourgeois little girls chewing gum on the top floor of a double decker bus (but she was too young to have seen them). Although such a complicated explanation wasn't strictly necessary, there's a very thin dividing line and everything is subject to vast upheavals – the reverse side of time, its dark back – you see it in life as well as in novels and plays and films, writers or wise beggars and kings without a kingdom or enslaved, princes shut up in towers and suffocated with a pillow, suicidal bankers and beauties changed into monsters, their faces scarred by vitriol or by a knife, noblemen drowned in huge earthenware vats of sickly sweet wine and the idols of millions strung up by their feet like pigs or dragged through the streets by a horse, deserters made into gods and criminals into saints, great wits reduced to the condition of obtuse drunks, and crippled kings who seduce the most beautiful of women, sidestepping their hatred or even transforming it; and lovers who murder the person they love. It's a very fine knife-edge, one false move and you could topple over on to the side you're trying to escape from, because the blade will cut you anyway and you'll end up falling one way or the other soon enough: all you have to do is to start walking or even just stay right where you are.

"So, how are you enjoying the driving?" Victoria asked, after another silence. "Are you in training for Formula 1 or are you still thinking about where you want us to go? Do you want me to look at the map? You're probably lost." And she opened the glove compartment to emphasize her remark with a gesture.

"Don't be in such a hurry, I've paid you for this time," I said curtly and slammed the glove compartment shut again. "And don't complain, you're better off sitting in here than freezing to death on that corner. How long had you been waiting there?"

"That's none of your business, I don't talk about my work. If I have to talk about it as well as do it, you can forget it." She was chewing vigorously on her gum and I wound down my window a little to get rid of the smell of mint which had become mingled with that of her own pleasant perfume, not Celia's usual one.

"Fine, so you don't want to talk about your work or about your family or about anything: that's what happens when you get the money upfront without having to work for it."

"It isn't that," she replied, "if you like, I'll give it back to you and you can hand it over when we've finished. But it isn't my job to teach you things, just stick to the rules, OK?"

"You're here to do whatever I tell you to do." I surprised myself when I said that, to Victoria or to Celia, it didn't matter which. We men have an ability to frighten women by a mere inflection of our voice or a few cold, threatening words, our hands are stronger and have maintained their grip for centuries. It's all bravado.

"All right, all right, don't go all stroppy on me," she said in a conciliatory tone. I calmed down when I heard her say "don't go all stroppy on me", it sounded rather cosy.

"You're the one who's been stroppy ever since you got into the car. God knows what went on between you and your previous client." It seemed to me that we were sliding into some absurd conjugal or adolescent argument. I added at once: "Sorry, I forgot, you don't like talking about your work, the lady likes to keep her professional secrets."

"I shouldn't think you want to talk about yours either," retorted Victoria. "Come on, what do you do?"

"I don't mind talking about it. I'm a television producer," I lied again, although I was on safe ground, because I know several and I could easily play the part of one for the benefit of a prostitute. I waited for her to ask what programmes I had made or to provide her with some proof, but she didn't believe me, so she didn't do either of those things (perhaps she didn't believe me because she was Celia, and in that case she would know the truth).

"At this time of night you can be whatever you like," she said, "As you yourself said, we're just here to please you men."

I decided to drive down the quiet, diplomatic streets that she had suggested in the first place, to find a space to park the car. I found it in Fortuny, not far from the German embassy, which appeared to be deserted at that hour, there was no light on in the lodge, perhaps the guard could see better like that at night, and it ensured that *he* wouldn't be seen. We passed two very obvious transvestites on the corner of Eduardo Dato, they were sitting on a still-damp wooden bench beneath the trees, surrounded by piles of fallen yellow leaves, as if they had frightened away a road sweeper in the middle of his work.

"How do you girls get on with them?" I asked Victoria, switching off the engine and indicating the transvestites with my thumb. Now we had both resorted to a depersonalizing plural form – "you men", "you girls".

"There you go again," she said. But this time she did give me an answer, she had to erase the impression of sourness, however minimally, you can't establish physical contact with someone in a sour atmosphere, however negotiated and codified and paid for that contact is: "Well, although we work the same area, we don't clash. They have this corner, but if, one night, neither of them turns up, we can use it, and then, if they turn up later on, we leave. They don't cause any problems, it's the customers who cause the problems."

"What, you mean we get stroppy?"

"Some of you guys are really frightening," replied Victoria. "Some of you are real bastards."

"Do I frighten you?" I asked stupidly, because, when I said it, I was conscious that neither of the two possible replies would please me. I couldn't frighten her if she was Celia, but she was behaving as if she wasn't. I, on the other hand, was behaving like myself, leaving aside a few white lies, although perhaps even that wasn't necessary either.

"Not at the moment, no, but who knows what you'll do," she said, as a kind of medium term, as if she had guessed my fleeting thought, or perhaps it wasn't that. "What do you want, a blow job?" and as she said that, she removed the chewing-gum from her mouth and held it between her fingers, uncertain whether to throw it away or not. That tiny blob would hold the imprint of her teeth, that's how they make a definitive identification of a corpse, if they can find the deceased's dentist.

"Doesn't it frighten you getting into a car with a complete stranger again and again?" I asked, and now I was asking out of genuine concern for Celia and also for Victoria, although less for Victoria. "You never know what you're going to find."

"Of course it frightens me, but I try not to think about it. Why do you ask, should I be afraid of you?" There was a touch of alarm in her voice, I saw that she was looking at my hands which were still resting on the wheel. Suddenly, every trace of sarcasm had gone, the idea of fear and my insistent questioning had made her feel afraid. How easy it is to introduce a possibility or a fear or an idea into the mind of another person, we are so easily infected, we can be convinced of anything, sometimes all it takes is a nod to achieve your aims, to pretend that you know something, or to suspect another person's suspicions about us and, out of fear, reveal ourselves without meaning to and reveal what we had intended to keep secret. Celia or Victoria was afraid of me now and I could understand that in Victoria, but how could Celia possibly be afraid of me? Or perhaps she could, if she suspected that I suspected her of avenging herself on me by imposing on me all those non-blood relationships, and without my consent or my knowledge. But how can there be consent? Perhaps she was going to make me become related to myself, Javier and Víctor, and then there would be consent.

"No, of course not," I said, laughing. But I don't know if that was enough, now that I had introduced the fear into her mind; women know that all they ever get from men are mere concessions – a voluntary surrender of their power, a temporary truce in their authoritarianism – which they can withdraw at any moment.

"Then why ask if it frightens me to get into a car with a complete stranger when that's just what I've done with you?" The sudden intrusion of fear had startled her, she was trying to shake it off before it took hold. She put the chewing-gum back in her mouth, she had been right not to throw it away. "You're just trying to wind me up, you're a stranger too, you know."

Why was she stating the obvious if I was I and she was Victoria, I wondered. Now I could see her face full on, badly lit by the yellowish light from a low street lamp, half-blocked or filtered by the branches, it was Celia's face but not her name. Celia was twenty-five then and Victoria seemed rather older, twenty-eight or twenty-nine, as if she were a short-term portent of a future Celia who had not yet come into being, an augury of the first lines on her face and of the weariness and panic in her eyes, a prediction of her ruined life or perhaps just a bad patch she was going through, her make-up too heavily applied for such a young young woman and the clothes that did not so much cover up as empha-size, her breasts accentuated and pushed up by the white body she was wearing, her legs bare underneath the tiny skirt crumpled by all that sitting in the passenger seats of indistinguishable night-time cars, and perhaps, later on, kneeling down or even crouching on all fours, her expression frightened or sour according to the moment, any friendliness suppressed or deliberately put on; I had enjoyed being with that woman for a time and I still did, I liked her shiny mac and her constant chewing and her bad manners, her eyes still wearing the dusky night and wearing fear too, fear of my hands and my desires and my imminent orders, what a disgrace it is to me to remember your name, even though I may not know your face today, still less tomorrow. I put my frightening hand on her thigh, I touched the strip of skin between stocking and skirt and stroked it.

"Am I?" I said, and with the other hand I took her chin and turned her face towards me, forcing her to look at me. She instinctively lowered her eyes and I said: "Look at me, don't you know me? Tell me you don't know me." She pulled away from my hand with a movement of her chin and said:

"Listen, what is it with you? I've never seen you before in my life. Now you really are frightening me. Look, I can't be expected to remember everyone, but I'm sure I've never been with you before, and, at this rate, I don't know if I'll bother. What's got into you?"

"How can you be so sure? How do you know you haven't been with me? You yourself just said that it isn't easy to remember everyone, for someone like you the faces must all get mixed up, or you probably do your best not to look at them, not to see them and then you can always imagine that you're with the same man, with your boyfriend, or your husband, you're probably married or have been."

"Do you think I'd be here if I was married? You must be mad. Besides, you're quite wrong, we make sure we get a good look at you all, front and back, to make sure we don't go with you again if you turn nasty or if things get ugly. The first time you go with a bloke, anything can happen to you, but the second time there's nothing to it. You can see right away what a bloke is after. So come on, tell me what it is you want and let's be done with it." The tone of that last phrase was again conciliatory, despite the impatient words.

"Are things getting ugly between us?" I said.

"Well, you're doing a pretty good job of it, talking about fear and asking me if you frighten me and if I know you."

"I'm sorry," I said.

There was a silence. She took the opportunity to remove her mac – another conciliatory gesture – she didn't just throw it on to the back seat, she folded it up and laid it down carefully, as if she were at the cinema. She wasn't wearing a bra, Celia always did.

"Look," she said, "we're all a bit paranoid around here at the moment. About a month ago, someone killed a young boy who got picked up in Hermanos Bécquer, just where you picked me up. That's why the transvestites don't use that corner any more, they think it's bad luck, and so they've given the corner to us. Until something happens to one of us, of course, then we'll clear off too, we're a superstitious lot when it comes to territory. He was ever so young, delicate, girlish, not like those great lumps," and she jerked her thumb backwards as I had done before. "He really did look like a girl. He'd only been here a short time, he'd just arrived from some village outside Málaga. He got into a Golf like this one, except it was white, he came to one of these streets to suck the bastard off, and the following morning they found him lying on the pavement with his head caved in and his mouth full of cum. He'd only just learned to walk in high heels, the poor thing, he must have been about eighteen. And what happens? The following night, we have to go out again and forget all about that, because, otherwise, we just wouldn't go out, we wouldn't and neither would they. So I'm really not in the mood for all these questions about whether I get frightened and whether or not I know you, do you understand?"

It couldn't be Celia, I thought; Ruibérriz or his friends must have seen this prostitute, Victoria, who looked so much like her, and must have wanted to think that it was her, and perhaps they even imagined that they had paid for sex with Celia, if they had done so with Victoria. She couldn't have changed that much in other respects, it couldn't be her; unless she was playing her part brilliantly, inventing gruesome stories to frighten me and worry me even more, so that I would want to rescue her from that life and from all those dangers by returning to her side, so that she wouldn't have to be here or anywhere or on that unlucky corner on Hermanos Bécquer (she herself had said: "Do you think I'd be here if I was married? You must be mad."). I hadn't read anything in the newspapers about a young transvestite being found in the street with his head caved in, I usually notice items like that because of my work. Celia did tend to embellish stories a bit and she was something of a liar, but she never went that far and she didn't normally invent misfortunes, she was optimistic and proud by nature. Nevertheless, I thought, if she was Celia, she would, by then, have spent some time working as a prostitute and would, therefore, be a prostitute, she would know that world and wouldn't have to invent anything, and that would explain her sour demeanour, her blunt vocabulary and her harsher way of speaking, it's easy to pick these things up. *She wouldn't, in fact, be pretending.* How could I possibly have any doubts, how could I possibly not be sure if I was with my wife or with a prostitute (with my wife who had become a prostitute or with a prostitute who felt like my former wife), I had lived with her for three years and known her for a year before that, I had woken up and gone to bed with her every day, I had seen her from every angle and I knew all her gestures and I had heard her talk for hours on end in every possible mood – once I used to gaze into her eyes as she lay with her head on the pillow – it was only four or five months since I last saw her, although people can change a lot in that time if that time is in some way anomalous, a time of illness or suffering or denial of what came before. I was sorry suddenly that she didn't have some scar or mark or easily visible mole, had that been the case I would have taken her home and undressed her, even at the risk of finding out her identity for certain. Or perhaps I just didn't remember those identifying marks on her body, we forget and never really notice anything very much, why remember if nothing is as it is, because nothing stays still, nothing lasts, nothing endures or is repeated or stops or persists, and the only solution to that is for everything to end and for there to be nothing, a solution which, at times, the Only One considered no bad thing, or so he had nihilistically said; and, on the other hand, everything is continually travelling on, everything is connected, some things drag other things along with them, all oblivious to each other, everything is travelling slowly towards its own dissolution the moment it occurs and even while it is occurring, and even while you're waiting for it to happen and it still hasn't, and you remember as being past something that is still in the future and perhaps won't even happen, you remember what has not been. Everything moves on apart from names, true or false, that remain for ever engraved on our memories as they do on gravestones, León Suárez Alday or Marta Téllez Angulo, they would have put Marta's name on the gravestone by now, and it would be no different from that 1914 headstone. I would have known that Victoria was Celia if Victoria had replied "Celia" when I had asked her what her name was, and I might then have answered "Víctor" when she asked me mine. And in that case, we would have recognized each other and perhaps embraced and we would not have gone to that street beneath the still-leafy trees and a yellow street lamp, but to our former home, which is now hers alone, or to my new home, and none of this would be happening in my car and she would not be frightened of me.

"Of course, I understand. I'm sorry," I said. "Did you know the boy well?"

"No, I'd seen him around a few times, I'd had the odd chat with him. He used to drag his high heels as if he were clinging on to his shoes with his feet, he wasn't used to it or perhaps he was ill, he seemed very fragile and somehow not quite with it. He was very sweet, very shy, very polite, he always said 'thank you' when he asked you something." Victoria remained thoughtful for a moment and stroked the end of one eyebrow with her index finger, as Celia Ruiz Comendador used to do when, in the middle of an argument or a story, she would stop to think about what she was going to say next, or when she was searching for the right word. The coincidence, however, did not strike me as important just then. "He was the sort of person that you don't really expect to live very long. You can spot them a mile off, they seem surplus to requirements, as if the world couldn't bear them and was in a hurry to get rid of them. But then it would be best if they weren't born at all. Because the fact is that they are born and there they are, and it's horrible when people you know die, even if you don't know them that well, it's hard to grasp that someone who did exist doesn't any more. At least I think it is. He called himself Franny, I suppose his real name was Francisco. What a way to die." Victoria turned her face to the street, revealing the back of her neck, she sat looking out at the pavement in Fortuny where we were parked, perhaps she was imagining the shattered skull of the young transvestite on that very pavement or somewhere nearby. "A horrible death, a ridiculous death," I thought, "his head between someone's thighs the moment before he died, the dying man's scorn for his own death. How awful, now I'll have to remember the name of someone whose face I don't even know: Franny," or at least that's how I imagined it would be written. Then I too fell silent while I sat thinking, leaning one elbow on the steering wheel and rubbing my thumb back and forth beneath my lower lip. But it was only a brief silence. Perhaps we were being watched from far off, from the dark lodge outside the German embassy.

"Do you fancy going in the back for a bit?" I said to put an end to her thoughts and to stop her making that gesture with her index finger. I put one hand on her shoulder, then I stroked the back of her neck. "You've still got to earn your money," I said, pointing to her handbag.

She looked at me and removed the chewing-gum from her mouth. This time she opened the window and threw it out on to the pavement.

IT'S TIRING HAVING always to move in the shadows, having to watch without being seen, doing one's best not to be discovered, just as it's tiring having to keep to oneself a secret or a mystery, how wearisome clandestinity is, constantly having to bear in mind that not all your close friends can be privy to the same information, that you have to hide one thing from one friend and something else from another, something the first friend already knows about, you invent complex stories for one woman and, in order not to betray yourself later, you have to fix the details of those stories for ever in your memory, as if you really had experienced them, to another newer woman friend you tell the truth about everything apart from certain innocuous, but embarrassing facts about yourself: the fact that you can happily spend hours in front of the television watching soccer or mindless quiz shows, that you still read comics even though you're now an adult, that you would happily lie down on the floor and play heads or tails – if you had someone else to play with, that you're hooked on gambling, that you fancy an actress you know to be odious and even offensive, and that you wake up in the morning in a foul mood and the first thing you do is light up a cigarette, that you fantasize about a particular sexual practice most people consider abnormal and which you dare not suggest to her. You don't always conceal these things out of self-interest or fear or because you really have committed some misdemeanour, it's not always a defence, often, it's to avoid upsetting or hurting someone or spoiling the fun, sometimes it's just common courtesy, it isn't polite or civilized to tell everyone everything, let alone reveal our obsessions and our shortcomings; sometimes it's our origins that we falsify or suppress, because most of us would have preferred at least one of our ancestors to have been somehow different, people hide away their parents and their grandparents and their siblings, their husbands or their wives and sometimes even the children who most closely resemble or take after their spouse, they silence some part of their own life, they detest their youth or their childhood or their mature years, in every biography there is some outrageous, desolate or sinister episode, one episode or many – or even everything – that it would be best other people did not know about, something that it is best to lie about even to oneself. We are ashamed of far too many things, of our appearance and of past beliefs, of our ingenuousness and ignorance, of the submission or pride we once displayed, of our transigence and intransigence, of all the many things we proposed or said without conviction, of having fallen in love with whoever it was we fell in love with and of having been a friend of whoever it was we were friends with, our lives are often a continuous betrayal and denial of what came before, we twist and distort everything as time passes, and yet we are still aware, however much we deceive ourselves, that we are the keepers of secrets and mysteries, however trivial. How tiring having always to move in the shadows or, even more difficult, in the half-light, which is never the same, always changing, every person has his light areas and his dark areas, they change according to what he knows and to what day it is and who he's talking to and what he wants, we are constantly saying to ourselves: "I am not the thing I was, I have turned away my former self." As if we had managed to convince ourselves that we are different from the person we believed ourselves to be, merely because chance and the heedless passage of time change our physical circumstances and our clothes, as Solo said that morning, when he was struggling to express his disordered ideas. And he had added: "Or perhaps it is the by-paths and the indirect crooked ways of our own efforts that change us and we end up believing that it is fate, we end up seeing our life in the light of the latest or most recent event, as if the past had been only a preparation and that we understood it only as it moved away from us, as if we understood it all completely at the end." But it is also true that as time passes and we become older, we hide less and recover more of what was once suppressed, and that happens only out of weariness and memory loss or because of the nearness of our own end, clandestinity and secrecy and shadow demand an infallible memory, remembering who knows what and who doesn't, what you have to hide from whom, and which of those people knows about each and every setback, each poisonous step, each error and effort and scruple and the dark back of time. Sometimes you read about someone confessing to a crime they committed forty years ago, people who have always led a decent life suddenly hand themselves over to the police or reveal, in private, a secret that is destroying them, and the naïve and the vengeful and the moralizers believe that these people have been overcome by remorse or by a desire for expiation or by a tormented conscience, when they have merely been overcome or motivated by weariness and a desire to be whole, by their inability to continue lying or keeping silent, to go on remembering what they experienced and did as well as what they imagined, to go on remembering their transformed or invented lives as well as those they actually lived, to forget what really happened and to replace it with a fiction. Sometimes it is only the weariness brought on by the shadow that impels one to tell all the facts, the way someone hiding will suddenly reveal himself, either the pursuer or the pursued, simply in order to bring the game to an end and to step free from what has become a kind of enchantment. The way I allowed Luisa to see me that afternoon after following her when she left the restaurant, or not exactly, after we had both accompanied Téllez to the door of his house, the three of us walked there because it was so close, she and I flanking that figure tottering along on tiny feet more appropriate to a retired dancer, bobbing like a marker buoy, luckily less so than he had been at the cemetery, although on that occasion it wasn't just his age and weight that unbalanced him. And there we all said goodbye, we watched the father open the door of the old lift and sit down on the bench so as to rest on his brief, vertical trajectory, he disappeared skywards in his wooden box like a sedentary god hoisted aloft, and then Luisa Téllez said to me: "Right, see you then" and I said "Yes, see you" or something of the sort, we both assumed that we would see each other again during the rest of that week when I would be coming to work for Téllez in his apartment.

She set off in one direction and I made as if to go in the other, but after taking a few steps, I stopped and turned round and, watching her move off, her back to me, her legs so like those of her sister Marta – or perhaps it was the way she walked rather than her actual calves – I decided to follow her for a while, until I got bored or tired. She strode confidently along for a couple of blocks, as if she knew exactly where she was going, but without being in any particular hurry, and only when she turned down Velázquez did she slacken her pace and begin to drift momentarily towards certain shop windows – one heel at a slight angle, the ground was wet – like someone merely locating where a place is and resolving to have a better look at it another day, then gradually the pauses became longer – her heels straight, the ground still wet – until, at last, she went into a clothes shop, and then I remembered that she had been charged with buying a birthday present for her sister-in-law, María Fernández Vera, on Téllez's behalf. I gingerly stopped outside the same shop and from one corner of the shop window I peered inside, especially when I saw that Luisa had her back to the street while she was talking to the assistant. Then she went over to the skirt rail and stood there looking at the skirts and touching them, still accompanied by the assistant – one of those young women who don't allow a customer time to think and are constantly trying to anticipate their tastes, she kept holding up skirts to which Luisa said no with a shake of her head – until at last Luisa chose one and disappeared into a changing room. She was careless or perhaps trusting, she left her handbag outside on what was more of a table than a glass counter. After a couple of minutes, she reappeared with the skirt on, still tucking in her blouse. It didn't really suit her, it was too long, and the colour was rather bland, her own skirt suited her better. She took a few steps forward and then back while she looked at herself in the mirror – the ticket still dangling – she looked at herself from the side, from the back, I could see from her face that she had decided against it, so I withdrew from my spying position and went off and stood perusing a nearby newsstand, waiting for Luisa to come out, I was forced into buying a foreign newspaper that didn't interest me in the least. She looked at her watch once she was out in the street again, perhaps she was killing time before another appointment, a skirt didn't seem a very suitable present for Téllez to give his daughter-in-law, it would be obvious that he hadn't bought it himself, although perhaps that didn't matter. Luisa continued on down Velázquez, and when she reached the corner of Lista or, rather, Ortega y Gasset (the street changed its name ages ago, but the old name prevails and, unfortunately for the philosopher, that's the one it's still known by), she went into a department store, large and diverse enough for me to follow her and observe her from a distance without being seen, if I was careful. I watched her walk through the book section, she picked up a book, quickly read the blurb on the back or the inside flap and returned it to its pile, she didn't even leaf through it (they mostly have new books in these places and a lot are wrapped in cellophane, which is a real drag), finally, she decided on one, I couldn't see what at first, and went over to the record department, I kept my distance, with my back to her, pretending to be poring over the videos, looking round every now and then in case she should leave without my noticing. In a moment of panic (she suddenly glanced over to where I was standing), I selected a video at random as if I were about to buy it, to give the appearance of doing something: an absurd gesture, it didn't matter what I was doing as long as she didn't find me out, or even if she did find me out. But Luisa was in no hurry or else was still looking for a present and, after a few moments, she walked off with her book but no record towards the food section, I followed after with my video in my hand and stationed myself by the magazines and started flicking through them, watching her out of the corner of my eye, still keeping behind her at all times, it's the one invariable rule when following someone. And then I thought that she must be intending to return home soon, or to Deán's home (to someone's home, whichever it was), because she took out two large tubs of Häagen-Dazs ice cream from the freezer where they were on display, when she opened the transparent glass door I saw her figure momentarily enveloped in the cold air, during the few moments it took her to choose the flavours, a cloud of cold air that seemed to make her blush. If she delayed going home, they would melt, it was the same ice cream that Marta had offered me at that supper at home and now Luisa was buying it too, or perhaps it was Eugenio who liked the ice cream and both sisters bought it for him – Marta had used it as a quick dessert, she hadn't known she was going to have a visitor until that evening. Ice cream in winter for such a small child, it didn't seem likely, I thought, correcting myself, not that I have much idea what children of that age or any other age eat, although Luisa would have to start finding out since she had offered to take care of him. That was when I wondered about the boy, who would he be with all that time, at that age – this I do know – they can't be left alone for a minute unless they're asleep, like that night in Conde de la Cimera when I went away and left him truly alone, nothing had happened to him. Perhaps his aunt and uncle were taking care of him for a while, María Fernández Vera and the brother Guillermo, while Deán and Luisa were having lunch with Téllez to discuss the child's future, a discussion I had partly prevented by my presence. Luisa also picked up a packet of good-quality sausages and some beer, Mexican beer, perhaps she was going to improvise a supper with those meagre ingredients, but not with me. She went over to the desk to pay, I followed, still making sure I kept out of sight, I went over to the section she had just left, I too chose a tub of ice cream from the freezer, I too was enveloped in the cold air, and then I imme-diately went to join the queue at the checkout so as not to be separated from her by too many other customers – luckily there was only one other customer between us – otherwise I might have lost sight of her on the way out. The guy between us wasn't very tall, so I could still see her. I was standing very close to her, I had a clear view of the back of her neck (fortunately, she didn't suddenly turn round). Then I saw the title of the book she had chosen, *Lolita*, an excellent choice, but, at the time, it seemed a little strange to me and not a particularly suitable present for her sister-in-law. Only when I was hurriedly paying for my ice cream and my video did I realize what I was buying, having chosen it blindly, *101 Dalmatians*, a cartoon, it didn't interest me in the least, but I didn't have time to run back and change it. Once out in the street, Luisa Téllez walked down Lista in the direction of the Castellana and, before she reached Serrano, she turned down another street and entered a clothes shop with large windows, much too exposed if I wanted to spy on her. I could wait in a nearby bar, but I preferred to watch her, so I decided to walk up and down outside the shop, glancing in as I passed, but without stopping, as if I were a character in a film repeatedly entering and leaving the field of vision, crossing the screen from one side to the other, that's how she would see me if, by chance, she noticed me, the first time she saw me would, for her, be the first time that I was casually strolling down that busy street, stranger things happen. The pavement was slightly uneven there and a puddle had formed, I had to avoid it each time I passed and, each time I did so, I took advantage of that brief pause to glance inside the shop, Luisa was talking to the idle shop assistants and was touching and looking at everything, she probably couldn't make up her mind. She picked up another skirt and a sort of elegant T-shirt (I saw how elegant it was later on) and went into the changing room, again leaving her handbag and her shopping bag behind, the women stood around yawning, their arms folded, waiting for her to re-emerge, there were no other customers on that afternoon of changeable weather, the assistants were wearing clothes from their own shop, which, I suddenly realized, was Emporio Armani. I was just beginning to get tired of walking up and down like that (I paused now and then) when Luisa emerged from the changing room wearing the T-shirt and the skirt, the skirt was quite short and deep red in colour and it suited her perfectly, even better than the one she had been wearing. I rapidly moved out of visual range and waited more than a minute before walking past again and, when I finally did, I caught Luisa in the middle of a double manoeuvre: she was turning to go back into the changing room, having looked at herself in the mirror and, on her way, she began taking off the elegant cream-coloured T-shirt. I glimpsed her bra, her arms in the air with the sleeves of the blouse turned inside out, I saw her smooth, clean armpits. I couldn't help but stop and stare and, as I did so, I stepped in the puddle with my right foot, soaking my shoe, I could feel the water in my sock and on my skin, horrible, such an unpleasant sensation. When I looked up, Luisa had disappeared into the changing room, but now I knew for certain that she was the woman I had seen undressing and looking out of the window of Marta's bedroom the night after my visit, Marta's sister, Luisa Téllez, who had perhaps also seen me as she looked out, while I stood there next to my taxi, pretending to be waiting for someone and thinking, for a second, that the silhouette in the window could be Marta still alive. I had thought that, knowing it to be impossible. One sister had ice cream already at home and the other was buying it now; one had an Armani top that I had helped to remove and the other was trying one on now, before my very eyes. I was still under the spell, I thought, or the spell was still working. But perhaps she was buying this new top for her sister-in-law, on behalf of Téllez, a father-in-law with money, he must have acquired it during the Franco era. I saw Luisa pay with a credit card (each article of clothing in a separate bag), and I moved out of the way so that I could follow her when she came out of the shop: she went back down Ortega y Gasset or Lista and walked as far as the Castellana, that avenue which is like a river flowing through the city, forming a long frontier with straight tree-lined quays, there are no meanders and no water, just asphalt, and the pavements or quays are not raised up. One of those trees had been blown over in the storm, it had been cut off at its base and the ground was scattered with splinters, the storm glimpsed from the restaurant must have been extremely violent, with almost hurricane-force winds, unless the tree had fallen over some days before and had still not been removed, the branches had not yet been sawn off, in Madrid imperfections are never corrected immediately. However it happened, it had fallen towards the pavement, not towards the road – the river – which is always full of cars, it could have killed some passer-by. We weren't far from Hermanos Bécquer, that is, from the corner of the Castellana where, nearly two years before, I had picked up Victoria and then deposited her back there afterwards, late into the night, that's what she had wanted, to be left where I had met her, so I did. Once we had climbed back into the front seats of my car and before turning on the engine again, I wondered whether I should offer her a bit more money and invite her to come back to my place until morning: if she was Celia she would be embarrassed or saddened, if she was Victoria she would be delighted to accept, a whole Tuesday night with the meter running, it probably didn't happen that often, it's probably considered to be a real stroke of luck. I didn't suggest it though, perhaps, again, because I did not want to be absolutely certain, and perhaps so as not to have to remember her figure in my bedroom, it is harder to rid oneself of ghosts that have been in your own rooms.

"Anything else?" she asked, while I was hesitating. That's what shop assistants ask you in shops.

"Do *you* want anything else?" I replied, trying my luck.

"Ah," she replied, in a slightly surprised, vengeful tone of voice, "remember now, I'm here to do what you tell me to do, you're in charge." She had picked up her mac from the back seat but she hadn't put it on, she had placed it on her lap, carefully folded, like someone preparing to leave. I said nothing, and then she took another piece of chewing-gum out of her handbag and while she was unwrapping it, added rather mockingly, studying the tiny rectangle: "And to think you could have killed me." She could allow herself this remark now because she was feeling calm and no longer afraid, she herself had said, "You can see right away what a bloke is after," and it was me she had seen.

"What a nasty girl you are," I replied and it was then that I started the engine again as if it were a continuation of that phrase or perhaps a full stop. The noise made the light in the porter's lodge at the German embassy go on, but only for a moment, darkness was immediately restored. Perhaps the guard hadn't even noticed our presence, perhaps he was dozing and the sound of the engine had woken him up from some bad dream. "Where shall I drop you?"

"Where you found me," she replied. "The night isn't over yet for me," and she put the chewing-gum in her mouth: this time it was a strawberry smell that mingled with the other smells in the car, there were newer, stronger smells now.

I wasn't expecting that last remark, I mean, it hadn't even occurred to me to think such a thing, and that was why I decided to follow her too or, rather, not to leave after dropping her on the corner which had not, for the moment, brought her bad luck. We were so close to the corner that I made a short detour before returning to Hermanos Bécquer in order to absorb that unexpected thought and to gain time. Before she got out, I gave her another note, I put it in her hand, money passing from hand to hand, that doesn't often happen.

"What's this for?" she asked.

"For the fright I gave you earlier on," I replied.

"You *are* conscientious, anyway, you didn't really," she said. "Still, it's received with thanks." She opened the door, got out of the car and began putting on her raincoat before stepping on to the pavement, her minuscule skirt was more creased than ever, but it wasn't stained or crumpled, not by me at least. I drove away quickly, when she still had just the one sleeve on. I turned to the right, now only one of the other two prostitutes was standing in a doorway in the Castellana, the ground was still damp and it must have been freezing.

I didn't go home though, instead, I turned off down the first street and parked there, next to the Dresdner Bank, with its broad lawn and its fountain behind the railings, I still think of it as the Colegio Alamán, which was near my own school, the garden then was a dusty playground where I would sometimes see boys my own age playing during break and I would feel that mixture of envy and relief that I wasn't them, which is how children always feel when they see other children they don't know. Opposite that bank or school there are three or four archaically frivolous bars where prostitutes from that whole area doubtless go to refuel when they need a drink or when they get drenched to the skin. I walked to the corner further up from the one where Celia or Victoria had taken up her position again, where the first stretch of the hill ended, the one I mentioned before – the false bridge – and where the second stretch, at right angles to that, began, the real continuation of Hermanos Bécquer according to the street name, in that part of that part of the street there were trees covered in creepers, the trunks thick with evergreen leaves and, above my head, ornate branches. I hid there and watched, I saw her lean back against the wall of the insurance-company building, wearily, patiently, immediately opposite her was another building, vaguely biblical in style, with a pretentious ramp reminiscent of the walls of Jericho as portrayed in paintings and films, although I couldn't see it from where I was standing, I couldn't see her very well either, it's quite a distance from one corner to the next, so I walked a little further down the same street in which she was waiting, General Oraa not Hermanos Bécquer according to the street sign, running the risk of her spotting me if she turned too far to her left, the side from which the cars would come, the cars which, like mine, might stop, open their doors and swallow her up. I paused outside a bar that was closed, the Sunset Bar, my light-coloured raincoat would be a visible stain in that night lit by the yellowish street lamps. I stood still for some minutes, keeping close to the wall, like Peter Lorre in the film *M*, the vampire of Düsseldorf, I've seen that too. There was even less traffic than when I had driven down there earlier, and I suddenly found myself hoping that no one else would pass, that no one else would pick her up so that, contrary to what she had thought and to what she had told me, her night would have ended. It was a perfectly normal thing to wish if I wasn't entirely sure that she wasn't Celia, but as I stood there, with my back against the wall, I realized that that was what I wanted even if she was Victoria and I had only just met her and wouldn't see her again, ever. What a strange contact that intimate contact is, what strong, non-existent links it instantly forges, even though, afterwards, they fade and unravel and are forgotten, sometimes it's hard to remember that they did exist that one night, or two, or more, after a while it becomes difficult. But not immediately after establishing those links for the first time, then they feel as if they were burned into you, when everything is fresh and your eyes still wear the face of the other person and you can still smell them, a smell for which one becomes, for a while, the repository, it is what remains after the goodbyes, goodbye passion and goodbye scorn. Goodbye memories. I could still smell the smell of Victoria or Celia which was not the same smell as that of Celia when she could only have been Celia and she had lived with me, I suddenly thought how absurd it was that I would never see her again or that she should get into another car, even though that was what her job involved and even though I didn't, in fact, want to have anything more to do with her, if she was Celia, I had stopped having anything to do with her out of choice and after a considerable struggle, I had consistently avoided her until she had grown resigned or weary, or perhaps she was merely recouping her energies and giving me time to miss her persistence, a postponement. She took a few steps across the pavement, dragging her heels, luckily for me, she walked towards the

Castellana rather than up General Oraa or Hermanos Bécquer where I was keeping watch, otherwise she would have seen me – I think – there was more traffic coming down the Castellana now and it was possible that, by then, the other prostitute in the doorway would have found a client while I was parking and turning the corner, and Victoria would not, therefore, be invading anyone's territory if she tried her luck over there. A couple of sinister-looking men came along the pavement, or tree-lined walk, and said something to her, I couldn't quite hear what, something unpleasant, I heard her reply boldly and they slowed their pace as if to confront her, I thought that I might have to intervene and, after all, be useful and defend her – the beneficent vampire – to meet her again despite everything and against all expectations, at least that night, one can't always avoid being involved in what happens before one's eyes, trying to stop a knife being plunged into someone's chest, if you see it coming, for example, or pushing someone out of the way and thus preventing their decapitation by a tree blown down in a gale, should you see it falling, for example. "Stupid fucking cunt," they shouted at her. "Oh, go fuck yourselves!" she shouted in turn, and that was that, the two men didn't stop, they staggered on, gesturing with their fingers, their bomber jackets billowing, they left the field.

And it was only two minutes afterwards that a car stopped alongside Celia or Victoria, it pulled up as I had pulled up, except that it hadn't come down Hermanos Bécquer but from the Castellana, it was another Golf, red, we Golf owners seem to be amongst the most solitary of night owls. She had her back to me now, so I moved a little closer, leaving behind me the shelter of the awning outside the Sunset Bar, although still sticking close to the wall like a lizard, I wanted to see and hear, it occurred to me that, with luck, they would be unable to reach an agreement, the bloke might be too mean or might make Victoria feel uneasy for some reason. She walked over to the kerb, I thought that he would open the passenger door for her and that I would not therefore see him, I did see him, though, because he opened his door instead and got out to talk to her from there, over the roof of the car, his left hand resting on the half-open door. Although I could only see her from behind, I recognized the lacklustre attempt at seduction, drawing her raincoat back with her hands in her pockets to show him more of that body with which I had just shared that strange, intimate contact that creates the immediate illusion of some real connection, even through a condom. I took off my raincoat so that I would be less visible if the man suddenly looked across and saw me standing there in the dark; I slung it over my arm, I shivered. "What would you charge me for a quarter of an hour? I'm in a hurry," I heard him say to Victoria across the car roof. I didn't hear her response, but it must have seemed reasonable, because the next thing I saw was the gesture he made with his head, a gesture that meant "Get in", with no hesitation, no pause to consider. The man got back in the car and so did Celia, she opened the passenger door herself and they zoomed off, they left the field, the bloke was in a hurry. He was about the age I am now, fair-haired and balding, he didn't look too bad, fairly well dressed and showed no signs of being drunk or desperate or malevolent, I thought he might be a doctor, perhaps he knew that he would be able to get to sleep more quickly and more easily if he went to bed after a quick screw or a blow job, his hands still on the steering wheel, something efficient and hygienic after eight hours on duty in a clinic full of exhausted nurses in white stockings with crooked seams. Then I felt a pang to be left there alone like the murderer and fugitive M, all the prostitutes had gone and, regardless of my wishes, one of them was about to make me the subject of that extinct verb *ġe·licgan*, or a participant of that forgotten noun *ġe·for·liġer*, while I was left on my own, or was about to make me for ever into that man's fictitious *ġe·brȳd·guma*, without my consent – but how could there be consent – she would have me lie with them, become a party to co-fornication and be the co-bridegroom of that imagined doctor whom I had seen for a moment from afar and who, unlike me, was in a hurry – I would have nothing to do with him again either. At that moment or during the next fifteen minutes, she would be forging an Anglo-Saxon relationship for me, by its very nature posthumous, a relationship I did not want, whose effects and exact meaning I would not know, since my language does not have a word for it, and from which I could do nothing to protect myself; and it's one thing to know about it and quite another to see it with your own eyes or to be a witness to the preparations, it's one thing to imagine the time during which events that displease or hurt us or drive us to despair are taking place and quite another to be able to say to ourselves with certainty: "This is happening now, while I'm standing here alone with my back to the wall, not knowing how to react in the middle of a night full of crushed, damp leaves, while I crunch back through them to my car parked next to the Dresdner Bank or the Colegio Alamán of my childhood and get into it and start the engine, a few moments ago, I was in this same car in Calle Fortuny accompanied by Victoria or Celia, enjoying that strange, intimate contact in the back seat or talking with her beforehand in the front seat, not daring to feel the certainty I now believe I feel out of jealousy, trying not to recognize the person I did recognize and at the same time not wanting to mistake my own ex-wife for an unknown prostitute. Now, on the other hand, I am possessed of a certainty unaffected by identity or name, I know that the woman is in another car and that her body is in other hands, the hands that touch everything without hesitation or scruple, the hands that squeeze or caress or investigate and also strike (I didn't mean to, it was an accident, don't hold it against me), the sometimes mechanical gestures made by the warm, expert hand of the doctor feeling his way over a body about which he is still undecided as to whether or not it pleases him. And while I drove along the same streets I had driven along before with her, trying to find where the red Golf had parked – down Fortuny itself and Marqués de Riscal and Monte Esquinza and Fernando el Santo, no sign of it in any of them – I thought too, with horror and suppressed hope, that I could not even be sure of that, since I would not be a witness to it: perhaps that fuck or that blow job, hands still on the steering wheel, would not take place if that man or doctor had hard, clumsy fingers like piano keys and decided to deploy them, before any further contact was made, on the throat or the cheekbones or the temples of Victoria or Celia, her poor temples, finally pushing her lifeless body out of the car on to the asphalt and the damp leaves. And while I gave up my search and finally returned home – the fifteen minutes were up, although that fifteen minutes was only a manner of speaking and the two of them might perhaps still be in the red Golf or the doctor could have decided to invite her back to his flat until the morning, I hadn't wanted to have that memory or ghost in my bedroom and now I was suffering for it – I thought that in the days that followed, I would have to study the newspapers carefully, my heart in my mouth, looking for and fearing a piece of news that would perhaps leave me a widower if Victoria was Celia, news that would make me regret all my fears until the end of my days if Victoria was Victoria. The car smelled of her and I smelled of her.

I arrived home in a state of extreme agitation, there was no way I would get to sleep now, I could have just driven off after leaving the prostitute on her corner and then what happened next would have been a matter of conjecture, a distraction, a pastime, conjecture is only a game, but actually having seen something is a serious matter, sometimes even a drama, it does not provide the consolation of uncertainty not, at least, until more time has passed. But I had seen myself with that woman in my own car and that was enough for me to be able to imagine her now with the doctor, my co-fornicator or, more accurately, co-fucker, perhaps *he* would frighten her. I turned on the television as I would two and a half years later in Conde de la Cimera, not knowing what to do while a woman lay dying by my side, not that I really believed it or felt particularly worried, the fact is she didn't believe it either; and as Solus too had turned on the television in his palace that same night, when he couldn't sleep and left his bedroom so as not to bother anyone and to try and summon up sleep while he watched the screen, in my case, it's what I normally do when I get home late, I suppose most of us who live alone do, those of us who are therefore no one, we watch to see what has happened in the world during our absence, as if we were not always absent from the world. It was already very late and only a couple of channels were still broadcasting, and the first thing I saw on one of them was a knight in armour on his knees outside a tent, commending his soul to God, it was obviously a film, in colour, but not, of course, new, the best programmes are always on in the early hours, when almost no one is there to see them. The scene immediately changed to show another man, this time lying down, fully clothed, a king, I thought, when I saw the flounced sleeves of his shirt, a king suffering from insomnia or who was perhaps asleep with his eyes wide open, he too was in a tent of war, although he was lying on his back in a real bed with pillows and sheets, I don't remember much about it, but I do remember that. And then, one after another, ghosts began to appear, superimposed on a landscape, perhaps the site of a future or imminent battle: a man, two children, another man, a woman, and another man bringing up the rear, shaking his fists in the air and crying out like someone calling for vengeance, all the others had sad, desolate faces, their hair had grown white and their bitter words were pronounced by pale lips that seemed to be reading something out in a quiet voice rather than speaking it, those who are now ghosts do not always find it easy to talk to us. That king was haunted or under a spell or, to be more exact, he was being haunted that very night by those closest to him, who were reproaching him with their deaths and calling down misfortunes on him in the battle that would take place the following day, they were saying terrible things in the sad voices of those who have been betrayed or killed by the person they loved: "Tomorrow in the battle think on me," the men, the woman and the children said to him one after the other, "and fall thy edgeless sword: despair and die!" "Let me sit heavy on thy soul tomorrow, let me be lead within thy bosom and in a bloody battle end thy days: let fall thy pointless lance." "Think on me when I was mortal: despair and die," they repeated one after the other, the children and the woman and the men. I remember those words clearly, especially those spoken to him by the woman, the last to address him, his ghost wife whose cheeks streamed with tears: "That wretched Ann thy wife," she said to him, "that never slept a quiet hour with thee, now fills thy sleep with perturbations. Tomorrow in the battle think on me, and fall thy edgeless sword: despair and die!" And that king sat up or awoke terrified and screaming at those terrible night visions and I too was afraid when I saw them and heard his scream coming from the television; I felt a shiver run through me – the sheer power of the performance, I suppose – and I changed channels with the remote control, I switched to the other channel that was still broadcasting and they were showing an old film too, this time in black and white, it seemed to be about aeroplanes, Spitfires and Stukas and Hurricanes and Messerschmitt 109s, as well as the odd Lancaster, the name of the dynasty of the two Henries; it was probably about the Battle of Britain, the battle that allowed Winston Churchill to utter one of his most famous phrases: "Never in the field of human conflict was so much owed by so many to so few," that's all that's ever quoted, like the phrase about "blood, tears and sweat" from which people always omit the word "toil". During the Spanish Civil War, Madrid was bombed by Stukas and Junkers, especially the former, people called them "turkeys" because of the way they lumbered across the sky bearing their devastating load, across the same sky that I could see from my window, the Republican fighters, on the other hand, were known as "rats", fast Russian Migs and old American Curtisses. I felt more comfortable in that unsupernatural world of aerial combat, and closer in time too, those other people on the first channel, in armour and flounced shirts, were doubtless nearer to the time when the verb *ȝe·licgan* or the nouns *ȝe·for·liȝer* and *ȝe·brȳd·guma* were still in use – words I had been forced to think about that night and which, perhaps, I had invented – although no closer to their meaning: I did not want to see them, whoever they were, I preferred to stay in my own century, with deaths brought about by war, although possibly on the other channel they too would be fighting a battle and the new dead might also be men killed in war, not murder victims, men, a woman and children. I was watching the planes while I was think-ing this, but while I was watching them, the curses of the ghosts in that scene of insomnia or troubled sleep were still resonating and floating in my head, and that's why I thought of or rather remem-bered them much later on, when I bumped against something in the darkness in the bedroom of Marta Téllez's son and saw, hanging from the ceiling, the miniature aeroplanes that had doubt-less belonged to his father, more numerous and far superior to any I had ever had in my own childhood, the aeroplanes hanging from threads, languidly preparing each night for a weary night-time foray, tiny, ghostly and impossible, a battle that never took place or took place only on sleepless nights, in my turbulent dreams.

What happened on those two nights remains etched on my memory, everything leaves a mark.

I wasn't sure whether to phone Celia or not, it was very late and if she was at home, she would probably be asleep, I hadn't heard anything from her, except indirectly, in about four or five months, and I preferred it that way, I didn't call her and she didn't call me, how could I explain my abrupt change of mind and that sudden impulse to call her without telling her everything that had happened to me, without telling her that the reason for my inopportune phone call was that I thought I had been with her until shortly before, that I had opened the door of my car to her and had given her money in the street, that I had taken her to a deserted place so that she could earn that money: to tell her that I thought I had fucked her; she would take me for a madman, if she answered at all. And yet it's very hard to resist making a phone call once you have considered doing so, just as the moment you get hold of a telephone number, you always feel tempted to dial it at once, that number that had been my number until not so very long ago. It was after three o'clock in the morning and the Spitfires, fired upon and pursued by the Messerschmitts, were hurtling across the screen as I picked up the phone and dialled the number, not allowing myself any further hesitations. If Celia answered, I would at least know that she was not Victoria and was not in danger, she wouldn't have had time yet to escape the hands of the doctor and return home, and, besides, her night might not yet have ended; but it would be worse if she didn't answer, my feelings of disquiet would grow and for two reasons, out of two fears: that Celia was indeed Victoria and that something bad might have happened to her, something so bad that one day she would appear to me on sleepless nights, or in my dreams, to tell me what then she could only tell me in dreams: "That wretched Celia, thy wife, that never slept a quiet hour with thee, now fills thy sleep with perturbations." Or fills it with spells and curses for having let her leave my life and for having left her that night too, when I could have brought her home under another name and thus saved her. It was a mistake to phone her, but I phoned her anyway: I heard the first ring, a second and then a third, it was still not too late to hang up and remain with my doubts unresolved. The answering machine clicked on and I heard her recorded voice: "Hello, this is 549 6001. I'm not home right now, but if you'd like to leave a message, please do so after the long tone. Thank you." She addressed the caller as "tú", the way young people do these days, she was young, so was Victoria. I heard two or three beeps left by previous calls and then the long tone, and I decided to speak out of pure fear, unlike that other time when I had dialled my old number while I was sitting at the foot of the bed getting undressed, one weary, melancholy night. "Celia," I said, "are you there?", answering machines often lie. "It's me, Víctor, are you in? I don't know, perhaps you're asleep and you've got the volume on the phone turned down low," I was in the middle of saying what I hoped would be the case when that wish was granted and the non-recorded voice of Celia interrupted me, she was at home and had picked up the phone when she heard my voice, so she wasn't Victoria, and not yet, not yet, I thought at once, not yet, because she was still alive. "Víctor, have you any idea what time it is?" she said. "Not yet," I thought, just as the time had not yet come for the pilot of that supermarine Spitfire Mk XII who could still see the world from up on high and was still fleeing. She sounded wide awake, I know what her voice sounds like when she's been asleep, just as I remember her sleeping face bare of make-up, the question seemed more of a formal reproach than a real one, I hadn't dragged her from sleep, that much was certain. "What's wrong?" she added. I hadn't prepared any likely excuse, how could I, if I didn't have one, and the state of excitement I was in had left me dumbstruck, so I said, just to gain time: "There's something I'd like to talk to you about. Can I come up and see you for a moment?" "Now?" she replied. "Are you mad? Do you know what time it is?" "Yes, I do," I said, "but it's urgent. You weren't asleep were you? You don't sound as if you've been asleep." There was a brief silence and before answering, she said: "Hang on a second," it might be the second required to reach for an ashtray if she had lit a cigarette, although I didn't hear the lighter, which you usually can down the phone, some smokers you can even hear inhaling. "No, I wasn't asleep, but you can't come over now." "Why not? It won't take long, really." Celia fell silent for a moment, I heard her give an exasperated sigh. "Víctor," she said, and I knew then, because when people call you by your name, you know they are not going to give you what you want, "do you realize what you're saying. For months you've been avoiding me, for months we haven't seen or spoken to each other, and suddenly you ring me up at half past three in the morning and want to come over. You've got a nerve!" That sort of remark always disarms people, "You've got a nerve!", she was right, I didn't say anything, I looked at my watch, it wasn't, in fact, half past, and then she added gratuitously, she did it simply to annoy me because I wasn't going to insist, she didn't need to tell me: "Anyway, you can't come over now, I've got someone with me." "Oh, right," I said, like an idiot. Celia let the phrase take effect, it isn't the same imagining what happened before or after as knowing about it when it's actually happening; then she spoke again, in a friendlier tone: "Call me tomorrow, late morning, and we can talk about whatever it is then. If you like, we can have lunch. All right? Call me tomorrow." Then it was my turn to say something simply to annoy her: "Tomorrow will be too late." And I hung up without saying goodbye. I was quite calm for a moment, I saw a pilot with a clipped moustache gazing up at the skies and saying: "Mitch! They can't take the Spitfires, Mitch! They can't take them!" He looked like David Niven to me and he was addressing someone who was dead; then the planes set off towards a sun crisscrossed with clouds and that quote from Churchill's came up on the screen, the battle was over and I changed channels again, suddenly curious or in a hurry now to know what the battle was in the other film and what the film was, in colour, historical, featuring ghosts and kings, but I found that it too had ended, I would never know. In its place, a few rachitic girls were doing some sort of gymnastics that involved twirling long, floating ribbons, with a commentary provided by a couple of hard-to-please lesbians who found fault with everything. I looked and listened for a few moments (I looked at the girls and I listened to the lesbians) then I returned to the aerial-combat channel, where, to my horror, a religious broadcast had just begun (I don't know the calendar of saints' days, so I don't know what it was they were celebrating) and a few hideous members of the faithful flock were standing in a church belting out "The Lord is my Shepherd" and other pontifical ballads. I turned off the television and looked for the newspaper to find out about the two films of which I had caught fragments, but the cleaning lady had already thrown it out, she had come that day in my absence and she always throws everything out too soon, as happens with Solitaire at the Palace and which irks him greatly, as I learned much later on. And that was when my brief moment of calm came to an end, it lasted little more than a moment, because my brain rarely rests and is constantly coming up with ideas and schemes: "If Victoria wasn't Celia and Celia had company," I thought, "both Celia and Victoria are making me the subject of that verb and the object of that ancient relationship, and I, in turn, have made her the co-fornicator of the prostitute Victoria who so closely resembles her, both verb and noun must apply to women too." And I suppose it was that feeling of being made a double subject, a double *ġe·brȳd·ġuma*, both at the same time – a disquieting feeling – that made me think further, and that new thought was worse still and completely undermined the partially calming effect of my phone call, calming only in respect of my two fears: Celia had picked up the phone and was, therefore, at home, but before I began to leave my message on the answering machine, there had been two or three beeps, indicating previous phone calls, so it was likely that when Celia picked up the phone, she had just come in through the door with her companion and would not even have had time to listen to those previous messages. It was again possible, therefore, that Celia *was* Victoria and that she and the doctor – a married man – had decided to go back to her place and had arrived at that very moment, shortly after I got home, perhaps after driving around the traffic-free city or after a brief halt in a quiet street, the man no longer in a hurry. And if that was the case, if her companion or the doctor was with her now, the danger was not yet over, not for Celia or for Victoria, not yet, not yet, but who knows, tomorrow or in a while, "Those who know me keep silent and in their silence they do not defend me". I couldn't phone her again, because now anything was possible and that is the price of uncertainty, it would have been ridiculous and I would have deserved her anger and her insults. In my present state, it made no sense my trying to sleep, I had to let some time pass, at least the time it would take for a fuck, or two simultaneous fucks, more or less the same amount of time, a fuck doesn't, in fact, take very long, half an hour, an hour with preliminaries, less than that with a whore with whom there are no preliminaries, perhaps more with a lover, longer still with someone new or if it's the first time, with Marta Téllez everything went on far too long, that's why I never came to form that relationship or link with Deán or with the gross, despotic Vicente, I don't have that link with them, or so I believe, although I do have the understandable feeling of having acquired it that night, it wasn't by choice that I did not acquire it or do not have it, nor ever will, it was not Marta's choice or mine.

I decided to go out again and go for a walk, to wander around for a while to distract myself and to tire my body out and at least not be in a bedroom while the others were, the other two or four. The city is never empty, but at that time of the damp night there were very few passers-by, two or three individuals who looked as if they had just got out of prison, the men hosing down the streets, who talk in loud voices as if no one else were sleeping and waste a lot of water, everything was still wet from the storm and it looked like it could easily rain again; the occasional ragged, itinerant old woman, a small group of noisy men and women who had doubtless been celebrating something at a nightclub or a discotheque, a stag night, a lottery prize, a birthday. I walked quite far, over to the west side of the city, not an area I like, in Calle de la Princesa and, later, down Quintana, I heard footsteps behind me, I heard them for three blocks along two different streets, for too long a time and over too great a distance for me not to wonder about it, whoever it was would be watching the back of my neck and was perhaps following me in order to mug me in the shadows, it was a night of fears and apprehensions, but nothing would happen as long as I could still hear them and they did not speed up, I didn't want to start running, so at the beginning of the fourth block I gave them the chance to overtake me, assuming they were the footsteps of someone inoffensive unable to walk any faster, I stopped to look in a bookshop window, I took out my glasses and put them on and, as I did so, I watched out of the corner of my eye, alertly awaiting his arrival, I heard the poisonous footsteps approaching and it was not yet, not yet, and still not yet: they passed by and, quite openly this time – for now I was the one looking at the back of his neck – I watched the figure moving off, a middle-aged man, to judge by his gait and the camelhair coat he was wearing, that was all I could make out in the darkness,

I smoothed down my raincoat and put away my glasses. I headed south-west, Rosales, Bailén, I like that area better, Rosales was the site of the Montaña barracks where, all those years ago, the third day of our war was so fiercely fought, now there's an Egyptian temple there. And it was just as I reached Plaza de Oriente that I saw two horses coming in the opposite direction, keeping as close to the pavement as possible so as not to get in the way of the few cars that passed. There were two horses, a stallion and a mare, and one rider, the man, wearing high boots, was riding the bay, whilst the dapple-grey mare, which was also saddled up, rode alongside, occasionally dropping back a little, they were moving along at walking pace, phlegmatic, Andalusian riding horses, their eight hooves echoed on the gleaming road, an ancient sound, hooves in the city, almost unknown in these arrogant times that have exiled these beasts which have accompanied man throughout his history, even during my childhood it was quite common to hear them, pulling rag-and-bone carts or the covered wagons of tradesmen, or carrying mounted policemen dressed in those long, sinister cloaks that made them look like Russians and concealed their elongated, rubber truncheons, or bearing some wealthy horseman back from his riding school. Animals were a common sight to people in the cities then, I even remember seeing cows crammed into basements, as a small boy, I was just the right height to see them through the barred windows of those dairies that gave off a penetrating smell, the smell of cow and horse and mule and donkey, the smell of manure, a familiar smell. That's why it seemed so odd to be standing in the Plaza de Oriente opposite the Palacio Real in which no one lives and to see those enormous horses, I felt something akin to wonder, despite the fact that I often go to the races on Sundays, but seeing horses parading round the paddock and then running round the track as part of a spectacle is not the same as encountering them in the middle of the city, on asphalt, next to the very pavement you're walking along, gigantic, lustrous and yet incomprehensible creatures with broad necks and muscular trunks and limbs, they have long memories and once they get into certain habits, these can be hard to eradicate, they know how to find their own way home when their masters are lost and they have an infallible instinct for distinguishing friend from foe, whether near to or far away, they would never confuse inoffensive footsteps with poisonous ones, they can sense danger before it even appears and before we have even imagined it. It was much too late for those horses to be out in the street riding past the Plaza de Oriente, it's true that a couple of times before, years ago, I had seen the occasional horse pass by at night or during the day in that area, but never towards dawn – or perhaps it was simply that I had never been in Calle Bailén in the early hours – perhaps they were horses from the Royal Palace and belonged to the king even though he doesn't live there, or they might be from the nearby Palacio de Liria, at any rate, they were definitely aristocratic horses. I watched, astonished, as they passed me, there they were so tall and immemorial, a stallion with a rider and a riderless mare in the night, there was a distant rumble of thunder and the mare started, though not the stallion, she made as if to rear up, she almost stood up on her hind legs for a moment like a monster, her two front legs raised as if she were about to fall on me and strike my head with those fantastic hooves and crush me beneath the weight of her immense body, a horrible death, a ridiculous death. The threat was shortlived, the horseman calmed her down immediately, with a word, a single movement. Many people, even the English themselves, believe the origin of their word "nightmare" to be simply that, a night mare, but it isn't so, that was another thing I looked into in my younger days, the word "mare" has two origins depending on whether it's on its own or combined with the word "night", when it refers to a horse it comes from the Anglo Saxon "*mēre*", which simply means "mare", whilst in the word "nightmare" its origin is, if I remember rightly, *mara* which means "incubus", the malign spirit or demon or goblin that squatted or lay on the sleeping person, crushing their chest and creating the oppressive sense of nightmare, occasionally engaging in carnal commerce with him or her, although if it's with a man, the spirit is female and is called a succubus and lies underneath, and if it's with a woman, it's male, an incubus, and lies on top: let me sit heavy on thy soul tomorrow, let me be lead within thy bosom and weigh thee down to ruin, shame and death, perhaps the Irish banshee, who used to announce imminent death with her moans and cries and canticles, had once been that kind of spirit, during my walk, I had seen a ragged, wandering old woman, perhaps she was a banshee who was not yet sure which home to go to that night in order to intone her lament, perhaps she would make her way towards what was once my home, I didn't live there now and so was safe, but Celia wasn't safe, because that was still her home and she wasn't alone there now, she had told me so, she was engaged in carnal commerce with someone. I thought all this very rapidly while the stallion and the mare were moving off, leaving in their wake their penetrating smell and taking with them, until who knows when, that childhood noise, superstition is just another form of thought like any other, a form that accentuates and regulates the association of ideas, it's an exacerbation, an illness, but, in fact, all thought is a sickness, which is why no one ever thinks too much, at least most people do their best not to.

I walked over to the kerb, trying to spot a taxi coming from either direction, I crossed the road and crossed back again, two cars passed and then a taxi that screeched to a halt, I was lucky, I gave my old address to the taxi driver, I hadn't been there or asked someone to take me there for a long time, though for three years that had been the norm, and when I found myself at the door I had entered on so many nights and left on so many days over a period of three years, I realized that I still had the keys on my key ring and I still had them with me – I took them out, some habits are hard to eradicate. If she hadn't changed the locks, I could go into the apartment, I could open the street door and take that familiar lift up to the fourth floor and I could even open the door to the right and see with my own eyes that nothing bad had happened that night, that no banshee had been prowling around, that Celia Ruiz Comendador was still alive and was safe in her bed, accompanied or alone – perhaps that was all Deán would have wanted to know, had he suspected something in far-off London; an hour and a half had passed since I went out into the street, time enough for a fuck or even two, if they were very impatient, it was what classical authors called the "conticinio", a Latin word meaning the time of night when, by mutual agreement, everything keeps silent – there was that prefix "con-" again – although, in Madrid, that time of night does not exist, perhaps Celia had

had company and was now alone, perhaps the doctor or whoever it was – the incubus – had left after the fuck, we male spirits don't tend to hang around to see the effect of our actions. And if he hadn't gone, I would at last be able to resolve my doubts about Celia and Victoria, I would see the man and I would see whether or not he was that fair-haired, balding man, or if he was someone else, a lover and, therefore, a co-bridegroom, whichever of them he was, he would get a terrible fright: the man who was still her husband bursting in, in the middle of the night, using his own key, surprising him in bed with the woman who was still, bureaucratically speaking, the other man's wife, for a few seconds the lover or customer would fear a scene worthy of a melodrama or a tragedy, covering himself with the sheets, he would glance at my raincoat pocket to see if I was about to take out a gun, a death more ridiculous than horrible. It was tempting to try it, for all kinds of reasons, serious and frivolous. I stood on the opposite pavement and looked up at what I knew to be the windows of the apartment, my own windows until not so very long ago, the bedroom window, the living-room windows, one of which was, in fact, a door that opened on to a large terrace, we often used to have supper out there in summer, during three summers of marriage. Everything was in darkness, perhaps Celia had made some changes since my departure and had moved the bedroom to the back, where it looked out on to a courtyard. There were no signs of life, it was the home of people either sleeping or dead, all was still, there was no one removing or putting on some article of clothing. I hesitated, not far off I heard the sound of breaking glass and urgent, muffled voices, someone was breaking into a shop, shortly afterwards, the alarm sounded, not that it stopped the glass shattering or the thieves ransacking the shop, everyone knows that, in Madrid, alarms go off of their own accord and no one takes any notice of them, they're useless, it must have been happening a few blocks away. The alarm stopped ringing and there was another roll of thunder, so close this time that it immediately started to rain, fat drops falling on the dead leaves and the damp ground, on the mud like half-dried blood or black, sticky hair, there was no one else in the street seeking refuge but me, the thieves were farther off and would have finished their job, I crossed over and took shelter in the doorway, once I was there, I couldn't resist trying my old key in the lock, it met with no resistance. And then, no need to think about the steps you have taken a thousand times, they almost take themselves or you do so mechanically, the lift, it was always on one of the upper floors, never downstairs, someone always arrived after the last of the people going out had left, some nightbird or myself and Celia, she was so young and loved going out at night, we came in and went out together, a real marriage. Now I went up alone, excitedly, my heart in my mouth, and at the same time, I felt amused, surreptitious behaviour is at once a source of diversion and anxiety, and when I put the key in the lock of the front door, I did so with great care to avoid making any noise, like a cat burglar who scales walls and sneaks in, that is what I was at that moment, although I wasn't going to make off with anything, only knowledge, and only in order to calm my mind with that knowledge that she was alive and was herself and no one else. But what if she wasn't alive, and what if she wasn't herself. If she wasn't alive, there would be no reason to walk on tiptoe, on the contrary, I would have to turn on all the lights and clutch my head in my hands and cry out in pain and remorse, try to revive her with my kisses, collapse in despair, I would have to call a doctor, call the neighbours, call her parents and the police, and explain my whole story. There wasn't a sound, not even once I was inside, I carefully closed the door behind me, I knew that door well, I had come in on other occasions when Celia was already asleep, some nights when we hadn't gone out together and I had come back late. I could walk in the dark in that house, it had once been mine and I knew the distances and I knew where the furniture was, the obstacles, where there was a corner and where something stuck out, I even knew which bit of the corridor would creak underfoot. I walked down that corridor and went into the living room, it was lighter there with the light coming in from outside, the street lamps, the odd neon sign, the sky which always provides some light even when it's overcast and wild, the noise of the storm would drown my footsteps, she or they would be unlikely to hear them above the thunderclaps and above the rain beating down on roofs and terraces and trees and on the fallen leaves and on the ground. It might also be that the clamour would wake her up or wake both of them up, independent of my inaudible, inoffensive footsteps and of the sense of someone being there which one has even when asleep, though not when dead. I was the incubus and the ghost come to disturb their dreams or to discover her body, it was me and it was no one, perhaps not so very inoffensive. My things were no longer there, I used to use part of the living room as my office sometimes, so as not to spend too many hours in the same room when the work piled up, I kept the scripts in my study and my commissioned speeches in one corner of the living room, which was quite spacious, the table I had installed there was gone, as, of course, were my typewriter, my papers, my pen, my ashtray and my reference books, none of which were necessary there now. In the semidarkness, everything else looked identical, Celia hadn't made any changes, perhaps she didn't have enough money to make the changes she would like to make. When we go back to a very familiar place, the intervening time becomes compressed or is even erased and cancelled out for a moment as if we had never left, it is that unchanging space that allows us to travel in time. I felt like sitting down in my armchair and smoking a cigarette and reading a book. But I couldn't do that, because I still didn't know and I was becoming increasingly agitated, my apprehension and my nocturnal fears were growing, as was my urgent need to find out and my fear of finding out and my desire for peace, I needed to untangle my associations and my ideas, to dispel my superstitions. And then I got up the courage to go over to the white sliding doors which led from the living room to the bedroom, when we went to bed, we always used to close them, even though there was never anyone else there but us, a gesture of intimacy and modesty towards the world that could not see us, and so we would cut ourselves off from the rest of the apartment to sleep or to lie in each other's arms with our eyes open. That was how the doors were now, closed, it was perfectly normal that Celia should keep that habit, whether alone or accompanied, it would be odder if the doctor or lover had closed them again after him, after leaving the bedroom, leaving behind him a cast-off, his work. That made me think that nothing could have happened and that gave me the courage to put my hands on the handles and very slowly to open the doors a crack, I looked through it, putting my eye to the crack, I could see nothing, it was darker in the bedroom, Celia had closed the blinds, taking advantage of my absence, she liked them closed and I liked them open, so eventually we reached an agreement, a compromise, we had them down but with the slats slightly open so that the morning light would not hurt her eyes and so that I would be able to tell if it was day or not when I woke up, I often wake up during the night, I never sleep very well or right through. I pulled the handles harder and kept on pulling until the doors were completely open, I wasn't sure that I wanted to do that, but I did it, one's actions move faster than one's will, a yes and a no and a perhaps and, meanwhile, everything has moved on or is gone, you have to fill up the insistent time that continues to pass without waiting for us, we move more slowly, and thus the moment arrives when we can no longer keep saying: "I don't know, I'm not sure, we'll see." I wanted to find Celia alone in the bed as if we had never separated or turned our backs on each other, to see her sleeping face that I remember so well, her left arm under the pillow, that's how she sleeps, breathing peacefully. There was no reaction, I heard nothing, I waited for the feeble light from the living room, which was the light from the stormy sky and the rain-flailed street, to dimly illuminate the interior of the bedroom and for my eyes to get used to the darkness so that I could discern something. I saw the white stain of the sheets, that was the first thing I managed to recognize, as she or they would have seen the pale stain of my raincoat if they had woken up at that moment and peered into the space before them. Much later, I stood like that at the door of a child's bedroom, but he had already seen me and had moved from wakefulness into sleep, not vice versa. And when my eyes had got more accustomed to the darkness, I was able to make out two figures in the double bed, two shapes beneath the sheets, Celia lay on the right-hand side and on the side that had been mine lay not me but another man, the same places occupied by different people, it's common enough, not only during our own allotted time span and in conscious or deliberate or imposed substitutions or usurpations, but also throughout the centuries of unchanging space, the houses of those who leave or die are occupied by the living or by the new arrivals, their bedrooms, their bathrooms, their beds, people who forget or have no idea what happened in those places, perhaps before they were born or were merely children with useless time on their hands. So many things happen without anyone realizing or remembering. So few things are recorded, fleeting thoughts and actions, plans and desires, secret doubts, daydreams, acts of cruelty and insults, words spoken and heard and later denied or misunderstood or distorted, promises made and then overlooked, even by those to whom they were made, everything is forgotten or invalidated, whatever is done alone or not written down, along with everything that is done not alone but in company, how little remains of each individual, how little trace remains of anything, and how much of that little is never talked about, and afterwards, one remembers only a tiny fraction of what was said, and then only briefly, the individual memory is not passed on and is, anyway, of no interest to the person receiving it, who is busy forging his or her own memories. All time is useless, not only that of the child, for all time is the same, however much happens, however much enthusiasm or pain one feels, it only lasts an instant, then it is lost and everything is as slippery as compacted snow, like the sleep being enjoyed now, at this moment, by Celia and the man occupying my place in the bed. That sleep vanished for ever before my eyes, although I was not the one to make it vanish, despite my being there: a flash of lightning followed by an even louder clap of thunder than before suddenly lit up the apartment, lit up the living room and the bedroom and my spectral figure standing there motionless in my raincoat, my arms outspread, holding open the white doors; it lit up the bed on which the two figures or shapes simultaneously and abruptly sat up or awoke, both wrenched from sleep, and Celia cried out like that king terrified by the visions he had seen, her eyes very wide and her hands over her ears, protecting them from the noise of the thunder or of her own cries. And I looked only at her, her naked torso like that of Marta Téllez, her firm, white breasts in which I had lost all interest until that night, when I thought she might also be Victoria of Hermanos Bécquer. The pale light showed me all that, as well as the clothes piled on a chair, his doubtless mingling with hers, removed at the same time, perhaps she had removed his and he hers. I didn't see the man, I didn't see his face, only the stain he made in the darkness, white like the sheets, I didn't see if he was the fair-haired, balding doctor or some other man I had never seen or glimpsed or someone I knew or a friend, Ruibérriz de Torres, for example. (Or Deán or Vicente, it would be another two and a half years before I knew their names and heard their voices and recognized their faces.) It could have been me. The brightness faded before I could see him, worse, I must have cried out too – perhaps shaking my fists in the air like someone crying out for vengeance, not that I deserved any vengeance – then I closed the doors, turned in terror and ran through the darkness of the living room and along the corridor – frightened of myself and of the effect I had had. I knew the terrain and there was no reason why I should collide with anything, even though I was fleeing like a soul being carried off by the Devil, as they used to say in my language, I could reach the front door before they had grasped the physical reality of the man in the raincoat who had spied on them from the doorway of their bedroom in the middle of the storm, and could recover from the panic of their awakenings, perhaps they would assume that they had shared a common nightmare, the same husband or incubus visiting them and oppressing them and finally tearing them, terrified, from sleep. They would not pursue me, they were naked, at least from the waist up, that much I had seen in the lightning flash. They were barefoot. I could and did reach the lift that was still waiting on that floor, I travelled down in it and crossed the hall and pressed the button and rushed out into the street lashed by the torrential rain that drenched me in a matter of seconds, and I ran and thought with relief that, although not alone, Celia was still alive and I would never know whether or not she was also Victoria. But while I was fleeing and going down in the lift and rushing out into the street and getting soaked and running away, my main thought was quite different, what I was thinking was: "How little remains of me in that apartment, how little trace remains of anything." The trees shook their branches like furious citizens in a popular uprising.

I CROSSED THE CASTELLANA behind Luisa, I had already
spent a good while staring at her legs and I no longer felt like
a scoundrel or ashamed to be looking at them, perhaps because I
did so at my leisure, unhypocritically and without witnesses,
perhaps because, as I followed her, I could not do or want anything
else, what more could I want? She went down the street full of
embassies in which, during the day, there are no parked cars with
people inside them, nor are there transvestites waiting patiently
and fatalistically on benches, she walked four blocks, moving from
one side of the street to the other, and on the fifth block, she went
in through the door of the house she had been heading for, from
the way she walked it was clear that she knew where she was going
from the moment she left the shop, preferring a zigzag route to the
strait and narrow, a way of making a familiar route more interesting. It was the most modest and neglected doorway in a good
street, an expensive area, and so was not, therefore, particularly
modest or particularly neglected, just a little run-down, in need of
renovation. There were no bars nearby where I could sit and wait
and watch for her to come out, however long that took, perhaps it
was her own apartment and she would not emerge for the rest of
the day, although it didn't seem like that to me from the way she
had gone in, you're usually already feeling for your keys in your
pocket, or in your handbag if you're a woman, I suppose, if you're
Luisa or Marta Téllez. I remembered Luisa's last words to Deán in
the restaurant, "I'll see you at home," I had assumed she meant
Conde de la Cimera, in fact it was ambiguous, "home" could also
be Luisa's home which this perhaps was. I decided to wait, I set
myself a limit of half an hour which I knew would stretch to three-
quarters of an hour if necessary, I moved a little further from the
door, I leaned on a corner so as not to be too obvious and so that

I could disappear in an instant, I lit a cigarette and started reading the foreign newspaper I had bought, it was *La Repubblica*, at least I could understand it, Italian and Spanish being related languages, and I let my thoughts drift. And I waited. I waited.

I was reading an article about the crisis in Juventus' game in Turin, possibly due to a widespread and growing interest in Satanism in that city, or perhaps I had let myself be misled by the apparent similarities between the two languages – that probably explains my loss of concentration and why I was not as alert as I should have been, or perhaps it was simply because I didn't have to wait as long as I had expected, not even a quarter of an hour had passed, which is why I wasn't on my guard – and when I glanced up at the doorway for the umpteenth time in those eleven or thirteen minutes and, instead of a blank – the door was open – or some unknown neighbour – two had come out in that brief space of time – I saw the face and astonished eyes of Luisa Téllez only a few steps away and another face and another familiar pair of eyes looking up at me from infinitely lower down, from the height of a two-year-old: Eugenio was well wrapped up and was wearing a quilted gaberdine cap with a strap buckled under his chin, reminiscent of those worn by pilots in the old days, although his cap had a small peak. He was holding Luisa's hand and she was far less loaded down now, in her other hand she was carrying only a handbag and one of the two Armani bags, she had left the other one upstairs – Téllez's birthday present, the top or the skirt – along with the bag containing *Lolita*, perhaps her own present, not much, a paperback book; either that, or a most unusual commission – and the beers and the sausages and the ice cream, those were doubtless the ingredients for the quick and simple supper that María Fernández Vera would not have had the time to buy having spent part of the morning and part of the afternoon looking after the boy, her sister-in-law must have promised to do some shopping for her and Guillermo on her way to collect their orphaned nephew. They were standing there before me, the aunt and the boy, they were two steps away, they must have come out just after I last glanced at the door and that had given them time to walk over, without my noticing, to where I was standing, reading about Satanism and soccer in Italian: they were about to turn the corner. Or perhaps there was a simpler explanation and I had actually allowed myself to be seen, tired of moving in the shadows. I wondered if the boy would recognize me, I don't know how much small boys remember or if it varies from individual to individual, it had been more than a month since he had seen me, but he had been with me over a period of a good few hours and on a night that for him had proved catastrophic, the end of his world: throughout the whole of a seemingly interminable supper during which he had played the role of guardian to his mother and had refused to go to sleep precisely because I was there. He had heard my name several times as I had heard his ("Come on, Eugenio, love," Marta had said at one point, "off to bed now, otherwise Víctor will get angry," and it wasn't true that I would get angry, although I was getting impatient), and he had seen me again when his simple dreams had been interrupted and he had pushed open the bedroom door that had been left ajar and, without his mother realizing, he had leaned in the doorway clutching his dummy and his rabbit, he had placed one hand on my forearm and I had led him away from there, concealing the bra, or trophy, which I still have, and preventing him from saying goodbye when he did not even know that he would have to, the end of his world and the last time that he would have seen her alive. Had it been otherwise, I would have let him come in, even though she was half-naked.

"Ictor," said the boy, pointing at me, he said it with a smile, he remembered my name. I think I found that rather touching.

Having recovered from her surprise, Luisa Téllez stood looking at me curiously, fixedly. Then it occurred to me how ridiculous both my presence and my appearance must seem, standing there reading a foreign newspaper with, next to me, on the ground, a bag containing a video of *101 Dalmatians*, which didn't interest me in the least, and an ice cream that would soon be melting, indeed, it probably already was, I realized then that it would be some time before I went home. I also had one sodden shoe that squelched every time I took a step, it was a sound more suited to the deck of a ship.

"What on earth are you playing at?" she said pityingly, and now she addressed me unhesitatingly as "tú", the way young people do and the way we all do when we address someone mentally, even when it is not to insult them or curse them or desire their ruin, shame and death, or to put them under a spell.

I felt embarrassed, I must have blushed a bit as she had when she opened the freezer door and was enveloped for a moment in that cold air, but I know that I also felt happy and relaxed, it meant an end to dissembling and an end to secrecy, at least as far as she was concerned, one less area of darkness for Luisa the sister.

"So, what did you choose in the end, the skirt or the top?" I asked, at the same time making as if to peer into the bag she was still carrying. I equally unhesitatingly addressed her as "tú" as well.

You can tell when anger could just as easily tip over into laughter, you spend your whole life watching for it, trying to get back into someone's good graces, in the broadest sense of the word "grace", trying to make sure that they don't notice your faults, outrages and abuses, the mistakes one makes and the disappointment they represent for those who trusted in you, the minor betrayals and minor insults. You can always tell who is going to forgive you, at least for a time, who is going to take no notice or turn a blind eye, to use a colloquial expression gradually falling into disuse, even idioms fade and disappear. Luisa would be like that, benevolent and lighthearted and practical and even frivolous if necessary, I saw it at that moment, I hadn't seen it before, during lunch, but then she had hardly paid me any attention at all and she was finding her brother-in-law and father somewhat irritating, the former with his inability to reach a decision on something that affected her directly, and the latter with his irksome, backward-looking view of life, a man from another time who didn't understand much and didn't try to, he was no longer of an age to make changes or to make an effort, in keeping with the character or person he had ended up as. And yet even then, I must have glimpsed something of her natural cheeriness and help-fulness, her tacit defence of Deán, the compassion she felt for him, even though she did not perhaps actually feel much sympathy or liking for him, her sense of duty towards the boy, her readiness to help and to change her habits – her life – her desire for recon-ciliation between the people close to her, her silence during the argument between the two men who got on so badly, her need for clarity and probably for harmony too, her ability to imagine the worst aspects of another person's death despite her own limited experience ("What would be frightening would be to think it," she had said, "and to know it"). She had paid me no attention, but during that lunch I had been merely an employee, an intruder, an inappropriate presence that had facilitated Téllez's careless indifference. Now, on the other hand, I was someone, not only my name had taken on considerable meaning in the boy's truncated pronunciation, I had suddenly become more interesting and had acquired, so to speak, a new place in the hierarchy. Now I was someone chosen by her older sister, Luisa had no way of knowing that I had played second or even third fiddle: I was someone with whom Marta had been in intimate contact during her last hours, hours which she could not have imagined would be her last, but which were, and that final moment had, in part, defined her for ever, we end up seeing our life in the light of the latest or most recent event, the mother believes that she was born to be a mother and the spinster to be single, the murderer to be a murderer and the victim a victim, and the adulteress an adulteress if she realizes, in the middle of the adulterous act, that she is dying and, assuming too, that the word "adulteress" has not also fallen into disuse. Marta did not know it, but I did and I am the one who counts, the one telling the story and the one who decides who will speak, "None that speak of me know me, and when they do speak, they slander me". It was also possible that Luisa had given her own partial, subjective, mistaken or even false version of the two sisters' adolescence, that was now her privilege as this is mine, there was no one now to contradict her, therein lies the pathetic superiority of the living, our temporary motive for triumph. Had Marta been present, she would doubtless have denied what Luisa had said and would again have called her a copycat, she would have said that Luisa was the one who could never decide and that she had only to show an interest in a boy for her younger sister immediately to become interested too, and thus the mechanism of usurpation would be set in motion. Either of the two things could be true, just as one might say: "I never sought it, I never wanted it" or "I sought it, I wanted it," in fact, everything is at once one thing and its contrary, no one does anything convinced of its injustice, which is why there is no justice and why justice never prevails, as the Lone Ranger said in his litany of disordered ideas: society's view is never that of the individual, it is only the view of the time and time is as slippery as sleep and compacted snow and always gives one licence to say: "I am not the thing I was", it's easy enough, while there's still time.

There was no laughter, not as such, just a half-repressed smile, I knew that, as well as being surprised and indignant, Luisa also felt flattered, I had followed her and spied on her, I had taken an interest in her, taken trouble over her, I had observed her and commented on her clothes and her purchases, I was someone chosen by Marta who was now turning all his attention on her, how that death gladdens me, saddens me, pleases me. "How easy it is to seduce someone or to be seduced," I thought, "we are satisfied with so little," and I felt safe and sound, my blushes and my embarrassment vanished, and I thought further, I thought something which, only a few seconds before, would never have occurred to me: "If Deán decided not to live with his son and Luisa went to live in his apartment, this child could, if I wanted, end up being mine, and then I would not be for him what I, at first, thought I would be, a shadow, a nobody, an almost unknown figure who watched him for a few moments from the door of his bedroom without his knowledge, without him ever knowing, and never therefore able to remember it, the two of us travelling slowly towards our dissolution. It wouldn't be quite like that, the reverse side of his time, its dark back. Or, rather, it would be, but it would not only be that, it would be other things too, the partial substitution of his doomed, lost world, the secret and compensatory legacy of one fateful night, a vicariously paternal figure – the usurper in short – the two of us nevertheless travelling towards our dissolution, only much more slowly and creating more work for the waiting oblivion. And thus I will perhaps be able to speak to him one day about what he was that night." And I thought further, I thought also of Luisa herself: "Perhaps I am the vague figure of the husband who has not yet arrived and who will help her to continue for many more years amongst the inconstant living, in a world of men, a world configured by comics and coloured prints and storybooks (and, above them, their model planes). We are united by more than one thing, we have both tied the same shoelace."

"Ah, I see," she said thoughtfully, her smile still hidden, "so you were there too."

"The skirt really suited you," I said. "Well, the top did too, but the skirt suited you best." I did not hide my smile, I had to get into her good graces, I had been a bachelor again for some time now.

"And now what? Now what do we do?" she said. She had grown serious again or had succeeded in making her angry feelings prevail, but she was betrayed by that use of the first person plural, "Now what do we do?", in the midst of her exasperation and severity which were simultaneously sincere and insincere.

"Let's go somewhere where we can talk quietly," I replied.

She looked at me distrustfully, but it passed, her wariness lasted only a short time, or was overcome by the other questions she was asking herself, unable to contain herself, she asked me one of those questions.

"What about the boy? I have to leave him at Marta's place, I was just taking him there now. You know the apartment well, don't you, inside and out? I saw you waiting by a taxi one night, it was you, wasn't it? The night afterwards. How could you have left the boy on his own?"

She still did not think of it as Eduardo's or Eugenio's place, it was still Marta's, it takes a while to lose the habit of using certain phrases that will eventually, albeit slowly, fall into disuse. There was more bitterness in that last question, a more scolding tone, she pouted her lips slightly, but she had little talent for anger, though, doubtless, more for regret. The child was still gazing up at me, a friendly look on his face, he had recognized me and had nothing more to say to me, he had no reason to make a fuss of me, he left that to the grown-ups. I crouched down and put a hand on his shoulder, he showed me a chocolate bar he was holding in his hand. I expected him to say: "chockit". His fingers and mouth were already covered in the stuff.

"He can come with us, it's not that late, you can tell Deán that you were detained here." And I indicated the doorway I had guarded so ineffectually. I was daring to propose to Luisa a concealment, it was inconceivable. I was replying not to her last question, but to her penultimate one. I added: "Or you can leave him at the other apartment and I'll wait for you downstairs. Yes, I imagine it was me you saw, assuming you were the woman in Marta's bedroom that night."

"Did she die alone?" she asked abruptly.

"No, I was with her." I was still crouching down, I answered without looking up.

"Did she realize? Did she know she was dying?"

"No, the thought never occurred to her. Nor to me. It was very sudden." How did I know what had passed through her head, but I said it all the same, I was the one telling the story.

Luisa remained silent. I took a handkerchief out of my jacket pocket, removed the chocolate bar from the child's hands with great skill and care so that he wouldn't get annoyed, then I wiped his mouth and sticky fingers.

"He is in a state," I remarked.

"I know. My sister-in-law just gave it to him," replied Luisa, "to eat on the way home. Ridiculous."

The boy started to protest, the last thing I wanted was to provoke his tears, I had to get into his aunt's good graces.

"Sh, don't cry, look what I've got for you," I said, and I took the video of *101 Dalmatians* out of my bag. "I know how much he likes cartoons, he's got one of Tintin, I was watching it with him," I explained to Luisa. She would never imagine that I had not, in fact, bought that video on purpose, that I had given not a thought to the child or to anyone, that it was pure accident. It would help me to get into her good graces, she would see that I was not entirely heartless. I looked for a nearby litter bin and threw away what remained of the chocolate bar and the wrapper, along with *La Repubblica*, which was beginning to annoy me, and the carton of ice cream and the bag, which was beginning to drip everywhere, it dripped on me and I used my handkerchief to wipe it off, the handkerchief was ruined by then. I threw that in the litter bin too, there; I thought: "What a bit of luck buying that video."

"You could have washed it," Luisa said.

"It doesn't matter." We didn't talk in the taxi that we took at my suggestion, my hands were free again, I opened the door, the boy sat between us, a quiet child, he kept studying the cover of

231

his video, he knew about videos, he was imagining what it might contain, he pointed at the dalmatians and said:

"Dog." I was glad he didn't say "bow-wows" or something like that, as I understand most very young children do.

I behaved well during the journey to Conde de la Cimera, I realized that Luisa Téllez wanted to think and to gain time and to get used to that unexpected association, she was doubtless reconstructing scenes in which she had played a part and scenes where she had not, my night with Marta and the following night, when Deán was still in London and she had probably stayed alone in the apartment with Eugenio, in the bedroom and the bed in which the death, the disaster, had taken place, though not the fuck – only she couldn't know that – she would have changed the sheets and aired the room, it would have been an awful night for her, one of sadness and dark thoughts and imaginings. I only risked a glance at her thighs out of the corner of my eye when I noticed that she was looking at my face out of the corner of her eye, she had had plenty of opportunity to look at it during lunch, but then she had hardly given it a glance, now she was putting my face to the person who, until that moment, had lacked a face, had been no one, a stranger without even a name – and my name is Víctor Francés, that's how Téllez had introduced me to Luisa, not as Ruibérriz de Torres, my whole name is Víctor Francés Sanz, although I never use the second surname: only in England have I been called Mr Sanz – now she could imagine Marta with me, she could even decide if we would have made a nice couple or if Marta could have imagined that she was going to die in my arms. I wanted to ask her questions too, not many, I could wait, I did not open my mouth except to speak to the child and to confirm to him:

"Yes, dogs, lots of dogs with spots." He probably didn't know the word "spots".

I said goodbye to him at the door of his or Marta's apartment, I patted his cap, I imagined that it would not be long before Deán arrived, if he hadn't arrived already, it was more or less the time when he and Luisa had arranged to meet at home, she told me that she had called him at the office from her sister-in-law's apartment to find out how much longer she was to have the boy. Deán would have said: "Go to the apartment now, if you like, I won't be long, I should be there around half past seven."

"If he hasn't arrived yet, I'll have to wait for him," Luisa said to me as we stood outside the familiar door in Conde de la Cimera. "There's no one else upstairs."

"I'll wait for you in the café over there, however long it takes," I said and I gestured vaguely towards the establishment with the Russophile name on the other side of the detached building, on the ground floor, where they would put out chairs and tables in the summer. There was a dry cleaner's there too, I think, or perhaps it was a stationer's, or both.

"And what if he wants a bit of a chat? He might need to talk about that scene with my father, get things off his chest."

"I'll wait, for however long it takes."

She was just about to go in with the child when she half turned round – her heel went over slightly, the ground was still wet – and she added thoughtfully:

"You do realize that, sooner or later, I'll have to tell him about you."

"But not now," I said.

"No, not now. He might want to come down and get you," she said. "I'll try not to be too long, I'll tell him I have things to do at home."

"You could tell him the truth, that you've got a date at, let's say, half past eight." And I looked at my watch.

She looked at hers and said:

"OK, let's say half past eight."

I waited in the café, from there I would not be able to see if Deán arrived nor would he be able to see me waiting – I was at the rear of the building – unless he came in to have a drink before going upstairs or in order to buy cigarettes, it was unlikely. I waited. I waited, feeling the lack now of a good article on demonology and soccer to peruse, then at a quarter to nine, Luisa Téllez appeared, still carrying her bag containing either the top or the skirt, I had waited for her for over an hour, she must have had a long chat with Deán or else he had arrived late. Not for a moment did I think she would fail me, nor that she would turn up with Deán without prior warning: she would tell him about me, but not now; I believed her. When I saw her, I felt suddenly tired, all that wasted tension, the two beers I had drunk, the whole day spent out and about, I hadn't been home, I hadn't listened to my answering machine or opened the post, the following morning, I would have to get up early to go to Téllez's house and continue writing the words that Only You would soon unleash on the public as if they were his, words in which no one believes anyway. I hoped it would not be another long night, there would be time enough for everything, not a night like that spent with Marta Téllez or with the prostitute Victoria and with Celia, my mind has decided in retrospect that they were not the same person: absurd, grim, endless nights. Celia was about to get married again and put her life in order.

"Right, where shall we go?" asked Luisa. It was already dark. I was still sitting at the bar as if I were Ruibérriz.

"Shall we go to my place?" I said. At that moment, what I wanted most in the world was to be able to change my shoes and socks. "I'd like to change my shoes," I said and showed them to her. White stains, like dust or, rather, lime, had appeared on them as they dried, especially on the right one. Her shoes were immaculate, though she had walked just as far as I had, and along the same streets. When I saw a flicker of doubt cross her face, I added: "I've got the tape from Marta's answering machine too, it might be a good idea if you listened to it."

"So it was you who took the tape," she said, touching her lips with two fingers. "I thought perhaps Marta had got rid of it, I didn't want to go through the rubbish that first night, so I just tied up the bag and put it out, so that Eduardo wouldn't look through it either when he arrived, besides it was already starting to smell. And what about his phone number and address, did you take that too? Why?"

"Let's go somewhere else and I'll answer all your questions." But I did answer one of her questions, because I went on to say: "I took the phone number and the address with me without realizing, I was going to copy it out, but I never got round to it, I thought perhaps I should phone him in London, then I couldn't bring myself to do it. Look, I've still got it." I took out my wallet and showed her the yellow post-it that Marta had not put away in her handbag or lost in the street, nor had it flown out of the open window or been swept up by the streetcleaners. Luisa didn't bother to look at it, she wasn't interested in seeing it, she just took it as read, she knew what it said. "Come on, let's go back to my place for a moment, then, if you like, we can go out to supper."

"No, let's have supper first, I don't want to go to a stranger's apartment."

"If that's what you want," I said, "but don't forget, it was your father himself who introduced us." She was on the point of smiling again, but she stopped herself, for the moment, she still needed to be strict and severe.

We went to Nicolás, a small restaurant where the people know me, so that she could see that I didn't always behave in that furtive, clandestine manner, the owners call me Víctor and the waiters, Señor Francés, there I have a name as well as a face and there I could, at last, tell her the story, I answered her questions and I told her other things that she didn't and couldn't ask me about, that was obviously the only thing I was after, to step out from the shadows and to cease being the holder of a secret, the keeper of a mystery, perhaps I too sometimes have a longing for clarity and probably for harmony too. I told the story, I told it all. And as I told the story, I did not feel as if I were stepping free from the spell I was under and from which I have still not escaped and perhaps never will escape, I felt, instead, as if it were beginning to mingle with another less tenacious, more benign spell. The person telling a story is usually able to explain things well and to explain himself, telling a story is tantamount to persuading someone or making oneself clear or making someone see one's point of view, that way everything becomes capable of being understood, even the most vile of acts, everything can be forgiven when there is something to forgive, everything can be overlooked or assimilated or even pitied, such and such happened and we have to learn to live with it once we know that it did happen, we have to find a place for it in our consciousness and in our memory where the fact that it happened and that we know about it will not prevent us from going on living. For that reason, what actually happened is never as dreadful as our fears and hypotheses, as our conjectures and imaginings and bad dreams, which we do not, in fact, incorporate into our knowledge, we dismiss them once we have suffered them or considered them for a moment, and that is why they continue to horrify us, unlike actual events which, by their very nature, precisely because they are facts, diminish in importance: since this has happened and I know about it and nothing can be done, we tell ourselves, I must try and understand it and make it mine or have someone else explain it to me, and the best person to do that would be the person directly involved, because he is the one who knows. You can even get into someone's good graces by telling them a story, that's the danger. The sheer power of the performance, I suppose: that's why there are defendants, that's why there are enemies who are murdered or executed or lynched without being allowed to utter a word – that's why there are friends whom one casts off, saying: "I do not know you", or whose letters one refuses to answer – precisely so that they cannot explain and slip back into our good graces again, when they speak, they slander me, so it's better that they say nothing, even though, in their silence, they do not defend me.

And then I, in turn, asked questions, not many, just a few things, out of pure curiosity, who came to the apartment and when, who discovered what I had kept silent all that night, how long the boy was left alone, when and how they managed to locate Deán in London and how long, from the time it happened, when he could have known about it, did he spend in ignorance, how many minutes had he spent in error, how much of his time had become something strange, floating or fictitious like a film you start watching halfway through on the television or in the cinemas of years ago, how much time was claimed by a kind of limbo. And Luisa answered my questions without any trace of suspicion or distrust – by then, she felt little of either, I had explained myself, I had made her see what had happened, I had made myself clear and perhaps even gained her forgiveness if there was anything to be forgiven (leaving the child alone, but it would have been worse had I taken him with me, that's what I told her: it would have been like kidnapping); and I had doubtless gained her sympathy. The boy had only spent the morning alone, from the moment he woke up until the time the cleaning woman arrived and let herself in, she used to clean the house and prepare a bit of lunch for the boy and for Marta and for the husband when he ate at home, and then she would stay with him while his mother went to her classes at the university – the same university where I studied – either in the morning or the evening, depending on the day. The boy did not seem to have realized that Marta was dead, because you can only recognize something you have known before and he did not know what death was, indeed, he still did not know and he would have had to assume that the unmoving body, indifferent to his calls and pleas, was asleep, he would have had to go back to that sleeping image in order to explain what happened that morning. He must have clambered up on to the double bed, he must have uncovered his mother as best he could, bearing in mind the weight of the bedspread and the sheets, he would have touched her, his hands would have touched her all over, he might perhaps have struck her, because small children do hit out when they get angry (you shouldn't hold it against them) and Marta would still have looked like Marta. No one knows if he cried or shouted angrily for a long time without anyone hearing him or perhaps choosing not to hear him, the fact is that he must have grown tired and got hungry, he ate the food from the eclectic platter I had improvised for him and he drank the juice, then he sat down to watch television, not the one in the living room that was showing *Chimes at Midnight* when I left, but the television in the bedroom that was still showing Fred MacMurray and Barbara Stanwyck, who were still on screen talking in subtitles, he probably preferred to be close to his sleeping mother, still clinging to the hope that she would wake up. That's how the cleaning lady found him just after midday, lying at the foot of the bed near his inert, dishevelled mother, watching with the sound turned down whatever programme chance offered him at the time, with luck, something for children. For a few moments, the cleaning lady did not know what to do – her hands still raised to her hat secured with the hat pin that she had not had time to remove since arriving at the apartment, still with her overcoat on, her initial thought, like a flash of lightning, was to curse the mess she had been left to clear up, she didn't know that Deán was in London, for the previous day, Marta had forgotten that he was going to be away until it was too late, she called his office and, unable to speak to Ferrán, she spoke hysterically to his secretary who understood little or nothing of what she said, then she found the sister's phone number, Luisa's, who was the first to arrive at Conde de la Cimera, in a taxi, out of breath, ten minutes later, Deán's colleague or partner at the office arrived, he had come in order to try and find out what was meant by the garbled message left with his secretary by the unfortunate cleaning woman. They looked in vain for the London address and phone number, they called a doctor they knew and while he was examining the corpse and advising them on its removal – I didn't ask what the cause of death was, because I still don't feel that it matters and life is unique and fragile, who knows, a cerebral embolism, a myocardial infarction, an aortic aneurysm, a meningococcal infection of the adrenal glands, an overdose of something, an internal haemorrhage caused by being hit by a car a few days before, any illness that kills swiftly, impatiently and unhesitatingly, meeting no resistance on the part of the dead woman who died in my arms as if she were a docile child, Ferrán stayed with her and Luisa took the child to her brother Guillermo's house – removing him from there as soon as possible, so that he would begin to forget and not ask questions – then to see her father in order to break the news in person, she asked the cleaning lady to wait but not to touch anything or throw anything away, they had to keep looking for Deán's address in London – the cleaning lady agreed to do so, but she kept grumbling about the time she was wasting idly in the kitchen, in her work clothes, knowing that they would expect her to get down to some hard slog later, outside her normal working hours. Luisa accompanied Téllez to María Fernández Vera's house as soon as her father was able to get out of the armchair he had fallen or, rather, sunk back into, since he was already sitting down – his face hidden in his mottled hands, seeking refuge – and as soon as he had drunk the whisky that his daughter had poured for him even though it was still morning, as it is in Madrid until lunchtime, at two or three o'clock: she probably tied his shoelaces properly before going out so that he would not stumble any more than he might otherwise do, his legs shaky with the news, he would walk as if he were walking in snow, just managing to extricate one foot, only to plunge back in again at every step, his dainty feet like those of a retired dancer. While Luisa was at her father's house, María Fernández Vera, who had been sobbing and clutching the child to her ever since they had brought him over, managed to free one hand long enough to call her husband at work, and he and Luisa returned together to Conde de la Cimera (or rather Luisa returned and Guillermo went there for the first time) to find another doctor at the apartment, a forensic one this time – sporting rather inappropriate sideburns, doubtless to compensate for his baldness – who certified that Marta was dead, and to find that Ferrán had disappeared: according to the cleaning lady, he had been very upset and had gone to the Russophile café downstairs to drink a few vermouths or a few beers. Luisa went down to get him and they diligently resumed their double search, Luisa, Guillermo and the cleaning lady were in charge of looking for the bit of paper with Deán's London address and phone number on it, his colleague was in charge of phoning round, trying to locate the English businessmen with whom Deán was supposed to be getting in touch during his stay there. But Ferrán barely spoke any English, that was Deán's province, which was why he did all the travelling, he couldn't get in touch with some of the businessmen and the one he did manage to speak to apparently said that he hadn't heard from Deán, that he didn't even know he was in London. They began making other phone calls to a few close friends, they had to hide the manner and circumstances – though not the cause – of her death from as many people as possible, it was best to tell only a few in order to limit the questions asked. Even so, the apartment began filling up with relatives and neighbours and friends and the kind of vulture who loves this kind of situation and who insists on embracing all the family – the young woman with the beige gloves was probably there too, but I didn't ask about her – a bearded judge arrived and, finally, the corpse was taken away to the morgue. Some people accompanied it, amongst them Guillermo and later María Fernández Vera; when Luisa managed to get back to María's apartment and pick up her father and the boy and free the latter from María Fernández Vera's embraces, she dropped Téllez back at his own apartment, having given him a sleeping pill, went back to her own place to collect a few things and then, alone now with Eugenio, who was absolutely exhausted, she returned to Conde de la Cimera for the third time that day at about eleven o'clock at night: she decided to sleep there rather than take the child somewhere else, in the belief that it's better for those who live in the home of a person who has died to go on sleeping and living there from the very first night, otherwise, later, they often don't want to go back, they don't want to go back there ever; that belief was shared by her more experienced father whom she consulted on the matter. According to the porter, the cleaning lady had left in high dudgeon, no one had told her what she was supposed to do or paid her the least bit of attention – Luisa had merely asked if she could borrow her key – it was hoped that, even so, she would turn up the next day to clean up the mess, that she would be understanding. Luisa put the exhausted child to bed – along with his dummy and his rabbit – his bedroom being the only room that remained intact, no one touched the aeroplanes, although all peered in as they passed by the open door, then she too took a sleeping pill. She tied up the rubbish bag and put it out, or did so subsequently, she searched, hopelessly and only superficially now, for the unfindable address and telephone number, at the same time tidying up a bit and changing the sheets on Marta's bed, which no one had bothered to do, the cleaning lady lacked initiative. She lay down and then she wondered about me, when she still didn't know that I was I, she remembered the message Marta had left on her answering machine about twenty-four hours previously ("I've got a date with a guy I hardly know, but I quite fancy him, I met him at a cocktail party and we arranged to meet for coffee the next day, he knows all kinds of people, he's divorced, he writes scripts and things, and he's coming over for supper; Eduardo's in London, I don't quite know what will happen, but something might and I feel a bit nervous about it"); she hadn't mentioned any name, no name, my name. She thought about her sister, she thought about her sister for a long time as she lay on her sister's bed, in her sister's bedroom, unable to understand what had happened, her abrupt dissolution, as if suddenly she could not differentiate between life and death, as if she no longer knew the difference between someone you can't see now and someone you will never see again, even if you want to (we don't see anyone all the time, only ourselves, and only then partially, our arms and hands and legs). "I don't know why I'm alive and she's dead, I don't know what either of those words means any more. I no longer have any clear understanding of those two terms." That's what she thought, or what I thought for her while she was telling me. She turned on the television, she wouldn't be able to get to sleep for some time even though she was exhausted by all the toing and froing and by the tragedy and the grief, she didn't even try, it was still early for her to go to bed, she didn't even bother getting undressed. Past midnight the telephone rang and it made her jump, it was then that she noticed that the tape in the answering machine was missing or, rather, immediately afterwards, when she saw that the machine was on, but went on ringing instead of operating as normal; she picked it up in a state of some distress, both wanting it to be Deán in London – making a routine call home with no clue as to what had happened – and dreading it: it was Ferrán, he had finally managed to talk to one of the English businessmen, who had told him the name of the lost hotel, the Wilbraham. He didn't want to phone Deán, he didn't dare, too many hours had passed for him to break the news to his friend just like that, in cold blood, and it would be in cold blood. "I'll do it," Luisa said, "but he's bound to want to call you afterwards, when he finds out that you arrived immediately after me and saw Marta that way." "If he wants to talk to me, that's different," replied Ferrán, "it's just that I don't feel capable of giving him the news now, myself, over the phone. Are you going to tell him that she wasn't alone?" "I'd rather wait until he's here to tell him that, but I'm not sure that will be possible, he'll ask me questions, he'll want to know all the details, how it happened and why she didn't call him as soon as she felt ill. Too many other people have realized what happened for us to try and hide it, he's bound to find out, it's best that he should know." And then, without any further delay, Luisa phoned the hotel (I didn't enquire as to whether she asked for Mr Deán or Mr Dean or Mr Ballesteros), so he already knew when I dialled his number from a public telephone at about one o'clock in the morning, only to hang up without saying a word, after hearing his voice say "Hello". He had just found out about it from Luisa, and his colleague had confirmed it, and some twenty hours of his time had to be corrected or cancelled or recounted, some twenty hours of his stay in London had to be converted into something strange, floating or fictitious, as will the images I retain of Fred MacMurray and Barbara Stanwyck, if I ever watch that subtitled film all the way through, as will the fragment of *Chimes at Midnight* that Only the Lonely watched on his sleepless night, when they get hold of the video for him, assuming Miss Anita bothers to do so. Or those scenes of Spitfire pilots and ghosts and kings that I saw on another night two and a half years ago, I still haven't managed to catch either of the films being shown simultaneously that night, I still don't know what the films were nor do I understand them, and yet that neither denies nor cancels their existence. Those twenty hours would have become for him the kind of enchantment or dream that must be expunged from our memory, as if we had not really lived through that period of time, as if we had to re-tell the story or re-read a book; they would have come to represent a period of time we find unbearable, a source of despair.

Luisa lay down on the bed again, once she had fulfilled her final duty of the day, a duty for which she had preferred to remain sitting up – it's difficult to tell someone about a death and to console a widower from a supine position – afterwards, she watched television for a long time until, inexplicably, sleep crept over her and, even then, she still had strength enough to get up and start to undress, without my help or anyone else's – how is it possible to sleep after the death of a loved one, and yet one always does – she went over to the window and stood there to take her sweater off, she crossed her arms, gripped the lower edges of the sweater and then pulled it up and off in a single movement – affording a momentary glimpse of her armpits – so that only the inside-out sleeves of the sweater remained on her arms or caught on her wrists. Her silhouette remained frozen like that for a few seconds, as if exhausted by the effort or by her day's work – the desolate gesture of someone who can't stop thinking and who gets undressed gradually in order to think or ponder between items of clothing, and needs those pauses – or as if, only after taking off the sweater – she was standing just behind the blinds to do this – had she looked through the blinds and seen something or someone, perhaps me with my taxi behind me?

"He's looking for you," she said, when she had finished telling me all the details I knew nothing about or about which I had only conjectured, "and I'll have to tell him that I've found you."

"I know," I said, and then I told her what I had chanced to overhear as I left the cemetery, I admitted to her that I had been there that morning when I had seen her for the first time and I repeated to her the words I had overheard from people who were, I told her, strangers to me: I didn't feel able to tell her the news if she didn't know it already, I wanted her to find out as I had, from the tape, although, in fact, I had heard it live. "Have they found out who the bloke was yet?" a man walking ahead of me had asked, that's what he had said; and the woman by his side had replied: "No, not yet, but they've only just started looking and, apparently, Eduardo is determined to find him." They were not complete strangers, their names were Vicente and Inés, and I had been on the point of becoming his co-fornicator.

There was no one else left in the restaurant, I had already paid, the owners were kind enough to pretend that they were closing the till and doing their accounts. We had eaten everything they had put in front of us barely noticing what it was, Luisa mechanically raised a napkin to her lips one last time, she had left it on the table after dessert, which already seemed an age ago, she had not wanted coffee but had ordered a pear liqueur instead.

"Yes," she said, "I imagine everyone knew, apart, luckily, from my father. I just hope he never finds out."

"Before you talk to your brother-in-law, I'd like you to hear the tape," I said. "There's something on it which you may not know about, and which he certainly doesn't. In fact, that's why I took it. Would you mind if we went up to my apartment for a moment? Then I'll take you home in a taxi." I paused and added: "You know me a bit better now."

"And may get to know me even better," I thought.

Luisa looked at me hard, frowning, as if she had heard my thoughts, she seemed to be struggling with a mixture of curiosity, tiredness and distrust – telling a story is very tiring – the two latter feelings were the weaker ones. She did actually look like Marta, especially when her face was not contorted as it had been at the funeral. She was younger – although, one day, she will be older – prettier perhaps and less dissatisfied with her lot. She said:

"All right, but let's go now, let's get it over with."

I knew and know that tape by heart, but for her, it would be the first time she had listened to it. She didn't want anything to drink at home, I asked her to wait in the living room a moment while I went into my bedroom to change my shoes and socks at last, with a feeling of immeasurable relief. She sat down in the armchair that I usually sit in to read and smoke and think, she perched on the edge, leaving her overcoat draped any old how over one of the arms, like someone anxious to leave a place the moment they arrive. She was perched on the edge like that from the start, but she leaned forward still more – as if shocked – when she heard the first steady, precipitate, monotonous voice saying: "Marta? Marta, are you there? Did we get cut off before. Hello." There was a pause and an irritated clicking of the tongue. "Hello? What are you playing at? Are you out? When I phoned you just now, you hung up on me. Oh, for Christ's sake, pick up the bloody phone"; and when the tormenting electric-shaver voice had concluded its message, I stopped the tape and she said, addressing both me and herself:

"That's Vicente Mena, a friend, well, a former boyfriend of my sister's. She was with him for a while before she met Eduardo, they remained friends, they often go out together, the four of them, he and his wife, Inés, and Eduardo and Marta. I knew nothing about this, Marta never talked to me about it, she never said that they'd started seeing each other again like that, and he's such a horrible man." She fell silent for a moment. She had inadvertently used the present tense, "they often go out together, the four of them," it takes us a while to get used to employing the past tense about the people who are close to us and who die, it takes us time to notice the difference. She was scratching her temple with one finger and she added pensively: "Perhaps they never really broke it off, how stupid."

"What shift would his wife be working?" I asked, to satisfy a secondary curiosity of mine, I might not be able to satisfy the major ones I could feel rising up inside me. "What does she do?"

"I'm not sure, I don't know them that well, I think she works at the courts," replied Luisa and then I played the tape with its second message, the beginning of which had been cut off, ". . . so", a voice was saying, the voice of the woman I now knew to be Luisa, because I had spent a whole evening hearing her voice, in a variety of tones, "make sure you call me tomorrow and tell me all about it," and Luisa closed her eyes and said: "That's me, returning the message she had left for me that afternoon, telling me about her imminent encounter with you. It seems such a long time ago now."

I stopped the tape.

"How come she told you about that but not about Vicente?"

"Well, she wasn't getting on very well with Eduardo, she had her fantasies, I had no idea that they were also realities, not until now: Vicente Mena, after all this time, how stupid," she repeated incredulously, disapprovingly. "Besides we've always told each other everything, or almost everything, she probably only told me about the fantasies and not the realities." "I'm a fantasy," I thought, "or I was before I went to Conde de la Cimera. And perhaps afterwards too, perhaps I was an incubus and a ghost, and still am." "Although it may not make much sense to you, we didn't judge each other, we didn't even advise each other, we just listened. With some people you always think that whatever they do is fine, you're just always on their side." Luisa was, without realizing it, still scratching her temple. "Marta, tell Eduardo that it's common to say 'we'll get back to you', he should say 'we'll return your call'," the end of the old man's message, flirting with self-pity at the end, "*povero me*", he said. "That's my father, poor him, poor him indeed," said Luisa. "He got on very well with Marta, she paid him more attention than I do, she used to listen to his stories about ancient quarrels with colleagues and about his little intrigues and privileges at Court. He would have been on the phone to her about you instantly, several times a day, it's a real event for him to have someone working at his apartment for a few days; that's why he wanted us to meet you, so that then it would be easier for us to imagine him in your company and we would be better placed to comment when he talked about it later on. Well, to me, not to Eduardo." She didn't realize the impossibility of Téllez ever having spoken about me to Marta, because I would never have wanted to meet Téllez if Marta hadn't died. "Marta, it's Ferrán," was the next message, and Luisa said nothing about it, it contained nothing new, she listened in silence and I didn't stop the tape, the next message or rather the end of it came on, the voice saying: "Anyway we'll do whatever you say, whatever you want. You decide." Now I was sure that it was not the same voice as before and therefore not Luisa's voice, although women's voices tend to be more alike than men's. Luisa asked me to rewind the tape so that she could hear it again, and then she said: "I don't know who that is, I don't recognize the voice, it's not a voice I know. I've never heard it before."

"So you don't know who it's for, Deán or Marta?"

"How could I?"

"Now it's my turn, this one's me," I told her quickly before the start of another incomplete message, the message I was ashamed of: "If you like, we can get together on Monday or Tuesday. Otherwise, we'll have to leave it for next week. From Wednesday onwards, I'm up to my eyes." How could I have said "I'm up to my eyes", I sounded such a phoney, I thought again glumly, any courtship looks pathetic when viewed from outside or in retrospect, now I was doing exactly that, and, worse, I was possibly engaged in another courtship, and thus incapable of seeing my words and my present attitude from outside or, indeed, from inside or in retrospect, sometimes we weigh each word in accordance with our, as yet, unknown intentions. "It all seems such a long time ago." I didn't stop the tape, Luisa let my deferential voice pass without comment, and then that electric buzz came on again: "Eduardo, hi, it's me. Listen don't wait for me to start supper," and so on until he asked them to save him a slice of ham and said an abrupt goodbye: "Right then, see you later," he said.

"That's Vicente Mena too," said Luisa, "The four of them often go out together or with other people." And again she used the present tense which had been inappropriate for a whole month now.

I stopped the tape and said: "There's one more. Listen."

And then that strident, continuous, undisguised weeping emerged from the tape, a weeping that has nothing to do with words or even thoughts, because it stops them or excludes them rather than replaces them – it impedes them – the grieving voice that could say only one intelligible thing: ". . . please . . . please . . . please . . ." and it was saying that not so much as a genuine plea intended to have some effect, but more as a conjuration, ritual, superstitious words, empty of meaning, spoken either to overcome or to fend off a threat, an immodest, almost malign weeping, not so very different from the more sober weeping of the female ghost who had uttered a curse with her pale lips as if she were reading something out in a low voice, while her cheeks streamed with tears: "That wretched Ann, thy wife, that never slept a quiet hour with thee, now fills thy sleep with perturbations." And it was only when I heard that for the umpteenth time, but also for the first time with someone by my side listening to it too, that it occurred to me that that child's voice, that infantilized woman's voice could be that of Marta herself, who knows, perhaps she had called Deán some time ago while she was away on a trip and had pleaded to him in her absence – perhaps he had been at home, sitting next to the phone, listening to her crying, but not picking up the receiver – she had left her tearful plea on the answering machine, a plea incorporated into her weeping as if it were just another of its possible modes, she had recorded her grief which was now being listened to by her sister and a stranger – possibly the vague, inconstant husband who had not yet arrived for that sister – just as Celia once left me three messages, one after the other, and by the end of the last one, she could barely speak or breathe. And I did not dare return her call, it was best not to.

"Who is it? Who's that?" Luisa asked me, frightened. It was an absurd question, provoked by confusion and by the infectious desolation of the voice, I couldn't possibly know who it was, even though I was the temporary and accidental owner of the tape (the thief or repository), and had listened to it so many times.

"I've no idea," I said, "I thought perhaps you might know. Who is this woman pleading with, Deán or Marta?" And again I gave expression to my doubts.

"I don't know. Him, I suppose. I hope," said Luisa. She was troubled, more even than when she had heard the first message from Vicente Mena with its grotesque revelation. She was scratching her forehead harder now, it was a gesture intended to indicate a calm she did not feel, or to keep a hold on herself. She reconsidered and added: "But I only think that because it's a woman's voice doing the pleading. I don't actually know."

I hesitated before mentioning what had just occurred to me that instant, and before I had even decided to do so, I had already done it, before knowing if I was right to do so or if I wanted to infect Luisa with the way of thinking that has become normal in me, dictated by the spell I am under and which is like an incessant beating in my thoughts (time does not wait for us):

"Could it be Marta?"

"Marta?" Luisa started, for those of us who live alone, it is not easy to imagine ourselves ringing our own number or other people ringing theirs. But I haven't always lived alone.

"Yes, couldn't it be Marta's voice? It could be for Deán that message or, rather, that call, she doesn't actually leave any message."

"Play it again, will you," she said. She sat back in my chair, no longer perched on the edge, she didn't seem so impatient to leave now, her eyes wide open, her eyes still wearing the dusky night, it was odd to see my armchair occupied by another person, a woman, it was nice. I rewound the tape and we listened to it again, the pleading, tearful voice so distorted that it was impossible to know who it was, if it was someone known to us, to me or her or both of us (we had only Marta and the child in common, and now Deán and Téllez as well), I wouldn't have recognized my own voice in that desperate state. "I don't know, it could be her, I don't think so though, it could be anyone, it could be the woman who phoned before, the one who said 'You decide'."

"Do you know anything about Deán's life?" I asked and the truth is that I asked that question less out of personal curiosity and more in order to endorse the questions that Luisa would be asking herself. I felt no curiosity, I did not want to know anything more about Marta, she was dead and curiosity does not affect the dead, it is not a feeling that touches them, despite all those films and novels and biographies that are investigations into precisely that, the lives of those who are no longer living, it's just a hobby, you cannot talk to the dead and that's all there is to it. I did not want to know anything more about Deán either (though I probably would want to know more about Luisa, but that was perfectly possible and would not now present any difficulties). Basically,

I knew that once I had found out what there was to find out (if there was anything), I would still not simply be able to resume my normal life and activities, as if the link established between Marta Téllez and myself would never be broken, or would take too long to be severed, far too long, leaving me perhaps for ever haunted. Or perhaps I just wanted to tell someone what I had already told once, that night, to Luisa during supper, telling a story as repayment of a debt, albeit symbolic and not demanded or required by anyone, no one can demand to know something when they are ignorant of its very existence and to hear of it from a person they do not know, something that they do not know has happened or is happening, they cannot, therefore, demand that it should be revealed to them or should stop. Until only a few hours ago, Luisa Téllez did not even know I existed. It is the person telling the story who decides to tell it or even impose it on another, the person who opts for revelation or betrayal, the person who decides when to tell, and that usually happens when the weariness brought on by the silence and the shadow becomes too great, sometimes it is the only thing that drives people to recount facts that no one has asked for and that no one expects, it has nothing to do with guilt or bad conscience or regret, no one does anything if they feel an utter wretch at the moment they do it, if they feel the need to do it, disquiet and fear come later, but not to any significant degree, disquiet or fear are more common than regret, tiredness even more so.

Luisa crossed her legs, her shoes were still immaculate, as if she had not spent hours walking along wet pavements.

"Do you think I could have that drink now?" she said. "I'm a bit thirsty." She wasn't in such a hurry now, she felt less awkward sitting in my apartment, we were bound together by what we had heard, by a tape that contained her voice and mine, as well as others which we did not entirely understand. We were brought close, too, by our weariness and by having told our stories, by having related something one to the other as in an exchange, things that vainly completed each other, she provided the after and I provided the before of something for which there was no help and that perhaps did not even interest us very much: besides, it was in the past, it had happened and was no longer happening,

249

it could be revealed, but it was over now. I got up and went to the kitchen to get her a whisky. She got up too and followed me, she leaned familiarly against the door frame, watching me as I got out the bottle and the ice and a glass and some water. That's how married couples sometimes continue a conversation, one partner follows the other through the house, while the latter tidies up or makes supper or does the ironing or puts things away, it is common territory where appointments have no place, there is no need to sit down to talk or to tell the other person something, instead activity goes on in the midst of the words and of accounts called for and accounts rendered, I know that because I have not always lived alone. "Well, as I said, they hadn't been getting on very well for some time," said Luisa, leaning in the doorway. "I suppose he must have had a few realities too, men can't put up with pure fantasy for very long. But I don't know anything concrete, the fact is, I don't know anything at all."

I wondered if now she was telling me the truth, shortly before, she had told me that she and Marta told each other almost everything, perhaps Marta hadn't known anything about it, which would explain why she had said nothing to her sister, it's best to say nothing as long as you can still give what is always the best reply: "I don't know, I'm not sure, we'll see," the consolation of uncertainty which is also retrospective. I gave her a glass of whisky and I poured myself a grappa. She didn't seem like a liar, but she might be being discreet.

"Cheers," I said, and then I got up enough courage to ask her something, to make even more of an ally of her than I had already, there's nothing like asking a favour of someone to win them over, most people like granting favours. It was a simple, justifiable request, but there was no reason why she should agree to it, there was no reason, as yet, why Luisa Téllez should agree to do anything for me. "Would you do me a favour and not tell Deán about me until I've finished the work for your father? It will just be this week. Could you wait until next week, as if you hadn't met me until then? Please. I'd prefer to finish what I've been asked to do, besides, I'm going halves with a colleague, and if Deán finds out about me, it will be difficult for me to finish the work. He might want to stop me doing it, he would be quite capable of telling your father everything, to distance me from him, from everyone, from Marta."

Luisa took a sip of her drink, the ice clinked in her glass, she took a step forward, she rested her left hand on the table in the utility room, her bracelet clinked, she was holding her glass in her right hand, she said: "What time is it?"

She was wearing her watch on her right wrist as if she were left-handed, it was a rhetorical question to gain time, or perhaps she was afraid that she might tip her glass over if she turned her wrist to look at her watch.

"Almost one o'clock," I said. I was just about to pour out my own drink.

"It's late, I'd better be going." I thought, "Our languages are just as subtle as the old languages, 'I'd better be going' indicates that she's not going just yet, she's going to wait a bit, at least until she's drunk half her whisky, although she'll drink it very quickly, now she's in a hurry again because I've asked her a favour and she won't want to risk my asking her any more. In a while, she'll say 'I must go' and later still, she'll say 'Right, I'm off' and only then will she actually leave." We went back into the living room on my initiative, I took the lead and she followed as if she were my partner and not a stranger. She remained standing, looking at my books and videos while she took rapid sips of her whisky. She had grown sombre, the tape or I myself had contributed to that. She had her back to me.

"Will you wait?"

She turned round and looked at me, she had avoided my eyes ever since she had asked me what time it was, her eyes now wearing the face of the other, my face.

"Yes, of course I can wait," she said. "But don't get the wrong idea, I don't think Eduardo wants to beat you up or anything. Not at our age, not at this stage of the game."

"Oh, really?" I asked ingenuously, perhaps in a tone of slight disappointment: an easing of tension, the reminder that we were not that young, "What does he want then? Why is he so determined to find me? What does he want? To know what happened? In that case you could just tell him everything that I've told you."

"I will tell him, I will, don't worry," said Luisa patiently, "I'll save you that initial repetition if you like, when I talk to him about you on Monday, if that's all right with you, I don't want to keep it from him any longer than is necessary. I know it's not easy for you." She was being understanding with me, she was giving me more than I had asked for.

"Monday's fine. I have to hand in my work by then anyway, your father will deliver it, so I'll definitely have finished. I'm really very grateful. What does he want though? Why is he looking for me?" I asked again.

"I think he's not so much interested in finding out anything as in telling you something. I don't know what it is, because he hasn't told me. But he's said several times that he wants to meet the man who spent the night with Marta so that he can tell him a few things. He wants you to know certain facts, I don't know what. Listen, I must go, I'm tired. He'll tell you whatever it is."

"Ah," I thought, "so he too has something to tell. He too is tired, weary of the shadows."

"I'll give you my number," I said. "You can give it to him any time after Monday if you want, that way he won't have to look it up or ask your father for it." I wrote it down on a yellow post-it, I have one of those little pads next to my phone too, almost every house has.

Luisa took the bit of paper and put it in her pocket. Now she really did look exhausted, the sorrow of the whole day had swept over her, she must be heartily sick of it all, of her father, of the boy, of Deán, of me, of her own sister alive and dead. She sat down in my armchair again with her glass in her right hand, as if she didn't have the strength to remain standing. With her other hand, she covered her face as she had in the cemetery, only now she wasn't crying: it was a gesture sometimes made by people when they feel horror or shame or want not to see or to be seen. I couldn't help noticing her lips – those lips – that her hand did not cover. She had not yet said: "Right, I'm off," not yet.

I WORKED WITH TÉLLEZ for the rest of the week and, on Sunday, I went to the races with Ruibérriz de Torres, now, I thought, I could reward him for his work, pay off my debt to him and tell him what had happened to me, more than a month before, with a woman I barely knew, he would enjoy the story, it would amuse him, that's all, in a way he would envy me: had it been his story, he would have proclaimed it to the four winds right from the start and it would have become a story that was half-macabre and half-jocular, half-absurd and half-sinister, a horrible death and a ridiculous death, something which, when it happens, is neither vulgar nor elevated nor funny nor sad can be any of those things when someone makes a story out of it, the world depends on its storytellers as it does on those who hear the story and occasionally influence it, I would not have dared to tell my story to Ruibérriz other than in the tone I used during the first two races – of little interest – that is, by turns sinister and jocular, interrupting the story now and then to watch the final straights through our binoculars, going from the grandstand to the paddock and from the paddock to the bar and from there to place our bets and then back up to the grandstand, nothing is ever told twice in exactly the same way or using exactly the same words, not even if the storyteller is the same each time, even if it's the same person. I told the story distractedly, adding a lot of gestures, in order that he should appreciate it to the full, I told it quickly, I couldn't talk to Ruibérriz about spells or enchantments. "You're kidding," he said a few times, "the woman snuffed it, just like that?" Yes, for him, that was what it was all about, nothing more, the woman had just snuffed it, just like that. "And you didn't even get your end away, bloody hell," he said, rather amused at my bad luck. And it was true that I didn't get my end away, and perhaps that was bad luck on my part. "And it was Téllez Orati's daughter? You're kidding," he said again, I remember. He listened to me with a mixture of hilarity and horror, as happens when we read in the newspapers about the inevitably risible misfortune of some unknown person who dies in their socks, or at the hairdresser's, still wearing a voluminous smock, or in a whorehouse or at the dentist's, or eating fish and getting a bone stuck in their throat, like a child whose mother isn't there to save him by sticking a finger down his throat, death as a performance or a show to be reviewed, that is how I talked about my dead person as I strolled around the racecourse that Téllez used to frequent when he was younger, outside the tote and in the bar and in the paddock and standing up in the grandstand watching through our binoculars, the horses swathed in a thickening mist, it was a month of almost constant mist in Madrid such as had not been known for over a century, there were more car accidents and delays at the airport, the horses, as they ran past us, appeared to have no legs, we watched their bodies and their spectral heads pass by, disputing the lead, like the horses on the merry-go-rounds we rode in childhood, those first horses had no legs at all, only a long transfixing pole to which we would cling while we rode round and round in a circle, without moving from the spot, faster and faster, just like in a race over turf or grass, until the music began to crackle and they slowed us to a halt. The new month had brought mists, the previous month storms. Ruibérriz was wearing a raincoat with the belt tightly knotted, the way posers do, I wore mine unbuttoned, we both had on stiff leather gloves, we looked like a couple of body-guards. The brilliance of his smile remained entirely undimmed, he curled back his lip in dissolute laughter, he watched the first, unim-portant trials disdainfully, he looked about him, even while I was telling him my story, in search of prey or of people he could greet or wheedle something out of, he was wearing a lot of cologne. I didn't tell him about more recent events, I didn't talk to him about the sister nor of what I foresaw happening, my debt was paid off with the story about the woman's death and the fuck that never happened. Then I told him that I had finished the speech the day before, I gave him a copy, after all, he would partake of the minimal profits, though when we would get paid was quite another matter, I had acted in his name.

"So, how did it turn out?" he asked, crumpling up the speech and stuffing it into his raincoat pocket without even looking at it.

"Oh, just as boring and inane as all the others, when he finally gives the speech, no one will pay any more attention to him this time either. Téllez forced me to behave myself and to be very conventional, he kept me on a tight rein, and the fact is he didn't have to change much either, I didn't really try anything new. You know how it is, the user of the product, or the public image you have of them, always somehow imposes his or her personality on you, and you just can't shake it off when it comes to writing for them."

I had worked until Saturday, Téllez becoming more excited and more familiar as the week progressed, visiting me, correcting me, inspecting me, advising me, preening himself on his knowledge of our employer's noble psyche. He certainly did not lack for distractions that week, he had a project in hand, responsibilities of state, a younger man who came every morning and placed himself at his disposal. Sometimes he would interrupt me to talk about other things, about the death notices in the newspaper which he always scrutinized minutely, about the catastrophic situation in this plundered country of ours, about the foibles and vanities of his most famous colleagues. He smoked a pipe when he was with me or cadged a few cigarettes, he held them inexpertly between thumb and forefinger as if he were holding a pencil or a piece of chalk, he puffed at them timidly and coughed a little when he inhaled the smoke, but he managed. He would wander off for a while to grind some coffee in the kitchen and then, mid-morning, he would force me to take a break, he would pour himself some port wine and pour a glass for me, then, with glass in hand, he would read out loud the pages we had finished and approved, keeping time with eloquent movements of his wine glass, adding a comma or replacing it with a semicolon, a sign he favoured, "it helps you to breathe," he would say, "and it stops you losing the thread". The phone almost never rang, no one needed him, no one sought him out, I would occasionally hear him talking to his daughter or his daughter-in-law, but he was usually the one who phoned them at work on various pretexts. His existence was a precarious one. On the last day, on Saturday, I ordered a huge arrangement of flowers to be delivered to him while I was there, from Bourguignon's, he wouldn't have settled for less. I had them sent without a card or message of any kind, I knew that would keep him intrigued for several days – until the flowers faded – it would help him feel my absence less keenly once I had finished my task and I no longer came to his house, not on Sunday or Monday or Tuesday or any other day. The ancient maid brought it in to the living room still in its cellophane and its bowl, she placed it on the carpet and Téllez lifted it up immediately to look at it, astonished, as if it were some strange beast.

"Open it," he said to the maid in the same tone in which Roman emperors would once have said to a servant "Taste it" regarding a possibly poisoned delicacy. And once the cellophane and the maid had gone (the latter disappeared carefully folding up the wrapping paper, so that she could use it later) he walked two or three times around the bowl looking at it with as much expectation as distrust. "Anonymous flowers," he said, "who the devil would send me flowers? Have another look, Víctor, are you sure there's no card? Have a good look amongst the stems. Very strange, very strange indeed." And he scratched his chin with the end of his extinguished pipe while I scanned the floor in search of something I knew we would not find. He pointed at them with his index finger as I had seen him point to his shoe in the cemetery, the thumb of his other hand cocked in his armpit as if it were a riding crop. He was about to say something, but he was too confused, too overwhelmed. He did not even go near the flowers, then, at last, he planted his swaying body heavily down in a chair, his chest puffed out, his face like a gargoyle, and he stared at the flowers in their bowl on the carpet as if they were a marvel. "It isn't my birthday, it's not my saint's day or any anniversary that I can remember," he said. "They can't be from the Palace either, we still haven't delivered the speech. I wonder if Marta and Luisa have any ideas, perhaps they can come up with a reason, I'm going to call Marta and tell her, sometimes she doesn't have a class until the evening and, besides, it's Saturday today, she's bound to be at home." He made as if to get up and go over to the phone, but stopped short and slumped into the chair again, leaning his neck against the chairback as if buffeted by an enormous wave or as

if he had received a revelation that had left him drained. Or
perhaps he felt dizzy and needed to hold his head back in order to
stop the feeling. He realized what he had done immediately and
apologized to me, it wasn't necessary: "I'm not mad, I'm not
losing my memory," he said to me, "it just takes time to get used
to it, you see. It's hard to grasp that someone who did exist
doesn't exist any more." He paused and then added: "I don't
know why I go on existing when so many have gone before me."
He didn't say anything more. He stood up again, leaning heavily
on the arms of the chair to push himself up, and then again took
a few cautious steps around the bowl of flowers. He was always
immaculately dressed when at home, as if he were about to go out
even when he wasn't, wearing tie, waistcoat, jacket and his street
shoes, one morning he had been railing against tracksuit bottoms,
which he found unspeakable. "I can't understand why politicians
allow themselves to be photographed wearing them," he had said.
"More than that, I don't know how they dare put them on, even
if no one's going to see them. And in summer, they go out
without any socks on, the vulgar creatures, such appalling taste."
He was neat and elegant, like a beautifully finished, rather ornate
piece of antique furniture. He put his pipe to his mouth and
added: "Anyway, about these mysterious flowers, I must make
some enquiries, I'll have to thank whoever sent them. But we'd
better get back to work, Víctor, otherwise we won't finish today,
and I always like to keep my promises." Then, taking me by the
arm, he led me back into his study next door, full of books and
pictures, jumbled and alive, where I was about to close my
portable typewriter that had sat there open all week. He didn't call
Luisa just then, he would do so later, as he would other people,
and with a good reason this time. I thought that he would, at
least, have some motive to live until Monday, he would go to the
Palace to deliver our transient piece of work, his and mine and
Only the Lonely's, under Ruibérriz's name, although probably
only Segurola and Segarra would be there to receive him, Only
the Lonely is not often available. Precarious existences rely on the
day-to-day, or perhaps all existences do. He could make conjectures about the flowers for a few days more, for a whole week if
he was lucky.

The third race was of no interest either, up until then, we hadn't won anything, our tickets torn up in anger and thrown scornfully to the ground, and Ruibérriz never leaves any game emptyhanded. While we were watching the horses for the next race parading round the paddock – again in a circle, like horses on a merry-go-round – he was busy regaling me with curious and obscene anecdotes about the latest poor sap of a woman to succumb to his Don Juanesque charms and who was currently satisfying his needs, when he turned round at the sound of someone calling out his full name preceded by the word "Señor" (until then, of our acquaintanceship, we had seen only Admiral Admira with his preordained name and his lovely wife, we hadn't even seen the bearded, bespectacled philosopher who never misses a race, he must have got held up in the fog or perhaps he would only get there for the fifth). He turned round, we turned round, he looked blankly at the woman who had uttered the cry and who was heading straight for me with her hand held out, calling me by his name in that absurd manner, "Señor Ruibérriz de Torres" sounds much too long. It was Señorita Anita, so devoted to the Only One, accompanied by a friend of the same stature and demeanour. The two of them had donned hats as if they were at Ascot, it's rare nowadays to see someone in a hat, they looked rather common, I could see that Ruibérriz did not approve; but he likes all women on principle, as do I more or less, we're no different in that respect, although we do differ in approach and method. I lose interest more quickly.

"May I introduce Víctor Francés," I said, referring to Ruibérriz. "Señorita Anita."

"Anita Pérez-Antón," she said. "This is Lali, a friend of mine." She did not honour her friend with a surname, just as Solitaire had neglected to do with her, in fact he hadn't introduced her at all, not only did he address everyone informally as "tú", he didn't mind his manners generally.

"I hope you don't have any problems with your tights today," I said as a joke, to see how she would take it, she seemed jollier than when she was at work. She took it extraordinarily well, and said:

"Oh, that was *so* embarrassing!" And she raised her hand to her mouth when she laughed, and added, explaining more for her friend's benefit than for the real Ruibérriz: "Can you believe it, I got this huge ladder in my tights and I didn't have time to change before meeting this gentleman who had an appointment with the boss. The gentleman was going to write a speech for him. Anyway, it just got worse and worse during the meeting, they were almost hanging off me by the end of it." And she made a gesture with her hands indicating the hem of her skirt, which again was very short and tight. Ruibérriz couldn't fail to notice this gesture, doubtless imagining something smutty. "I was absolutely mortified, there I was with my tights in shreds and no one saying a word, talk about sang-froid."

"Sang-froid" was rather an old-fashioned term, but then she worked in a place that was, by definition, old-fashioned. More and more words are falling into disuse, they get discarded more and more rapidly. I drew her aside a little and said:

"By the way, I've finished the speech, Señor Téllez will take it to him tomorrow." Ruibérriz heard and understood, I imagine that this only increased his interest in the young women, not that he needs much incentive, the older he gets the more readily he runs after any woman with a bit of charm. But if the four of us were to stay together, one thing was certain, he would have to pair off with Lali (possibly an orphan with no surname). Besides, it was unlikely that we would find their company amusing for more than one or two races, until the fifth. The same went for them. It would be better to arrange to meet one night, the four of us together, two or four.

"What do you mean tomorrow?" said Señorita Anita, recovering her professional air for a moment. She looked awful in that red hat. "Didn't anyone tell you that the Strasbourg thing's been cancelled? I gave orders for them to phone Señor Téllez and warn him. Don't tell me they didn't do it."

"We were working on it until yesterday, he didn't say anything to me," I replied, after a few seconds' pause. "Perhaps Señor Téllez forgot to tell me, he is getting on a bit, after all." I felt sorry for Téllez, at first, for his wasted Monday at the Palace, then it occurred to me that perhaps he had known and hadn't said anything to me in order to detain me there for a few more days, keeping him company at home. That speech would end up in a drawer and stay there for good, they're written for specific occasions. I didn't like the idea, even if I was only a ghostwriter. I thought: "Poor old man, he certainly knows how to look after himself, how to get by from day to day."

The four of us headed for the tote, I cupped Señorita Anita's elbow lightly in my hand, a protective gesture, Ruibérriz was a little behind me, obliged now to talk to Lali, whose hat had even less to recommend it.

"I'm sorry you did all that work for nothing," said Anita. "But you'll get paid, you'll get paid anyway, make sure you send us your bill." "It's just like the scripts I write that never come to anything," I thought, "more wastage. At least people give me work, though, at least I'm not unemployed like so many others." Señorita Anita dropped her programme, I crouched down to pick it up and she crouched down too, more slowly, and, as I stood up, I deliberately brushed against her bent head (again she was slower than me, her skirt rather too short for such endeavours) and managed to knock her hat off. I crouched down again to pick it up, furtively wiping it on the ground in order to be able to regret it having got so dirty. "Oh, shit," she said. I don't know if she would dare say such a thing at the Palace.

"Oh, I'm sorry, it's absolutely filthy now, the ground here's disgusting. Don't worry, I'll hold on to it until we can get something to clean it with, the race is just about to start. Anyway you look prettier without your hat." It was true, she did, she had a pleasantly rounded face and nice dark hair, but, basically, I just couldn't bear that hat, there are some things I get quite obsessive about.

The four of us placed our bets, they bet small, amateurish sums, we bet higher, they must have thought we were rich, in today's terms we are in a way, I'm richer than Ruibérriz, I work harder and I don't live off someone else. He gave advice to poor, disinherited Lali while I passed a hot tip on to Anita the courtier. We returned to the grandstand with our tickets, they kept theirs clutched in their hands as if they were objects of great value which they were afraid to lose. We put ours in the breast pocket of our jackets, the one intended for a handkerchief, worn, of course, with just a corner showing, I never have a handkerchief in mine,

Ruibérriz always does, brightly coloured ones, he had unbuttoned his raincoat to show off his pectorals. He was reverting to his polo-shirted self, we had removed our gloves. They hadn't brought any binoculars with them and, out of gallantry, we had to lend them ours, we would certainly have to divest ourselves of their company by the fifth and most important race, we didn't want to have to guess at the result of that one. What with the mist and now deprived of our binoculars, we couldn't see a thing, we had no idea what was going on, Lali got confused and declared that a horse had won when, in fact, it hadn't, she wanted her horse to win at all costs, the horse on which she had pinned her penury. We all lost, we immediately tore up our tickets with the appropriate mixture of scorn and rage, they held out a little longer, hoping for a late and unlikely disqualification that would benefit them. Now it was time to go to the bar by the paddock, the same steps repeated again and again after each of the six races, that's the charm of it, the half-hour wait between each race, and then they're over in a moment, but occasionally they're memorable.

"How come Strasbourg was cancelled?" I asked Anita who now had a Coca-Cola in her hand. I was still hanging on to her hat, it was a real nuisance. "I thought it was supposed to be important, and I imagine your boss's diary is arranged a long time in advance and must be pretty well immutable."

"Yes, it is in principle, but he's so exhausted, the poor thing, that sometimes we have no option but to cancel something at one fell stroke, just like that." (I imagine she was confusing "at a stroke" and "at one fell swoop".) "Better that than just postpone it and mess everything up or try to come up with some compromise, that really would be a muddle."

"Surely the people affected protest," I said. "They must feel they've been victimized, discriminated against. Aren't there diplomatic incidents over such things?"

She looked at me impatiently, disapprovingly (she pursed her painted lips) and replied loftily:

"Well, tough shit, he already does much more than he should. He's in demand from all over, it's just outrageous. What they don't bloody well realize is that there's only one of him." She was distinctly foulmouthed, but then these days everyone is.

"Is that why they call him the Only One?" I asked. "Do you call him that, when you talk about him, I mean?"

She was touchy about that question, she obviously didn't like the fact that other people knew the nicknames used by the inner circle.

"That, Señor Ruibérriz de Torres, would be telling," she said. The real Ruibérriz, standing a little further along the bar, couldn't help but crane his neck slightly when he heard his name. He wasn't getting anywhere, friend Lali was positively verbose, a regular chatterbox.

"I do hope the cancellation of the speech doesn't mean that your boss has had some mishap."

Señorita Anita was more reserved regarding her own feelings than regarding the life and customs of the Lone Ranger. She replied to this question without hesitation:

"No, nothing like that, touch wood." And she lightly tapped the toothpicks in the little porcelain jar on the bar. "He's just completely worn out, he doesn't pace himself, and people won't leave him alone, he wants to please everyone, and he's not been sleeping well lately. He's never had that problem before. And obviously it affects him badly, he's feeling very low, he's a bit of a wreck actually. He may get over it, this last week has been particularly bad. He says that he starts thinking just as he's going to sleep and that the thoughts stop him drifting off. Or else he goes on having the thoughts while he's asleep and then they wake him up."

"That's what insomnia's like," I said, knowing what she meant, "thoughts take precedence over tiredness or sleep, and if you do manage to get to sleep, you don't so much dream as think."

"Well, it's never happened to me," said Anita. She was a very healthy young woman, I wasn't surprised that Only the Lonely liked having her by his side.

"But surely he takes something, there are sleeping pills he could take, he must have a battalion of doctors ready to prescribe them for him."

"He tried Oasin, do you know it? Oasin Relax, I suppose the name comes from oasis." I knew a tranquillizer called Oasil Relax, I imagined that was what she meant. "But it's too weak and had no effect whatsoever. Now they've prescribed him some drops from Italy that work better, EN or NE they're called, I don't know what the name means, they help him get off to sleep quickly enough, but then he doesn't sleep through. So no one knows how long this is going to go on for." The expression "he doesn't sleep through" was almost maternal.

"He mentioned something about it, I believe, on the day we were there," I said. "And what does he think about? Has he made any comment? Not that he doesn't have plenty to worry about, but then he always has had."

"He says he thinks about himself, that he has doubts. We're all a bit worried about that."

"Doubts? What about?"

Señorita Anita grew impatient again, she had quite a temper:

"Doubts, dammit, doubts, what does it matter what they're about? Isn't that enough?"

"It seems quite enough to me, especially for someone in his position. What does he do when he can't sleep? Does he catch up on work? He should try not to worry about it, I say that because I've suffered from occasional bouts of insomnia for years now."

"Oh sure, so you'd have him up working all hours too, would you?" She said this in the same tone that Only You had used when addressing the painter Segurola, Anita was a victim of mimetism, it was only natural that she should be. "No, he tries to rest even though he can't sleep, he lies down and puts his feet up, he reads, watches television, although not all the channels broadcast after midnight; he throws dice to see if he can bore himself to sleep."

"Dice?"

"Yes, dice." And Señorita Anita made a gesture as if shaking a pair of dice, blowing on her fist as if she were in Las Vegas, she must have seen a lot of movies, Las Vegas, Ascot. "Come on, give me my hat back," she said. "I'm going to dab it with a bit of water. Honestly, what a bummer." If she allowed herself this expression, it was obviously because she had forgotten that I was responsible for that particular bummer.

I handed it back to her in order to get rid of it, but there was no way I was going to let her ask for some water:

"You'll spoil it if you get it wet," I said.

"Hey, let's go down to the paddock, the horses came out ages ago," said Ruibérriz, momentarily interrupting the unstoppable torrent of talk from Lali.

We barely had time to see the horses parade round, we had to run to place our bets, there was a queue at all the windows, the race track was packed like everywhere in Madrid always is, it's a city of crowds. The two women were staring stupefied and uncomprehending at the screens showing the prices.

"Hey, Ani," her friend said to her, "wasn't it in the fourth race that you were supposed to put that big bet on for him?"

"You're right, it's lucky you remembered, this is the fourth race, isn't it?" replied Anita. She hurriedly opened her handbag (she had painted fingernails), took out a piece of paper with a few numbers written on it, along with a thick wad of notes. They looked like new notes, fresh from the Mint, they still had a band around them (before the Civil War, they were made in England: Bradbury and Wilkinson of London were the people commissioned to do it, I've seen notes dating from the time of the Republic and they were in perfect condition; before the Civil War, the race track was in the Castellana, not outside the city as it is nowadays and as it has been for decades, it's an old and honoured place now, La Zarzuela). It was an enormous sum of money, it's hard to judge how much when the notes have never even been folded. That was no amateur bet, it came from someone who has a tip from a very good source and wants to win a bit of money to set himself up for the year. I felt rather ridiculous holding the two miserable notes I had earmarked for my bet, now it was the turn of Ruibérriz and me to look like beginners. I let her go ahead of me, out of normal politeness and because it suited me to do so.

"All this on number 9, to win," said Anita to the man at the window. "And I'd like to put this on number 9, the same thing." And she gave him another large note, separately, doubtless her own bet.

I looked at the price of the horse or rather the mare: Condesa de Montoro, it wasn't amongst the favourites and the odds were still high, but, at this rate, we would soon lower them. Anita, inexpert in these matters, should have made her own bet first. I took out a third note and bet the same amount on a horse that wasn't number 9, so as not to be too obvious. But with the notes I had out already I unhesitatingly imitated Anita.

"I'm going to copy you," I said.

Ruibérriz missed none of this, despite the continuing torrent of words in his ear. He simply let Lali talk and then followed our example, four notes, he bet double what I did, and the price was already reflecting our injections of confidence.

The two young women put their tickets away very carefully in their handbags, they looked at each other, laughing excitedly, covering their mouths with their hands. Anita said to me:

"You trust me then, do you?"

"Of course, or rather I trust the friend you're placing the bet for, you don't risk sums of money like that willy nilly. Who is he, an expert on the horses?"

"Very much so," she replied.

"And why doesn't he come to the races himself?"

"He can't always manage it, but sometimes he does."

Solitary games of dice, risky bets, I didn't want to link the two things: if we won, it was definitely a hot tip, that is, a scam that not even Ruibérriz was in on. I preferred not to associate the Only One with fraudulent practices, but those crisp new notes . . .

As soon as we returned to the grandstand, we again lost our binoculars to the two young women. The mist hadn't lifted but it hadn't got any worse either. The mass of spectators was blurred and looked even more like a mass, there were no edges to anyone, there was still a few minutes before the start of the fourth race, the horses were entering the boxes, I noticed that Condesa's rider was a deep red smudge, his hat too, that would help me follow his trail, doomed as I was by my own unending gallantry to watch with the naked eye. We would dump the women for the fifth race, we had had quite enough of seeing nothing.

"Did you manage to get the video for him?" I asked Anita suddenly.

"Who for? What video?" she replied and her surprise or confusion seemed genuine.

"For your boss. That film we talked about, don't you remember? He was telling us about the sleepless night he'd had about a month earlier, he'd been watching television, he saw a film that had already begun, *Chimes at Midnight*, I was the one who told him the title. He had only caught the second half and he said that he'd like to see the whole thing one day, he was very impressed, he watched it to the end, he was telling us about it."

"Ah yes." Anita finally understood what I was talking about. "The fact is I haven't done anything about it, we've been so worried about him not sleeping that we haven't had time to think about things like that, you know how it is, there are always a thousand and one other matters to deal with, and when he's feeling down, well, you can imagine, no one even thinks about anything else." Sometimes she used a plural which was not the royal "we", but a rather modest "we" into which she dissolved, one that included a lot of people, doubtless the family and Segurola and Segarra, perhaps also the woman with the feather duster and the broom who had slowly traversed the room on her dustered feet, humming, the old banshee. "And he hasn't asked me about it again either," she added, as if justifying herself. She remained thoughtful for a moment and then said: "Although he can't have forgotten about it completely, because, it's odd, yes, now I remember: that was the first time he mentioned 'partial sleep' and he's often used that expression recently, 'Our friend partial sleep failed to visit me again last night, Anita,' he's said to me on a couple of mornings. How was it in the film, can you remember?"

"Well, that's all it was I think. The old King, Henry IV, can't rest and he inveighs against sleep, who visits so many other places but not his palace, who bestows herself on the humble and the evil and even on animals," I don't actually remember that last category, but I thought I might include it since we were at the race track, "and yet refuses to bless his crowned and ailing head. The King is dying and eventually he does die, tormented by his past and by the future in which he will not participate. And that's what he says to sleep: 'thou, O partial sleep'. That's all, as far as I can remember, the fact is I remember more of what your boss said the other day than of the film itself, I saw it years ago."

Anita pursed her lips again, biting the inside of her cheek, looking very thoughtful.

"Yes, yes," she said, "that may be what it is. It's probably that film that's to blame for his present insomnia. Perhaps I should get him the video so that he can see the whole thing, that way he'll have the whole story and can stop thinking about it, I suppose."

"Maybe, who knows. It's worth a try."

"Anyway, thanks for reminding me, it had gone completely out of my head. What did you say it was called?" And she quickly took out of her handbag the same piece of paper on which she had noted down the numbers for her bets. "Can you hold my hat for a moment, please."

"I think you wrote it down the other day," I said, once more taking charge of the infamous hat.

"God knows where that's got to. Now what was it again?"

"Look, it's *Chimes at Midnight*," I repeated again. "It was filmed here in Spain, some of it in Madrid. It won't be difficult to find, the television company must have a copy of it."

"There they go," shouted Lali and she immediately began to cheer. "Come on, Condesa de Montoro, come on." It was too long a name to be shouted out, she should have just called it Condesa.

Señorita Anita hastily stuffed the piece of paper back into her handbag and shut it before she had time to write down the title, then she raised my binoculars to her pretty, painted eyes. She too began to urge on the mare, but she, rather inaccurately, called it Montoro.

"Come on, Montoro, whip him," she said. She must be a fan of wrestling or boxing.

I couldn't see a thing, but even so I couldn't not watch the race, not so much because of the amount of money I'd bet on it as out of curiosity: I wanted to know if the friend's tip was a good one, perhaps she had been given the tip by a rather shady boyfriend of hers, she was just the kind of healthy young woman who often goes for good-for-nothings, a way of balancing her own honest, open character. The four of us stood up, I glanced at Ruibérriz and he made a gesture indicating that he had no idea what was happening either, his binoculars were also in the hands of the fair sex, that's how men used to refer to women when it offended no one, when there still were things that caused offence. At the beginning of the final straight, I managed to make out the dark red stain of our jockey's shirt, all the horses were still bunched together, apart from two or three who had dropped back and had no chance of winning, the Condesa wasn't amongst them. You could see the breath of thousands of spectators, which did nothing to help the already difficult visibility. Suddenly there was a collision and a fall, two riders rolled to the ground and covered their heads as soon as they had come to a stop, their brightly coloured caps sent flying, one of the horses rode on riderless, the other one slipped on the turf with its front legs spreadeagled as if it were skiing over slippery, compacted snow, a third took fright and gave a few hesitantly artistic steps before rearing up like a monster and wheeling round, like that horse in Calle Bailén two and a half years before, when I was out on a night-time walk, thinking about Victoria and Celia and their carnal commerce, and perhaps my own. *Mère. Mara.* The others speeded up so as to leave the collision behind them as quickly as possible and not become entangled in it, at that moment the race was split, every mount rode away from there as fast as it could, some moving away from the rails, others towards them, most lost their impetus or were reined in or held back. The horse bearing the dark red stain on its back was the only one that kept straight on without swerving, a path opened up along which she advanced unopposed, galloping smoothly onwards, the jockey didn't even have to use the whip. "Come on, Condesa, come on," I surprised myself thinking, I don't usually shout in public places.

"Come on, Montoro, come on," Anita was yelling at the top of her voice. "Yes, yes, yes," she repeated excitedly. I reckoned there would be no disqualifications, despite that fall and possible irregularities. If the race was fixed, it had been done in an extremely risky manner.

The young women were leaping joyfully in the air, they embraced each other three times, they shouted "Hooray for number 9!" Lali dropped Ruibérriz's binoculars and didn't even realize she had, he picked them up ruefully, one lens was broken. He didn't say anything, though, he was obviously overjoyed, he never leaves any game emptyhanded, and today was no exception. In the distance, I saw the Admiral tearing up his tickets with obvious annoyance, as was the incredulous philosopher who had arrived by then, everyone was tearing up their tickets. But not us, I was pretty much set up for that month, especially as I was unlikely to be paid for the speech.

"Right, goodbye then, we're off now, we're in a bit of a hurry. Nice to see you, Señor Ruibérriz de Torres, Señor Francés. And thanks for your company," said Señorita Anita, hastily saying goodbye to us both at the same time. They were in a hurry to get their money, I imagine that for that amount of money, they'd need to show some proof of identity, I don't know, I've never won that much. Perhaps they wouldn't even stay for the fifth race, the friend or good-for-nothing would be waiting for them in order to celebrate their win. We weren't of any interest to them now. She gave me back my binoculars, I returned her hat which was the same colour as the winning jockey's shirt. I watched her walk away, watched her nice legs with their plump thighs, her short skirt revealed where they began, she had sustained no runs in her tights at the races. She hadn't, in the end, written down the name of the film, she would forget again, the Only One wouldn't get to see it all the way through and so would keep remembering it, and continue to be bothered by vexatious bouts of insomnia.

"What a pair," said Ruibérriz, tugging on his trouser belt with both hands and filling out his chest as they disappeared amongst the moving mass. And that was all he said by way of farewell.

We decided to go and collect our money later, we were really interested in the fifth race, we wanted to go straight to the paddock to study the best horses at close quarters, we could watch the race without worrying about the outcome now, we would emerge with a profit anyway, thanks to that pair, to the girls. We got a good place at the bar from which we could see when the horses left the starting post. The race track, by then, was packed, whatever happened they wouldn't dare to cancel the fifth race, visibility didn't matter.

"Did you see that wad of notes?" I said to Ruibérriz.

"I should say, an absolute fortune, where do you think she got that? And they were new notes too, weren't they?"

"Brand new, I'd say."

"Bloody hell," he said.

I don't know if he was going to say anything further, he didn't get the chance, because, just opposite us on the other side of the bar, we suddenly saw that a guy with a scarlet face and bulging veins had smashed a bottle and had grasped it by the neck, he was brandishing it in the air, the foam from the beer gushing out like urine. We just had time to see another man in a camel coat advancing on him with a knife clasped in his hand, those poisonous steps, we hadn't heard the verbal part of the argument, in Madrid everyone talks so loudly anyway, the man with the knife tried to plunge it into the chest of the man with the bottle, an upward movement, he missed, nothing was torn, the jagged edge of the glass aimed at the throat or neck missed too, each caught hold of the other's armed hand with their free hand, other men took advantage of the struggle to hurl themselves upon them and separate them and immobilize them (doubtless some pickpocket took advantage of the mêlée), then some policemen intervened, they would ask for documentation from every living soul on that side of the bar, the two rivals were hauled off, they were beaten with truncheons, their heads bleeding, we saw it, Ruibérriz and I went on taking sips of our beer, one sip, then another and another, it all happened very fast and the mist was growing thicker.

EVERYTHING HAPPENED very fast on Monday and on Tuesday too, the way everything seems to when it finally happens, then you have the feeling that it has all happened in a rush and is over in a flash and that the run-up to it was much too short, that it could easily have happened even later; everything seems as nothing to us, everything becomes compressed and seems as nothing to us once it is over, then we always feel that we were not given enough time, that it did not last long enough (we were still considering, still hesitating, how few letters and photographs and memories remain to me), when things come to an end, they are countable, they have a number, although what has happened to me is not yet over and may perhaps never be over until I am over and, on meeting death, I find rest and contribute to death's salvation, like all the other centuries that have played their part, that monstrous riddle of 1914. And meanwhile, another day, how dreadful, another day, how fortunate. Only then will I cease to be the thread of continuity, the silken thread without a guide, when my weary will grows tired and withdraws and no longer wants to want or wants anything, and when what prevails is no longer "not yet, not yet" but "I can't take any more of this", when I interrupt myself and I travel along the reverse side of time, or along its dark back where there will be no room for scruples or error or effort.

It all happened very fast because not everyone is aware that the recent present can suddenly seem like the remote past: Deán was not aware of this and he doubtless considered that he had already spent far too much time waiting to know what he finally learned from his sister-in-law Luisa on the agreed or stipulated day, she was kind enough to phone me on Monday evening – or perhaps it was already night, the blurring mist of the previous days continued – to confirm that she had spoken to him, she had just done so, she had unmasked me and for Deán I had become somebody in all respects, that is, someone with a face and a name who had confessed to certain deeds, or to warn me of that other phone call from the husband or widower which would come very soon, she thought, that same night, the moment we hung up and my line was free, or the next day at the latest, if Deán decided to spend his sleeping hours coming to terms with or pondering his newly acquired knowledge. I realized that Luisa had dialled my number immediately after giving it to him, perhaps to protect me for a few more minutes, perhaps to stop him making use of it the moment he had the number. She had been at the apartment in Conde de la Cimera talking to him, they had seen each other as they did almost every day about something or other to do with the child, now she was talking to me from the Russophile bar downstairs, where she had gone immediately after leaving the apartment. At least Deán had not rushed to the phone while she was coming down in the lift and turning the corner of the building and getting out her card or coins to warn me, if I wanted, she said protectively, I could leave the answering machine on all night, if I wasn't yet ready to confront that voice, to confront Deán.

"How did he take it?" I asked.

"I think he was surprised, but he concealed it very well. He must have been thinking it was someone else. But listen," she said, "I didn't say anything to him about Vicente Mena, it suddenly felt too much, too many useless revelations, he's a friend of his, I don't know, what does it matter what happened if nothing can possibly happen now. I'm telling you this so that you don't feel you have to tell him either, if you don't want to." She remained silent for a second, then she added in a detached way: "Although you'll probably have to tell him, I don't know, see what happens, it doesn't really matter what he thinks of Marta any more. In fact, I don't know if I should worry about her good name, one doesn't really know quite what to do with the dead, I just feel terribly confused."

"People used to venerate them or at least their memory, and they would go and visit their graves with flowers, and their portraits would preside over their homes," I thought, "people spent a period in mourning and everything stopped for a while or slowed down, the death of someone affected the whole of life, the dead person really did take with them a part of the lives of their loved ones and, consequently, there wasn't such a separation between the two states, they were related and they were less frightening. Now people forget the dead as if the dead were plague victims, sometimes they use them as shields or dunghills in order to blame them and make them responsible for the terrible situation in which they have left us, often they are loathed or they receive only acrimony and reproaches from their heirs, they departed too soon or too late without preparing the ground for us or without leaving us free, they continue being names but not faces, names to which all manner of villainies and cowardices and horrors are imputed, that's the current tendency, and thus they do not find rest even in oblivion."

"Don't worry, I won't say anything to him about Vicente if that's what you want, I trust your judgement and I've no objection to keeping it quiet," I said. "I didn't know of his existence when I went to supper with your sister, I might not have known about it when I left, it would have made no difference. One of these days, I'll throw the tape away, I'll throw it away today, it's of no help or benefit to anyone. Anyway, don't worry about me, somebody's possible anger doesn't mean that there has to be a culprit, nor does somebody's possible pain, no one does anything convinced that what they're doing is wrong, it's just that often one simply can't take other people into account, we would be unable to do anything, sometimes you can only think about yourself and about the moment, not about what comes afterwards." In fact, I was feeling nervous and rather frightened. Perhaps I didn't know what I was saying, we often speak without knowing what we're saying, merely because it's our turn, impelled into speech by the silence, as happens in dialogues in plays, except that we are constantly improvising.

There was a silence at the other end of the line, but I didn't go on, I was patient enough to wait. "Other people," I thought, "other people have never quite done," I thought while I was waiting.

"Just one thing," Luisa said at last, "if he suggests to you that you should meet tonight, I would say no, if I were you. It would be better if you met during the day and, if possible, when the boy isn't there, if he wants you to meet at his place. My sister-in-law María will pick him up in the morning and won't be back until the evening, it's her turn tomorrow. As I said before, what Eduardo wants most of all is to tell you something, but even so I think it would be best if the situation were as different as possible to the one you experienced, the one he now knows about. I gave him a fairly faithful account of what you told me, and I gave him your version of events. He hardly said a word, he just listened, but I think what he finds hardest to understand is why you didn't tell him about it, why you didn't tell anyone. The fact is I really don't what state he'll be in." Luisa paused and then added, "Will you tell me how it went?" She sounded a bit frightened, we're always afraid when we've set something in motion. She was giving me advice and was worried about me, perhaps because she saw that she owed it to me, I was the one who would have to listen to any reproaches and to bear someone's anger and to be called to account. Marta wasn't there to share it.

"He'll tell you about it himself, I imagine."

"I'll know how it went for him, but not for you. It's different."

That left the way open for us to see and phone each other again, to talk, how unfortunate and how lucky, one step leads to another step quite innocently and, in the end, they become poisoned, not always, perhaps not the steps that I might take towards her or Luisa towards me, perhaps not this time, we think and go on thinking until the end of the time allotted to us, our conclusion. I hung up, we hung up and I sat down to wait for the phone call. I didn't just sit by the phone, I got up, I moved around, I went to the fridge, I opened a bottle, I took a sip, I went back to the living room, I picked up the tape in order to throw it out as I had told Luisa I would, but I didn't, I left it where it was, on a shelf, you don't always have to do what you say you'll do, there's always time, later on, no period of waiting is long once it's over. After three minutes, the phone rang, I let the machine answer first, I was sure it would be Deán. Instead, I heard Celia's voice beginning to leave me a message. We're talking to each other again, we even see each other occasionally, but we talk fairly often, a telephonic relationship now that cohabitation is over, that way the only temptations are verbal ones. Apparently, she's going to marry again, then I'll stop sending her cheques or giving her cash when we do see each other, she'll have a wealthy husband of whom I am doubtless already a co-bridegroom, he's the owner of an expensive restaurant which I will never visit, or so I think, no needs unmet, or so I hope. I picked up the phone and spoke to her, my line was busy again and I was safe for a few more moments, just a few, she was about to go out and just wanted to tell me something that I already knew: the tedious actor for whom I sometimes work had left me five messages on the answering machine, he was trying to get in touch with me urgently – I didn't want him to find me that day – when there's no other way of getting hold of me, some people still try to locate me through Celia as if she were still my wife (just as Ferrán tried phoning Marta when Deán had gone to London without leaving his address, I was a later ear-witness to that). Now we know little about each other's lives, Celia and I, we don't ask each other any questions, we wait until the other tells us something, perhaps the last time any concrete questions were asked was two and a half years ago, the day after my furtive night-time visit to her home which was once my home, she called me despite having suggested the previous night that I should be the one to call her in the morning to arrange to have lunch together and then talk about whatever it was, not at half past three in the morning as I wanted. That's what she had said, but she didn't mention any possible meeting when she phoned, she wanted to talk about one thing only, she asked me very seriously: "Listen, Víctor, you've still got the keys to the apartment, haven't you?" "No," I lied, "I threw them in the rubbish ages ago, in a fit of rage, one day when I got angry. Why?" "Are you sure?" she said. "Are you sure that you didn't use them to get into the apartment last night?" Normally, I would have hit the roof or asked her if she had gone mad, it was one thing phoning her at some unearthly hour after months of silence, saying that I wanted to see her and quite another that, despite her refusal, I should turn up there with no warning, without even ringing the doorbell, I could have answered her in an offended tone: "Are you mad? That's hardly my style." Instead I replied soberly, too soberly not to betray myself, I think: "No, why, what happened, it wasn't me." Sometimes I lie and not always very well, I still have those keys, although she would doubtless have immediately had the locks changed, that very day. I still have the tape too, I haven't thrown it out, and Marta Téllez's bra that I took with me by mistake, from time to time I sniff it, but it doesn't smell of anything now, and the yellow post-it that says "Wilbraham Hotel", I might stay there next time I happen to go to London. What doesn't remain, though, is Marta's smell that lingered after her, smells don't last very long and are hard to remember, although one does remember other things through them very intensely when they reappear, though it's unlikely that the smells associated with the dead will ever be repeated. Celia didn't insist, she just said "Fine" and hung up, just as I said "I know, if he bothers you again, just tell him that you've no idea where I am," when she told me about how impatient the tedious actor had been, and then I didn't hang up, we both hung up at the same time, we get on well now, at a distance. I don't usually like talking about Celia.

I took a sip from my bottle, I went to light a cigarette but the gas in my lighter had run out, I looked for matches in my bedroom and from there I heard the phone ring again, I reached it at the same time as the answering machine leapt into action with my voice saying: "This is a recorded voice. If you want to leave a message, please do so after the tone. Thank you." That's what Deán heard before he began speaking and he said this, which was recorded on the tape: "It's Eduardo Deán. I've spoken to Luisa and now I want to speak to you." I realized at once that he was addressing me as "tú" the way one does when one feels superior to someone or one is owed something or one feels insulted, then, one tends to do so only mentally. "I know you're there, lurking somewhere, a few seconds ago the line was busy, it's up to you if you pick the phone up or not." He paused to give me time to do so and I took advantage of that pause, I picked up the phone and said ridiculously:

"Yes, hello, who is it?"

"I've just told you who it is," said the exceptionally deep and now rather irritated voice, perhaps he had grown irritated while I was on the phone and he had tried to dial several times, or perhaps the irritation was more deepseated than that, it was as if he had said: "I've just told you who it is, you idiot," it made no difference that he had omitted the last couple of words, he was clearly thinking them. Perhaps he was going to continue treating me like an employee, like an underling, his voice on the telephone had more depth and weight than that of Vicente Mena, his co-fornicator, it was like fingers playing a double bass, he kept his composure, his irritation was well under control.

"I'm sorry, I was in the other room and I didn't manage to hear what you said to the machine. Who is this?" Perhaps this time I lied better, the truth was not so far from the lie.

"It's Eduardo Deán. I've spoken to Luisa and now I want to speak to you." He said exactly what he had said before: perhaps he had been rehearsing it for a while before dialling my number. "Could we meet tomorrow?" It wasn't really a question, more of a communiqué: "We could meet tomorrow," like someone making a concession, not consulting or asking.

"Fine. What time? I'm free in the late morning and then for a while after lunch."

"That's impossible," he replied, "I'm working all day. It would be best if you could come to the apartment at about eleven o'clock at night, the boy will be in bed by then." Those were clearly orders, I could either refuse or obey. "You know where it is," he added.

"All right," I said obediently. "I'll see you tomorrow then."

But he had already hung up. It was exactly the opposite of what Luisa had recommended I do, I was tempted to call her later on to tell her about our failure and thus make it hers too in effect, but it was best to take no further steps unless they were entirely justified (any courtship looks pathetic, the false front covering up something that is pure instinct), I would prefer her to take any unjustifiable steps.

I got out of the taxi in Conde de la Cimera, like the first time I had gone there and unlike the second time, both times at night. I had arrived a little early, at ten to eleven, I looked up and I saw the now-familiar lights in the living room and the bedroom, the balcony illuminated from within, I preferred to wait until the exact time arranged in case Deán was still putting Eugénio to bed, although that night the child would have no reason to delay things or keep guard, he would not have to fight against sleep again for the sake of a woman until he was grown up, or at least an adolescent. Using my matches, I lit a cigarette and went over to the doorway, and walked calmly up and down in front of it, I had spent a week preparing myself for this, possibly longer. I had snorted a line of coke before leaving the house so as to feel more alert, I'd slept very badly, I hardly ever use cocaine, but I had asked Ruibérriz for a quarter of a gram when we were at the races, he's usually got some ("Do you want a snort?" he asks me sometimes), unusual situations or situations you have simply thought about too much call for unusual measures. The effect wouldn't last, the alertness would wear off after a while, perhaps precisely when the conversation became more difficult and when I most needed to be alert. I stood in the fog smoking, then flicked the cigarette end away. I was just getting ready to press the intercom button, when I saw the lift doors open and two figures emerge from it in the half-darkness, they turned on the light in the doorway and came towards me, I didn't press the button, I waited for the young woman with the gracefully centrifugal gait and the beige gloves to open the door for me after pressing the bell which, some nights before, at a much later hour, had taken me a while to find, she was accompanied by the same man who had said he couldn't take it any longer and whom she had told to piss off, words are nearly always rhetorical or exaggerated or metaphorical and, therefore, inexact, he obviously could take it and she both clung on to and put up with him, they were still together, they were going out together while I was going in, the opposite way round this time, she must be the most active of the tenants, always up and down, by this time she must take me for a fellow tenant, she recognized me and said spontaneously, smiling: "Hello," and I said "Hi," the good-looking man didn't greet me today either, he was either extremely unfriendly or just distracted, perhaps he was still absorbed in the kisses they had exchanged upstairs and even while they were waiting for the lift, still with the front door open, even though neither of them would be staying behind this time or separating, they were going out together. Perhaps he was thinking of the rumpled bed from which he had just emerged and about his own neat bed.

I went upstairs and rang the bell and Deán immediately opened the door as if he had been waiting for my arrival and spying on the comings and goings of the lift through the spy hole. He was in shirtsleeves but still wearing a tie – slightly loosened – like a husband who has just got in from work and has only had time to take off his jacket. If Marta had been alive, I thought, she would perhaps have been in the kitchen with her apron on (I saw her in an apron), scraping off the plates or bustling about the house, with him following her from room to room while he told her things or they argued or he asked her something, I haven't always lived alone. He ushered me in without greeting me, although he offered me his left hand to shake and said "Sit down", pointing to the sofa on which the boy, small as an ant, had watched his videos of Tintin and Haddock and had fallen asleep after his long and finally fruitless battle, he asked me if I wanted a drink, I said I'd like a whisky with ice and water if possible. The apartment hadn't changed, I thought, men never change anything, I didn't want to look too hard, it didn't seem proper, I didn't want to remember or recall her there. At the table at which Marta and I had eaten our slow supper, there was still a pudding plate, empty – the dirty teaspoon still in it, askew – on a small table cloth the size of a large napkin: Deán still had enough energy and was in good enough spirits to sit down and eat whatever was left for him by the disgruntled cleaning lady or by his solicitous sisters-in-law, I almost never have lunch or supper at home, but if I do make myself something, I eat it quickly, standing up in the kitchen, a sign of debility and depression, it's bad for the stomach. He cleared away the plate and the table cloth before pouring me a whisky, all I'd had to eat was a McChicken at McDonalds, I lack his aplomb or perhaps it's just that my cleaning lady is lazy and I don't have any sisters-in-law, nor do I have a child to inspire pity and to make me a participant in the feelings he inspires. Deán returned from the kitchen and poured me a whisky, he rolled up his shirtsleeves – usually a threatening gesture, or so it always was traditionally – he poured another for himself, without water, he still didn't sit down, he remained standing up, with one elbow resting on a shelf, looking at me, I tried to hold his gaze, all this had happened in silence, silence is permissible as long as one of the people keeping silent is busy doing things, even if they're only getting out a bottle and a couple of glasses, he was holding his glass in his hand. From the moment I'd walked through the door, my eyes had drifted involuntarily towards the corridor, towards the open door of the boy's bedroom, he would be sleeping now, dreaming the weight of his father, utterly alone, and, perhaps, of his young aunts, of his eternally young mother, growing increasingly tenuous, her image ever more nebulous. Deán suddenly asked me if I wanted to take my raincoat off, I still had it on, creasing the seat of it, the suggestion made me lose all hope – this wouldn't be a matter of minutes – I handed it over to him together with my scarf, he went out and hung them in the wardrobe where the scarf had hung once before along with my overcoat, it had been colder then, on these misty days you only need a raincoat. I remembered the pith helmet I had seen in that wardrobe, Teobaldo Disegni de Túnez, it was from the 1930s, I was on the point of asking him where he had got it, but I didn't, a remark like that would be tempting fate. He came back into the living room, he leaned one elbow on the shelf again, he was looking at me in exactly the same way as he had in the restaurant, when I was still no one, and there was a silence between us then too, a silence made more bearable because the others were talking, Luisa and Téllez. He looked at me, therefore, as if I held no secrets for him, or perhaps he was weighing me up, he was doubtless trying to view me through Marta's eyes, when she was alive, he was trying to find out where my attraction or charm lay, trying to understand what his wife had sought and wanted that night. For the moment, there was no sign of scorn or anger or mockery, nor of curiosity either, he looked at me with penetration and apprehension, as if, from his great height, he were absorbing or verifying something and taking it all on board, I was looking up at him from the viewpoint of a low-angle shot in the cinema – Orson Welles was the master of that – his Tartar eyes, the colour of beer, seemed expectant and incredulous, the kind of eyes that force one to go on talking – except that I had not yet started – his cleft chin tilted as if he were awaiting a response, the lines or threads or incisions in his woody skin clearly visible, it would be like tree bark one day or was already on the way to that, his comminatory face gradually coming to resemble the scarred surface of a schooldesk.

But when he finally spoke (and he began with a question), the irritation or tension of the previous night's telephone conversation instantly reappeared, as if he had kept it alive and intact during the twenty-four or more hours since he had hung up, as if he had not gone to bed or been to work or seen anyone in the meantime and had merely been waiting for me all night and all day, pacing up and down, occasionally peering through the spy hole and punching the palm of one hand like a boxer before a contest or as a film director told me once that the actor Jack Palance used to do between takes during filming so as not to lose concentration and energy, whilst another famous actor with whom he worked, George Sanders, would smoke cigarettes, reclining in a hammock, one hand behind his head, two very different methods, one born of nervousness and the other of indolence, but both produced excellent results on film; Sanders ended up committing suicide in Barcelona, having written a note in which he told everyone to go to hell (a horrible death, a foreign death, "Stay where you are, in the shit," was what he was saying), I think Palance is still alive or else enjoyed a long life.

"So she didn't die alone, then?" Deán said at last, and immediately took a sip of his whisky: it was a gesture intended to cover his mouth and make it seem as if he himself had not spoken, as if the words had been uttered by no one or by the television, although that was switched off. The way he asked the question meant that I couldn't be sure what answer he was looking for.

"No, I was with her, surely Luisa told you that," I answered, and I, in turn, took a sip of my whisky, doubtless in order to cover my mouth too and to get my turn over with as quickly as possible.

"What was the last thing she said, can you remember?"

"Oh God, the child," I thought.

"She expressed her concern for the child," I said.

Deán stroked one cheek with his hand, as if pretending to think deeply.

"Ah, the child," he said, "that's logical. And then you neither called me nor anyone else. It didn't occur to you, which is perfectly understandable, isn't it? Perfectly understandable."

There was an example of Deán's infinite understanding or he may have been putting it on, enough time had passed for him to be able to resort to irony.

"Look, the fact is I did call you, perhaps Luisa didn't tell you that." I decided to continue to address him formally as "usted", at that point I didn't foresee insulting him in word or thought, and I could always start calling him "tú", as he had done with me from the start, if I needed to. It was a great help being able to refer to Luisa. "I found your number, you know that, I got through to your hotel in London even though it was very late, they said that there was no one by the name of Deán staying there, that there was no room reserved in that name. Only later did it occur to me that they might have booked you in under your second surname, if you give two surnames in England, the one that counts is the last one, you know, on your driving licence or your visa. But I didn't dare to ring again that night." I could have lied, I could have said I didn't know his second surname (there was no reason why I should know even the first) and that, therefore, it would have been impossible for me to try again anyway, that way I would have been free of all responsibility as would everyone else, I wasn't in fact responsible, nobody was, and that is why, perhaps, I told the truth. "What could I have said to you?" I added. "Think about it for a moment. What could I have said to you?" It didn't seem to matter much to him that I had been with Marta (I was the one who alluded to her), or perhaps he had simply had much more time to come to terms with that fact than to acquire understanding or irony, and he merely took his anger for granted, that is, there was no need to express it or show it, no need for any dramatic gestures.

"What could you have told me?" he repeated. "Exactly. What would you have said if they had listed me under my first name and had put you through to my room that night? I was there, I would have listened to you." I didn't say anything. "You still don't know."

"You didn't save us," I thought. "You saved neither her nor me."

"My phone call would have been anonymous," I said. "I would probably just have said: 'Phone home.' No one would have answered here and you would have been alarmed, you would have sent someone over. Or maybe I would have hung up before I spoke, that's what I did the following night, when I asked for Mr Ballesteros and someone answered. I hung up without saying anything."

"Yes, I know someone answered," repeated Deán. He stroked his cheek with his hand again, this time as if checking to see that he had shaved; but he was extremely well shaven, certainly not half-shaven. "But it didn't matter by then, it was too late. Everything had already happened and I had just found out about it, two misfortunes instead of one, or instead of what, until then, was not merely a misfortune. Not pure misfortune."

"Why don't you sit down?" I said. I felt diminished before that extremely tall man standing opposite me. "I can't hear you properly. I don't understand you."

"I'm fine here, I've spent all day sitting down," he said. He had rather hairy arms, he scratched his right arm with the stiff fingers of his left hand, perhaps it was going to sleep, leaning on the shelf. "You can hear me perfectly well, but it's true that you don't understand me, you don't know my rôle in all this just as I didn't know yours, up until yesterday, I could only hypothesize. Your rôle and mine do not complement or complete each other, they are not mutually necessary, they merely cross each other unwittingly, or rather yours does, not mine, mine continues along the track of ignorance and yours crosses it, there are some things that one should know about at once, if you had rung someone that night, they would have rung me, don't you see?"

"We can't bear those close to us not to know about our troubles," I thought, "we can't bear them to go on believing what is no longer true, not for a minute, for them to believe that we are married when we have just been widowed or that we still have parents when we have suddenly become orphans, that we have company when that company has just left or are in good health when we have suddenly fallen ill. That they should think us still alive when we are dead or should believe us dead when we are still alive. But I am not close to him."

"I don't understand," I said again, only this time it wasn't quite true.

He waited a few seconds, he ran his hand over his hair, he wore it combed to the left like an old-fashioned child (perhaps himself as a child), and when he spoke again, his voice was even deeper, gravelly and hoarse as if he had an asthmatic chest or as if he were speaking from inside a helmet, he said this:

"But you will understand. I want you to know what happened during that period when I did not know that Marta had died, what I did and didn't do and what I was about to do and what happened anyway. It wasn't your fault, it didn't happen because of you, I'm not blaming anyone for the way things turned out. Things just happen, that's all, I know that, perhaps it's a question of good or bad luck, sometimes no one intends anything or seeks or wants anything. But those things always happen to someone and there is always someone else, their paths cross, often without their realizing it, usually without their even getting the chance to know. It doesn't matter. No one expects it. You crossed my path, though how, you don't know, you don't know me, I'm a matter of indifference to you, now you *can* know all that and it's best that you do, then you will understand me. It won't take long, don't worry, it won't be a long story, I'll tell it quickly."

"Ah, yes," I thought, "he is weary of the shadows. He too wants to escape from the enchantment, he's in a hurry to be done now. But what's he talking about, he's saying what Solus said, no one dies of their own accord, we don't usually find out about those who die because we pass too close by or too far off, normally we all follow the course of ignorance, it's the only course there is, I've done my own share of hypothesizing too, but what death is he talking about, everything is continually travelling on, everything is connected, some things drag other things along with them, all oblivious to each other, what death is he talking about?"

"That would be best, I haven't got much time," I said, though that wasn't quite true, all that awaited me the following day was my tedious actor, I would have to phone him, he would give me work. And perhaps I could call Luisa too, a justifiable step, she had asked me to.

Deán picked up the remote control for a moment and switched on the television, at the same time turning down the sound. He flicked swiftly through the channels and turned it off again, a nervous, mechanical gesture, a habitual gesture for someone on his own, we all do it sometimes to find out what is happening in the world in our perpetual absence.

"I wasn't alone in London," he said then, "it's not difficult to imagine, nor is it hard to imagine that I was alone, I could have been either of those things, no one knows about it. I've had a lover for a year now, a young nurse who works in the hospital next door," and with one restless hand he pointed vaguely outside, towards the balcony. "It was nothing special at first, she was no one special, just as you wouldn't have been particularly special to Marta that first night, you were still no one and, for good or ill, that's how you remained, you didn't get any further than that, you didn't even get as far as that, I didn't know that until yesterday, I only had suspicions, hypotheses. Anyway, there were the uniforms, a few words exchanged in a nearby pub, a drink paid for from the other end of the bar, some shared laughter, the hugely influential laughter of her colleagues, a brief walk together ("Those inoffensive footsteps," I thought from my enchanted state, the incessant beating in my thoughts), the feet that stroll along together and stop at the traffic lights where the faces suddenly meet in a kiss, and so the next day you go and pick her up when she comes off her shift, you take her out to supper and you end up back at her apartment ("She takes off her white stockings with the lumpy seams"). Nothing special, nothing important, a reaction against the daily grind until, foolishly, those steps are repeated, with no witnesses now, no encouraging laughter and, imperceptibly, they become habits, minimal habits that consist in almost nothing, in phoning at around the same time whenever you phone her, in always having the same thing to drink when you're with her, in inadvertently memorizing her work schedules, there is always someone who sees such things as signs, as meaningful data, the other party has no hidden agenda, he or she means nothing by them, at least sometimes. But each of us understands things as we choose to, we tell our own stories, no two stories are the same even if they recount a common experience ("And, besides, they don't belong only to those who were present or to those who invent them, once a story has been told, it's anyone's, it becomes common currency, it gets twisted and distorted, and we all tell our own version"). And far too often you end up back at her apartment and it takes longer and longer to say goodbye, what burdens things with significance is repetition and secrecy, not any one gesture or word, the flesh makes people over-confident, and then habits become confused with rights, people call them acquired rights, ridiculous, you long to go home and yet, a few days later, you return to the very place you wanted to leave and where you were detained by caresses and kisses and protestations of love and lamentations, I suppose it pleases and cheers us to know that we are loved ("One's eyes already wearing the face of the other: I stay too long by you, I weary you")."

Deán stopped talking and went over to the coffee table to pour himself another whisky, he was drinking as he talked, he wasn't talking slowly now, he really was telling the story quickly.

"Did your wife know?" I ventured to ask, taking advantage of the clatter of ice and liquid. But I didn't dare call her Marta in his presence. He returned to his post by the shelf.

"No," he replied. "No, no." People always answer questions thrown in like that. "That is, I don't think she did, I don't know, she and I never asked each other questions, we waited for the other to tell us whatever there was to tell. Naturally, I did everything possible to ensure that she didn't know, as soon as the affair became a habit, I never again walked down a street with Eva, I never went to meet her at the end of her shift, I didn't take her out to supper after that first night, nothing, we met only in her apartment, she wasn't allowed to call me at mine, our affair was an area closed off from everyone, hermetically sealed, especially from her colleagues, I had my life and I couldn't run any risks, I didn't want to continue the affair, although it did continue ("And now I too will have to remember that name," I thought. "Eva"). I don't know, I don't think so, although, recently, on a couple of nights, I did hear Marta crying into her pillow thinking that I wouldn't hear her, I didn't say anything the first time, it didn't last long, the second time I asked her: 'What's wrong?' and she said: 'Nothing, nothing.' 'But you're crying,' I said. 'Sometimes, at night, I have dark thoughts, fears.' 'Fears about what?' I said. 'Uncontrollable fears,' she said, 'that something bad will happen to us, to you or me or the child.' 'But what could possibly happen to us?' I said.

'I know, I know, I'm just tired at the moment, weak, it will pass, when you're feeling like this everything looks black, don't worry, it doesn't happen during the day.' I didn't give it any further thought, but who can say, maybe she did know in some way and that's why you're here." And Deán stood looking at me with his chin slightly raised as if he had asked me a question. But he hadn't.

"I don't think she did," I allowed myself to say, more than enough, I think. "She talked about you quite naturally all the time, I don't think there was any premeditation on her part. When you called from London and spoke to her, neither of us had any firm intentions, I'm sure. As you yourself said, things just happen."

"I'm not asking you about that, Luisa told me everything yesterday, I don't want to know any details," said Deán, instantaneously angry, gripping his glass harder, but without quite showing his anger fully. "I'm not asking you about that," he repeated and loosened his grip. "Remember, I'm just telling you a story, all you have to do is listen to me." He could be violent that man, like Jack Palance.

"I'm well aware of that. Go on, I'm listening."

Deán seemed a little ashamed of his reaction. He paced across the room, drumming his short, hard nails against his whisky glass, doubtless trying to distance his story from that interjection, to avoid contamination. The wooden floor creaked. Then he went on and I continued listening, his lips seemed to grow thinner, from where I was sitting, I could barely see them:

"The night I called her, everything was as it should be, in so far as that was possible. Three weeks before, the nurse had told me that she was pregnant, you can imagine, we'd always been very careful, but there's no such thing as absolute safety, I thought it had been a deliberate mistake on her part, I wanted to stop the affair, the prearranged visits and the endless goodbyes, I didn't want Marta to cry any more or to have any reason to be afraid, even if she didn't know what it was she needed to be afraid of, everything was becoming more and more complicated with Eva, I couldn't manage to leave either, the flesh exercises a great pull as long as that pull lasts, a year isn't long enough for it to wear thin, for it to give, I still hadn't made the break, I hadn't said I was leaving, and then I was faced with that pregnancy, she was a nurse too, so there was no possible room for doubt. Women traffic in their own bodies, they manipulate them, they have that extraordinary capacity to transform them, to have something grow inside them as a result of their dealings with any man, anyone, even the most inhuman or most abject of men, their bodies can do that, can you imagine ("*Ġe·licgan,*" I thought, "If that was the verb, it disappeared; perhaps it isn't easy to accept the act that it describes and it's therefore better not to name it"), something that wasn't there before and that is not only there now but is changing, and then they expel it when it has done its duty of making them mothers and of providing them with a link that will last for ever in another form which, though changing, is visible, for an indefinite period and which, under normal circumstances, will survive them, they've always got that as a last resort, it's not just their prolongation, it's their grasp on the world, I've seen it, I have a son and he doesn't mean the same to me as he does to his mother ("The mother believes that she was born to be a mother and the spinster to be single, the murderer to be a murderer and the victim a victim: they all believe this from their ghostly positions"). I begged her to have an abortion and she didn't want to at first, she threatened to talk to Marta, I told her I would deny everything, I would even deny knowing her ("I know you not, old man, I know not who you are, nor have I ever seen you before"), she laughed because today a child's paternity can be proved beyond doubt, so I threatened her with the only thing I had left, with never seeing her again and with not loving her. I don't mean to boast, but she loved me a lot, in fact, she would have done anything for me, it's inexplicable, sometimes we take irrevocable decisions about a person and no one can change our minds, she would have done anything for me, but first, she had to play her hand and see what she could get." Deán paused for a moment and cadged a cigarette from me, I had put the packet on the table, I was chainsmoking. He picked up my matches and held one in his large hand; before lighting it, he went on: "She didn't get very much, feelings enfeeble us, you know, they're our ruination ("Feelings or loyalty or inexplicable decisions"), so she backed down in exchange for a few vague promises, and we decided to take advantage of a business trip of mine to London, being a nurse she knew that London is still the safest and most hygienic place for these things, and that way I could accompany her. It sounds ridiculous, but it occurred to me too that there we would be able to walk down the street together again and eat in restaurants, although it seemed prudent to me that we should stay in different hotels, I found her one near mine, in Sloane Square, better than mine in fact, my stay was being paid for by the company and I might have to receive the occasional colleague at my hotel, it made sense for us to stay in separate establishments. I gave her money to pay her bills, for the hospital too, the trip didn't cost her a penny. No one knew we were together, not even her colleagues, they would have been worried and they would have asked her to bring things back for them. The first night I took her out to a very amusing Indian restaurant in order to distract her as much as possible from what awaited her the following day."

"Yes, the Bombay Brasserie, I know it," I said, I couldn't not say it.

"How do you know that?" said Deán, displaying his natural capacity for surprise, his nostrils flaring, suggesting vehemence or perhaps inclemency.

"You told your wife when you called, she remarked on it, she asked if I knew it."

"I see, and you do, do you?"

"I have dined in its vast colonial-style rooms on a couple of occasions, a pianist in evening dress sits in the foyer, and there are respectful waiters and maîtres d'hotel, and huge ceiling fans winter and summer, it's a very theatrical place, rather expensive by English standards, but not prohibitively so, a place for friends to meet and celebrate or for business meetings, rather than for intimate, romantic suppers, unless you want to impress an inexperienced young woman or a girl from the working classes, or your wife or your mistress whom you never or almost never take out (the wife stuck at home in Conde de la Cimera as she is every night, although tonight she has company for what is clearly a romantic supper, the mistress usually stuck in her apartment, but who, today, is on a trip, a trip paid for by someone else, a trip she was obliged to make) someone likely to feel slightly overwhelmed by the setting and to get absurdly drunk on cocktails and Indian beer, Bombay Sunset, Bombay Skyline, Pink Camellia, Bombay Blues, someone you won't have to take to some intermediate place before hailing a taxi with fold-up seats and going back to your hotel or your flat, someone with whom there will be no need to speak after the hot, spicy supper, you can merely take her face in your hands and kiss her, undress her, touch her, framing that bought, fragile head in your hands in that gesture so oddly reminiscent of both coronation and strangulation, I thought all this while I was standing in the shadows looking at the planes hanging from the ceiling of the child's bedroom and while Marta Téllez was still ill but not yet dead, they would be there now, in the room next door, the planes would be watching over his sleep while they prepared for that night's weary, anachronistic foray, that tiny, ghostly, languid battle, hanging by threads, the inert, passive oscillation, tomorrow, despair and die."

"Yes, I like it immensely," I said. "I've been there on two or three occasions, some time ago."

"It's recommended in all the guides," said Deán earnestly, as if making some excuse. "I took her there, we drank and laughed quite a lot despite what would happen the following morning, the drink would help her get to sleep that night, as it would me, I would take her to the entrance of the hospital, I'd wait outside in case there were any problems or she got into a panic, a couple of hours she'd told me, although it was unlikely that anything unusual would happen, she was a nurse and she had seen it all before, nurses get very depressed, it's only logical, although, obviously, it's not the same having it done to oneself. I found it odd that they didn't want to take her in before or keep her in afterwards, for a night, a few hours, but she knew better than me, she had made all the arrangements from her clinic here, it worked out cheaper hospital to hospital she had said. She could get by in English, so can I."

"I read English at university," I said; it was an absurd remark that Deán ignored. I poured another whisky, he let me do so, he continued as if he hadn't heard:

"That night I took her back to her hotel in a taxi after supper, we both chose not to go up to either of our rooms, there was something in her body that would not be there the following day and it was best not to be reminded of it. She didn't seem particularly affected by it or she pretended not to be, the cocktails must have helped, she even seemed contented, affectionate, perhaps my promises made up for everything else. At the door of her hotel, she gave me one of those grateful kisses, how can I put it, an enthusiastic kiss, I felt sure that she would bear me no ill will for that awful experience. I walked back to my hotel, a short distance away, and then I called Marta from my room to confirm that I had arrived safely and to find out how things were, she didn't say she was having supper with you or anyone, I thought she was alone with the boy, and you really believe that there was no premeditation, you've got a nerve." Deán was still standing, he stopped talking and stood there looking at me, I saw a hint of cruelty in his frank eyes, he struck a match and lit the cigarette that he had cadged from me, as if he didn't want to get sidetracked down the other possible route that our conversation might take, he had dismissed it from the start; then the glint disappeared. "The fact is I didn't sleep well that night, I slept badly, I kept waking up, I blamed myself and Eva, but not Marta, although I thought about both of them, what was happening in London was happening because Marta existed, there are certain spaces in one's life that are occupied, which is why people do everything they can to create a space for themselves or to replace instantly those who leave ("You didn't sleep very peacefully on the island, then, on neither of your two nights on the island did you have a quiet night's sleep," I thought. "But the rustle of your own sheets here didn't reach you either, sheets I never touched, nor did the clatter of your own plates bearing Irish steak and ice cream, or the clink of your glasses filled with red wine, or the rattle of death, or the boom of anxiety, or the creak of malaise and depression, or the buzz of fear and regret, or the sing-song hum of weary, much-maligned death, you heard only the traffic driving on the wrong side of the road and the tall red buses, the night-time bustle and the reverberating chatter in various languages at the Indian restaurant, and the echo of other, possibly mortal, sing-song voices: you speak of your Eva in the past tense"). If I had known, if I had known that night what you knew ("I knew it, you fool, because I saw it and experienced it and I was afraid and I could do nothing to stop it, I was a witness to it and I took her in my arms so that she might die as well as possible, I wasn't the one who should have been by her side," and again I addressed him as "tú" as I had at the entrance to the restaurant in order to insult him the way one does in one's thoughts, his complaint, which sounded like a reproach, irritated me, he had gone off with Eva to resolve his affair without Marta's knowledge, what did he expect)." Deán came over to the armchair, which matched the sofa, and he sat on the right arm as if he had lost his footing on the slippery snow, I had seen him falter like that before, indeed more dramatically than that, at the open grave, he got spattered with the earth dug up by the gravedigger, it spattered his raincoat. Even sitting down he was still very tall, he didn't cross his legs, he kept them straight, he seemed to me more vulnerable in that position. "If I had known, everything would have been different in London, I would never even have allowed her to go to the hospital the following morning, there would have been no reason to, a brother or sister for Eugenio and a new mother, why not, given the circumstances, you love things and people according to what you have or haven't got, according to the spaces they leave, our needs and desires vary according to what we lose or to whether we are abandoned by someone or dispossessed, the same goes for our feelings too, as I've already said, irrevocable decisions can be taken and, in part, that's the basis for everything, we base them on incompatibilities and on what we need at the time." He was contradicting himself about feelings or perhaps, before, he had been speaking for Eva and, now, he was speaking for himself.

"I've told you already," I said, "I didn't dare to call you twice, I lost my nerve after talking to the porter. There wasn't anyone called Deán there, for all I knew there might be no Ballesteros there either. In fact, I don't know that I achieved a great deal by finding out what your last name was."

"How did you do that?" asked Deán.

"There were letters around, I looked for one from the bank."

"At least you're resourceful, not everyone would have thought of that." He was calling me "usted" all of a sudden, an unexpected sign of respect, a moment of belated hesitancy, or perhaps he had picked it up from me. But it only lasted a matter of seconds, after a few sentences, he reverted to "tú": "Look, I'm not blaming you for anything, I'm just telling you what happened because I didn't find out in time, how I spent those hours, quite a few hours, during which I was in a state of complete misapprehension. I'm not even blaming you for having left the child alone, for example, as an embittered, resentful widower might do: nothing happened to him and it would be wrong to accuse you of what might have happened but didn't, everything depends on the end result, doesn't it, and that includes everything, even if it's only an instant in time, one particular action varies depending on the effect it has, a bullet that hits the target is not the same bullet if it misses, nor is a blow with a knife if it fails to strike home, it's as if we had held nothing in our hand and yet we acted as if quite the opposite were true, we're always so full of intentions, I wonder if they really are what count or precisely what do not count, it's also true that sometimes we have no intentions, maybe you didn't ("A yes and a no and a perhaps and, meanwhile, everything has moved on or is gone, the misery of not knowing what to do and of having to act regardless, because one has to fill up the insistent time that continues to pass without waiting for us, we move more slowly: having to decide without knowing, having to act without knowing and yet foreseeing, and that is the greatest and most common of misfortunes, foreseeing what will come afterwards, it's a misfortune generally perceived as quite a minor one, yet experienced by everyone every day. It is something you get used to, we take little notice of it")." Deán stubbed out his cigarette before he had finished it and, as he did so, he slid down on to the seat of the armchair, now he was almost at my height, his shirtsleeves resting on the arms of the chair and his tie looser, although, even then, he lost none of his composure. "But things did happen here" – he continued, I wasn't sure I wanted to hear the whole sordid tale, it had nothing to do with me, but that man was telling me the story, he had chosen me to listen to him, perhaps it did have something to do with me, to some degree – "I wonder if things would have turned out the same if you hadn't been in that bedroom with Marta." And he gestured with his head towards the corridor that led to the bedroom, I knew the way. "I don't mean her death, but

I wonder if, then, she would have called someone when she felt ill. Perhaps not me so as not to alarm me when I was so far away, but her sister or a friend or a neighbour or a doctor, to ask for help. I wonder if she didn't call because she was with you, perhaps she hoped that it would pass and you could resume the party ("You're mad, how can I possibly phone him, he'd kill me," I thought, "that's what Marta Téllez said to me when I suggested she should warn this man in London, Deán may be right, she might have called someone if I hadn't been here. But that wouldn't have saved her, it would only have saved him from his enchantment, his shadow, given what he's been saying"). Things happen, it's true, it always happens to someone and not to others, and those it happens to bemoan the fact that it does ("And even if there's nothing, something moves us, it's impossible for us to remain still, in our place, the only safe option would be never to say or do anything, and even then: inactivity and silence might have the same effects, produce identical results or, who knows, even worse ones, as if vacuous resentments and desires, unnecessary torments, emanated from our very breath. The only solution is for everything to end and for there to be nothing"). It doesn't matter, it happened to you and to me, and more especially to the two women. The following morning, I went to the hospital with Eva, it was a good hospital, with everything as it should be, not too far from our hotels, Sloane Square, Sloane Street, towards the river, I'm sure you know the area, all very nice and clean. I didn't go in with her, there was no need and she preferred it that way, I told her that I would be in a café opposite, reading the newspapers, I would stay there just in case she needed something suddenly, she'd be a couple of hours at most, not long, it's the least I could do, I had put off a work engagement until after lunch, there would be time for my other meetings the following day, we were to be there for three nights, we wouldn't go back until Friday, each with our own ticket, we had booked them separately though on the same flight, we thought it best to do things that way. When I said goodbye to her, I saw how pale she was, I noticed for the first time that she was frightened, perhaps she regretted what she was about to do, but it was too late now. I gave her a hug, I kissed her on the cheek. 'It'll be over soon,' I said, 'I'll be thinking of you all the time, I'll be right here.' I watched her disappear into the crowd in the foyer, hospitals are even fuller than hotels, she was wearing a long overcoat, a headscarf and pair of low, rather childish shoes. I bought several Spanish and English newspapers and sat down in the café, it was a pleasant morning, cold but clear, not that the weather was likely to last in London. Contrary to what I had said, I tried hard not to think about her and about what would be happening, but I ended up keeping my promise despite myself, it imposed itself on my thoughts albeit bereft of images, I have no very clear idea of what happens in these cases, nor do I want to. The truth is that I was thinking about similarities, but we won't go into that." Deán raised a hand to his forehead, he rubbed his forehead with his stiff fingers as if he had an itch, then he put one hand over his eyes and pinched the bridge of his nose as if he had just removed his glasses, only he didn't wear glasses. "After one endless hour, I couldn't stand it any longer, I couldn't bear sitting there trying to read a newspaper that I wasn't in the least bit interested in. I got up, paid my bill, walked slowly across to the hospital, went hesitantly into that foyer crammed with people waiting or passing through and coming and going, it was swarming with people, an enormous clinic, I saw Eva's counterparts, they're always busy, she would have felt at home with them. I went over to the reception desk and in my acceptable English I asked where I could wait for Eva, Eva García, I said, I spelled the name, she was having an operation, I hadn't been able to get here earlier to be with her, I lied ("And now I too will have to remember that surname together with that first name," I thought). I was upset and a bit worried, I didn't want to do anything or change anything, I just wanted to be near to her, so that she would see me as soon as she came out of wherever she was, there were several floors. The nurse asked me when Eva had come in, I said an hour ago, she asked if it was an emergency, I said it wasn't, it was an operation that had been arranged beforehand, she had been given an appointment for that morning. 'That's not possible,' she said, while she searched the computer, presumably for the name García. 'If she had an appointment for an operation today, we would have taken her in yesterday anyway,' she said. 'It's not a serious operation,' I explained. The nurse looked up and asked me what I was afraid she was going to ask me: 'What sort of operation is it?' I didn't want to use the word, I said, translating literally: 'An interruption of pregnancy', I don't know if there is a more suitable euphemism in English, but she understood anyway, and said: 'That's impossible, they would have taken her in yesterday, I'm sure.' She again searched on the computer, tapping the relevant keys to find the list of people who had been taken in yesterday, I suppose, then the same thing happened to me as happened to you, I suggested that she should also look under the surname Valle, which was her second name. Eva García Valle. 'There's no García and no Valle, either yesterday or today,' she said firmly after consulting the screen, 'there's no one in the hospital with those names.' 'Are you sure?' I insisted. 'Absolutely,' she said and cleared the list from the screen, there was no arguing with her. She sat there looking at me. 'Are you her husband?' she asked. I don't know if that was a momentary flash of humanity or a desire for gossip; since Eva wasn't there it made no difference to her what I was. 'Yes,' I said, 'thank you,' and I withdrew, she watched me with her neutral eyes. I waited in the foyer not knowing what to do, watching the doctors and the nurses and the patients and the visitors pass by, I wondered if perhaps Eva had registered under another name, but that was impossible, they would have asked to see her papers. I noticed a particular door through which visitors kept disappearing, I followed them, I saw a large room, apparently a waiting room, again it was chock-a-block with people sitting on battered armchairs. I peered in, I glanced around. I was confused. And then I saw her in the distance, Eva was sitting there, eyes downcast, having taken off her overcoat and scarf, as I got closer, I saw that she had her legs crossed and was reading a magazine, she seemed quite calm, there must have been some delay, I thought, that was why she hadn't yet registered. But I thought other things too as I approached her. She was reading a glossy magazine, a weekly, she didn't look up until I was by her side, brushing against her with my coat, I put my hand on her shoulder. 'What are you doing here?' I said; I wasn't sure whether to add 'Haven't they admitted you yet?', but I didn't want to give her an easy way out or tempt her into more lies. She jumped, a whole hour had passed since we had parted, for me, it had seemed like a century, she became flustered, she placed a hand on my forearm, she immediately closed the magazine, she tried to stand up, I prevented her from doing so, my hand on her shoulder, I sat down beside her, I gripped her wrist, I repeated, this time angrily: 'What are you doing here? In reception they told me that your name isn't even on the list, what is all this about?' She looked away, her eyes glazed over, she couldn't speak, as if she were choking, she said nothing. 'So there's no operation, then?' I said. She shook her head, her eyes glittered, but there were no tears. 'There's no abortion, no pregnancy, nothing?' I said. She picked up her scarf from the chair beside her and burst into tears, covering her face with the scarf. We left there at once, walking quickly across the foyer, I still had my hand on her wrist, almost dragging her after me." Deán paused to take a sip of his drink, the first in ages, momentarily covering his mouth again.

"It's so easy to live in a state of delusion, or to be deceived," I thought, "indeed, it is our natural condition: no one is free of it and it certainly doesn't mean that one is stupid, we should not struggle so hard against it nor should we let it embitter us." That is what Deán had said, although he had added: "And yet, when we do learn the truth, we find it unbearable."

"There's still a link," I said.

"Yes, that's it," replied Deán, "a link, which is still there even though what might have existed no longer exists, on the contrary, perhaps there's an even stronger link, perhaps the renunciation of what might have been and was common to you both unites you more than its acceptance or accomplishment or its unfettered development, it is frustration, failure, separation or the end of something that bind us together most strongly, the small scar lingers for ever like a reminder of abandonment or want ("Or of exile," I thought), and that scar keeps reminding us: 'I did this for you, you are in my debt.' There is a link too with what has been lost from sight, with what one imagines and with what never even happens ("With the dead too"). If I hadn't got worried, if I hadn't gone into the hospital, Eva would have come across to the café after two hours looking shaken and slightly unsteady on her feet, like a heroine who has passed her trial by fire and I would have consoled her then until the end of my days, I'm sure, she doubtless had ready in her handbag a bit of bloodstained cotton wool to show me, as if by chance, to make me feel even more in her debt, women can always come up with some blood when it's needed ("I saw a bit of bloodstained cotton wool in the rubbish bin here in your wife's apartment, after she had died"). We went back to our separate hotels without saying a word, I dropped her off, I didn't even get out of the taxi, I just opened the door in silence and bundled her out. I wanted to be alone, I went out for a walk, to buy some presents for Marta and the boy ("A reward for waiting or a message from some new conquest or intended to ease a guilty conscience, who knows, they arrived too late"), I didn't want to see Eva ever again, we would be taking the same plane back, but there was no reason why we should sit next to each other, I wanted nothing more to do with her. After a bite to eat, I went back to the hotel, I discussed business with the colleague I had arranged to meet, I couldn't take in a word he said to me, I was absorbed in my own thoughts, I was reconstructing the three weeks I had spent in that state of delusion, the arguments, the threats, the preparations, the trip, how stupid I've been, I thought ("And yet we really shouldn't find that so very painful, it is simply a period of time that has become strange, floating or fictitious"). Eva had called me three times, I didn't return her calls, it didn't occur to me to call here, I was too upset to talk to Marta and I preferred to wait, most unfortunate, at that very moment, everyone was desperately trying to find me, you had gone off with the piece of paper with my address on it and no one knew where I was ("I didn't mean to, it was an accident, don't hold it against me"). I went out again, I was just as agitated, even more so, in fact, I caught the underground into the West End, I wandered about some more, I bought more presents, more junk, I went into a cinema in Leicester Square, I don't understand enough English to be able follow a whole film and, besides, my mind was on other things, I was absorbed in my own thoughts, I left halfway through, I didn't get back to my hotel until half past eight and in the foyer, waiting for me, was Eva, I've no idea how long she'd been there, again she was leafing through a magazine. She stood up, raising her hands to her chest as if to parry a blow. 'Let me talk to you,' she said, 'please, please, just let me talk to you.' She hadn't eaten a thing all day, I had hardly had anything to eat either, she had spent the day locked in her room, she was unsteady on her feet and looked as if she had been crying, I said that I was prepared to listen to her, but that it would make no difference, we looked for a place nearby, it was a bit late for supper in England, the Bombay Brasserie stays open late, so we hailed a taxi and went there, only this time there was nothing special about it, we were like someone lost and disoriented in a new city who returns to the one place he knows. It was an act of revenge too, I suppose, taking her there again, repeating it all, for the night before I had been all attentiveness, you see, I had made an effort. This time we didn't even notice the piano or the exotic waiters or the décor, we ordered for the sake of ordering, in fact, we found it hard to eat anything, but we did order and drink several cocktails, I drank one after the other, I drank quite a lot, in fact, I got thoroughly drunk on cocktails and Indian beer, it packs quite a punch, I wouldn't find it easy to sleep that night either. If I had known that Marta was dead, I would not have hated that nurse so much, more than that, I would probably have forgiven her. Just then, you see, she would have been all I had. You tend to be more understanding with the person you are left with."

"What did you talk about? What did she say to you?"

Deán got up, as if prompted by my question, and returned to his initial position, one elbow leaning on the shelf, a decorative pose, a thin man, a tall man. His face grew even more sombre, his energetic chin turned away as if in flight, his beer-coloured eyes glinting wildly as they had when he had left the restaurant and Téllez wouldn't let him pay the bill, but we were not lit now by the greenish light of a storm, only by electric light and, outside, fog which, in the city, looks yellowish or whitish or reddish, it depends.

"Nothing, what could she say? She tried to placate me, she pleaded, she explained, she tried to justify what could not be justified, as if the love people bear you could wash away certain things, there are people who believe that the intensity of their feelings is some sort of guarantee, having exalted feelings becomes confused with acting honourably. Perhaps I would have seen it like that too had I known what was going on here, I was behind with the news."

"We can never know for certain that we have acted honourably," I said, venturing an opinion, perhaps myself acting improperly. The effects of the cocaine were wearing off, I was less alert now, at least less alert in relation to myself.

"You're right, I can't say that I acted honourably any more than you can." Deán cadged another cigarette off me and, this time, he lit it straight away, he took two puffs, he probably wasn't really a smoker and he was smoking now in order to accompany the narrative act by some physical gesture, the person telling a story barely moves. That is what I thought and that is how I remember his talk, he had ideas, but he found it hard to put them in any kind of order. But then who doesn't? "She insisted on explaining the process, her thought process, it wasn't necessary, I understood it already. She could see that I was distancing myself from her, or trying to, and she didn't want to lose me, it made her desperate just to imagine it, she considered getting pregnant but that wasn't easy, as I told you before I was always very careful. She couldn't trust to her flesh to keep me, one year isn't long, but two might be enough for it to wear thin, for it to give. She said that it broke her heart when she saw how impatient I was to leave her apartment and go back to mine, I hadn't been like that in the beginning, then I hated having to leave, maybe I was the one who was clinging then, it's true that I used to find it hard to say goodbye to her, that was shortly after I had met her, I can hardly remember it now ("The kisses of the one who is leaving, standing at the front door of the one who is staying, become confused with those of the day before yesterday and those of the day after tomorrow, there was only ever one memorable first night and it was immediately lost, swallowed up by the weeks and the repetitive months that succeeded it"). I know it was like that once, but I can't remember it. I was different now, she said, irritable and abrupt, as if she had suddenly become a stranger, it's perplexing and upsetting when things change so radically, but one hasn't oneself changed ("I do not know you, nor do I know who you are, I have never seen you before, do not come to me asking favours or calling me sweet names, for I am not the thing I was, and neither are you; that is what people always say, sooner or later"). Then she thought up this little drama, she believed that an abortion might also bring us together, that I would admire her sacrifice and respect her for her powers of renunciation, and her reasoning was quite sound, it would have been like that had I kept my cool and obediently finished reading my newspapers and not moved from that café, I had promised her that I would stay there just in case she needed me and there I sat for more than an hour, pretending to read, but all the time thinking about her and the doctor's hand on her, and about similarities. It had seemed like an eternity to me and all the time she had been calmly reading magazines, can you understand that?"

"The person telling a story is usually able to explain himself," I thought, "telling a story is tantamount to persuading someone or making oneself clear or making someone see one's point of view and, that way, everything is capable of being understood, even the most vile of acts, everything can be forgiven when there is something to forgive, everything can be overlooked or assimilated or even pitied, such and such happened and we have to learn to live with it once we know that it did happen, we have to find a place for it in our consciousness and in our memory where the fact that it happened and that we know about it will not prevent us from going on living." I also thought: "Sometimes, telling a story can even get you into someone's good graces."

"I think I understand how you felt, I think it's understandable," I said.

"When we left the restaurant a storm broke and a terrific wind got up, we were both a bit unsteady on our legs, I because of the amount I had drunk, she out of desperation when she saw that none of her explanations or pleas had any effect on me, made no mark on me, I had responded only with cruelty and sarcasm. The fact is that then they genuinely didn't move me. Afterwards . . . But there was no time." Deán fell silent, I didn't say anything this time, there was no question in that pause, not even an implicit one. He seemed sunk in thought just then, it was impossible to know what transformation or distortion to expect from that face, although his almond eyes looked at me, but did not rest on me, it was as if they merely skirted round or passed over me; his rebellious chin was lowered, an edgeless sword. "I hated her," he said. "I hated her and yet it wouldn't have been the same if I'd known,

I might even have felt sorry for her and her drama, I would have been more indulgent. Poor Eva, poor Marta." The distortion or promised transformation took the form of pity, it accompanied his words. "We got soaked through in a matter of seconds, we stood on the kerb to hail a taxi, there wasn't one, it was rather late for England and, as happens everywhere, taxis always vanish the moment it rains, the underground appeared to be closed and we didn't bother crossing the road to find out, we walked on a bit, not knowing what to do, perhaps going in the opposite direction to the one we needed to go in, a taxi passed, it was free, but the driver chose not to stop when he saw us, maybe our unsteady steps inspired mistrust, I couldn't stand still without staggering slightly, I felt more in control when I was walking, I protected myself as best I could by turning up my coat collar, she vainly covered her head with her scarf, a present from me, it clung to her hair, it was completely soaked, at least that way her hair wouldn't be ruffled by the wind. She wanted to wait in the shelter of an awning, I again grabbed her wrist and pulled her along, I wouldn't allow her to take shelter. The rain was not as strong as the wind, it was falling obliquely, the street was deserted. A double decker bus stopped at the traffic lights, it must have been on its final run, the open platform looked inviting, Eva broke away for a moment and leapt on, I followed and managed to get on too, grabbing the rail when the bus was already moving off, it didn't really matter where it was going, she had seen it as a kind of refuge. I paid the conductor, who was Indian or Pakistani, 'The last stop, please,' I said, that was simplest, we went up to the empty top deck, I saw, out of the corner of my eye, as I was climbing the stairs, shoving Eva ahead of me, that downstairs, there were only a couple of passengers, 'Are you stupid or what? You're crazy,' I said, 'we don't even know where this bus is going.' 'What does it matter?' she replied, 'anything is better than being out in the street in this gale. When we see an area with more traffic about, we can get off and then we'll find a taxi. Or else when it's not raining quite so much. I'm drenched, do you want us both to catch pneumonia?' She sat down, took off her scarf, shook it and wrung out her hair a little, she took a Kleenex out of her handbag and dried her face and hands as best she could, she offered me one, I refused, I didn't sit down beside her but behind, like some lout about to set upon his victim, the wind had made my mood wilder, hers too, the wind does madden people, she had suddenly had the gumption to answer me back. We smelled of wet wool, our sodden overcoats, an awful smell. The bus sped on through the rain the way they do at night, there was hardly any traffic, it made a monstrous noise when it braked at bus stops or at traffic lights, sometimes it brushed against the branches of the trees at our height ("The foliage"), sometimes it sounded like a whiplash, at others, more like drumming, when there were several branches all in a row waving like furious arms in the wind as the bus passed ("And I always wondered how she managed to avoid the branches of the trees that stuck out over the pavements and thudded against the high windows as if in protest at our speed, as if wanting to reach through the windows and scratch us," I thought, "and I don't know if that thought is mine or Marta Téllez's, or if it is just a memory"). In front of me, Eva was again wringing out her curly hair as if it were a piece of fabric, I had often seen her do so when she emerged from the shower in her apartment, in her dressing gown. She didn't turn round, she kept her back to me ("The back of her neck"), I got the impression that she was acting offended now, perhaps it was a change of tactic, she wasn't pleading any more, or perhaps she considered that what she had done was not that serious and was attempting to play another hand, when the fact was that she had played all her cards. Maybe she thought that I had gone too far in my revenge and that now it was her turn to call me to account for my cruelty and my sarcasm and my mistreatment of her all that day ("Everything becomes creased or stained or crumpled"), that's why she had allowed herself that haughty response. I couldn't bear it, it was just the idea of it, how dare she, I had sat waiting, thinking about her and about similarities ("What is truly unbearable is that the person one recalls as part of the future should suddenly become the past"). I was drunk, but that's no excuse, you can be drunk in as many different ways as you can be sober. It was unpremeditated but I knew what I was doing, I was aware of what I was going to do because I remember thinking that no one would see me from the street or from downstairs, they install round, convex mirrors on all the buses, so that the conductor can see what's going on upstairs, but in order to do that, he has to be looking and that Indian or Pakistani wouldn't be looking at anything on this final trip of the day, he would be exhausted, and tiredness drives out curiosity. Nowadays, some buses are fitted with a camera instead of a mirror to keep an eye on the upper deck, but that bus wasn't one of them, a number 16 or 15, I'm not sure, or another bus altogether, I turned round to check, there was no camera, that's how I know that I thought about myself and about what might happen afterwards, about the possible consequences ("You thought about tomorrow"), that's why I know that I knew what I was doing when I put my hands around her head and squeezed it violently between them ("You squeezed my cheekbones and my temples, my poor temples"), I held her and squeezed her hard so that she couldn't turn round, her damp curls beneath my hands ("My large hands with their hard, clumsy fingers, my fingers like piano keys"), because now she did want to turn round but couldn't, for a moment, she still thought I was playacting or joking, she still had time to say to me in an irritated voice: "What are you doing, stop it," and then she must have sensed that I was serious, I was hurting her, I must have hurt her a lot with my thumbs, in what was a matter of only a couple of seconds, I could easily have crushed her temples had I kept up the pressure, but in order to stop her crying out, I quickly lowered my hands to her neck and her throat, which were also wet ("Her old-fashioned neck traversed by striations or threads of black, sticky hair, like half-dried blood or mud"), and I put pressure on her throat too, the pressure on her temples had almost made her lose consciousness, she was limp, I hardly felt any resistance in her hands as they struggled lamely to loosen my grip ("Like children who put up no resistance to the swift, impatient illnesses that so effortlessly carry them off"), she would remain lying on the seat of a London bus that would continue on its night journey through the wind and the rain and I, on the other hand, would get off, there was no door to stop me ("A foreign death, a horrible death, and on an island"), I couldn't see her face, I couldn't see her eyes, only the back of her neck and her hair, but I knew she was rapidly dying ("What disappears is not only who I am but who I have been, not only me, but my whole memory, everything I know and have learned, all my memories and everything I've ever seen, the thousand and one things that passed before my eyes and are of no importance or use to anyone else and become useless if I die"). I don't know if it was the bus suddenly squealing to a halt and stopping with a jolt that made me release my fingers, as if my actions depended on the bus continuing to advance and on the wind that seems less strong when you're standing still. Or perhaps it was fear or a kind of regret that surfaced simultaneously with the act that provoked it ("A yes and a no and a perhaps and meanwhile everything has moved on or is gone"). I immediately released my grip, I withdrew my hands, I suddenly let her go without taking her life ("Not yet, not yet, and as long as it is not yet, I can go on thinking about the daily battle and looking at this foreign landscape, and making plans for the future, and you can still go on saying goodbye"), I put my hands in my overcoat pockets at once as if I wanted to hide or erase what they had been about to do, but had not, actions are not the same if they do not last long enough, they depend on their effects ("The thread of uninterrupted continuity, my silken thread still intact but without a guide: another day, how dreadful, another day, how fortunate"), Eva was alive instead of being dead ("And I don't know what either of those words means any more. I no longer have any clear understanding of those two terms"), I got up, I walked round her to look at her, I gazed down at her from my superior height, in her distraction her legs had parted, she raised to me her battered, injured head, she looked at me for a moment and her eyes still wore my face and the dusky night, I saw depression and pity and exhaustion more than fear or resistance ("Without the consolation of uncertainty that cannot always be retrospective, even though the recent present can suddenly seem like the remote past"), as if, more than by her possible death to which she had come within a hair's breadth, she was saddened to think that of all the people living I should be the one who had tried and wanted to kill her ("The dying woman's scorn for her own death confronted by the pathetic superiority of the living and our temporary motive for triumph: I stay too long by you, sweet boy, I weary you"). And then she ran down the stairs in the high heels that she had put on in order to wait for me at my hotel, to plead with me, she ran down the stairs so that she could jump off before the bus started up again, I don't know where we were or what street we were in, I didn't follow her, I merely opened a window that let in a gust of wind and oblique rain and I leaned out in time to see her jump off ("And I still see the world from on high"), the bus was pulling away and picking up speed when, from the back window, to which I moved immediately afterwards, I saw her overcoat and her entirely un-childish shoes on the asphalt and I saw her, in an obviously confused state, trying to cross the road, fleeing from me, the man who might be pursuing her to continue trying to kill her, or fleeing perhaps from the sorrow of what she had felt and seen. She tried to do this without looking, still concealed by the bus which was just about to draw away but had not yet done so, she didn't reach the opposite kerb because a black taxi came racing up from the other direction and hit her, an Austin taxi like a rhinoceros or an elephant, the traffic in London drives on the wrong side of the road. I saw this with my own eyes from the back window as I moved off, I saw the tremendous blow, it hit her full on so that she was thrown not upwards but straight ahead at the height of the snout ploughing into her, and I saw how the taxi was unable to brake even after it had hit her and saw how it ran over her after she had dropped to the ground. A fatal blow that came without warning, my bus was either not aware of it or preferred not to be, the moment after the crash, it made as if to brake, but didn't actually stop, it went on its way, picking up speed by the yard, perhaps neither the sleepy driver nor the Indian had heard it, or perhaps they had and decided that it would make them too late getting off work if they found themselves involved in an accident that they hadn't seen and in which their vehicle had played no part. The last I saw, before the bus went round a corner and the scene disappeared from view, was the taxi driver and his passengers – the taxi had finally managed to stop – who had all opened their doors and run towards the body. The woman and the man were sheltering from the rain beneath a newspaper, the taxi driver knew already that the body was a corpse, because he was carrying in his hands a kind of rug with which to cover her, her face too, at least she wouldn't get any wetter I thought ("But, on the other hand, the smell of metamorphosis would begin"). I did nothing, I mean, I didn't get off at the next stop or at the next set of traffic lights in order to go back and find out what I already knew or to accompany the dead Eva and to help with the formalities. I would have done if I had known now what had happened here, almost twenty hours before, but I didn't. But no, that's not true, I wouldn't have got off even then. I had washed my hands of it. Strictly speaking, I hadn't killed her, the taxi had, but a minute before, I had wanted her death and sought it and now it was done, and by my own wavering will, if not by my hand ("She didn't die of her own accord," I thought, "and the fact of someone dying while you remain alive makes you feel, for a moment, or for a lifetime, like a criminal, what a terrible curse, now I will have to remember that name too, the name of someone whose face I do not even know: Eva García Valle"). Or perhaps it was her will bowing to mine so as not to be in the way ("The will that steps aside and grows tired and, by its withdrawal, brings our death, as if the world couldn't bear us and was in a hurry to get rid of us"). In those moments, as the bus moved off and I lost sight of the scene, the thought uppermost in my mind was that no one knew that she was with me. The tickets bought separately, the different hotels and, at the hospital, she hadn't registered because there was no need ("And, as if it was just another insignificant, superfluous link, the murder or homicide is simply lumped in with all the crimes – there are so many others – that have been forgotten and of which no record remains and with those currently being planned and of which there will be a record, even though that too will eventually disappear"). Her death was just that of another tourist over in London from the Continent who, yet again, forgot to look in the right direction after getting off a bus on the left-hand side and then trying to cross the road, forgetting that the traffic was coming from the other direction ("A ridiculous death, the improbable death of someone who is just a visitor to the city, like someone dying, crushed or decapitated by a tree split in two by a lightning bolt in a broad avenue during a storm, it happens sometimes and we just read about it in the newspapers and laugh"). She had nothing to do with me, she was a stranger, I threw her bus ticket out of the window, the Pakistani wouldn't remember that I had paid for her as well as myself. There would be no reason why he should even remember her. And besides, I hadn't done anything, no one had, a mere accident, a misfortune. There was her scarf still on the seat, still wet. It still smelled of her, of her black hair ("The smell of the dead lingers when nothing else remains of them. It lingers for as long as their bodies remain and afterwards too, once they are out of sight and buried and disappeared: let me be lead within thy bosom, let me sit heavy on thy soul tomorrow, bloody and guilty"). I put it in my overcoat pocket. I still have it." Deán fell silent and then added: "That was what happened to me, do you understand?"

"We are so easily infected, we can be convinced of anything, we can always prove ourselves to be right and everything can be told if accompanied by some justification, some excuse or by some attenuating circumstance or even by its mere representation, telling is a form of generosity, anything can happen and be said and be accepted, you can emerge from anything unharmed, or more than that, unscathed. No one does anything convinced of its injustice, not at least at the moment they do it, it's the same with telling a story, what a strange mission or task that is, nothing that happens has ever completely happened until you tell someone, until it is spoken about and known about, until then, it is still possible to convert those events into mere thought, mere memory, nothing. But, in fact, the person telling the story always tells it later on, which allows him to add things if he wants, to distance himself: 'I have turned away my former self, I am not the thing I was nor the person I was, I neither know nor recognize myself. I did not seek it, I did not want it.' And, in turn, the person listening can listen to the end and even then give what is always the best answer: "I don't know, I'm not sure, we'll see.'"

"I think so. What happened then?" I said. "I should be going, I really must be going."

Deán had not moved for some time. When I asked him this, he adjusted the knot on his tie and began slowly to roll down his shirtsleeves, as if he were preparing to put on his jacket, as if he were the one who had to leave. I was the one who had to go. "I'm going to go," I thought, "I've heard what he has to say and I won't forget it."

"I got off at traffic lights a long way from where the accident had occurred, in an area with more traffic. There was no one else on the bus now, I saw that there wasn't out of the corner of my eye during the second that the lower deck appeared before me, between the last steps on the staircase and my leap down into the street. I stood on the pavement, the conductor probably didn't even realize that someone else had just got off the bus at the wrong spot. I quickly found a taxi and went back to the hotel, it had stopped raining during the journey, the wind had dropped too, and I had sobered up after those Indian cocktails. I went up to my room, there had been no messages. I turned the television on and I watched for a few moments, switching channels, I barely understood what they were saying, so I got up from the bed and opened the window and I leaned on the window sill and, despite the cold, I looked out of it for a long time, I don't know how long ("Deán looks out of his wintry hotel window through the veteran dark of the London night at the buildings opposite, or at other rooms in the same hotel, most are in darkness, staring at the brightly lit attic room of a black maid getting undressed after her day's work, removing her cap and her shoes and her stockings and her apron and her uniform, then standing at the sink and washing her face and under her arms, he too can see a half-dressed and half-naked woman, but, unlike me, he has not touched her or embraced her, he has nothing to do with that woman who, before going to bed, has a perfunctory wash, British-fashion, at the wretched sink of one of those English rooms whose tenants have to go out into the corridor to use a bathroom shared with other people on the same floor. Deán cannot smell her at her distant, high window but he might still know her smell, perhaps he has already passed her in that corridor or on the stairs with his already poisonous footsteps, the day before or that evening. He hears the phone ringing in his room, it echoes and bounces out across the night to that half-dressed, half-naked maid and alerts her to the fact that she can be seen, in bra and pants, she takes a few steps over to her window, opens it and peers out for a moment as if to make sure that no one is climbing up towards her, and then she closes it and very carefully draws the curtains, no one must see her in the midst of her desolation or fatigue or exhaustion, or half-dressed or half-naked or sitting at the foot of the bed with the inside-out sleeves of her uniform still caught on her wrists, perhaps she had already been seen like that without her realizing it, while she was combing her hair and singing some unidentifiable song or a dirge, like a young banshee, the sing-song hum of weary, much-maligned death proffering a prediction about the past, time passes heedlessly. I don't know any of this, I don't know it for a fact, we'll see or, rather, we will never know, the dead Marta will never know what happened to her husband in London that night while she lay dying beside me, when he comes home bearing gifts, she won't be there to listen to him, to listen to the story that he has decided to tell her, possibly fictitious and very different from the one I have heard. The dead person who haunts and watches and revisits him is different from my dead person, the person who lives in his thoughts as mine does in mine like an incessant beating, awake or asleep, his unfortunate wife and his unfortunate lover mingled and both lodged in our heads for lack of anywhere more comfortable, struggling against their own dissolution and seeking embodiment in the one thing that remains to them if they are to preserve their validity and maintain contact, the repetition or infinite reverberation of what they once did or what happened one day: infinite, but ever wearier and more tenuous. And his dead woman, like mine, belongs to the very recent past and was neither powerful nor an enemy, yet her unreality grows apace"). Until the phone rang," said Deán, "and they told me the news. Some twenty hours had passed. There are certain things that we should be told about immediately so that we do not, for a single second, walk about the world believing something that is utterly mistaken, when the world has utterly changed because of them ("It's so easy to live in a state of delusion, indeed, it is our natural condition," I thought again, "and we really shouldn't find that so very painful: you'll go on hearing Vicente's electric-shaver voice, you'll go on seeing him")."

"I'm going to go now," this time I said it. I had used that verb before in that house, but never quite that, I had never said to anyone "I'm off", I had never said that.

When I was putting on my scarf and raincoat in the hall, I glanced surreptitiously down the corridor at the open door of the child's darkened bedroom, I couldn't believe that Deán would keep him. Tomorrow, I would have to phone the woman who was now both older and younger sister, I looked at my watch, it wasn't that late, perhaps I would be justified in calling her that same night when I got home, in taking one still-innocent step, after all, I might be the vague figure of the husband who has not yet arrived and who would form part of her world amongst the inconstant living. And that child could come and live with us, I couldn't believe that Deán would keep him. In that event, his planes would come with him too, although they belonged to his father's far-off childhood, I had never had that many, I quite envied him, fighters and bombers from the First and Second World Wars all mixed up together, some from the Korean War and others that had attacked or defended Madrid, years and years ago, during our Civil War. When things come to an end they have a number and the world then depends on its storytellers, but only for a short time and not entirely, they never fully emerge from the shadows, other people are never quite done and there is always someone for whom the mystery continues. That boy will never know what happened, his father and his aunt will hide it from him, I will too, and it doesn't really matter because so many things happen without anyone realizing or remembering, everything is forgotten or invalidated. And how little remains of each individual in time, useless as slippery snow, how little trace remains of anything, and how much of that little is never talked about, and, afterwards, one remembers only a tiny fraction of what was said, and then only briefly: while we travel slowly towards our dissolution merely in order to traverse the back or reverse side of time, where one can no longer keep thinking or keep saying goodbye: "Goodbye laughter and goodbye scorn. I will never see you again, nor will you see me. And goodbye ardour, goodbye memories."

January 1994

DARK BACK OF TIME

Called by its author a "false novel," *Dark Back of Time* begins with the tale of the odd effects of publishing *All Souls*, his witty and sardonic 1989 Oxford novel. *All Souls* is a book Marías swears to be fiction, but which its "characters"—the real-life dons and professors and bookshop owners who have "recognized themselves"—fiercely maintain to be a roman à clef. With the sleepy world of Oxford set into fretful motion by a world that never "existed," *Dark Back of Time* begins an odyssey into the nature of identity and time. Marías weaves together autobiography, a legendary kingdom, strange ghostly literary figures, halls of mirrors, a one-eyed pilot, a curse in Havana, and a bullet lost in Mexico.

Fiction

WHEN I WAS MORTAL

Stories

A dozen stories by Javier Marías, "the most subtle and gifted writer in contemporary Spanish literature" (*The Boston Globe*). Victims of mistaken identity, sponging relatives, amateur sleuths, eavesdroppers, professional liars, assassins, and failed bodyguards populate the short stories in *When I Was Mortal*. Plots turn on curious exigencies—a woman about to star in her first porn film; a night doctor who adds new meaning to "specialist"; a ghost whose neglect is greatly resented.

Fiction